Monday's Child

MONDAY'S CHILD

Caroline Jones Lewis

Monday's Child

Caroline Jones Lewis

Copyright © 2013 by Caroline Jones Lewis

Caroline Jones Lewis the author asserts the moral right to be identified

as the author of this work. All rights reserved.

This novel is entirely a work of fiction.

The names, characters and incidents portrayed in it are the work of the author's imagination. Any resemblance to actual persons, living or dead, events or localities is entirely coincidental.

All rights reserved under international and Pan-American Copyright Conventions.

Monday's Child

Caroline Jones Lewis

CONTENTS

Chapter One   *We Three*

Chapter Two   *Breaking Up*

Chapter Three   *Where from here?*

Chapter Four   *Revelations*

Chapter Five   *Disillusion*

Chapter Six   *Out of control*

Chapter Seven   *Scandals*

Chapter Eight   *A step forward and a step back*

Chapter Nine   *Survival*

Chapter Ten   *A time for healing*

Chapter Eleven   *Moving forward*

Chapter Twelve   *Falling back*

Chapter Thirteen   *Danger or deliverance?*

Monday's Child

Caroline Jones Lewis

Monday's Child is fair of face
Tuesday's Child is full of grace
Wednesday's Child is full of woe
Thursday's Child has far to go
Friday's Child is loving and giving
Saturday's Child works hard for a living
But the child who is born on the Sabbath Day
Is bonny and blithe and good and gay

'The swinging sixties' they called them, the decade that changed the order of things in a Britain in the throes of a youth revolution. Youth music, young fashion, a generation with cash in its pocket and the belief that it could change the world. And for some, it was true. Their lives would never be the same again - for better, or for worse.

Chapter One – We Three

Lizzie

I remember the start of it so well, the start of all the changes. It was as if the world had shifted slightly on its axis and in so doing had set in motion a chain of events that changed our worlds too. Just a tiny shift to begin with, so small it was barely perceptible at all if you weren't taking notice, which of course most of the time we weren't. All too busy living our everyday lives. I noticed, just little thing to begin with. But then I notice lots of things other people miss. I noticed lots of things that year at Abberley – but not enough as it turned out.

Change was inevitable, of course. Nancy and I were awaiting our A-level results, me with the intent of going to university if I had the grades I hoped for. My passion was economics which was considered unusual for a girl so I would be competing mostly with boys for the place I wanted. It wouldn't be easy. For that reason I was only

Monday's Child

Caroline Jones Lewis

intending to stay at Abberley for two weeks that year instead of the whole of the summer break. I wanted to be at home when the results came through, ready to make the necessary 'phone calls if my results were what I hoped for – and I already had a job for the rest of the holidays to earn some cash, whatever the outcome. And Nancy? Well, no-one knew what Nancy wanted to do – including Nancy. I'd made suggestions but nothing seemed to fill her with lasting enthusiasm. She flitted from one idea to another in no time at all. She's quite arty and she's always loved fashion – clothes and hairstyles and the like. So I had suggested art school. Perhaps a course on design. She was quite keen for a while but then as ever the enthusiasm seemed to fade and disappear. No-one could have guessed, though, the turn her life would take in the coming months.

We were sitting in the garden after lunch, Nancy, Hugh and me, Hugh being all grown up with his glass of gin and tonic in his hand because of course he is older than Nancy and me. Nancy was sunbathing on the lounger, trying to get a tan because that was the fashion. I was sat with my head in a book. I always had a book on the go, not just because I liked reading – and still do – but because it was an easy escape route when I got bored with the conversation, which was often at Abberley. I have always loved both my cousins but I have to admit that in those days I sometimes found their conversation rather banal and self-absorbed. How arrogant I was. I know better now. Little did I realise then what lurked beneath that banality with Hugh. Dear Hugh. If his behaviour was a little bizarre that year it was understandable. We would have understood had we known but we didn't at the time. None of us did.

"Do you think," Nancy had drawled. "Do you think anyone would mind if I took the boat out on my own for the afternoon?"

Monday's Child

Caroline Jones Lewis

"Since when did you care if anyone else minded anything?" Hugh had chuckled, shooting a glance at me. "Of course I mind," Nancy had protested, pouting her ample rosy lips in the way only she could do. "Of course I do. You make me sound like a selfish little strumpet, Hugh," – which of course she was and we all knew that she was and that she would take the boat out anyway.
Nancy, she would boast, had been named after one of the Mitford girls by whose writing her mother, my aunt, was very taken at the time of her pregnancy. She had just read 'Love in a Cold Climate', Nancy told us and was smitten by the author's name. As if by a deliberate stroke of fate, Nancy – our Nancy – had seemingly been endowed with the same strength of mind and will that were the characteristics of her namesake. Not always to the benefit of those around her.
"That girl's thoroughly selfish," her father would complain to my aunt. "She needs taking in hand." But I don't think either he or my aunt were up to a task left a little late in the day.

Nancy had always been considered spoiled by my parents and by that year, in the closing stages of a stormy adolescence, it would have been difficult for a change to have been accomplished without a great deal of angst.
"At least when the time comes she'll marry well, one hopes. At least her face will be her fortune – if there's any man alive willing to take her on, that is," Uncle James was heard to exclaim. Marriage, it seemed, was his only hope for her future – not that marriage was on Nancy's agenda, so far as I was aware.
"I wanted to call her Phoebe," I once heard him mutter into his Financial Times, his newspaper the barrier he used to distance himself from the vagaries of domesticity that he strove to avoid. At Abberley he would read and reread his newspaper from cover to cover until it was like a threadbare old garment, in the quiet of his study or a deserted corner of the garden. He had the art of escapism

Monday's Child

Caroline Jones Lewis

honed to perfection. "Far more suitable name for a daughter," he had concluded.

Nancy had risen from her seat and flounced past Hugh with a deliberate toss of her head and sway of the hips. She crossed the lawn towards the house to change into her sailing gear.
"Damned cheek," she exclaimed indignantly as she past me. "Hugh of all people, probably the most selfish person you could ever meet in your entire life. Damned cheek."
Not true, of course. Hugh was nothing of the sort.
Hugh had watched her receding form through eyes squinting against the midday sun. He had grinned at her peak and winked at me. Nancy was and always has been very beautiful, more than ever when her cheeks were tinged pink with an annoyance that also put a glint in her clear blue eyes. But her moods were only ever temporary and by dinner that evening we fully expected that she would be restored to her usual light-hearted humour and wit, regaling us all with an account of an afternoon indulged in a pastime which, to her, was a source of joy. That was the trouble with Nancy. She was mercurial in temperament and her lapses in good humour never lasted long enough for anyone to remonstrate with her. And so she got away with it and everyone loved her no matter what she did. I think I envied her a little. No, actually, I know I did. I envied her a lot. I've never had her charisma – or her looks. And clothes just looked fantastic on her, naturally stylish, like a second skin no matter what she wore.

I was the quiet one in the family. The studious one. And I was never confident of fashion and such so I always felt in the shade when we were together. It didn't matter to me at other times. There always seemed more important things to consider than hair styles and the length of one's skirt. We were as different as chalk and cheese. But when I was

Monday's Child
Caroline Jones Lewis

in Nancy's company I felt that I should care about those things, that I should make an effort to be more fashionable.

On this day, though, there seemed something different about Nancy's mood. She seemed fragile. Brittle. As though at any moment she would not so much snap into an ill-tempered spoiled-brat tantrum as plunge into a bout of despair. It was a different mood unlike the usual Nancy and one with which I was not familiar. At the time I was unsure as to whether I was imagining it and certainly Hugh gave no indication that he had noticed anything untoward. That's what I mean – about noticing things other people missed.

I had never known Nancy to be unhappy in all the years of our childhood. She had never had reason to be, of course, but then to my knowledge she had no reason to be at that moment in time. Unless, I thought, Aunt Miranda, Nancy's mother, was ill. I had also noticed that during this particular holiday Aunt Miranda had excused herself from our company more than usual, saying she felt unwell and needed a rest or a walk to clear a headache which was not like her as she was not given to country walking. Perhaps that was it, I mused. Perhaps Aunt Miranda was ill and no-one had yet told us.

Aunt Miranda is my mother's sister, younger by just one year, both daughters of an Oxford scholar with not much money. She had become a secretary after school and married her boss, a former public schoolboy ten years her senior in business in the City. He owned a substantial property in a fashionable part of London and of course Abberley which he had inherited from his grandmother. My mother, by comparison, had become a nurse and married a doctor who was clever and dedicated, passionate about the National Health Service and therefore overworked and poor by Aunt Miranda's standards though we didn't consider ourselves as such. Resisting regular

Monday's Child

Caroline Jones Lewis

suggestion by my aunt and uncle, my father steadfastly refused the very idea of private practise.

Despite the difference in their circumstances, my mother, Emily, and my Aunt Miranda had remained close. They had married within a year of each other, were pregnant at the same time and had both produced daughters of whom they were inestimably proud. Neither had had more children. I had spent most of my summer holidays at Abberley with Nancy and Aunt Miranda while my own mother worked and sometimes we would be joined by my Uncle James and by Hugh who, poor chap, has no parents at all.

Hugh is the only son of Uncle James' sister and brother-in-law who had been killed in a car crash when Hugh was only six years old. He had been brought up in childhood by his paternal grandmother but had always spent most of his long summer holidays with us at Abberley - to give his grandmother a break, Aunt Miranda had said. By that summer, though, he lived in London in a flat of his own and worked in a bank in the City. He was quite successful, I believed, though I wasn't sure what he did as he travelled a lot. An investment bank, he took pains to point out to Nancy and me, not a high street clearing bank though the difference still eluded us to a degree. Mum would visit as often as her shifts would allow and she and Aunt Miranda would take us out for cream teas and visits to the cinema. Then she would leave and I would miss her terribly until she fetched me home again at the end of the holidays.

Home was in Kent in a little cottage on the edge of a village. From my bedroom window I looked out over apple orchards to the west that were clouds of blossom in the spring and rosy with fruit by the end of the summer and to the east over hop fields that were harvested in autumn. In the distance I could see the oasthouses of the farm that owned the orchards and hop fields. In late summer they

Monday's Child

Caroline Jones Lewis

employed students still on holiday from university who came to earn money to help fund their living expenses. They picked the apples and harvested the hops and kept us amused with their singing and laughing, their flirting and antics around the village. But the work was back-breakingly hard and they earned every penny they made. It was a happy childhood and though I enjoyed my holidays in the comparative luxury at Abberley and my time with my cousins I loved being at home more. Home with my parents was always where the heart was – comfy, familiar home with Mum and Dad.

Abberley is a large old detached house that sits in expansive lawned gardens overlooking a bay on the north Cornish coast. Unlike Aunt Miranda's London home, which boasts every modern convenience on the market, Abberley still lags behind in modernity. It was only a decade or so since the village had been connected to the national grid. Lighting before then had been by oil lamp, which had been a great novelty to us as little children in the summer months but which my mother said had been tedious through the winter months. It did by this time have a twin-tub washing machine which Mrs Hale, the housekeeper, adored and a small refrigerator to store the most vulnerable foods. A toaster had appeared since our last visit but the only source of heating was still the old Rayburn on which Mrs Hale produced the most mouth-watering of foods and which heated the water. All of this was rather prohibitive to winter visiting except in the most clement of weather. Aunt Miranda sustained a vigorous campaign for Abberley's modernisation, a campaign which Uncle James resisted good-humouredly but with equally fierce determination on the grounds that a return to a simpler lifestyle was good for the soul. This reason, Aunt Miranda assured us all strongly but without the slightest impression on her husband, was nothing more than an excuse not to spend the money. So Abberley remained untouched.

Monday's Child

Caroline Jones Lewis

The gardens at Abberley were hedged on either side - by tall, dense hedging on the east side shielding it from the neighbouring property and by a lower level hedging on the west broken by a rough gateway into a lane beyond that led down to the shingle beach. Along this boundary, bridging the front and rear gardens, ran a pergola that, from early summer through to late autumn, was heavy with the scented blooms of roses. The boundary at the bottom of the garden was sealed with rustic trellis fencing, low-level to optimise the view of the bay and grouped at its centre stood a wrought iron table and chairs at which, on that day, we had all been seated and indeed at which Hugh and I remained. Nancy reappeared changed into shorts and blouse and her deck shoes. I heard her swing through the gate in the hedge into the lane beyond, heard the gate clatter closed behind her and saw the tip of her blonde head bob by as she swayed down the lane to the narrow beach ahead. Then came the thud of her footsteps as she bounded down the wooden steps onto the beach and the crunch of the shingle beneath her feet as she crossed the beach to the jetty. Her boat was moored there bobbing gently in the afternoon swell. Her posture as she hopped into the boat seemed to suggest a rise in spirits from her earlier mood, a light-heartedness that then had been missing. Sailing always did that for her, transported her to a place she loved to be. I watched her unfurl the sail, slip the mooring rope and push the boat away from the jetty. She turned the stern seaward and made ready to head out to sea. I watched her from the lawn above, we both did, Hugh and me. Nancy and the boat rounded the headland to the east of us, disappearing from sight to leave the tranquil glistening expanse of sea empty again. Hugh returned to sipping his gin and tonic and I to my open book while we awaited her return.

When I think of that summer it is always that afternoon I return to, to the clear light over the shimmering sea, the

Monday's Child

Caroline Jones Lewis

scent of the roses carried on the breeze and the gentle shush shush of the surf caressing the shingle. How I wish I had known then, as I do now, that Hugh was wrestling with his own demons. Perhaps I would have talked to him, given him my care and attention instead of burying my head in my book again. It was selfish of me – and unsociable. Not that it would perhaps have changed the course of events but at least he would have known there was someone he could turn to, who would care. I hated knowing later that he had tried to cope alone. How I wish that Nancy could have confided her worries to me, too. I should have asked her what was wrong, if I could help. Looking back, it was a shame that three young people who had been so close in their growing years spent that holiday so preoccupied each with their own agenda that they could not communicate with each other. And I had no excuse. Apart from waiting for my A-level results, I had no worries at all. I had noticed so many things were different that holiday but to my regret I failed to notice the pain of my cousins and in so doing I failed them both.

******

Nancy

That holiday is still as fresh in my mind as if it were yesterday, those weeks that changed my life in a way I had never dreamt of. It was the first time in my entire life that I had felt anxiety. Until then worry of any kind had definitely not been my style. I suppose I had lived a charmed life, a privileged existence though I hadn't fully appreciated it then. Both my parents doted on me, each in their own way and I had the best of both worlds with our life in London and those school holidays at our beloved Abberley – sometimes Christmas and Easter too but especially those wonderful long summers.

Our main home was in London where I attended private school. I suppose it's true to say I was a spirited scholar,

Monday's Child
Caroline Jones Lewis

above average academically but always up to pranks with chums that sometimes got me into trouble. I caused my parents a degree of concern but nothing really serious. Just high jinks. Unless you count the time I was almost expelled for instigating a demonstration against homework. It was supposed to be peaceful but things got a bit out of hand. Daddy always said it was my name that was the problem. Calling me Nancy, he said, had been a guarantee of trouble. He had wanted to call me Phoebe but my mother had insisted on Nancy – after Nancy Mitford, she said, who was bright and spirited and wrote so wonderfully. So I suppose she was right about that much because spirited is definitely me. I think my main trouble then was that I lacked any real direction or conviction to any one thing so I got into mischief instead.

On this one day in the holidays I was lounging in the garden. It was a beautiful hot day, clear blue skies and a light breeze, just enough to keep the temperature at a perfect level. Hot but not oppressive. I was with Hugh and Lizzie, my cousins, who spent most of the summer holidays with us at Abberley. Hugh was trying to impress Lizzie and me with his grown-up-ness which I thought really tedious and Lizzie, as ever, had her nose stuck in a book. She was always a bookworm. We were both waiting for our A-level results, Lizzie and me. Lizzie was desperate to get her grades. She was planning to go to university. I had no idea what I wanted to do which irritated Daddy immensely. My mother was much more relaxed about it all. She argued that no girl of my age could possibly be sure what they wanted to do with the rest of their life but of course Daddy retorted that that couldn't possibly be true since Lizzie obviously did. I had put the whole matter out of my mind. This was holiday time. I'd think about the future later. I tried to relax and sunbathe. All my friends were sporting a tan that summer so I wanted to return to London looking bronzed. My friend Jacqueline was coming the next week and then was going

Monday's Child
Caroline Jones Lewis

to Spain with her parents on holiday. We were all envious
– that is, me and my friends. Jacs was the only one of us
going abroad on holiday but then she had relatives who
lived there and we didn't. So I wanted to be tanned when
she came. You can get a really good tan in Cornwall, just
as good as Spain. But I couldn't settle. Something was
niggling away at me, disturbing my calm.

I've always been a bit temperamental but this was
different. I didn't feel volatile. More depressed and
irritable. It was unusual for me to feel troubled. At 18
years of age, having had this wonderfully carefree
childhood, an only child born at the close of war to doting
parents, I had wanted for nothing in life. My father earned
a more-than-adequate living in the City so I was somewhat
indulged materially and I knew how to get just what I
wanted anyway. My mother, of course, didn't have a
career. It would have been frowned upon in her social
circle, but she devoted a great deal of her free time, of
which there was plenty with household staff to attend to all
those domestic duties, to appropriate charities. Holidays
were spent at Abberley on the Cornish coastline. I've
always loved Abberley – and Cornwall – and when I was
small my father had taken me sailing and taught me how to
handle a boat of my own. I had a dog there too, which I
couldn't have at our house in London; Cassie my spaniel
who lived with our housekeeper when we weren't there. I
loved it there and I loved the change from our life in
London but Mummy, I think, found it a little too quiet and
unsophisticated though I know she enjoyed being with her
sister, my Aunt Emily, and my cousins. They're quite
alike in many ways, my mother and Aunt Emily. They
look alike a little though my mother is more sophisticated
than Aunt Em. Comes from having more money to spend
on herself, I suppose. People tell me I'm very like my
mother, which is lucky for me because Mummy is very
beautiful and graceful. And I'm a Monday's child, as my
mother likes to remind me – fair of face and all that so I

Monday's Child

Caroline Jones Lewis

suppose I'm doubly blessed. Lizzie is a Thursday's child and Hugh is Friday. Mummy and Aunt Emily are both Tuesday and Daddy is a typical Wednesday. He always has something to complain about – like Eyore. Aunt Emily is more sort of pretty than beautiful. I suppose Lizzie must take her looks from her father because her hair and complexion are darker and her features are more rounded than our mothers. I think in temperament, though, I'm more like Daddy. I'm certainly moody like him but at times he can be much more fun than my mother. At least he used to be. But lately, just before that holiday, he had seemed much more tetchy than usual. And pre-occupied. I knew he was irritated with me at times for not having any direction in life but I hadn't thought it serious until now. By the time of that holiday I was really starting to wonder what was wrong.

A few days before that afternoon with Hugh and Lizzie, there had been an incident with my mother that had bothered me. It had left me with a suspicion that things were not right but then I wondered if I was over-reacting. I was prone to do that at times so I wasn't sure if it was just me. I had tried to speak to Mummy about this incident and she had given me an explanation but somehow it hadn't rung true. And that had bothered me even more. I hadn't had the chance to pursue it because then Lizzie had arrived and I didn't want her to see my concern. If there was something wrong I hadn't wanted Lizzie to know about it. Lizzie's parents were so devoted to each other and to Lizzie that I envied her. I knew my parents loved me but they didn't show it in the way that Lizzie's parents did. With my parents it was material things but with Lizzie's it was hugs and kisses and a special sort of communication between them, familiar and unique. Like they knew what each other was thinking. Something I seemed to be losing with my parents in recent times. So pride made me keep my worry to myself.

Monday's Child

Caroline Jones Lewis

Several days before I had entered the rear garden from the conservatory that ran the full width of the back of the house. From the corner of my eye I had briefly caught a movement to my left, just fleetingly, near the rose pergola that stretched between the side gate and the archway into the rear garden. But when I turned my head I could see no-one, not even Cassie. I had hesitated for just a moment, then propelled by curiosity I had ventured towards the pergola to investigate, moving as quietly as possible across the lawn which was becoming dried and crackly with the hot summer sun. As I came near I could hear the soft hush of voices, a man and a woman engaged in conversation and a soft, girlish giggle. I don't know why but I didn't want them to see me so I paused as I reached the pergola, crouched against the foliage of the roses wrapped around the timbers and I peered between the tangle of glossy leaves and stems. I remember that the scent of the blooms made me feel heady – it was so strong in the midday heat. Whenever I smell roses now I remember that moment. I could see my mother in profile only feet away from me and a man I didn't think I knew, though his features were partly obscured by the blousy yellow blossoms. They weren't touching but there was something about the way they faced each other that suggested familiarity, even intimacy. My mother was smiling and as I watched I was sure the man's hand lightly brushed her cheek. I pressed my face further into the foliage to see and as I did so a thorn caught the flesh of my arm, stopping my movement and holding me firm. A globule of blood bubbled on my skin and I let out a cry of pain. I couldn't help it. Then, afraid they might hear me, I hurriedly disentangled myself from the thorn, reaching into the pocket of my dress for a handkerchief. As I fumbled to unravel it from the other contents of my pocket, I dropped the handkerchief to the ground. Blood was trickling down my arm and I suppose I panicked a little. I let the handkerchief fall, more intent on getting into the house and out of sight.

Monday's Child

Caroline Jones Lewis

Inside the kitchen Mrs Hale, our housekeeper, clucked and fussed when she saw what had happened. She fetched the first aid kit from the pantry and gently dabbed my arm with cotton wool saturated with TCP to cleanse the wound. That smell still makes me retch. Her plump fingers pressed the flesh to stem the bleeding and I sucked in my breath as the antiseptic stung.

"There now, young lady. You'll live," she said. Her broad Cornish drawl was homely and comforting. "You'll just be a bit sore, that's all. No worry. How the dickens did you manage to do this, luvvie? You're usually so agile. Chasing that dog of yours, I'll be bound."

I shrugged and pretended she was right, shooting a glance at Cassie who sat watchfully in her basket in the corner of the kitchen.

"I just wasn't looking where I was going, Mrs H," I lied. Not really a lie, I told myself. Just not the whole truth which I didn't want to tell.

Our conversation was interrupted by my mother's arrival. She swept in from the conservatory with an anxious expression on her face and in her hand she clutched my handkerchief.

"Heavens, Nancy. What have you done to yourself?"

Mrs Hale answered for me. I was grateful, for at that moment I didn't want to say a word.

"Caught 'erself on a rose bush, ma'am. Nothin' serious though. I've cleaned it with TCP and it's stopped bleedin' already, see. Best put a plaster on it, I reckon."

"My handkerchief," I said, reaching out to take it from my mother.

"Yes," my mother replied. "I found it on the lawn."

She handed it to me, looking away as she did so as if she were avoiding my eyes. My mother inspected the wound and agreed with our housekeeper about the plaster.

Nothing more was said at the time but later, when we were alone, my mother and I, sitting in the living room having tea, I asked her.

Monday's Child

Caroline Jones Lewis

"Mummy, I thought I saw you there, at the pergola – just before I hurt my arm."
"Me? Oh, really?" I thought she hesitated for a moment. "Well, yes," she continued. "I remember now. You're right. I was there. I was looking to see if there were any dead blooms on the roses that needed removing," but again she looked away as she said it and straightened the hem of her skirt which didn't in the least need straightening. I was sure she was deliberately avoiding my gaze and that she blushed. She was hiding something. I was sure she was.
"You were talking to someone," I insisted. "A man, I think. Who was he?"
Again the hesitation.
"Oh, yes," she answered. "Some man saw me from the lane and came to ask the way to the village. A newcomer to the area. He'd been to the beach and wanted to know if there's a café nearby. He's here on holiday, I believe. Quite a pleasant man," and she smiled at me, a strange, crooked sort of smile that was unconvincing.
"Oh, I see," I said. "It's just that I thought you seemed to know him."
"Goodness no. Whatever gave you that idea," and she leaned forward to place her tea cup back on the table.
I said no more, didn't mention that light brush of her cheek. After all, maybe I had imagined it. Got it wrong. I felt a bit awkward, a little silly. What was I suspecting after all? It was probably my imagination, I decided. It's always been over-active – everyone said so. Nancy the drama queen, that was me. So I said no more. My mother rose from her seat and went to the bell pull.
"Shall we have more tea?" she asked. "Your father's coming with Lizzie and Hugh this evening so dinner's going to be late."
There was an awkward sort of pause.
"This cake of Mrs Hale's is delicious," she went on. "Would you like another slice?"
The clue had been there, of course. But I didn't pick it up at the time. If I had been wrong she would have been more

Monday's Child

Caroline Jones Lewis

challenging, more inquisitive as to my thinking but she didn't. Instead she moved the conversation on to another subject.
Of course, I thought, it's Friday. Daddy and Lizzie and Hugh would be on the train from London and Mr Hale would pick them up from the station. So the moment passed and I said nothing more. But the unease remained.

I didn't really believe Mummy's explanation but I didn't really know why. It was plausible, after all. Perhaps I **had** imagined that brush on the cheek. I relived that scene over and over – I was sure I'd seen it, those fingers lightly stroking her skin. So had my mother lied to me? Surely she had and mothers aren't supposed to lie to you, are they? They're supposed to be honest and perfect human beings. But surely my mother had lied. That feeling had stayed with me over the days no matter how I tried to ignore it and the same questions came with it. Was my mother having an affair? If so, did Daddy know? Probably not or he would have stopped it. What if they were going to end up divorced? So many of my school friends had parents who were divorced or divorcing. It was almost becoming fashionable. Cynthia Hargreaves said she got more attention from her parents since they were divorcing – and loads more presents. But Amanda was devastated by her parents' split. It was really acrimonious, each one trying to turn her against the other. Amanda had cried for weeks and now refused to talk about it, pretending that it wasn't happening and her father was just away on business, even though we knew – her friends, that is – that it wasn't true.

So on this afternoon I was feeling confused and restless. My usual habit of flying into a temper tantrum was not appropriate here. It was too big an issue and my conviction was shaky. I decided to take the boat out. I needed some time alone. Being out on the sea with only the wind and the sun for company always calmed my spirit

Monday's Child
Caroline Jones Lewis

– put life into perspective. It was my usual thing when I was in a temper about something trivial and needed to snap out of it. I accused Hugh of being beastly and rude when really he was only teasing. Hugh is the kindest gentlest person I know, a much nicer person than me. He was being a bit superior which wasn't really like him but it was only in a teasing way. I had no idea then of his problems, neither did Lizzie. Had we known – well, poor Hugh.

As soon as I was ready I hurried out of the garden down towards the beach and the boat and my worries seemed to lift and float away on the wind. I hopped onto the boat, releasing the sail and loosening the mooring rope as I went, then headed out of the bay. Out at sea I manoeuvred the boat around the rocky coastline. It was only a small boat, light and easy to handle and the sea and gentle breeze presented no problem at all. In the distance I saw Joe Higgs coming in from the rocky spit, collecting his lobster pots. "Lo Nancy," he called. "You 'ere for the summer?" "Yes," I replied, lowering the sail and making fast beside his boat. "Mummy and I came last week but the weather was so awful the first few days we hardly set foot outside the door except to shop."
"Aye, it was that," Joe agreed. "But it's good for the lobsters, that sort of weather. Churns the sea up and gets 'em movin'."
"Did you get many today?" I asked him, leaning across to peer into the pots he was lifting onto the jetty.
"Not bad," he said. "Arf a dozen or so. Not bad. But not as good as last week, mind."
I helped him carry the pots ashore, following him to the cottage where he lived with Maggs, his wife. His progress was slow, a gammy leg hindering his progress. The damage had been done during the war and never really repaired. But it was only the visible evidence of far greater injury. Blown up in a tank in the desert, his injuries had been severe and his life had hung in the balance for some time. They were scary days for Maggs, she had told me;

Monday's Child
Caroline Jones Lewis

her in Cornwall waiting for news and Joe all those miles away. And just across the water in the islands were the Germans. If they came – what then? No-one knew. Scary days they had been, Maggs said. Seriously wounded, the telegram had told her; seriously wounded in action. Only dedicated nursing care had seen Joe through. The leg had been saved, albeit stiff and unwieldy but a greater blow to a newly married couple was that they couldn't have children. In the early days it had been a great source of sadness but gratitude to still have life had overruled that sadness and time had gradually eased the disappointment. "I still 'ad Joe, that's what mattered to me most," Maggs told me and she had told him over and over, she said, until at last he had believed her.

I had known Joe and Maggs since I was little. They were like an aunt and uncle to me so it was natural for me to follow Joe into their cottage for tea.
"Ay ay, Maggs," he called to his wife. "Best put kettle on. We've company."
"So I see. Better find some biscuits, then, I reckon. 'Lo Nancy. Back for the summer?"
Their ageing black retriever was at Maggs' side and lolloped, tail wagging, to greet me, an absent friend returned. I dropped the lobster pots to the ground to ruffle the fur around the dog's neck and tickled his ear.
"Yes," I replied. "I came last week and Hugh and Lizzie have just arrived. But the weather's kept Mummy and me indoors until now. I've never seen such rain, Maggs. Have you? Mrs Hale said a whole scout camp was washed away round at Craggy Head."
"So I 'eard too," said Maggs, rising from her seat. She secured the needle in the fabric she had been sewing and placed it tidily on the table. She swayed her ample hips towards the stove and set about the tea and biscuits, the scrummy homemade cookies that were her speciality.

Monday's Child
Caroline Jones Lewis

"Well, I 'ope we shall see Hugh and Lizzie while they're 'ere. You will tell 'em, won't you? I do like to see 'em, such nice young people, they are."
"Yes I'll tell them," I promised. "I'm sure they'll come."
"Your friend Jacquelin' coming this year, is she?"
"Yes, she's coming next week. Only for two weeks, though. She's going to Spain with her parents after that."
"Oh, Spain, is it?" exclaimed Maggs. "Going by aeroplane, I suppose. One of them new fangled 'olidays?"
"Yes, they are," I answered, not adding how envious I had been when Jacs had told me. "We're flying," she had said. "Daddy said the 'plane is a 707."
I was a bit miffed too because she wasn't staying as long as usual. Lizzie was lovely but she wasn't as much fun as Jacs, always more serious and bookwormy, interested in museums and history and such and she was very anti-war especially against Vietnam. And the Berlin Wall, oh, that really got her going. The wall had been built the previous summer. She was outraged.
"The Germans have divided families, Nancy," she had fumed. "There are parents who may never see their children and grandchildren again. Just think how you would feel if you could never see your parents again. How would you feel?"
I could understand what made Lizzie so angry. The thought of it made me a bit angry too. But what could we do about it? There really was no point in us agonising about it.
With Jacs it would be make-up and hairstyles and fashion and pop music. We both liked Cliff Richard and then there was this new group The Beatles, that our Dads tut-tutted about. Jacs liked John but I thought Paul was really, really dreamy. We'd be learning the words to all their new records while Lizzie was writing protest letters about Vietnam.
"Nice girl, Jacquelin'," Maggs mused. "You're still good friends, then?"

Monday's Child
Caroline Jones Lewis

I nodded and munched on one of her cookies and we chatted about people and events in the village.

Everything was fine until Maggs asked how Mummy was. "Fine," was all I could say. I sort of froze, not knowing what to say which was unusual for me.
"That girl has too much to say for herself," my father would grumble. But not on this day. My worry resurfaced and niggled at the back of my mind and I wasn't sure but I thought I caught a look between them, Joe and Maggs, that added to my discomfort. A raised eyebrow, was it? Or a knowing glance.
"I must go," I blurted abruptly. "Mummy will get anxious if I'm out on my own too long."
Hurriedly I made my farewells to a couple who looked startled by my sudden departure, promising to come again soon with Hugh and Lizzie and Jacs. I rushed back to the boat, waving goodbye as I went.

I remember it like it was yesterday, that day, that holiday, that year. It was like the last day of my childhood, my youth, of my life and my world as I had known it. The next few days were to propel me into a whole new world and a whole new awareness.

******

Hugh

1962 was a strange year all round. It began well enough, I suppose, but the summer months were, for me, a time of facing reality. I could not have known during those days I spent at Abberley how close the coming months would bring me to losing my life. But the die was already cast and indeed it was at Abberley, during those warm sunny days of Cornish tranquillity, that I accepted for the first time the reality of my own sexuality. It was a lonely time, too, since I could hardly confide my thoughts and anxieties to two adolescent girls, my cousins Nancy and Lizzie.

Monday's Child
Caroline Jones Lewis

Homosexuality was then still an offence punishable by, at worst, imprisonment and at least by loss of employment and ostracism by those who considered themselves pillars of decent society. It was considered a mortal and moral sin.

I had first suspected my sexual persuasion several years earlier when I had had a major crush on a male colleague. But I had pushed it from my mind, convinced myself that I simply admired and respected him and wanted him as a friend. He quite obviously was more interested in our female colleagues in an intimate way. I had even actively attempted relationships with girls but always held back from anything physical which others, of course, attributed to me being a perfect and honourable gentleman. I knew, however, that I never felt a physical attraction to any of them and again managed to convince myself that I had simply not met the right one. The girls, of course, soon became frustrated with the lack of progress in the relationship and simply lost interest and moved on. But the positive was that in virtually every case we remained friends, even to the extent that for some I became their shoulder to cry on when future relationships hit a rocky patch or dependable old Hugh to whom they could turn for advice. It was a comfortable position that I enjoyed. I would be teased about my lack of girlfriend, fiancée, wife – but I would always reply that I had yet to meet the right one, and there was plenty of time for romance at my age when I was concentrating on establishing my career. There was some truth in that for I was indeed always too busy to seriously contemplate involvement with the many attractive and successful young women I met in business around the world.

I didn't want to be homosexual. I didn't want to be different from other male members of my family and social circle. I wanted the same aspirations as they had; marriage; children; what was considered to be a normal

Monday's Child

Caroline Jones Lewis

life. So it was a difficult crossroads I found myself at that summer when love for another man had exploded the subterfuge I had carefully constructed around my life, as much for my own benefit as for anyone else. My denial had been complete until now but love, intense and urgent, had changed all that. And I was ill prepared to cope with it. My escape to Abberley was meant to restore the pretence, the status quo. I would convince myself that it was simply an aberration, that like the crush on my former colleague it would evaporate once I removed myself from the scene; that my former persona would be restored. I would enjoy the company of my cousins; share the usual jokes with my Aunt and Uncle about my lack of girlfriends. But it was a hollow joke and while I pretended to them that I was a confident, easy going man of the world at ease with life I was in reality reeling from the sea change that was overtaking me and from which, I was beginning to comprehend, I would be unable to escape.

I had come to Abberley by train the previous Friday with Uncle James and Lizzie, planning to stay about a week before returning to business. Uncle James had returned to London on the Monday morning and on this weekday afternoon Nancy, Lizzie and I were in the garden. Nancy for some reason was unusually tetchy. We were all used to her volatility, her volcanic tantrums over seemingly trivial matters that subsided as rapidly as they began. But that was not her mood on this afternoon. This time Nancy was not so much volatile as irascible, anxious about something though she denied when asked that anything was wrong. What with Nancy's mood and me behaving like a prize fool only Lizzie seemed her usual self, calm and studious as ever. Dear Lizzie. What a rock she and her family were to be in the weeks and months ahead, both to Nancy and me. Lizzie, as one would expect of her, was taking life in her stride, ready and excited to meet the challenges ahead. She was so grounded but then she was lucky. Her home

Monday's Child
Caroline Jones Lewis

and family were so secure and loving without the indulgences that had been heaped on Nancy.

I, of course, hadn't known that secure family unit after my parents died, despite the best intentions of my dear Grandma. She gave me all the love and care she could but it could never have been the same. I don't think I had ever been reconciled to the loss of my parents despite my age. They had been such warm, loving parents and at the time of her death, my mother had been heavily pregnant so there had been the excitement and expectation of a new baby brother or sister ahead, a new baby much awaited and longed for by my parents. With only weeks to go to the happy event, they had gone out that evening to celebrate their wedding anniversary while I was cared for at home by my grandmother. My last memory of my parents was my mother hugging and kissing me goodnight as they left, smiling and radiant with happiness, my father standing in the doorway urging her to hurry or they would be late for their booking.

"Night, champ," my father said. "Have fun with Grandma. See you in the morning."

There are times when I still feel the soft warmth of my mother's lips on my cheek, still smell her perfume that had lingered on the air after they left, still see my father's smile and hear his voice as he wished me goodnight. They were torn from me in an agonising instant. Then came the shock, the pain, unfamiliar sounds that roused me from my sleep, sombre voices in the hallway and my grandmother's anguished cry as I crouched behind the banister staring down on the policeman standing beneath me. There were comings and goings that night, the opening and closing of doors as people came and went and my aunt and uncle and neighbours I barely knew. And the question I heard on their lips; how do we tell Hugh?

I don't remember crying, not even at the funeral, but I'm sure I must have. They had tried to save the baby, the

Monday's Child
Caroline Jones Lewis

doctors, Grandma told me. A girl, my baby sister. But she was too small and it was too early and the shock of the accident and all that. She lived just a few hours and my grandmother had her christened. Ella, she called her – not knowing what name my parents had chosen. My baby sister Ella. And they took a photo which we still keep in a little silver frame at my grandmother's, beside the one of my parents. I went to live with my grandmother, a strange new life with strange new people and a new school. So I didn't have the privilege of constancy and security that Lizzie grew up with. Memories come back sometimes in a jumble of nightmare. I think after that I always felt insecure.

But I digress. Where was I? Nancy. Oh yes, Nancy – on that afternoon.

Nancy flounced off to the boat. It was her usual thing when she needed an escape. It usually worked though. She would return from sailing in good humour, the angst that had sent her off in the first place completely forgotten. I probably didn't help that afternoon, trying as I was to be 'normal', whatever that means. Looking back I probably over-compensated for the dawning recognition of my sexuality by trying to be macho-man. I think I came over as a self-righteous chauvinist prig, which annoyed Nancy immensely. Somehow I couldn't help myself. I was churning inside. Perhaps if I hadn't been so flippant she might have confided in me. Perhaps. Perhaps not. I'll never know now.

She was gone for several hours and when she returned she wasn't in her usual high spirits after sailing. More in the same mood as she'd been in before she left. I think at the time I put it down to the life changes the girls were going through – waiting for their exam results, leaving the shelter of school and about to launch into the rest of the world; academia or whatever. And of course Nancy was getting a

Monday's Child

Caroline Jones Lewis

fair amount of nagging from her father over her apparent lack of direction career-wise made all the more glaringly obvious by Lizzie's clear-headed focus. He must have felt despondent given the considerable amount of money that had been spent on Nancy's education. My Aunt and Uncle had been good to me since my parents died. Uncle James was an executor of my parents' will and Trustee of the Trust Fund that had been set up to provide for my needs. But it's strange, isn't it, that while they were both so clear-thinking where other people's lives and finances were concerned, they seemed myopic when it came to Nancy and had never really been able to channel her considerable energy into a positive direction. She had been spoiled and over-indulged materially since the day she was born. Maybe, I thought, it was just beginning to dawn on her that people in the wider world would not make excuses for her short-comings in the way her parents had. Lizzie and I had commented to each other that the disciplines the rest of the world lived within might come as a shock to Nancy after a school life where her parents' generous contributions to school funds had resulted in the overlooking of certain pranks and misdemeanours that might otherwise have resulted in expulsion. Whatever the cause for her state of mind, Nancy's mood still hung around her that day impregnating the atmosphere at dinner. Both Nancy and I, it seemed, were in turmoil.

Aunt Miranda did her best to dispel the atmosphere, without much success.
"Will you still be here at the weekend, Hugh? When James arrives?"
"I'm not sure yet, Aunt Miranda. Can I let you know once I've spoken with my office? I have to be in Edinburgh for Monday morning so I may have to go back to the flat for the weekend to prepare. To be honest, I've been so relaxed here that I haven't worked out my timetable yet."

Monday's Child

Caroline Jones Lewis

"Of course, dear," my aunt replied. "It's just that I think James wants to talk to you about the Trust Fund at some point soon. But I don't think it's urgent."
My Trust Fund matured on my 25th birthday when the proceeds legally became mine to do with as I pleased. My birthday loomed ahead in the autumn but, engrossed as I had been with other matters, it had hardly crossed my mind. I knew that, handled right, the fund would provide me with security for the rest of my life, a fortunate situation to be in, but I regarded this as a bonus as I fully intended to make my own way in life through a successful career. I think I answered her with what sounded like disinterest, preoccupied as I was. She must have found my attitude strange as it was a significant event in my life.

I was becoming increasingly desperate to return to my London flat and the man I was missing. I needed to know if he was missing me, unsure as I was of his commitment to what I saw as our relationship but what he might regard as simply a bit of fun. Simon was everything I wasn't. He was blonde with hair down to his shoulders, outrageously good-looking, but most of all fun and exuberant. He worked at the local rep with all those artistic people, a much more exciting environment than banking. His flat, which he rented, was always in disarray because he never had time for tedious things like housework. How boring, I wondered, did he view me with my mousy brown hair, ordinary looks and quiet personality and my flat that I tidied compulsively.

The next morning I made a telephone call to my office and feigned an urgent return to London on Friday morning, giving no further thought to Uncle James or my Trust Fund, or to Nancy and her anxiety whatever the cause. Looking back I just wish I had paid her more attention. Hindsight is a wonderful thing, is it not?

Monday's Child

Caroline Jones Lewis

Chapter two – Breaking Up

Friday morning opened in a flurry of activity in contrast to the sedentary nature of the previous days. Hugh needed to be at the station by 10 am. Mr Hale would therefore take him and on a round trip would call at the village quay to buy fish for supper. He would return to the station again that evening to collect Mr Carlisle from the London train.
"Are you sure you have everything, Hugh?" Miranda asked, her eyes roving around the drawing room to check that nothing of his was left in the room. "You've checked your room?"
"Yes, thanks, Auntie. And the bathroom," he replied anticipating the routine. He edged towards the hallway where his suitcase already rested near the front door. "Thank you for having me, Auntie. It's been lovely to have a break."
"Well, you must come again, dear. Before the summer's over. You know you're always welcome," replied his Aunt as they moved out into the hallway. "Your room is always ready. Just give me a call."
She kissed him on the cheek as he edged out of the doorway, watched by Nancy and Lizzie who stood outside ready to wave him off.
"Don't work too hard," called Miranda as he turned and walked out of the door.
"Bye, Hugh," chorused Nancy and Lizzie as he tossed his suitcase into the boot of the car.
He turned to kiss them both on the cheek, then bounded back to the car and climbed into the passenger seat next to Mr Hale. In no time the car was moving forward, the tyres crunching on the gravel driveway as it went and Hugh looked back with a smile and a wave as it disappeared around the corner into the road beyond. In months to come they would recall that moment, the kindness and affection in that poignant smile and hazel eyes, the nut brown hair that flopped, as ever, across his forehead and the brush of

Monday's Child
Caroline Jones Lewis

the hand as by habit he pushed it away. And then he was gone.

The girls turned to go back into the house where Nancy's mother stood framed in the doorway.
"So," she exclaimed. "What have you two planned for the day?" she asked cheerily as they all went inside.
"We're going swimming, aren't we, Lizzie?"
"Mmm," Lizzie nodded lazily.
"We thought we'd have a picnic on the beach. Are you coming, Mums?"
"Oh, I don't think so, darling. Not this morning, anyway. I have things to do."
"What things?" questioned Nancy, a shadow falling across her smile."
"Oh, just odds and ends. I thought I'd walk into the village. Mrs Hale will be here if you need anything. I'll help you do your picnic before I go, though."
"You could join us afterwards, though, couldn't you?" Nancy pressed. "You won't be that long in the village, surely?"
Miranda hedged.
"I'm not sure, darling," she said. She paused for thought, then continued.
"I may call on old Nanny Sophie if she's up and about. Mrs Hale tells me she's been quite poorly since Christmas. She's getting old, poor thing."
Sophie Baines, or Nanny Sophie as she had always been referred to, was the former post-mistress of the village, now retired and living in a small cottage near the green. Widowed in the second world war, she had never remarried since no man on this earth could ever live up to her long-departed Charlie. It was naturally incumbent on the residents of the community to look after one of their own in times of sickness. Miranda, who liked to think of herself as one of that community in a way that in reality she could never be regarded by the villagers, included herself in that responsibility.

Monday's Child
Caroline Jones Lewis

"But we could do that tomorrow, couldn't we?" Nancy insisted. "We could all go. Or perhaps we should come with you today and picnic tomorrow. What do you think, Lizzie?"

Miranda interjected before Lizzie had chance to reply. "Oh, Nancy, that would be boring for you, two teenage girls visiting a sick old lady. And who knows what the weather will be like tomorrow. No, really, darling. You carry on and have your picnic. I'll be back as soon as I can and then I'll join you on the beach. You'd rather that, wouldn't you, Lizzie?"

Lizzie stood between them, piggy-in-the-middle. She had the feeling there was more going on here than she could fathom. She hesitated and then,

"Swimming sounds fine," she offered. "Come on, Nanc. Let's go and see what Mrs Hale has for our picnic."

Nancy conceded, doing her best to sound light-hearted. But she was reluctant. She followed Lizzie through to the kitchen, smothering her disappointment. She had wanted to stay close to her mother but still did not want to let Lizzie know anything of her fears. Just at this moment there was nothing she could do.

"Still," she thought, "Daddy will be here tomorrow. Then he and Mummy will be together again and everything will be fine."

Miranda helped them with their picnic, a veritable feast produced by the ever-resourceful Mrs Hale, interrupted only by a telephone call which Miranda took in private and from which she returned without comment. Nancy's stomach took another lurch but, with Lizzie within earshot, she resisted the temptation to ask who was on the phone. In due course, the girls set off for the beach equipped with picnic basket, swimwear and – in Lizzie's case – the inevitable book whilst Nancy took the latest edition of "Jackie" magazine. As soon as they had left, Miranda went to her room and spent ten minutes or so carefully touching up her make-up and tidying her hair. Then she,

Monday's Child

Caroline Jones Lewis

too, left with only the briefest of words to Mrs Hale and no mention of where she was going and for how long. The housekeeper said nothing – but she thought all the more.

When Miranda returned a little after 3 o'clock, just in time for the reappearance of her daughter and Lizzie, she gave the deliberate impression that she had been home for a while.

"Mums, you didn't come to the beach," Nancy pouted.
"I did think about it, darling, but decided it wasn't worth it," Miranda replied. "I was sure you'd be back home soon so by the time I'd fetched a towel and changed into my swimsuit you'd be on your way back."
She diverted the conversation deftly.
"I'll bet you're both starving after all that fresh air and swimming. Did you have a good time?"
"Famished," agreed Lizzie emphatically, seemingly unaware of the tension creeping in between her cousin and her aunt.
"Shall I ask Mrs Hale to put the kettle on, Auntie?"
"Please, dear," Miranda replied and Lizzie left the room and headed for the kitchen.
"So," Nancy began, unable to leave matters rest any longer. "Did you visit Nanny Sophie then?"
"I tried but she obviously didn't hear me," her mother lied, suspecting she detected tension in her daughter's voice. Or was it just guilt fuelling her imagination, she wondered?
"She was probably asleep. So I took a nice long walk along the coast path towards the Gap instead. It was beautiful up on the cliffs today."
"That isn't like you, Mummy," Nancy observed, reluctant to concede. "I've never known you go walking much before."
"Well, perhaps it's time I began," countered her mother. "Maybe it's time for a change from the bright lights. Something closer to nature, don't you think? You and Daddy love it so, don't you? Perhaps I should try to join in."

Monday's Child
Caroline Jones Lewis

Nancy was silent, lost for anything further to say without confronting her mother directly.
"Have you been to see your lover?" she wanted to ask. "Are you having an affair?"
But why should she? On what grounds should she think there was such a person, except there was that light brush of her mother's cheek and a certain smile on her mother's lips that, in the briefest of moments that now seemed so distant, had triggered the suspicion. Now she wasn't sure what she had seen. Perhaps she had imagined it, or misinterpreted the whole episode. Perhaps she was being paranoid. She would put it out of her mind right now – before Daddy came. It was going to be a lovely weekend and on Monday, Jacs was coming. It would be fun. Her mood visibly lifted and Miranda inwardly heaved a sigh of relief.

James Carlisle arrived that evening to the sound of laughter and a dinner of freshly caught and cooked halibut, fresh vegetables grown by Mr Hale in his garden and cooked by his wife and strawberries from the local market. All should have been well – except that he, too, felt tense.

After dinner, Lizzie decided to have a bath before bed. She had done her best to wash the salt off her skin after swimming, but it had not been sufficient. Her skin felt sticky and hot and her hair felt positively rank. It was a bath that was needed, she decided. And some soothing cream to cool her skin which was threatening to redden with sunburn.
"I'll get you some of my cream, dear," her aunt promised. "You must take care of that lovely complexion of yours. Sunburn is so ageing."
Lizzie blushed. She had never thought of her complexion as lovely, or any other part of her, come to that. Nancy was the pretty one. No, not pretty even – beautiful. That's what Nancy was. Beautiful. Miranda fetched a plethora of

Monday's Child

Caroline Jones Lewis

bottles from her room and bundled them into her niece's arms. Lizzie departed, giggling, for the bathroom.
"I'll be in there for hours," she declared.
"Well, it's alright if you are, Liz," Miranda assured her. "Take as long as you like. Wallow in it," and her aunt laughed.
Nancy decided to go up to her room.
"I'm going to play my new record," she announced.
Nancy followed her cousin up the staircase and left Lizzie heading along the long landing towards the bathroom for her luxurious bubble bath while she continued to her own room in the other direction. The dining room door had closed behind them.

Silence fell across the table between James and Miranda seated at either end. The house seemed strangely quiet with Mrs Hale gone for the evening and the girls both quiet upstairs. Miranda felt the tension increase; there was clearly something wrong. She hesitated, thinking perhaps James would speak but he said nothing, leaving it to her to break the silence.
"James?" she asked.
"What?" her replied stonily.
"There's obviously a problem. Are you going to tell me what it is?"
James considered for a moment. Did he want to raise this now – at Abberley with the girls upstairs? His face was stern, his jaw set rigid and his eyes dark with anger beneath the thick brown lashes. Unable to resist and urged on by the rawness of his pain, he raised his napkin from his lap and slapped it onto the table.
"You're seeing him again, Miranda."
It was a statement, not a question.
"No," she began but James stopped her, brushing aside her attempted denial impatiently.
"Don't lie to me, Miranda, for God's sake. I've had enough of your lies. You're seeing him again, aren't you?"

Monday's Child
Caroline Jones Lewis

She hesitated, then answered in a hushed voice.
"Yes."
"You promised me it was over. You promised me you would never see him again."
They fell silent. Miranda was caught on the back foot with nothing in reserve for her defence. She had not expected this, had thought she had covered her tracks adequately. She hated the deceit, the lying but equally she hated the idea of hurting James, something she had hoped to avoid without any idea of what she wanted for the future. James glared, apoplectic with hurt and anger. He could think of no way of putting into words all that he was feeling. From an upstairs window strains of Cliff Richard floated down on the breeze from Nancy's bedroom and in through the open French doors.

> The young ones
> Darling, we're the young ones

For some seconds neither moved a muscle, tongue-tied, neither knowing what to say next. It was an emotional dam that was about to burst.

Upstairs in her room, Nancy laid stomach down on her bed, head and shoulders propped up by her elbows, long legs bent up at the knees and ankles crossed, swaying in time to the music. She mouthed the words to the parts she knew and hummed the parts she didn't. Her mouth felt dry, she was thirsty, dehydrated after the beach and the sun, from the salt of swimming and carried on the breeze. She noted with pleasure that she was developing a glowing tan. She rolled over contentedly and sprang to her feet, crossed the room to make her way down towards the kitchen to fetch herself a drink of water – or maybe Mrs Hale would have made some fresh lemonade and left it cooling in the 'fridge. Barefoot she slipped silently down the stairs, still humming quietly, and padded along the cool tiles of the hallway. As she neared the dining room, she

Monday's Child

Caroline Jones Lewis

heard her father's voice raised in fury, her mother's angry response. She stopped in her tracks, paused outside the door and froze, silent, listening to a storm raging between her parents inside the room. Their earlier silence had broken and a raging torrent flooded the space between the two people still seated at the table.

"How could you, Miranda? After all we said before. How could you?" James ranted. "You promised me it was over."
"It was," began Miranda. "It was. Truly. But then … "
"Oh, spare me the details," James raged. "Don't tell me. True love, is it? You couldn't live without him."
Her feathers ruffled now, Miranda took the bait.
"Well, maybe that's right," she countered, her voice rising and she rose to her feet. "Not just sex like it was with you, James. But I suppose that was alright. Sex is alright as long as there's no love involved, is that it? But I suppose what's good for the goose is definitely not good for the gander."
"That's not fair," James retorted, rising from his chair to meet her gaze equally. They confronted each other across the room like birds in a cock fight.
"It was different. The circumstances were different," he continued. "You accepted that at the time. All that time you rejected me after Nancy was born. I've never done that to you. There's no reason for this. No reason at all."
"Oh, is there not? So you think that you and our marriage are perfect, do you?" Miranda was raging now, the guilt and shock of discovery replaced by self-righteous indignation.
"While you can justify your infidelity down to my shortcomings, your little peccadillo, you of course are perfect. You can see no justification for mine."
James turned his face away from her, stung by the challenge.
"So that's all it is, then? A peccadillo."
"That isn't what I meant and you know it."

Monday's Child

Caroline Jones Lewis

"So what is it that's so bad, then, Miranda. Tell me. What is it that is so bad in our life and our marriage that you need another man to satisfy your needs?" he asked bitterly. Miranda was silent. She didn't know how to put what was in her heart. She was hurting him enough already. She didn't want to hurt him more. Yet her memory insisted on reminding her of how he had hurt her by *his* affair; how it had broken that special bond she had thought was between them. Now she needed Michael. He was like a drug to her and she a junkie.

"Tell me," James continued, his voice flat and cold. "Would you have married me if you hadn't been pregnant?"

Miranda did not answer. James waited for a moment but then pressed her, impatient for a reply.

"Come on, Miranda. Tell me," he insisted. "At least be honest about that. Would you have married me?"

"I don't know, James," she protested. "How can I possibly answer that now – after all these years and all that has happened between us."

"Well, there *is* the answer, isn't it?" James insisted. "There *is* the answer. If you had really loved me you would know the answer, wouldn't you?"

"Maybe," she replied in a whisper.

"So there we have it," he shouted angrily. "There's the truth of it. You only married me because you were pregnant. Perhaps you even regretted not having the abortion . Perhaps I should never have persuaded you." He turned away, his face twisted with pain and wishing now that he had not asked the question.

"No," Miranda began hotly. "No. I've never regretted that. How could I?" but James was not listening. He stormed across the room and flung open the door to leave. Both he and Miranda were shocked to see an ashen-faced Nancy on the other side.

"Nancy," he gasped.

Nancy turned and fled back up the stairs to her room.

Monday's Child

Caroline Jones Lewis

"Nancy, darling. Come back," he pleaded, rushing after her with Miranda close on his heels. She stopped at the bottom of the staircase and sank onto a stair, groaning, shaking, head in her hands.
"Oh, no. Oh, God, Nancy," she gasped. "I'm so sorry, darling. I'm so sorry."

Lizzie, who had heard nothing, emerged from the bathroom wrapped in her bathrobe and was surprised to see her Uncle James pleading anxiously at Nancy's bedroom door.
"Nancy, darling. Please open the door. Please. Let me just speak to you."
"Is something wrong, Uncle James?" she asked.
"Go away. I don't want to speak to you. I hate you, both of you. I hate you," came Nancy's reply shouted from behind her bedroom door.
James shrugged at Lizzie in an attempt to minimise the drama taking place.
"God forbid Lizzie should know all this", he thought.
"You know Nancy," he said weakly.
Lizzie grinned and nodded.
"Can I help?" she asked. "She'll listen to me sometimes."
James shook his head.
"No, it's alright, Lizzie. Thanks all the same. You carry on with what you're doing. She'll soon snap out of it. Probably be right as rain in the morning."
He smiled wanly, wishing desperately that this was truly likely but knowing full well it was a vain hope.
"Goodnight Uncle James."
"Goodnight Lizzie."
"Goodnight Nanc," called Lizzie. There was no reply.

Nancy, of course, was not as right as rain in the morning. Neither were her parents. After several attempts by each of them that evening to prise Nancy out of her room to talk, and her stubborn refusal, Miranda had retired to the master bedroom to spend a restless night and James to the

Monday's Child
Caroline Jones Lewis

spare room where he failed to sleep at all. Each spent the darkness hours tossing and turning punctuated by trips to Nancy's bedroom door to listen for any sound. There was none. No ranting, no crying, nor any other sound discernible. Neither did she appear for breakfast. James excused her to Lizzie.
"Too much sun yesterday, I think, Lizzie. I think that's why she was so out of sorts last night. Not that it takes much, as you know."
"Shall I go up and see her," Lizzie asked.
"I think she's sleeping at the moment," interjected Miranda. "I went up to her just now and she was firm."
Lizzie wondered at the dark circles under Miranda's eyes and a slightly unkempt look that was not usual for her elegant and well-groomed aunt.
"Perhaps she is ill as I thought", wondered Lizzie. "Perhaps they've just told Nancy and that's what's upset her."
But her thoughts were broken as her aunt continued.
"Jacqueline arrives tomorrow. Nancy will soon perk up when she's here and she has both of you for company."
Much as Lizzie found her cousins prattle banal and tedious at times, the thought of the entire day without her was strange and uninviting. And what if Nancy were still out of sorts tomorrow? She felt that she and Jacqueline had little in common, Jacqueline's interests more in tune with Nancy's than her own. Uncle James would no doubt retire behind his newspaper and Aunt Miranda, well, Lizzie could hardly relish the thought of the entire day in her aunt's company alone. Whatever would they say or do for an entire day? Or even two! With Hugh gone, there was no other company, no alternative. She considered her options and since they were few, she took herself down to the beach with a sunbed, a beach umbrella from the garden shed to protect herself from further sunburn and a book borrowed from Uncle James' bookcase since she had finished her own the night before. The day passed slowly and still Nancy failed to appear.

Monday's Child

Caroline Jones Lewis

James and Miranda, having agreed to postpone further discussion between them until they had coaxed Nancy from her room, kept their distance from each other, each trying to hold a stilted conversation at dinner with a vexed Lizzie. The atmosphere was strained. Grateful when the meal was over, Lizzie excused herself as soon as the pudding dishes were removed. Even Mrs Hale was uncharacteristically lacking in jolly chit chat, sensing the atmosphere was not conducive. It was a shaken but thankful Lizzie who took a telephone call from her father after dinner telling her that she needed to come home.
"Dad, what's wrong?" she asked.
"Your mother's not well, Liz. She needs you here to help look after her for a few days. I'm so sorry to cut your holiday short. Do you mind terribly?"
"Of course I don't," she told him.
"Sure?"
"Positive. I'll get the early train in the morning. Aunt Miranda can call you to let you know what time my train will arrive. Will you pick me up at the station?"
"Of course, love. See you then."
"Dad – what's wrong with Mum?"
Her father paused.
"She's had a miscarriage, love."
Lizzie gasped.
"Oh, Dad. I had no idea."
"No, well. We hadn't wanted to tell you yet. Early days and all that. It wasn't planned. We'd always wanted more children but when the years went by and it didn't happened, well, we just accepted it and thought it wasn't meant to be. We had you so we were lucky in that. This baby came as a bolt out of the blue." He laughed weakly. "Sadly this wasn't meant to be either."
"Is Mum ok?"
"She'll be fine, she's just weak and upset. She needs time. And she'll be glad to have you home. It's all been a bit of an emotional roller coaster."

Monday's Child
Caroline Jones Lewis

"Oh, Dad. I'm so sorry. Give Mum my love and a hug from me. Tell her I'll spoil her rotten when I get home."
"Ok, love. But please don't say anything to your aunt and uncle. It's up to your mother to tell them when she's ready."
"OK. See you tomorrow. Love you, Dad."
"Love you too, Liz."

Nancy appeared briefly to see Lizzie off to the station. She looked dreadful, Lizzie thought. Just dreadful. She obviously was not well.
"Time of the month," Nancy lied ruefully.
"Oh, poor you," Lizzie sympathised. "Hope you feel better soon," and they hugged goodbye at the door.
"I'm sorry you're going, Liz," Nancy blurted suddenly. "I hope your mother's better soon, too".
Lizzie turned back to face her.
"Me too. I'll ring you," Lizzie promised – and she was gone.
Nancy felt sad and alone. She turned to face her parents standing together in the hallway, glaring at them angrily before sweeping past them and returning to her room.

With Lizzie gone and Mrs Hale on her day off, there was nothing to stem the tide of anger that Nancy had been stifling. When she was finally forced from her room by hunger, it erupted in a tempestuous flood of accusation. Miranda was attempting normality by preparing their traditional Sunday roast but nothing was going to hold back the anger and distress that Nancy was feeling. She slammed around the kitchen collecting cake, biscuits, an apple, a glass of milk, anything she could grasp to take back to her bolt hole. As she moved around the room, she spewed forth a hail of penetrating and precise questions like a torrent of red hot lava. They left her parents reeling and defenceless. So who was her mother's lover - the man in the pergola? So her father had had an affair, too. Why, when, with whom and for how long? Their marriage was

Monday's Child
Caroline Jones Lewis

obviously nothing but a sham and what of her? How could they expect her to believe they cared about her? So her mother had considered aborting her. So did she regret having had her? And was her father really her father? Her mother had lied, not just to her father but to her too, to Nancy. Her father had lied, too. In fact their entire marriage was a lie. Her accusations she considered indefensible.

"So I wasn't premature, then – the longed for baby that arrived early. I was just a mistake. A mishap you weren't even sure you wanted to keep."

"No," Miranda tried to protest. "No, you weren't premature but that was only an excuse to hide that I was pregnant when we married. You must understand, in those days …"

"Is there nothing you don't lie about?" Nancy spat at her. "Were you that ashamed you were having me?"

"Nancy, listen to me – please," her mother begged but Nancy's anger seemed inexhaustible. They could say nothing to placate her.

"What for?" she shrieked. "For more lies? How can I believe a word you say; either of you. I hate you. I hate you both," and she fled back to her room, her parents trailing in her wake.

James and Miranda stood on the landing silent and shaken, neither knowing the next move to make.

"We should ring Jacqueline's parents," Miranda suggested as she slowly descended the stairs. "We can't have her coming in the middle of this. She'll be leaving soon to catch the afternoon train."

"I agree," said James. "I'll ring them. We'll have to make an excuse. Illness, or something."

"Tell them a lie, you mean," snapped Miranda. "Another lie."

Fate conveniently intervened. Before they had even had time to find the phone number for Jacqueline's parents, another call resolved the difficulty. There was illness but it was Jacqueline's.

Monday's Child

Caroline Jones Lewis

"Nancy, Jacqueline's on the phone," Miranda called outside Nancy's bedroom door. "She's in hospital. She's had her appendix out so you'd better come and speak to her. She can't stay on the phone for long."
The bedroom door was flung open and Nancy flew past her mother down the stairs to the telephone in the hallway.

"Jacs. Oh, Jacs. What's happened?"
"I've had my appendix out, Nanc. Yesterday. I'm in a private room but I can't stay on the phone for long. It was agony. You wouldn't believe. And I threw up all over the place."
"Oh, Jacs, that's awful. I'm really sorry. I was so looking forward to seeing you. Lizzie's gone too because her mother's ill. I'll *really* miss you."
Nancy ached. If there was a time she needed her friend it was now.
"We can't even go to Spain, Nanc. Can you believe it? Look I'll have to go. We'll have to meet up when you come back to London. I'll be better by then. We can go to a film. "The Young Ones." Everyone says it's brilliant. I'm dying to see it. Cliff Richard. Hey, sexy or what? Have to go Nanc. See you soon," and the line went dead.
Nancy replaced the receiver feeling bereft. She returned to her room. Everything felt so unreal. Everything was going wrong. She felt ill. She had hardly slept for the last two nights and had eaten very little except to sneak down to the refrigerator when the house was quiet and find some ham and cheese to stick in a roll. She didn't want to go anywhere. She didn't want to see anyone. She crawled into bed and pulled the eiderdown over her head. There she stayed for the rest of the day while her parents fretted downstairs.

"I'll ring the office in the morning. I'll tell them I'm sick," James decided.

Monday's Child
Caroline Jones Lewis

"No," said Miranda. "No, I think you should go. Maybe she will at least open up a bit if there's only one of us. Perhaps I can get her to talk to me."
"Oh, fine. A chance for you to get your story in order, no doubt," James spat.
"I won't. I promise I won't," Miranda insisted. "I'll just try to get her to calm down a bit. Try to get her to eat something substantial."
"Perhaps we should all go back to London," James suggested.
Miranda considered. Michael was here; that cat was out of the proverbial bag. He had rented a cottage for the summer months to be near her. She wanted to stay but it was a dilemma. The important thing was to pacify Nancy. She must come first.
"Maybe when I've had chance to calm her down," Miranda suggested. "But she loves it here. She may want to stay. It should be her decision."

In the event, the matter was taken out of their hands. James left for the station in the morning with Mr Hale to catch the early morning train. Nancy made no appearance to say goodbye. When Nancy failed to make an appearance of her own volition, Miranda finally tapped on her bedroom door later in the morning in the hope of coaxing her out of her room. She found the door ajar. It swung open to reveal a room in chaos. Of Nancy there was no sign, nor of her holdall into which she had obviously stuffed some of her clothes which were missing, her toiletries, make-up gone from the dressing table and odd personal items. The family photograph Nancy normally kept on her bedside table, of herself and her smiling parents taken on the boat, lay smashed on the floor. In panic Miranda rushed from the house to search for her daughter. She ran first down to the boat but it rested calmly at its mooring, rising and falling gently with the incoming tide. She headed for the village, checking the bus stop and the taxi rank and asking people in the village

Monday's Child

Caroline Jones Lewis

if they had seen Nancy as calmly as she could without giving away her considerable concern. Desperate and distraught she returned to the house to ring James. "She's gone," she told him. "Nancy's gone."

Monday's Child

Caroline Jones Lewis

Chapter Three – Where from Here?

Letting herself into the house quietly, Lizzie parked her suitcase in the hallway and checked the downstairs rooms for her mother but there was no sign. Making her way deftly up the carpeted staircase she headed for her parents' bedroom, whilst in the bedroom Emily Hayne heard her beloved daughter's key in the lock and her footsteps down the hall.

"Lizzie's home," she thought. "My lovely Lizzie," and tears of gratitude welled in her eyes. She breathed deeply and waited expectantly for the tap on the door.

"Mum," Lizzie called and popped her head around the door to see her mother propped up on the pillows of the bed looking pale and dishevelled from tears and sleeping.

"Lizzie," breathed her mother and turned to face her daughter, smiling wanly.

Lizzie crossed the room. She hugged her mother and sat beside her on the bed.

"Mum, I'm so sorry," she began. "Dad told me – about the baby. I'm so sorry. I had no idea you were pregnant."

"We decided not to tell you yet," Emily explained. "Until I was past the first twelve weeks just in case. And well - here we are."

She sighed and a tear squeezed from the corner of her eye.

"We were so excited, Liz. Just for a few short weeks …. "

She paused, unable to say more. Her lip trembled and another tear escaped to roll slowly down her cheek, then another and another until they came in a flood.

Lizzie clasped her mother's hand in her own but said nothing. She could find no words or know how to comfort her mother in her distress. Thoughts and emotions had overwhelmed her, too, in the last 24 hours. Despite her maturity the fact that she had almost had a new brother or sister, a new life that had failed to survive, had been a shock that had impacted on her perception of life and their family unit. How different would their world have been had that baby been born? During her journey there had

Monday's Child
Caroline Jones Lewis

seemed to be babies everywhere around her, gurgling, crying, sleeping in their mothers' arms or in their pushchairs or being wheeled along pavements in coach built prams. She had tried to imagine both the positives and the negatives having little experience as she did of the practicalities of a baby in the house. But overall the idea had been exciting to her too. That excitement had quickly dissipated into sadness for the loss. Compassion for the mother she so loved caused a physical ache in her chest. Now in the quiet of the bedroom and the poigniancy of the moment, words would have been an intrusion.

They remained in silence until Emily, anguish subsiding, rummaged for a handkerchief under her pillow. She mopped her eyes and snuffled into its crumpled softness. "We'd always wanted more children," she went on. "But it just seemed it wasn't meant to be. All those years we were hoping. We just consoled ourselves with having you, Lizzie. Lucky us. There are so many couples who don't even have one child. They eat their hearts out year after year. We have you and you're everything we could ever wish for," and she squeezed Lizzie's hand affectionately. "All the same, it was exciting, just for a little while, the prospect of another child even at our age."
She paused again, struggling with emotion.
"Do Nan and Grandad know?" Lizzie asked.
Emily shook her head.
"They would only want to come. All that long journey. You know what your Nan is like."
Tom's parents had retired to Harrogate several years before from his childhood home in Leeds. It was normally Tom, Emily and Lizzie who made the journey to them and not the other way around, particularly as the parents were not overly fond of the hustle and bustle of London where they would have to change trains.
"We decided not to tell them too early. I'm not sure there's any need for them to know at all now. But I did

Monday's Child
Caroline Jones Lewis

want you to come home, Liz. I hope you didn't mind too much."

"Of course I didn't, Mum," Lizzie assured her. "I wasn't really enjoying myself that much at Abberley this year so it was no sacrifice at all."

"Oh," Emily was surprised. "That's not like you. You've always loved your summers at Abberley. What was the problem?"

"I don't know really. Maybe it was me. Because I'm waiting for my exam results. I'm really excited about going to university and until I get my results I can't be sure. I just want to get on with it. Nancy just seemed in a funny mood and ..."

"So what's new there," Emily laughed.

"No, not like usual. Not tantrums. Nothing like that. She just seemed edgy. And Hugh was – well, I'm not sure how Hugh was," she said, shrugging her shoulders. "I don't really think he wanted to be there at all. He didn't say but I just had this feeling. Perhaps we're all just growing up, growing apart because our lives are changing and going in different directions. I don't know – it just all seemed different."

"Hmm, I suppose things are bound to change. Your lives are all moving on, aren't they? Not children any more."

Lizzie nodded.

"I hope we don't grow too apart," she exclaimed. "That would be awful."

"Oh, I'm sure that won't happen, love," Emily reassured her.

How sad that would be, she thought. But all the same, their lives were moving in different directions and in recent years the three cousins had developed as very different people. Who knew what the future had in store?

"I'm going to get up now," announced Emily, her voice thick and nasal from the effects of emotion. "I need a wash. I feel such a mess," and she looked up into Lizzie's face. "And you must be tired after your journey,

Monday's Child

Caroline Jones Lewis

sweetheart. When I come down from the bathroom you must tell me all about Abberley."
"I'm ok," Lizzie insisted. "You needn't get up yet if you don't feel like it. How about a cuppa? I could do with one. Why don't you rest a bit longer and I'll bring one up?"
"Good idea," Emily agreed. "The great British panacea. Works every time."

Downstairs in the kitchen Lizzie gazed absentmindedly out of the window at the courtyard beyond. The geraniums in the pots along the fence were wilting, she noticed, their blossoms limp around the rim, obviously overlooked in the present disruption of her mother's routine and suffering from the dry heat of the long August days.
"I'll water them later," she told herself. "When the heat of the day has died down a bit."
The whistling of the kettle on the stove jolted her out of her reverie. She turned off the gas and poured the boiling water onto the tealeaves in the teapot already prepared on the tray. She found some biscuits in the cupboard and placed them on a plate beside the cups and saucers. Then she carried the tray and its contents back upstairs to the bedroom. Quite unexpectedly a weariness crept over her, a longing to sink into the soft chintziness of her own bed. It had been a week like no other, not just here at home but at Abberley too. It had not been the relaxing carefree interlude of previous years. There had been tensions she did not fully understand. But she was home now and first she would look after her mother and then prepare for what she hoped lay ahead – when her results came in. It was only days away now and the thought of her hoped-for bright new future both excited and intrigued her. A slow smile crept across her mouth. When she re-entered her mother's bedroom, a glow of anticipation radiated from her.
"Lizzie?" her mother questioned.

Monday's Child

Caroline Jones Lewis

"I'm sorry, Mum," Lizzie began. "I'm being selfish, I know but I just can't help being excited. My results will be through in a few days and I worked so hard. I just hope it was enough. I think it was. I can't help feeling excited. Am I being selfish?"

"Of course not," her mother protested. "That's what we have to do, Liz. Concentrate on positive, happy things. And if I know you, you'll have done it. We'll be celebrating. I don't doubt it."

Lizzie poured the tea, tingling with excitement. Changes were afoot and the start of the next phase of her life was only days away.

******

It was early evening when Nancy arrived in London. The journey had seemed interminable, a slow train that had stopped at virtually every station along the route and by the time it pulled into Paddington the anger that had driven her was subsiding. She felt drained. She had rarely travelled alone before and never for so long a journey, had always been in what she thought the safe company of her loving family.

"What a joke," she thought.

They had never really wanted her; she had been an accident, a mishap and their marriage a sham because of her. Her whole life had been a lie. Hurt and anger flared simultaneously and spurred her on. It was too late now, she decided, to go to the house. Her father would be home from his office. She did not want to see him. So checking the funds she had, she searched for and found a bed and breakfast for the night near the station, modest but clean. In a cheap café she drank lukewarm tea and ate a sandwich as thick as a doorstep. But the bread was good and it assuaged the hunger that had crept up on her during the journey.

Monday's Child
Caroline Jones Lewis

The waitress studied Nancy with curiosity as she cleared the formica-topped tables and wiped them clean of crumbs and tea stains with a grubby dishcloth.
"Not from round here, that's for sure," she thought. "Obviously out of place in an area like this." The cut of the jeans, the crisp white cotton blouse and classy suede shoes shouted Knightsbridge, so much in contrast with her own market-stall clothing, the cheap bri-nylon of her overall and the low-heeled black patent shoes form Marks and Spencer with their ribbed ribbon bows.
"Wonder what the story is there," she mused as she whisked away the stub-laden ashtrays that reeked of nicotine and tar. She breathed in the scent of expensive toiletries appreciatively as she passed Nancy by.
"Hmm, nice," she thought. "You can always tell money, they always smell nice, people with money."

Nancy finished her food and sat dejectedly at the table. With her anger cooled she felt confused and lost, part of her regretting her haste in leaving but the rest of her determined never to see her parents ever again. The jukebox, fed by a scruffy youth in working clothes who had consumed a mountain of food at a nearby table, jerked into action as his coins dropped with a clatter into its innards.

> Only the Lonely
> Know the hurt I feel inside.

The words were too much for Nancy and unable to stand the melancholy they threatened to invoke, she left and made her way back to the B & B. She collapsed exhausted onto the bed fully clothed and fell into a deep sleep.

It was early morning when she awoke. Her tawdry surroundings reminded her of recent events and she sat on the bed crumpled and confused. What to do next? Everything seemed unreal, like a bad dream from which

Monday's Child
Caroline Jones Lewis

she would awake at any moment. But the anger was still there, sparking and crackling in her brain like a firecracker. She checked her watch. It was only 7.30, still too early to venture far. What would Lizzie do, dear organised clear-thinking Lizzie?
"Stupid question," she told herself. "As if Lizzie would be ever in a situation like this.
First things first, she thought. A wash and a change of clothing; that was where to start. She delved into her holdall for clean underwear, a change of jeans and blouse, toothbrush and toothpaste, soap and towel and deodorant, the bag's contents littered across the bed. But she congratulated herself for having brought everything she needed, that in her anger and panic to leave without being noticed, she had managed to achieve that much. She washed in an ageing basin in the corner, avoiding cutting herself on a chip in the corner but not wanting to use the shared bathroom across the landing that smelled of bleach and carbolic except for the toilet which was unavoidable. Once freshened a little, she planned her next move. She would wait until her father had left for his office, then go into the house for more of her belongings. The daily didn't come in today so she could take time for a bath and shampoo her hair. She would find her savings book and diary in which all her contacts were written, then ring the friend who she hoped might invite her to stay. She couldn't ring Jacs, obviously and didn't think it right to ring Lizzie, at least not at the moment. Hugh was away if she remembered rightly, and in any case he would probably simply tell her to go home. She ruled him out and concocted in her mind a story for her friend that would be acceptable. With a reasonable plan for survival in place, at least for the short term, she felt better, more confident. She went down to the dining room and ate all she could of the breakfast she had paid for, surprised at how hungry she felt. The landlady eyed her with curiosity but there were no questions asked. Returning to her room, she re-packed her holdall and left.

Monday's Child
Caroline Jones Lewis

Nancy took a bus to the familiarity of Knightsbridge. On the way she stared blankly out of the window panes at passers-by hurrying along the pavements on their way to work. It still felt unreal, bizarre, like she was sleep walking or wandering through the set of a movie. She walked the rest of the way to the house but when she turned the corner into Wilton Place she was shaken to see her father's car still parked at the kerb. He should have left by now. He must be waiting for her, she thought, expecting her to return home. She shrank back behind a furniture van just inside the street. Now what? She turned quickly and retraced her steps hurriedly until she found herself on the corner of Sloan Street where she stopped. For a moment she froze, staring vacuously ahead of her. The blast of a car horn brought her to her senses and she crossed the street heading for a coffee bar on the other side. If she had enough money, she thought, she would stop for a coffee in the hope that her father would go out soon. Taking her purse from her holdall, she was checking her money when a voice broke into her train of thought.
"Wow, Nancy. Hi. I thought it was you. I haven't seen you for ages. How are you?"
Nancy spun round and for a moment, and in her agitated state, she struggled to identify the owner of the voice. Then recognition dawned. Catherine was the daughter of a former neighbour who had now moved to the country. It must have been about a year since their move. Catherine's appearance had changed dramatically, adding initially to Nancy's confusion. The hairstyle had become fashionably sleek instead of the soft fluffiness that Nancy remembered and she wore a short, flowered dress that shrieked of Mary Quant. God, Mary Quant, thought Nancy. How she had nagged and cajoled her mother for a Mary Quant outfit instead of the twinsets and skirts that made her look like a miniature version of her mother. All she had managed to elicit was a promise of something fashionable for Christmas.

Monday's Child
Caroline Jones Lewis

"They're so short," her mother had protested. "The skirts are so short. They give out all the wrong messages to the boys."

Nancy and Jacs had been planning a shopping trip when they returned to London after the hols, Carnaby Street and the Kings Road, BIBA and all the new hotspots for fashion. They wanted mini skirts and boots right up to the knee and Jacs wanted a peaked cap, red and shiny that would look great against her glossy dark hair. The sight of Catherine reminded Nancy of all the things she and Jacs had planned to do. She instantly coveted Catherine's look. "Oh, Catherine, hi. I hardly recognised you – you look so different," she exclaimed. "I'm fine, thanks. Really great."

Under other circumstances, Nancy would have been delighted to meet up with her again but right at this moment it was an interruption she hardly needed. She wanted to get away and delved desperately into her mind for an excuse. Catherine, however, was intent on catching up with the news and gossip.

"it's just great to see you again. How are the family? You must be leaving school by now. Are you going to university?"

Nancy attempted to answer but the questions fired one after the other as Catherine prattled on.

"Heh, how about a coffee? Have you got time?"

"Well, actually," Nancy began, "I was just thinking of going for one but I've come without enough money so ..."

"Oh, no problem," Catherine effused. "They're on me. Come on, we can catch up on the gossip over an expresso."

Relaxing a little, Nancy accepted gladly and allowed herself to be ushered inside the coffee bar without another word. She had always liked Catherine, though her mother had not been keen, Nancy recalled. Flighty, her mother had said. And a bad influence. So who was she to talk? Well, I like Catherine, Nancy decided defiantly, and to hell with her. I can do what I want now. My mother's no longer in control.

Monday's Child

Caroline Jones Lewis

Keeping a low profile and choosing a table away from the window, Nancy dropped her holdall to the floor and settled herself on a chair while Catherine ordered the coffees. For the next hour or more the two girls chattered and reminisced and compared notes on the neighbouring families. Catherine, it transpired, had returned to London on her own.

"You didn't like the country, then?"

"No," Catherine said bluntly. "All that fresh air – it isn't natural," she laughed, screwing up her nose.

"So where do you live now?"

"I've got my own place. It's quite small but I like it."

Nancy's interest intensified.

"But how can you afford it?" she asked. "I mean, London's so expensive, isn't it?"

"Oh, I earn enough," Catherine winked conspiratorially. She leaned towards Nancy, lowering her voice in the cavernous echo-chamber of the near empty coffee bar.

"I work in this nightclub," she went on. "I'm a dancer – well, sort of. We get all these wealthy clients in; all top drawer people. The management are fussy, they don't just let any old riff raff in. If they like you they tip well."

"Oh. I didn't know you were a dancer," said Nancy.

Catherine giggled.

"Oh, I'm not, not really. But it isn't anything demanding," she explained. We do a bit of a cabaret and there's a singer. Really I want to get on the stage. I shall audition when the right thing comes along. There just hasn't been anything yet."

"There's nothing, well – you know ..." Nancy asked.

"Underhand – sex you mean?" Catherine asked. She laughed.

"I'm not a stripper, Nancy."

Nancy felt embarrassed at what was in her mind – but she had to ask.

"No – nothing like that," Catherine continued. "Well, none that I'm aware of. As far as I'm concerned it's all above board. There may be others up to stuff but not me."

Monday's Child

Caroline Jones Lewis

She sipped her coffee, then leaned forward to whisper as if confiding a dark secret.

"The owner of the club is my boyfriend. He wouldn't like anything that wasn't above board. Only – we have to be discreet. He says it wouldn't be fair if the other girls knew. There might be jealousy, or the other girls might think I was being treated differently if they knew, that sort of thing. So nobody has to know about us, for now anyway. It will be different when we're officially engaged but by then I won't be working there any more. He's going to get me a job elsewhere, hopefully on the stage. He knows plenty of the right people. We're just waiting for the right thing to come along. And anyway, when we're married I won't work at all."

During a pause in conversation while Catherine sipped her coffee, Nancy considered for a moment, then voiced the questions that were begging to be asked.

"How long have you worked there?"

"Six months or so," came the reply.

"Is it easy to get that kind of work? I mean, not a dancer but anything, like waitressing, or in the bar or something. Only, well – I need a job," she shrugged, trying to appear nonchalant.

"You," Catherine said aghast. "Needing the money. But your Dad's loaded."

"It's nothing to do with him," Nancy retorted. She paused, unsure of whether she should confide in Catherine and if so, how much. Then, taking a deep breath, she continued, "I've left home. I need to find work – and a place to live. I was thinking of going to an agency but I don't have any experience of anything. And until I have an address and a phone number... well, it's difficult." She rushed on "I thought I could stay in bed and breakfast for the time being but it's expensive and I've got savings but they won't last long if I can't get a job. So I wondered ..."

"Wow, hang on a minute," Catherine stopped the flood of explanation. She put down her coffee cup and placed her hand on Nancy's.

Monday's Child

Caroline Jones Lewis

"Have you really fallen out with your parents?"
Nancy nodded.
"So that's what's with the holdall, then?"
Nancy nodded again.
"When did all this happen?"
"Yesterday," replied Nancy. "But it's for keeps. Not just for today."
"Are you sure you can't make it up with them? I mean, it isn't easy being young and on your own in this town, you know. You're leaving so much, Nancy. It's ok for me because I've got Adam. But are you sure you can't go back home and …"
"No," Nancy interrupted. "Absolutely not."
"That bad an argument?"
"That bad," confirmed Nancy.
Catherine studied Nancy steadily. She was so young, only two years or so younger than herself but she seemed so much younger somehow - not very wordly. But on the other hand, she thought, she has class and beauty. Adam would be over the moon if Catherine were to introduce Nancy to his club. She was sure to be a hit with the clients. She thought for a moment. Was it the right thing to do or should she try to persuade Nancy to return home? She had not been entirely honest about the club. There was a lot more going on than she had admitted. Not herself, of course. She was a good girl – except with Adam. But there were others; oh yes, there were others more willing than herself. What the hell, she decided. It's her choice. I'm not her keeper.
"Well, if you're sure," she said to Nancy.
"I'm sure," Nancy replied. "It sounds fun," and she smiled as convincingly a smile as she could manage.
"Sure," Catherine told her. "It can be. Hard work sometimes but then what job isn't. And we can find you somewhere to live easy enough. Adam has all the right contacts. At a push you can use my sofa for a night or two. Perhaps," she added hesitantly, not wishing to compromise her situation with Adam.

Monday's Child

Caroline Jones Lewis

It was agreed. Catherine would mention Nancy to Adam that evening and in the meantime, Nancy could stay at Catherine's where she could use the bathroom and relax after the stress of the last few days. Catherine paid for the coffees and the two girls set off together, hailing a taxi at the kerb. For Nancy, a black cloud had lifted, at least for the moment, and she put everything else out of her mind.

******

At the house in Wilton Place James Carlisle sat in the study, head in hands. After discussion on the phone with Miranda that morning, he had walked to the nearest police station to report his daughter missing. In the streets outside, the genteel traffic of a genteel neighbourhood passed the windows intermittently, so unlike the scene that had played out before him only an hour or so before at the police station. A prostitute released from the cells had let forth a torrent of abuse and foul language as she reclaimed her possessions, then tottered towards the exit in her skin-tight skirt and stilettos, hair tousled and make-up smudged clown-like. James' heart had sank at the thought of his beautiful daughter loose and vulnerable in the streets of a city she knew far less than she believed. It was in frustration he had returned home having been told that since Nancy was 18 and therefore an adult in the eyes of the law and had left of her own volition, there was little they could do other than register her as a missing person. And worse. She had left as the result of an argument, though he had given little detail, describing it simply as a difference of opinion between them, so his concern was virtually dismissed. He had explained that she could be emotional and volatile and was prone to days of protest but that she had never been missing from home before and certainly not overnight however angry. If she had stormed off on previous occasions she had always come back an hour or so later, which was why he and her mother were so

Monday's Child
Caroline Jones Lewis

concerned this time. It was all to no avail. The officer would not be moved.
"She'll probably come home of her own accord, sir" the officer had assured him. "Once she gets hungry and starts missing her home comforts."
He had not been unkind; merely unconcerned.
"'They'," James had fumed. "This is not 'they' we're talking about. It's my daughter. My beautiful young headstrong daughter who is hurt and angry. God knows what she might do."

******

Miranda had ascertained that Nancy had bought a ticket at the station. Though the clerk remembered her, for obvious reasons, he was not sure quite which train the ticket was for though he thought it was the 10.45 to London, information she had immediately relayed to James. It therefore made sense for Miranda to return to the London house, too. She would, she told James, catch the afternoon train.
"I'll pick you up," he told her.
"No," said Miranda. "I think you should stay at the house – just in case she comes home. She must need things from home surely. I'll get a taxi."
"Does she have money with her?"
"Yes, I think so. She had some £10. notes but I'm not sure how many. I don't really know how much."
"She'll need her bank book from home, then. She'll need to come home."
Home, thought Miranda. Home indeed. There is no home any more. Not for me. Maybe not for Nancy. It's a nightmare. Where will it all end. And it's all my fault. James sounded dreadful; his breathing was erratic, laboured, as though his chest was constricted by the stress.
"Shouldn't we ring Lizzie?" she suggested. "Nancy may contact her. Or Hugh."

Monday's Child
Caroline Jones Lewis

"Not Hugh," James answered. "He was going away on business. Nancy knew that. Maybe Lizzie but I'm not sure. We couldn't ring them and ask without having to explain, could we? And if she comes home soon on her own she won't thank us for having told other people. In any case, if she went to Lizzie and Emily, they would let us know straight away so I don't really see the point. Same with Jacqueline. We know she can't be with her. What about her other friends? We could concoct a cover story between us, surely?"

"Perhaps we should decide when I get back," Miranda suggested. "I don't want to upset family unless we really have to. Especially Emily. She isn't well herself, is she?"

"What's wrong with her?"

"I don't know," Miranda confessed. "I should have asked Lizzie before she left. She's my sister and I didn't think to ask. God, this is such a mess."

"Who's fault is that?" James retorted.

*****

Hugh returned to London from Abberley with both excitement and trepidation. He took a taxi from the station to his flat and dropped his suitcase in the lobby. Scooping up his post from the doormat on his way he hurried to the study and the phone on his desk to ring Simon. He sank into a chair and waited hopefully as the ring tone buzzed but there was no reply. He dropped the receiver back into its cradle. It had been a vain hope that Simon would be at home just when he called but it had been worth a try. Hugh checked his watch impatiently. On the journey he had speculated over and over the outcome of their reunion, firstly to his liking and then not. Perhaps they would meet for a drink this evening, or a meal at a nearby bistro. Whatever the venue in his impatience his expectation had been that it would be immediate - today. He was suddenly horrified to realise that he could spend the whole evening on tenterhooks, indeed the entire weekend, as he

Monday's Child
Caroline Jones Lewis

remembered that Simon often went out straight from work on a Friday or even went to friends out of town until Sunday if it were his weekend off.

Stupid of me, he thought. I should have let him know I was coming back today, but ringing from Abberley would have been difficult.

Simon had friends in Brighton that he sometimes visited for weekends and who he had previously taken Hugh to meet. Simon may have gone already. Faced with potentially the whole weekend of uncertainty after his rush to get home, Hugh sighed - and then hoped for the best. He wandered through to the kitchen to make himself a coffee and considered the options. He could think of only two. He could wait and do nothing more than keep trying Simon's number – not a good option, he decided. Or he could go to Simon's flat and leave a message for Simon to call him if/when he returned home, not much better as either option entailed hanging around the flat waiting for a call. He seesawed between the two versions, not wanting to appear too keen, then convincing himself he should be more bold. A third option popped into his mind. He could go to the theatre where Simon worked. But this could make known to others the relationship between them and he was not sure that it was the right thing to do. He dismissed the idea and decided on option two.

He drank his coffee and munched on a biscuit while he pondered the contents of the note he would leave if Simon were not home. What to say? Again he was apprehensive about appearing too keen which could put Simon off. He mulled it over, then went to his desk for pen and paper. After several attempts that ended screwed up and tossed into the waste paper bin, he wrote a note with which he was content, folded it neatly and put it into his breast pocket. He glanced at his post abandoned haphazardly on the otherwise immaculate desk and considered that he should open it before he left. There may be something important that needs attention, he thought, but in his

Monday's Child
Caroline Jones Lewis

impatience he knew he could not give it serious attention now. His brain was fizzing with anticipation, more intent on making contact with Simon.
"I'll deal with it over the weekend," he promised himself. "There can't be anything *that* urgent."
He went to the bathroom, washed his hands and face and cleaned his teeth. Then folding the towel neatly and replacing it on the towel rail, he returned to the hallway, grabbed his jacket from the coat stand, checked his pocket for his keys and wallet and left to walk to Chelsea, a fair distance but no hardship on a lovely summer afternoon such as this.

Hugh lived on the edge of Regents Park in a nineteenth century terrace designed by John Nash and steeped in history. He loved this part of London and felt fortunate to live there, a prestigious address. When Nash had seen his terrace built, horse drawn carriages would have deposited their fashionably-attired passengers onto the pavement and the picture that presented, of begloved ladies in floor-length dresses and their escorts in top hats and frock coats strolling leisurely about their day, appealed to the romance in Hugh's nature. The terraces were criss-crossed by narrow side streets and stylish mews properties stretching southwards to Westminster and the river beyond. His route took him southerly, along the green swathes of Regents Park. On this lovely day the lawns of the park were dotted with holidaying families and courting couples strolling hand-in-hand or stretched languorously on the grass in the coolness of shade beneath the trees. Squirrels darted across the path ahead of him effortlessly scaling the trees to escape an occasional marauding dog or inquisitive child. It was a scene that pleased him, a tableau of contented lives.

The park gave way to the columned facades of Park Crescent and the side streets into Westminster, then through the famous plane trees of Berkeley Square. Hugh

Monday's Child
Caroline Jones Lewis

hummed to himself, a tune about nightingales here in this square, smiling as he walked. The afternoon sun was warming on his face and shoulders and he felt good about life, full of hopefulness and skittish good humour. He veered off westerly, skirting Hyde Park and crossing through great rivers of traffic around Marble Arch and Park Lane, then headed southwards towards Sloan Street. Passing the Duke of York Barracks and heading down the Kings Road he began to scan passers-by in the hope of seeing Simon somewhere in the vicinity, anticipating that Simon was not likely to be home. But he reached Simon's front door with disappointment for Simon was nowhere to be seen and when he rang the doorbell, much as he had expected, there was no reply. Simon, he knew, was rarely home for long. With a sigh and a last vain glance around him, Hugh took the note from his pocket, took a last glance at what he had written, then pushed it through the letter box in the front door. He turned away and began to retrace his tracks.

Feeling too restless to return home immediately, he continued southwards towards the embankment and found a café to take tea. Barely had the pot of tea been set on the table in front of him before he was fretting to return home to wait in case the phone should ring. He tried to steady his impatience and drank his tea thoughtfully, but unable to contain himself any longer, he tossed a handful of coins onto the table to cover his bill and left, hailing a passing cab at the kerb.

When once more he stood at his own front door a while later, laden with two brown carrier bags of shopping bought along the way, he planned his itinerary as he fished in his pocket for his key. While waiting for Simon's call, however long that would be, he would fill his time with practicalities – first opening his post, then unpacking his bag from Abberley, and of course planning his itinerary for Monday. Cooking an evening meal would be a pleasure as

Monday's Child
Caroline Jones Lewis

cooking to Hugh was an enjoyable task. But as he entered his flat the ringing of the phone greeted him already and it was all he could do not to drop the shopping on the floor in his haste to reach it before the caller rang off.
"Hugh, old chap. Hi."
Hugh warmed at the sound of Simon's voice.
"Simon," he glowed.
"Thanks for the note, old chap. I must have missed you by minutes and I've been ringing ever since. You've been an absolute age, dear heart. Did you walk back?"
"No, I took a cab," Hugh explained, "but I stopped to buy food on the way. Cupboards being bare after being away – you know how it is."
"Oh, don't I just. Well, you know me. My cupboards are always bare. Organised is just not me, as you well know. So what's the plan, old bean? What did you have in mind?"
Hugh considered quickly.
"Well, I wondered if you were free this weekend? This evening maybe?"
"I've got nothing planned and it's my night off so my time is my own. Shall we eat somewhere? Or do you know where there's a good party, you dark horse, you?"
"No, nothing like that," Hugh muttered apologetically, wishing he was not so boring, so conservative. With friends he would go to a concert or the theatre – coals to Newcastle to Simon. He was not part of the swinging scene of music and pop and parties.
"Well, how about coming here?" he suggested. "I've just bought food and to be honest, it would be nice for me to be at home after being away all week. That's if you don't mind. How would a light supper suit with something alcoholic to wash it down?"
"Sounds good to me," came the reply. "Just need a quick wash and brush up and then I'll be on my way. About an hour do?"
"An hour's fine. See you then."

Monday's Child

Caroline Jones Lewis

Hugh replaced the receiver in a state of euphoria, then flew into action – travel bag into the bedroom, clothes neatly put away or flung into the linen basket for washing. Food was hurriedly put away in the kitchen, ingredients placed ready to cook a meal and a bottle of Chablis in the 'fridge. He switched on the radiogram in the lounge and lingered over his collection of LPs, trying to decide which to play. Ella Fitzgerald or Count Basie, and of course the classics, he pondered. None of these were likely to be Simon's taste. Simon was more into the modern stuff, The Beatles, The Rolling Stones, but he had none of those, so on balance he decided that Count Basie may be a better choice than Ella. Checking his watch he knew he had time for a quick wash and change into fresh clothes. Clean and fresh and smelling of his favourite cologne, he was laying the table tastefully when the doorbell rang.

Dressed as theatrically as ever in a navy velvet jacket, frilled shirt and flares and a silk paisley scarf flung around his neck despite the warmth of the evening, Simon stood in the doorway grinning broadly, a bottle of Moet tucked under one arm and a black Russian cigarette glowing in a holder posed dramatically in the hand of the other. Hugh, also as ever, felt eclipsed in the flamboyance of Simon's presence. Shyly he invited Simon in. Needing little encouragement, Simon flounced past him, flirtatiously planting a kiss on a crimson cheek as he passed and made for the sitting room. Placing the champagne on the coffee table, he dropped elegantly onto the sofa.
"So, Hugh, dear," he began. "What did you do in sunny Cornwall?"
"Oh, just family stuff – you know how it is," Hugh replied.
"Lucky you," responded Simon and just for a moment, a sadness clouded his normally brilliant blue eyes.
"Don't you," Hugh asked as he sat in the chair opposite. "With your family, I mean?"
Simon shook his head.

Monday's Child

Caroline Jones Lewis

"Black sheep of the family, old chap. Can't be doing with a queer in the family closet. Skeletons are ok but not queers. Oh, dear me, no. Whatever would the neighbours say?"
He drew deeply on his cigarette and bounced to his feet to deflect a subject that was raw.
"Come on, old chap. Get the glasses then. I'm celebrating."
"Oh, right. What's the celebration," Hugh asked, fetching the glasses from the kitchen.
"Just the illusion of wealth that payday brings," Simon answered grinning. "You have to catch it quick. It doesn't last long."
Before he had chance to produce the carefully prepared supper he had planned, an inexperienced but willing Hugh found himself manoevred to the bedroom, complete with champagne and seduced by his much more experienced guest. It was only after breakfast the next morning that Simon left for duties at the theatre, promising to return later in the day. Hugh glowed with love and happiness and in anticipation of the remainder of the weekend, he consigned to the back of his mind for the time being the implications of the path he was taking. He was beyond such care. Even the shambles that Simon had left behind him did not detract from the euphoria of the moment.

Hugh set about repairing the damage, the washing-up left overnight after their eventual supper, the bedding awry and Simon's scarf draped across the dressing table mirror. He crooned to himself as he worked.

> Every time we say goodbye I cry a little
> Every time we say goodbye I even die a little
> There's no love song finer
> But how strange the change from major to minor
> Every time we say goodbye

Monday's Child

Caroline Jones Lewis

He planned to deal with his post and to put his clothes and papers ready for Monday morning before Simon returned in the afternoon. Then he could commit his entire weekend to being with Simon. It came as a shattering disappointment therefore when he received a call from Simon mid-afternoon to say that he was needed at the theatre for the rest of the day and for the evening performance.
"Sorry, old chap, but the floor manager's gone off sick so I have to stay. Nothing I can do about it I'm afraid, and it will be late before I'm finished. Call you tomorrow. OK?"
"You're not free tomorrow?" Hugh enquired. "I'm away on business for several days from Monday."
"Sorry, dear heart. Promised to see friends tomorrow."

Hugh made conciliatory noises to cover the sinking feeling in his stomach. He replaced the receiver and sat at his desk in disappointment. He felt a sudden loneliness. He had never felt lonely before, even when his own friends were busy and he had spent a weekend alone. Now he felt lonely, a yearning for company but dismissing the thought of contacting friends. He was lonely for Simon's company – no-one else's. He heard nothing further from Simon over the weekend which he spent quietly reading or attending to domestic duties and reluctant to leave the flat in case he should miss Simon's call. But the promised phone call did not come. He left for business on Monday morning feeling glum, relieved that the weekend was over and with a sneaking suspicion that this could be the shape of things to come.

Monday's Child

Caroline Jones Lewis

Monday's Child
Caroline Jones Lewis

Chapter Four - Revelations

Several days after her return home, a surprised Lizzie responded to a knock on the door to let her Aunt Miranda into the hallway. Why she was here and not at Abberley was a mystery. She once again noted that her aunt was looking less than her usual immaculately groomed and dressed self.

"How is your mother?" began her aunt as they edged towards the kitchen. They were interrupted by the sound of Emily's voice from the top of the stairs.

"Miranda," she exclaimed. "What a lovely surprise. I didn't realise you were back from Cornwall. We tried to call you earlier. We got no reply and thought you might be on the beach or something but now we know why," and she came steadily down the stairs to greet her sister.

Stilted conversation accompanied them as the three made their way along the hall. Miranda hardly knew how to approach the questions she needed to ask and the explanation she had to give. Her sister and niece's demeanour suggested they knew nothing and had no more idea of Nancy's whereabouts than her own. Emily and Lizzie, sensing a source of distress, anticipated the reason for the visit with apprehension.

"Coffee time, don't you think?" suggested Emily, indicating the clock face showing mid-morning and Miranda nodded her reply.

Lizzie had returned from school earlier bursting with joy. "Three straight As, Mum."

"Oh, Lizzie. Well done," and Emily had kissed her daughter with pride and joy.

"Penny got two As and a B and Kate got three Bs so we're all going to uni. We're going to have a celebration. I need to ring Penny later."

Quite obviously, Nancy's results had not given rise to similar celebration but surely that was no less than expected and was unlikely to be the cause of Miranda's agitation.

Monday's Child

Caroline Jones Lewis

Seated at the kitchen table, Emily cut through the small talk and posed the question directly.

"Miranda, what's wrong," she asked her sister. "You look dreadful. Are you ill?"

"I knew it," thought Lizzie.

Miranda's resolve crumpled and the tears began to flow. "It's Nancy," she began breathlessly. "She's run away. She's been gone for days now. I don't know what to do. James and I are at the end of our tether. I had hoped she might have come to you, or at least phoned you but I can see she hasn't."

Aghast at the news, Lizzie and Emily exchanged glances and Emily moved around the table to comfort her tearful sister.

"We would have let you know," she assured her. "We would have known how worried you were. Whatever's happened."

Miranda snuffled and gave a brief but simple explanation of 'we had a dreadful row and the next we knew she'd gone. She's been missing for days."

Emily and Lizzie were shocked. Nancy had pulled some stunts in the past but never anything like this. Emily chose not to ask the nature of the row at this moment, which seemed inconsequential. The important thing was to find Nancy. Where to start? What to do?

"What can we do to help find her?" she asked.

"I wondered whether Lizzie had any idea, any friend she thinks Nancy could have gone to," Miranda pleaded but Lizzie shook her head.

"Jacqueline's the only one really," she offered, "but she was coming to Abberley, wasn't she. Is she still with you?"

Miranda explained about Jacqueline's surgery and the recollection reminded her of her own sister's illness.

"Oh, Emily," she exclaimed. "You've been ill too and I haven't even asked how you are. I'm so sorry. Are you better? What was wrong?"

Monday's Child
Caroline Jones Lewis

Emily revealed to her shocked sister the loss of the baby. It was her turn now to receive sympathy and comfort. It fell to Lizzie to produce the coffee.
In the hallway the telephone shrilled.
"Can you get that, Liz?" Emily asked. "It's probably your Dad. He said he would ring to find out about your results. He'll be in clinic, though, so he won't have much time."
Lizzie left her mother to pour the coffee and hurried to take the call.
"Now. Come on, Mie," she said, using the childhood knickname. "I know you. There's something you're not telling; more to this than you're letting on. What's going on. You can tell me, you know that. And it will go no further. Is there a boy involved? Has she run off with someone?"
"No. No – not like that," Miranda answered. She paused, hesitant to spill the beans and incur her sister's censure but unable to resist. She needed to tell someone. It had to be Emily, who after all was also her best friend. She could indeed tell her anything, or so she hoped.
"It's me," she blurted. "I've been seeing someone and Nancy found out. She heard James and I rowing and everything got really out of hand. Lots of things came out, about me being pregnant with Nancy before we were married. And James let out that I had considered an abortion. That really hurt Nancy. She just went overboard. You know how difficult she could be at the best of times. This time she had good reason."
"You mean – an affair? You've had an affair?"
Miranda nodded. Emily was temporarily stunned into silence.
"Oh, Mie, does this mean that you and James are splitting up?"
"I don't know. We haven't talked that far, not yet. The first thing is to find Nancy, we're both going out of our mind with worry. We're sure she made her way back to London but after that we have no idea. Suppose she's been taken by some unscrupulous individual. She thinks she's

Monday's Child
Caroline Jones Lewis

grown up and worldly but she isn't. Not really. She's still just a child and ...."
Miranda stopped, overwrought and Emily tried to calm her.
"Oh, come on, now. Calm down. Your imagination's running riot. Let's just think about this logically, about where she could be and how to go about finding her," Emily soothed, though mentally she also panicked at the thought of her beautiful young niece alone and loose in the capital.

Lizzie returned from her phone call to find her aunt distraught, head bowed and resting in her hands. Her mother quietly waved her away and she went upstairs to her room. She sat on her bed, staring out of the window and agonising as to what she could do. She remembered Nancy's strange mood that day and wished desperately she had found a way to talk to her about whatever was troubling her, berating herself that she had been so absorbed in her book and in considering her own future that she had not given Nancy a thought.
Should she ring Hugh, she wondered, but then remembered that he was away, though it might be worth a try just in case he had not gone. But no, she decided. Nancy would not have gone to Hugh, Lizzie was sure. There had been that abrasive edge to their exchanges this summer. Most unusually Hugh had teased Nancy in a way she had been unable to take. Under the circumstances it was unlikely Nancy would turn to him. There was little else she could think of to do.

A while later, when Miranda had recovered her composure, Lizzie returned and together the three considered how to go about finding Nancy. What to do? Where to look? They sat together racking their brains about the next move.

******

Monday's Child

Caroline Jones Lewis

Catherine's flat was far nicer than Nancy had expected; small – little more than a bedsit – but in a tidy block tucked away off Kensington High Street with an entry system for security. It was sparsely furnished in a contemporary style, moulded plastic chairs like Nancy had seen in her mother's copies of Practical Householder, and a fitted wardrobe in the bedroom – so much more chic than the dated décor of Abberley or the expensive antiques of Wilton Place.
"It's great," Nancy exclaimed, wandering bemused from the lounge-cum-kitchenette to the bedroom. One door of the mirrored wall to wall wardrobe swung slightly open allowing her a tantalising peek at the clothes hanging inside; new mini skirts and dresses in the height of fashion like the one Catherine was wearing. On the dressing table amongst the expensive brands of make-up was an almost new bottle of Chanel No 5 and a new pair of sling-backs rested against the side of the stool, one of them tipped onto one side.
If Catherine can afford to live like this, thought Nancy, so can I. All recollection of the dingy bed and breakfast of the previous night vanished from her memory together with the fear of the future it represented and the suspicion that she had been too hasty in her actions. Now she began to believe in a different future for herself. She would show them – her parents. She did not need them. They would see.

It was agreed that Nancy should stay at the flat while Catherine went to work that evening.
"You can sleep on the sofa, just for a night or two," Catherine told her, and promised that she would speak to Adam straight away to find out if there were any vacancies at the club. Secretly she knew very well that Adam would not turn Nancy away but she made it sound to Nancy as if she may have to persuade him to give her a chance, as though she were doing Nancy a favour.
"What if he says no," Nancy asked. "Can't I come in and ask him for myself?"

Monday's Child

Caroline Jones Lewis

"All in good time," Catherine insisted. "Let me speak to him first. You just relax here. You've had a rough few days. You want to look your best for an interview, don't you? You can have a nice, relaxing bath. Help yourself to the stuff in the bathroom. Smells wonderful. Adam bought it for me."

"What he's like?" Nancy asked.

Having attended to the preliminaries, they sat in the lounge curled up on the sofa, nibbling on apples and biscuits.

"Well," Catherine began, glowing at the very thought of him. "He's not exactly tall, dark and handsome. More medium height, dark and handsome," she giggled. "Very charming. Smart. He's older than me which I suppose is why he's so experienced at everything. I like that. I find boys of our own age so stupid. So full of themselves. Adam is really sophisticated and he makes me laugh. And," she added blushing, "he's very good in bed."

"Naturally," grinned Nancy.

"He is. And he's mine so hands off," exclaimed Catherine, with a smile of jest but with a serious undertone.

"I wouldn't dream of it," Nancy assured her.

"Do you have a boyfriend, Nanc?"

"No."

"Have you had?"

"Not exactly. I did go out with someone a few times but it wasn't steady, or anything like that."

"Are you a virgin?"

"Catherine," Nancy protested.

"Oh, go on. You can tell me."

"Well, no, actually," she admitted. "But it was only the once."

"Well, you little dark horse, you. Bet your Daddy would be shocked," Catherine teased. "I know mine would be if he knew. He thinks I'm still pure and unsullied, waiting for the right man," and she laughed, her laughter a little brittle either from bravado or embarrassment, Nancy wasn't sure which.

"Does he know about Adam?"

Monday's Child

Caroline Jones Lewis

"Oh, God, no," Catherine exclaimed. "He's not exactly what my father would welcome as son-in-law material. I don't think he'll be over the moon when I tell him. Nor my mother. But I'll still marry him anyway. I'm supposed to marry someone successful in the City, give up work and have 2.5 children," and she grimaced with distaste.
"Do they know about the club?"
Catherine shook her head.
"They think I work in an office. I did when I first came back to London but I didn't earn enough. I had to share this grubby flat with two boring girls. Then I met Adam and everything changed. I just didn't tell my parents."
"How did you meet him then?"
Nancy was curious and storing information for her own use should Adam reject her at the club.
"I went to the club one Friday with a friend. He chatted me up, I suppose you could say. And the rest, as they say, is history."
She glanced at the clock.
"I'm going to have to move," she said, stirring from her seat. "I need to bath and get ready for work."
Nancy remained seated, thoughtful about her future prospects.

She slept fitfully through a night that was humid, having spent a tedious evening trying to amuse herself. Catherine had the latest edition of Jackie which Nancy flicked through absentmindedly but was unable to concentrate on anything for long. She rifled through Catherine's collection of 45s and LPs and played some Elvis and Motown on the Dansette in the corner but it was mostly slushy romantic stuff which was not to her taste. The one still on the turntable was obviously a favourite of Catherine's and one which, Nancy realised, was apt to her relationship with Adam.

> Our day will come
> And we'll have everything

Monday's Child
Caroline Jones Lewis

We'll have the joys
Falling in love can bring

The irony of it irritated Nancy and she put it aside, sighing with exasperation. Bored with the selection on offer she eventually fell into an exhausted sleep on the sofa.

When she awoke the next morning, initially disorientated and forgetting where she was, she struggled to recall the events of the previous day, what day it was now and what she had to do. Realising there was little she could do until Catherine emerged from the bedroom, the door to which right now was tightly closed, she sank back against the cushions and closed her eyes.

It was almost 11 o'clock by the time Catherine appeared from the bedroom, bleary eyed and dishevelled from sleep. Nancy had washed and dressed and brushed her hair liberally, rummaging in her holdall, now deposited in the cupboard in the hall, for clean clothes and make-up. She had made herself coffee and helped herself to a bowl of cereal while the kitchen clock had slowly ticked the minutes away. Seated at the coffee table bored and impatient for Catherine's appearance she had watched the passers-by and traffic in the street below for a short while. But time had seemed to drag more and more with each passing hour. Catherine's eventual appearance was a relief.
"Hi, Nancy," she yawned. "Did you sleep ok?"
"On and off," Nancy replied, impatient to ask about Adam and the club but aware she should not push too soon. "You look tired," she offered.
"Yeah – really late night," Catherine yawned again, filling the kettle for a much-needed fix of caffeine.
"Here – let me," Nancy insisted, jumping up and taking the kettle from her.
"Did you get chance to mention me to Adam?" she blurted. She could wait no longer.

Monday's Child
Caroline Jones Lewis

"I did," Catherine replied. "He wants me to take you to the club at 2."
"Oh, great. I look forward to it," Nancy beamed, trying to hold down her excitement.

The Club was a smart establishment in a side street in Belgravia that smelled of a cocktail of cigar smoke and expensive perfumes. Even at 2 in the afternoon it was well patronised, mostly by City businessmen in pinstripes entertaining clients or simply playing hooky from their offices and dining on expenses. A pretty girl whose looks outweighed her talent was attempting a Peggy Lee number at a microphone on a small stage – a passable performance but no more. A backing group swayed behind her, three equally pretty girls in long slinky halter-necked dresses. Nancy followed Catherine through to a door at the rear which led into Adam's office, the progress of the pair tracked appreciatively by several pairs of eyes around the tables. Catherine was, as usual, immaculately groomed and dressed in a blouse and mini skirt which did justice to her shapely legs and figure. Nancy, armed with only the sparing selection from her own wardrobe that remained clean, had borrowed a blouse from Catherine which she wore over her jeans, accentuating the length and slimness of her own legs. She wore little make-up, sporting a natural golden tan and had brushed her long blonde hair into a fashionable sleekness. When they entered Adam's office together, he suppressed a whistle at the sight of her. "Good girl, Cathy," he thought. "She's a stunner. A definite winner. Knocks you into a cocked hat, sweetie." Concealing his eagerness, he rose leisurely from a black leather chair behind an expensive mahogany desk, holding out his hand formally to greet her. Catherine, unsure of whether she should greet him as her boss or her boyfriend in Nancy's presence, hung back and allowed Nancy to step forward to take his hand. Nancy, too, was unsure of how to behave in the unfamiliar environment of a job interview

Monday's Child
Caroline Jones Lewis

but had no intention of letting him know. Adam immediately put her at her ease.

"Nancy, I take it," he began. "Nice to meet you," and he instructed her to take a seat, indicating the chair in front of his desk. He looked at Catherine, not unkindly but with an air of dismissal.

"I'll leave you, shall I?" she ventured awkwardly.

Adam nodded and she turned to leave, smarting at what felt like a denial of her special status – a brush off.

e has to, she consoled herself. He has to behave like that in front of others.

But she wished so much they could be done with the secrecy, that she could take her rightful place at his side openly and in public. She wanted him to parade her in full view of the world, not just these clandestine visits to her flat after the club was closed leaving in the early hours before the rest of the world was up and about, or the stolen moments in his own flat above. It was not as if his marriage mattered any more. It was over. He had made that quite plain. She was not breaking up anything. But of course he had to be careful if his greedy and cruel wife was not to take him for every penny he owned.

She had to be patient, she reasoned. It would come – all in good time.

Back in the office Nancy studied Adam as he studied her. He was dark as Catherine had said and not bad looking, she decided, but not the handsome that Catherine had described. More to the point, he was old – at least by Nancy's standards. He looked nearer her father's age than her own. His hair was dark and wavy and had a sort of unctuous quality, his skin sallow and deep pools for eyes were fringed by luxurious ebony lashes beneath dark thick eyebrows. He dressed conservatively and in pristine neatness, a sparkling white shirt with a burgundy silk tie and crisply pressed pin-striped suit. Not for him the frilled shirts and flares that were the incoming fashion of the day. On his left wrist he wore a gold watch with a wide black

Monday's Child
Caroline Jones Lewis

leather strap that looked expensive and gold cufflinks glinted in the cuffs of his shirt. Everything about him spoke of money. New money. He was of medium build but a little spongy around the waistline and there was something else that particularly impressed itself on her. That smile, it was what her mother would call smarmy, false, the smile of a politician on the campaign trail switched on for all and sundry but meaning little.
Well, she thought. So what. We're not going to be bosom buddies. I want a job. He's got one. Two can play at that game, and she smiled her most charming smile. He was smart, though; immaculate and he smelled nice and she liked that She liked, too, that Adam asked her about herself. What could she do? Could she dance? Not very well. Could she sing? Definitely not. Could she hold intelligent conversation with clients? Absolutely. They were superfluous questions. He knew he wanted her in this club and he knew what for. At the very least she was top drawer window-dressing, at best a great deal more. He knew she needed this job. Everything else was unimportant. It was all arranged in no time at all.

Over the ensuing months Nancy was indoctrinated into club life as a hostess. The clients, as Adam had known they would, loved and lusted after her. She spotted several well-known faces, a politician, an actor or two, a musician, one or two others that were pointed out to her. The clientele, as Catherine had promised, were of the social elite and Nancy loved rubbing shoulders with the well-to-do. She moved into a flat in the same block as Catherine's, the rent deducted weekly from her wages but which she realised must be subsidised by the Club. She did not care. She was an asset and no doubt Adam recovered his money by the prices charged to the clients for her company. He was not a fool but neither, she told herself, was she. Housework came as a shock to her system but she found ways to manage and determined to find herself a lady-that-did as soon as finances would allow. She had never

Monday's Child
Caroline Jones Lewis

cooked, not so much as boiling an egg, so did not know how and bothered little. Evening meals were provided at the club which she used to full effect and snacked the rest of the time. She trained herself to always have milk in the morning, bought from the corner shop each day before she went to work, so that cereal for breakfast became the norm and lunch was just a nibbled bar of chocolate or a pastry of some kind. She found a launderette where, for an extra 6d., an ironing service was offered and her smalls she rinsed out in the kitchen sink and draped, smoothed neatly, on a clothes-horse that she stood in the bath. That much she had learned from Mrs Hale. Cleaning she deemed to be a chore and behaved accordingly so her flat lacked the pristine femininity of Catherine's and resembled more a charity shop on the eve of a jumble sale, though she did take care with her clothes. She regarded with scorn the sight of Catherine, hands encased in a pair of Marigolds, dusting and polishing, scouring and titivating in readiness for a visit from Adam when clearly, she scoffed, it was not Catherine's domestic skills that were of interest.

The two girls made visits to Carnaby Street and the Kings Road, tried out new make-up and nail polish and clothes they did not intend to buy. Or they simply lolled around on wet days discussing hairstyles and fashion, men – or in Catherine's case Adam – and playing the latest records until Catherine intimated to Nancy that it was time to leave. Clearly the dreamy smile and warm glow signalled that a visit from Adam was imminent, which Nancy increasingly found irritating. It was inevitable that what Nancy saw as Catherine's uninspiring company would soon become tedious and that she would look around for more stimulating friendship. To this end it was natural and convenient that she struck a friendship with Eve, another hostess at the club, a feisty no-nonsense girl from the East End.

Monday's Child
Caroline Jones Lewis

The surreal quality of life continued for Nancy as though one day she would wake from a long and deep dream. There were times when she missed home and family but all thoughts of contacting her parents were vigorously resisted and to combat those moments she immersed herself in the excitement and opportunity of the present. She told herself she was too far down the line now to do otherwise and pride would not allow her to do other than succeed under her own steam. She had to see it through. She still had no idea of how well, or otherwise, she had done in her exams but they were the past. This was her present and future. She enjoyed life at the Club basking in the adoration of the clients. Even of Adam, giving rising to a niggling jealousy from Catherine. From time to time, however, she found herself balking at the patronising indulgence of some of the men and had to bite her tongue not to rile against it, aware that what would have given rise to retaliation in her previous life would be detrimental in this one where her well-being depended on pandering to the male ego. The years of practise on her father were invaluable and she cajoled and flattered profusely. All was going well as Christmas approached, a time she feared would strengthen the pull towards home.

******

Life had taken on the nature of an emotional roller-coaster for Hugh. Simon kept him guessing from one day to the next, one moment the ardent lover then broken promises and unexplained absences. He always offered excuses but they were so ambivalent as to leave Hugh doubting and confused as to Simon's true feelings and intentions. Distracted by unanswered questions Hugh found himself preoccupied when his mind should have been sharply focused on business matters. Speculation in his office was rife. At the outset of the relationship, with a permanent smile on his face and a noticeable spring in his step, the secretaries were sure that at long last love was in the air.

Monday's Child

Caroline Jones Lewis

"Never seen him so happy. I wonder who she is. Has he told you anything, Pat?"
"Not a word," Pat regrettably had to admit. "But I'll wheedle it out of him when I can, don't you worry," she assured them, the switchboard operator, a buxom and bedizened blonde with a 50s hairdo that was back-combed to gigantic proportions and lacquered so stiffly that even a gale force wind would have difficulty dislodging it. A little past her prime, she now satisfied her lust for gossip in pursuit of details of everyone else's life. She was not averse to the occasional listening-in to a private call, deftly flicking the switch to cut her eaves-dropping dead when interrupted but suspicion hovering over her by those who suspected they had heard that little tell-tale click on the line. So it was she held the dubious reputation of hub of the office gossip machine and it was believed without question that in time she would reveal all.

On occasional weekends off from the theatre, Simon took Hugh to visit friends in Brighton. Chas and Edward lived together in a large bay-fronted first floor flat overlooking the sea front. Chas was a sticklike as Edward was rotund, an odd couple in their late thirties but devoted and who had been together for years. They all went together to the Parakeet Club, in reality a gay club but crudely organised by a clientele of both sexes who would hastily pair into couples when tipped off by a police insider, himself a closet gay, that a police raid was in the offing. The club was tucked away in a side street off the promenade where, to Hugh's dismay and embarrassment, Simon's behaviour would become outrageously coquettish. He would flirt with all and sundry, deliberately abandoning Hugh to the company of his friends.
"You won't take Simon seriously, will you, old chap?" Chas ventured to Hugh on one such occasion and in recognition of Hugh's obvious discomfort. "He isn't the type to be taken seriously, you know. He's like a spoiled

Monday's Child
Caroline Jones Lewis

child who is used to getting everything he wants so values nothing."

He wanted to say more, to say that Simon had a need to destroy, to be cruel, to push the boundaries of a relationship to see how far he could go before driving his partner away whilst seemingly oblivious to their pain and remaining emotionally unscathed himself. He and Edward had seen it all before. It was difficult to resist confiding this to Hugh who both he and Edward had taken a great liking to, more so than some of the other lovers Simon had previously brought to visit. But Edward would have chided him for disloyalty to Simon, their long-standing friend and whose own pain they understood.

Hugh had shaken his head, doing his best to appear nonchalant in the face of what he felt was public humiliation.

"Of course not," he had replied. "We're just having fun." But he had smarted inside and longed for the evening and the farce to end.

During the days following these weekends, when he was more subdued than usual even for Hugh, the office speculation took on a different tone.

"It's funny he never mentions anyone by name. Do you think she's married, Pat?"

"Well, there must be something, mustn't there? Otherwise he would be boring us all with the details. Must be something amiss," proclaimed the oracle as she honed the blood red finger-nail of her little finger with an emery board, deftly plugging in to take an incoming call and deflect the speculation to which she had no answer.

Simon, of course, would be penitent and affectionate on their return to London.

"Sorry, luvvie," he would say off-handedly to Hugh. "You know what I'm like when I get amongst the others. But it doesn't mean anything. You know how much I care about you."

Monday's Child

Caroline Jones Lewis

Hugh would acquiesce mildly for fear of losing the relationship altogether. And so it would continue for the coming months until events were to intervene.

Monday's Child
Caroline Jones Lewis

Chapter Five – Disillusion

Hugh had heard about Nancy's disappearance from Lizzie and had paid a visit to his aunt and uncle's home in Kent. He, too, was worried about Nancy being alone in the capital and out of touch with her family. Her parents, he had learned, had spent frantic hours wandering aimlessly through the crowded streets of the West End. James had visited various nightspots frequented by the young and trendy, feeling like an ancient relic as he weaved his way through the jiving, twisting, smooching couples on the dance floor to music that throbbed and pulsed loudly and created near deafness to anyone within its reach.

> She loves you, yeah yeah yeah
> She loves you yeah yeah yeah
> She loves you yeah yeah yeah yeah

"Whatever happened to music?" James had muttered irritably. "Real music written by a genius and played magnificently by a full orchestra."
This was not real music, not to him. But to the young it was the real thing and it seemed right now as if the young were taking over the world, an unstoppable rabble army arguing with anything and everything that his generation believed in; challenging everything, tearing down the whole fabric of the society they had created and replacing it with what? Not for the better, that was sure, if this travesty was anything to go by.
Their clothes, he thought,"are ridiculous. Boys in frilly shirts, flared trousers, the girls' skirts halfway up their backsides. And Nancy is loose in this somewhere. Vulnerable and we're not there to protect her. Panic consumed him at the thought. As a last desperate measure he visited the Salvation Army hostels dotted about the capital though he could hardly see Nancy venturing through their doors. Again it was without success. No-one he had approached had seen her.

Monday's Child
Caroline Jones Lewis

Hugh phoned his aunt and uncle often and offered whatever help and support he could give to prop up their flagging morale but frankly had little more idea than they did as to what shape that could take. The stress in the Carlisle household was clearly taking its toll. Miranda was a shadow of her former self – thin, drawn, consumed by guilt and sinking daily further into depression. She would sit for hours in Nancy's bedroom, smoothing the bedclothes that were washed and clean ready for her return and fingering the precious belongings that had marked the rites of passage of Nancy's growing years. The drug that had been the passion of her affair with Michael had now been replaced by another and far more potent one – the longing for Nancy to return home.
"I really don't know what to suggest, Liz," Hugh confided to his cousin. "Other than just more of the same. It's disappointing the police won't do anything. Perhaps we should have some leaflets printed and hand them out in bars and coffee houses. What do you think?"
So they tried, but with no response. With Christmas and the New Year approaching, the two cousins could only hope that Nancy would be drawn home.

******

The relationship between James and Miranda was disintegrating daily. In the early days following Nancy's disappearance they had worked together to try and trace her. But as the days had stretched into weeks and months the need to blame had erupted. Miranda's tears and self-recrimination, which at first had elicited sympathy and support from James, now simply prompted anger.
"Well, it is your fault, isn't it?" If you hadn't been behaving like a whore none of this would have happened."
"How dare you call me such a thing. How dare you. And if you had not had an affair in the first place maybe I wouldn't have needed one. But then it's ok for the men, of

Monday's Child
Caroline Jones Lewis

course. Just makes them one of the boys – men being men. Just as long as women don't follow suit," and the slamming of doors had reverberated through the building as each retreated to their now separate bedrooms. It was clear the situation could not continue indefinitely and already each was contemplating an alternative. The festive jollity normally generated by the approach of Christmas was replaced this year by a dread of the emptiness it would magnify even further if Nancy failed to appear.

******

Amidst the trauma of Nancy's disappearance Lizzie had begun her first term at university. She was lucky to be near home but even so, along with her fellow freshmen, she lived in halls. It seemed as if her life was split into two parts, the first of which was the exciting half of being in a new and challenging environment, the whole new world of learning in a different setting to school and the extra curricular activities like the debating society, the students union and the widening social circle with new-found friends. On Friday evenings, when she was not going home for the weekend, she fell into the habit of visiting a bar where discussion of current affairs or events at uni were often the source of sometimes passionate but friendly debate.

The other half of life was the problem of Nancy's disappearance which belonged to another time and place and mostly the full impact of it only returned for Lizzie when she was with family. As the Christmas break approached, she and her mother discussed the domestic arrangements which invariably would be different this year. It had been their usual practice as a family to visit Miranda, James and Nancy on Christmas Day for lunch or supper, whichever was best suited to the weather. On one or two occasions, the weather had been so mild and unseasonal that the entire family had taken the opportunity

Monday's Child

Caroline Jones Lewis

to celebrate for a day or two at Abberley, a special treat which meant a stroll along the beach each day with the dog. The usual venue, however, was the house in London where the elegant sitting room was large enough to accommodate all of them comfortably, James, Miranda and Nancy, Hugh and his grandmother and Tom, Emily and Lizzie and still allow space for the opening of presents around a tall and beautifully decorated tree. On Boxing Day Tom, Emily and Lizzie would make the long journey to Harrogate on alternate years to Tom's parents and the intervening years for the parents to visit them. This year, Emily suggested the family should all be invited to Kent on Christmas Day.

"Let's invite them all here."

"How on earth would we fit everyone in?" Tom exclaimed.

"Eight of us around the dining table."

He considered for a moment.

"Well, I suppose that might be possible," he conceded, "but what about the rest of the time. It would be a bit of a squeeze in the sitting room – and no hope of a tree in there. There wouldn't be room to swing a cat. And it's the first time for years I won't be on call. Much as I sympathise with James and Miranda I really would like to enjoy this Christmas with my family."

"Oh, come on, Dad. We could manage," said Lizzie. "We could put the tree up in the hallway, not as big a tree as we'd have at Aunt Miranda's but that wouldn't matter. If we took the bureau out of the sitting room and swapped it with the small sofa in the spare room, we could seat everyone, couldn't we?"

Tom sighed and acquiesced. So it was agreed to propose the idea to James and Miranda. In the event, however, Miranda would not hear of it.

"Christmas," she said emphatically, "is the time Nancy is most likely to come home. We have to be here. No, you must all come to us as usual."

"Are you sure, Mie?" Emily asked her.

"I'm sure," came the reply.

Monday's Child

Caroline Jones Lewis

While the family planned their Christmas around Nancy's hoped for return, Nancy was planning her Christmas to suit herself.

******

One evening, just as the Club was closing, Adam moved across the floor to where Nancy sat at a table she had earlier shared with a client.
"Well, Nancy," he began, taking the seat opposite to her. "How's it all going with you? You seem to be enjoying yourself here."
"Yes," she replied, with an assurance that had been growing in her time at the Club. "I am," but not for ever, she added silently for her own benefit.
"Good," he said and smiled that smile to which she had become accustomed and which no longer seemed quite so suspect – just Adam being Adam.
"We've got a special booking coming up," he went on. "I thought you might like to be included – and of course it pays well."
He knew instantly he had caught her attention for it was easy to see by her expensive taste that Nancy liked money.
"We have a special client who lives on a country estate near town. He gives dinner parties at odd times for favoured friends but he's a bachelor and lives on his own. Sometimes he needs some glamorous female company to balance the guest list, so to speak. Just some gentle social chit-chat – that sort of thing. That's all that's needed. So one or two of our girls go along. He provides a limousine for the travel and there's an overnight stay – in luxurious surroundings, I have to say. You'd need something nice to wear but I can let you have an advance if you need one. What do you think?"
Nancy nodded. It sounded a good opportunity. Anything could come of it if the clients at the Club were anything to go by.
"Sounds fine to me," she agreed.

Monday's Child

Caroline Jones Lewis

"Good. His name's Stephen. I'll introduce you next time he's in."
Adam beamed expansively and rose to leave.
"Better get some beauty sleep," he added and winked. "Mustn't spoil that beautiful schoolgirl complexion, must we? And those lovely eyes of yours."
He would handle Nancy carefully, he thought. She was different to Catherine. Beneath the calm exterior she presented to the world, having studied her intently he guessed there lurked a volatile nature within. She was intelligent, educated and erudite and was a clever mimic with a great sense of humour. She was also becoming increasingly independent which showed in her demeanour, so unlike Catherine who was malleable, easily manipulated, gullible, none too bright and whose increasing tendency to cling was becoming a chore. More than that – not only was Nancy a beautiful and intelligent young woman but she had that indefinable quality that was class. It was a winning combination.

Nancy's mind was racing. This could be the break she needed, her chance to get in with the right sort of people. She had seen little of Catherine in recent weeks, far too busy and wrapped up in her new friendship with Eve, a tall, slim brunette whose looks were striking rather than classically beautiful or pretty. Eve was tough and intelligent, funny and with a heart of gold to those that earned her loyalty. Nancy and Eve shopped together in the Kings Road boutiques and went to Vidal Sassoon to have their hair done. With Eve's contribution, Nancy's appearance, like Catherine's, had been transformed – a modern hairdo and a new and fashionable look to the clothes that formed the nucleus of a newly acquired wardrobe. Nancy glowed with the confidence that her new persona gave her. Eve had admitted openly to Nancy that she had slept with clients for money. She wanted to earn money, she had told her; lots of it to take her out of this life into the life she intended to have. With little in the way of

Monday's Child
Caroline Jones Lewis

academic achievement she recognised her options were limited.

"But only if I like them," she had added. "And so what. It's only sex. I'm not called Eve for nothing." She had grinned. "These men, they're so weak where sex is concerned. They just can't resist taking a bite of the apple. That Catherine does it with Adam for nothing. At least, she thinks it's for love but she's kidding herself. And she thinks no-one knows, poor disillusioned cow. She follows his every move with those puppy dog eyes of hers. It's nauseating. Does she really think he will leave his wife for her? He'll drop her like a ton of bricks if she doesn't shape up the way he wants – with the Clients and that."

"Wife," echoed Nancy. "I didn't know he was married. He doesn't wear a ring, or anything."

"So what. That doesn't mean anything, does it? Lots of the men who come to this club don't wear wedding rings but I'd bet a pound to a penny most of them are married. Of course he is," Eve guffawed. "Ring's tucked away in the drawer of his desk. He puts it on when he goes home for the weekend. Wife and two kids tucked away in Essex. Great big house, they've got, set in its own grounds. The trouble is the wife's the one with the money so he's got to keep her sweet."

"How do you know all this?"

"My Mum's sister works for her. His wife, I mean. Cleaning. That's how I knew about this place. She told my Mum that when Adam wanted to buy the club there were all sorts of rows. His wife didn't want him to buy it but Adam needed her money so he had to persuade her. My aunt reckons the wife would be glad to see the back of him if she had a good excuse. Separate bedrooms, they have. Not much of a marriage that, is it? She'd divorce him in a flash if she knew about Catherine – and all the ones before. He's getting bored with her already. You can see how he brushes her aside now instead of the cosy little chats they used to have. He tried it with me. Can you

Monday's Child

Caroline Jones Lewis

imagine? Adam and Eve! I wasn't interested in a bite from his apple, thank you."

They burst into raucous laughter. Eve had confirmed to Nancy what she had already begun to suspect and from the change in Catherine's demeanour what Catherine herself was beginning to understand. When Nancy had last seen Catherine she had noted the change in her. The chirpy confident person Nancy had bumped into that day in Sloane Street was now transformed into a shadow. Actually, she recalled, she had asked Catherine if anything were wrong but since Catherine was adamant everything was fine Nancy had been happy to believe her, far too occupied with her own life to give it more thought. So Nancy had dismissed it in her mind as perhaps time of the month or simply tiredness from the unsociable hours of the job. Now, however, it made sense and as the days wore on, Eve's summary of Catherine and Adam's relationship seemed glaringly obvious. Love's young dream was no more than an illusion and the fairy-tale engagement would never happen. Catherine, Nancy concluded, was not included in the special dinner and she pondered whether she should mention it to her at all.

"We keep it to ourselves, just those of us included," Eve told her. "Just for the sake of peace. You know how jealous some of the girls can be."

When Nancy met Stephen she liked him at once; suave and sophisticated, charming, intelligent and easy company. Nancy looked forward to this dinner party. A few days before it was to take place, Adam approached her as she sat at the bar.

"What are you wearing to the dinner?" he asked her.

She told him what she had bought with the advance he had given her.

"I'd like to see it," he insisted curtly. "Bring it in tomorrow. We do want you to look your best, don't we?"

She nodded, irked a little by his tone. He had been quite specific about the type of outfit she should buy which had

Monday's Child
Caroline Jones Lewis

irritated her somewhat at the time. Did he really think she didn't know what to wear for such an occasion, coming from her background? Was he that stupid? She had wanted to cut him down to size with a biting retort but conscious of her need to keep Adam sweet for the time being, she bit it back, pursing her lips to seal within the words that were threatening to spill from her mouth. It was, after all, an important client to him and an occasion that might serve her purpose well. So in his office she modelled for him the little black dress which fitted her like a glove and received gracious approval in a tone in total contradiction to his manner the previous day.
"You look stunning," he assured her. "And just to complete things, you can borrow these," he added, taking from the drawer of his desk a black velvet box which he passed across to her. Nancy opened it to find inside an elegant pearl necklace and earrings. The muscles of her stomach knotted. She didn't want to wear them, almost thrust them back across the desk as though they were hot and singeing her fingers. They were a near replica of her mother's favourite pearls, in looks, in size, in colour. She tried to speak but the words would not come so she fingered them to cover her angst. Then, "they're lovely," she told him. "Thank you," and hurried from the room clasping the box tightly in both hands.

That night sleep would not come as readily as usual and when it did, it was spasmodic and disturbed by uninvited images – of her mother, of Adam, of a broken string of pearls tumbling around her, a mirage of imaginings bombarding her subconscious. When at last she lay fully awake in the early hours, she lay watching the light of dawn sneaking around the curtains. The effect of her dreams stayed with her for days.

The weekend of the dinner party arrived, as did the limo. Nancy and Eve were driven to the venue, a picturesque lodge in the grounds of a beautiful manor house north of

Monday's Child
Caroline Jones Lewis

the City. Two other girls had arrived already, Suzanne, who Nancy had seen at the Club and who seemed as new to the surroundings as she was herself and Christine who Nancy had never met before and who seemed totally at home. Nancy revelled in surroundings that were undaunting to her. An elegant tiled hallway led to a wide and winding staircase of rich dark rosewood, carpeted in deep pile burgundy. Paintings on the walls were instinctively recognisable as originals. Christine led the girls to a dressing room off the landing where they left their coats and bags. They tidied their hair and retouched their make-up with giggles of excitement and examined their overall appearance in a long gilded mirror before rejoining Christine on the landing. She led them to their bedrooms further along the corridor, passing open doors on either side that revealed luxuriously decorated rooms. Each had a large sumptuous bed and tall, deep windows draped and pelmetted in rich fabrics. Outside lush floodlit lawns and gardens swept into the distance like swathes of emerald velvet. Carefully dressed in her new black frock with the sheen of the pearls lighting her skin, Nancy glowed with self-assurance. She had become increasingly aware in recent years that she was more than average in the beauty department.

"Truly a Monday's Child," her mother would tell her with pride and affection.

Now in these surroundings amongst what she understood to be wealthy and influential people, her awareness and confidence in her physical attributes was palpable. Christine eyed her with disdain.

There were three men in the party apart from Stephen. They were introduced to the girls as they entered the warmth and glamour of a sitting room brought to life by a blazing fire; a French businessman, handsome with that seductive accent that made women drool, an English diplomat home on leave from a far eastern posting and a Russian attaché about whom they were told nothing more

Monday's Child
Caroline Jones Lewis

than his name – Ivanov. Nancy was surprised he was there. Even someone as apolitical as Nancy was aware of the Cold War antagonism between the two countries. She remembered her father's opinion of the Russians, mistrusting and convinced they still had sinister motives. Ivanov, however, Nancy found charming, an easy companion and one whose eyes rested easily in her direction. She enjoyed his attention through dinner, flattering and flirting with her in impeccable English. Conversation between them flowed with ease.
"Tell me, Nancy," he coaxed, "how does a beautiful young woman like you come to know this reprobate?" and he nodded in Stephen's direction. "Are you his mistress?" Stephen pursed his lips in a non-commital grin to Nancy, cocking his head to one side in an invitation for her to reply as she wished. She laughed and mimicked outrageous indignation in the manner of a Victorian housemaid accused of indiscretion with her master.
"Why, sir," she began with a wide-eyed purity that managed at the same time to be flirtatious, "I'm sure I don't know what you mean, casting aspersions on a pure unsullied maid like me."
The men smiled and the girls giggled. Ivanov's eyes twinkled in amusement and he raised his glass to her in salute.
"Oh, do please forgive my impertinence," he pleaded. Wit as well as beauty, he thought to himself. A rare combination. Enchanting. But is she his mistress? Or is she free?
Stephen winked at Nancy, aware that she had neither admitted nor denied the suggestion leaving the Russian's curiosity unsatisfied. Stephen wondered how successful his scheme for the evening might be, whether Adam's assessment of Nancy's vulnerability was correct. He did not see it and already it seemed to him that she may indeed emerge as the one in control. The thought intrigued him and caused an enigmatic smile to cross his lips. She

Monday's Child
Caroline Jones Lewis

denied the Russian any further comment on the subject and the conversation moved on.

The food came and went. The wine flowed gently. Conversation and good-humour stretched into the early hours as the group migrated from the dining table to the drawing room, blatantly pairing into couples. Nancy found herself drawn quite naturally to Ivanov by whom she had become enchanted. And so to bed.

In Ivanov's room instead of her own, caressed by soft words and kisses that left her eager for more, resistance did not so much as occur to Nancy. It was not until the next morning, late and alone and in the haze of a light hangover, did the realisation of how she had been manipulated impress itself upon her. Ivanov was long gone. She lay amongst the sumptuous sheets and pillows, closing her eyes to soothe the dull thud of her head – and considered. The evening had been great fun and her companion charming and amusing. She felt no regret at the way the evening had ended. On the contrary, the sex had been wonderful and satisfying with so experienced a lover, unlike her previous experience of fumbled coupling with a schoolboy no more experienced than herself. She had no illusion that love had anything to do with it. But surprisingly it did not matter to her. She had enjoyed it and more – she wanted to do it again. But not just with anyone, only with someone that appealed to her. Like Eve, she thought to herself. She was surprised at herself. She thought of her parents and how horrified they would be. But then what was so different between her and her mother? Her mother had behaved like a whore, hadn't she? A supposedly respectable married one but still a whore. The reminder of her mother's affair sparked her anger again and with it came the defiance that had compelled her all these months. With Christmas approaching, nostalgia had been creeping in of late. There had been moments when the desire to speak to her parents

Monday's Child
Caroline Jones Lewis

had almost overwhelmed her but she had cut the emotions dead - like a severing of the umbilical cord. They probably didn't miss her anyway. She had been a mistake in their lives, their excuse for marriage. She did so now, shut out the thought of them. The hardest part, though, was shutting out Lizzie and Hugh who had done nothing to her and who she was beginning to miss more than she would ever have thought possible. It was in her mind that perhaps she would ring Lizzie at Christmas. Well, maybe, she thought. She would think about it, perhaps do it on a spur-of-the-moment decision.

Agitated by the recollection, she stirred from the bed and walked naked to the window, opening it to breathe in the sweet fresh air. Oh, yes, she thought. That's how it's going to be. I'm in control now. The naïve young girl was no longer. In her place was a determined young woman who would be no-one's fool. She would live her life as she wished. The way *she* wanted. Doing what *she* wanted. There was a toughness about her now that had not been there only weeks before. And the Adams and Ivanovs of this world were there for her benefit and not the other way around. From the corner of her eye she thought she saw a movement in the grounds below. She peered but could see no-one. But she turned from the window anyway and walked steadily to the bathroom, stepped into a warm shower and let the warm rivulets of water cascade over her body. In the grounds below Stephen stood concealed beneath the branches of a tree smoking a cigarette as he watched her naked at the window. Already putting together a guest list for the New Year, Nancy, he decided, was a definite.

On the drive back to town, Eve and Nancy compared notes in whispered voices, arms linked and laughing.
"There is one thing, though," Nancy began in a more serious tone.

Monday's Child
Caroline Jones Lewis

"Precautions. I didn't even think if it, Eve. What do I do? I don't want to get pregnant. But I daren't go to my old GP and I haven't registered with a new one."
"You go to a clinic," Eve assured her. "You don't need to go to your doctor now. You can get the pill at a clinic. Don't worry. We'll get it sorted."

******

Christmas week arrived in freezing temperatures and a flurry of snowflakes. A white Christmas was a distinct possibility. Hugh sat in his sitting room the weekend before, his dressing gown wrapped around him and a mug of steaming black coffee cupped in his hands as he watched the comings and goings of the morning in the street below. His anticipation of Christmas fluctuated from pleasurable to despair with every twist and turn of Simon's inexplicable behaviour. Then there was the worry about Nancy and the angst from which his aunt and uncle were suffering in their failure to trace her. All in all, it was not likely to be the best Christmas the family had spent together.

He wished there was something he could do to help his aunt and uncle. He had done a certain amount to help, visited likely parts of town where she might be, but like everyone he had drawn a blank. He was invited, as tradition, to spend Christmas Day at his aunt and uncle's London home. It would undoubtedly be a subdued occasion without Nancy but at least it precluded any possibility of being let down yet again by Simon who would probably abandon him at the last moment in favour of more illuminating company. Hugh wished he could pull himself free of a relationship that was so detrimental to his well-being but although he had tried each time that Simon had let him down, he had not yet found the emotional strength to do so. He had lost weight, along with his appetite and his usually neat and tidy home and person

Monday's Child
Caroline Jones Lewis

were frayed around the edges. He had see-sawed between a strident determination to end this farce of a relationship and get on with his life and the slough of despair at his inability to break free. He craved Simon's love and attention like a junkie needing a fix, all the time knowing it to be destructive. Over recent months he had neglected other friends who knew nothing of these events, avoiding their company and turning down invitations he might otherwise have accepted on the excuse of family matters, in particular Nancy's disappearance. He had been open to friends and colleagues on the matter of Nancy in the hope that the more people who knew of her disappearance, the better the chance of finding her. But it was not an excuse he could use forever.

He had become aware that the girls in the office were probing; in a kindly way, but still probing.

"Nice weekend, Hugh? Anything special? Anyone?" the font of all knowledge had ventured.

He had smiled and waved dismissively but what would they think of him if they knew? A pervert? A freak? He would become a social outcast, a pariah. His boss, a self-confessed homophobe, would undoubtedly turn against him. Since his relationship with Simon was so tenuous there was no point in risking such ostracism. It was painful enough to deal with privately without public condemnation as well; and for his future since his job would undoubtedly be at risk. Then there was his family to think of, in particular his dear Grandmother. After all she had done for him he could not bear the thought of the pain his sexuality would cause her. And as for Simon – he was unlikely to change, barring a miracle. Chas' warning to Hugh had stayed with him – his description of Simon as a spoiled brat used to getting everything he wants and valuing nothing. In quiet contemplation Hugh came to recognise that Simon's malaise would have to run its course. And he with it. Come the New Year, he decided, he would pull himself together and invite his valued friends to the flat for drinks.

Monday's Child

Caroline Jones Lewis

The ringing of the 'phone interrupted his train of thought bringing him back to the problem of the moment - Nancy. His aunt's voice at the other end of the line was tremulous as they discussed the arrangements for Christmas Day.
"Are you sure you want to do this, Auntie? Under the circumstances."
"Especially under the circumstances, Hugh. I couldn't bear not to be with you all this Christmas. And maybe remembering that we'll all be together might ….. "
"Draw her home?" Hugh finished.
"Yes. Maybe," his aunt replied in an emotional whisper.
"Let's hope so," Hugh responded.
Miranda hesitated, suddenly unsure of herself.
"I don't know," she went on. "Perhaps I'm being foolish."
"No, no," Hugh reassured. "Of course not. You're right. It makes sense. The thought of us all being there together, it might just be what she needs. Let's hope so. And we'll be here for you, you know that."
Miranda sighed.
"Thank you, Hugh. You're such a dear."
Hugh replaced the receiver with a new purpose to his day. It was time, he decided, to do the Christmas shopping he had neglected too long, so absorbed in his obsession with Simon. He would spend today buying presents for his loving family and friends who he had so failed in recent weeks.
"Thank you, Aunt Miranda," he thought to himself and headed for the bathroom and the shower. He was halted in his tracks by the ringing of the 'phone. To answer or not to answer, he thought. It was likely to be Simon. In this moment of strength and determination, he assured himself, he would not be available for Simon today. He would answer, he decided, but his resolve would not melt away. He would show Simon that he was not going to be messed around this weekend. He turned back and lifted the receiver.
"Hello… Hugh?"

Monday's Child

Caroline Jones Lewis

A female voice. And in the flash of a second, the penny dropped for Hugh.
"Nancy," he gasped. "Thank God. Nancy, where are you?"

******

Lizzie's suitcase stood packed near the front door of the room in halls that she shared with Sarah. She was looking forward to being at home for Christmas. Her first term at university had been so exciting and she had loved every minute of this new phase of her life. The time had flown by, the only thing that marred the experience was the anxiety about Nancy. She had wished fervently that Nancy would get in touch with her, or with Hugh – or with anyone else in the family if she could not bring herself to ring her parents. She had given her telephone number here in halls to Hugh to pass on to Nancy should she get in touch again as Lizzie had guessed if Nancy were to contact anyone in the family, in the absence of a number for herself, it would be Hugh.
Lizzie's roommate burst into the room.
"Your taxi's downstairs, Liz. Want a hand with anything?"
"Oh, great. Could you just manage the carrier with the presents in? I'll take the suitcase. It's a bit on the heavy side."
"Sure."
The two girls clattered down the staircase to the front door, exchanging good wishes for the Christmas and New Year festivities until Lizzie settled herself in the taxi along with bags and baggage.
"See you in the New Year, Sarah. Hope you have a lovely time," she called and leaned out of the cab window to kiss her friends cheek just as the taxi began to pull away.
Sarah bent forward to receive the kiss.

Monday's Child

Caroline Jones Lewis

"You too. And I hope you have news of Nancy," she replied. "That would be the icing on the Christmas cake, wouldn't it?"
Lizzie nodded, wrapping her ample scarf around her neck against the cold and waving as the taxi swung away from the kerb.

Lizzie's excitement bubbled to the surface. She could hardly wait to see her Mum and Dad again. There was so much to tell them. Despite the anxiety of Nancy, she had thrown herself wholeheartedly into university life and learning, the goal she had aimed for for so long. Now and then she felt a pang of guilt in the light of Nancy's absence. Nancy could be in all kinds of trouble. But she could not help herself. She had worked so hard for this for so many years and all her hopes and dreams for the future depended on what she achieved here. She rubbed the frosted window pane with her gloved hand and peered out at the passing hubbub, puffing a cloud of hot breath against the cold of the glass. She tingled with anticipation.

As her train pulled into Tonbridge station she slid down the window and searched ahead of her. From the platform, her parents' beaming faces came into view and she waved, returning their smiles with one of her own. Hauling her bags down from the luggage rack she was ready to propel them onto the platform the second the train screeched to a halt. They kissed and hugged on the platform and her father scooped up the luggage Lizzie had dropped at her feet, then placing their arms around her shoulders, they guided her to the car park and the car to take her home.
"You look wonderfully well, love," Emily enthused. "You must be eating alright."
"Oh, Mum. I have so much to tell you. I'm not sure three weeks will be long enough," Lizzie laughed.
Tom stowed the luggage in the boot of Emily's car, then bent to kiss Lizzie on the forehead.
"Have to tell me later, love. Got to dash."

Monday's Child

Caroline Jones Lewis

"Oh, Dad," Lizzie began to protest. "Why?"
"I'm on duty, Liz. As ever. Only managed to get cover long enough to come and meet you. We're really short staffed. You know what it's like at this time of year. 'Flu, bronchial problems all the usual winter stuff. I'll see you later. We can catch up over dinner."
"Ok, fine. See you later then," Lizzie said and quickly hugged and kissed her father before he climbed into his own car and drove away. "Thanks for coming," she called at the disappearing car.

The cottage was the usual warm and cosy home Lizzie had been looking forward to. She and her mother peeled off their outer clothing and hung their coats on the stand in the hallway, then shuffled along the hallway to the kitchen, chatting and laughing as they went. While Emily filled the kettle to make tea, they launched into a conversation about much that Lizzie had experienced in her first term, her studies, her room and roommate, the Students' Union, the debating society, the bars and the male students, oh, yes, the male students.
"Male chauvinist students, mostly," Lizzie giggled.
Their conversation was interrupted by the ringing of the 'phone.
"I'll get it," Lizzie chirped, leaving her mother to pour the tea. "I'm dying to catch up with everyone," and she swirled along the hall with a flurry of anticipation. She was not to be disappointed.
"Hugh," she crooned. "Oh, Hugh, how lovely to hear from you. I'm so dying to see you. How are you?"
But his voice sounded tense and she paused, unsure of whether he was troubled.
"I'm fine, Liz, thanks. Lovely to speak to you, too."
He paused and Lizzie waited.
"Liz, I've just had a call from Nancy," he blurted.
Lizzie gasped.
"Oh, Hugh. Thank God," she replied. "Is she alright? Where is she?"

Monday's Child

Caroline Jones Lewis

"She sounded alright. She wouldn't say where she was. Only that she's safe and we're not to worry. Look, Liz. I know you've only just got home and all that but would you mind if I came down. It's shaken me up a bit hearing from her like that. I'm not sure what I should do. What should I tell Aunt Miranda and Uncle James? I'll have to let them know she's ok but she's insistent she doesn't want to talk to them."

"Did she say why?"

"No. Look, Aunt Emily is probably the best person to talk to them. Is it ok with her for me to come."

"I'm sure it will be, Hugh, but let me just check with her that she has nothing else arranged. Hang on, she's only in the kitchen."

After a brief discussion with her mother, she returned to the 'phone.

"Mum says it's fine. She says why don't you bring your toothbrush and stay over for the night. Then we can have a real catch up."

"I'm not sure," Hugh replied. Simon hovered in the background of his thoughts.

"Maybe. I'll see," remembering his earlier resolve. "I'll catch the earliest train I can and get a taxi from the station."

"Ok. See you later then."

Christmas shopping once more on hold, Hugh showered, dressed and headed for the station.

******

After the first dinner at Stephen's that Nancy had attended, Adam was intrigued at her reaction. He knew what had transpired from a conversation with Stephen and he had wondered how the experience had sat with Nancy, but she demonstrated no change of demeanour and made no comment on the matter other than that she had enjoyed the evening. She accepted without question the generous

Monday's Child
Caroline Jones Lewis

bonus he paid her cash in hand but she made no comment on that either and Ivanov's name was not mentioned.
"I have another Client who is planning a small dinner party for the weekend before Christmas," he told her. "He needs a few female escorts to make up numbers. Are you interested?"
He watched her face intently. She was sitting at the bar sipping a glass of tonic, her thick glossy hair swept up into a slide. She turned and faced him with an enigmatic smile that revealed nothing of her inner thoughts.
"Fine," she replied. "Just let me know when and I'll be there."
"Good," he said, turning and walking back to his office. He sucked on the Havanna gripped between his teeth.
"Excellent," he whispered under his breath.

Nancy attended an appointment at a birth control clinic that Eve had told her about.
"Tell them you're in a serious relationship," Eve had advised her, "but that you don't want to have to marry because you're pregnant. It's not that you don't want children, just not now. You want to plan things properly and marry at the right time, for the right reason. They'll like that. It will impress them with your responsibility. Not that they ask many questions anyway, but it will sound good. Don't worry. It will be fine."
"Well, it is true," thought Nancy dismissing thought of any further explanation. The irony of her situation struck her. If her mother had been able to do as she herself was doing when she was young, her mother might never have become pregnant, her parents may never have married and she, Nancy, may never have been born.

Nancy and Eve were driven to the Client's in the Jaguar. A bright full moon glowed down on a landscape glistening white with frost like the icing on a Christmas cake. Illuminated in the headlights of the car, the hedgerows along the driveway sparkled like the conversation and

Monday's Child
Caroline Jones Lewis

laughter between the two girls inside. Like any teenagers out for an evening's fun, they giggled and speculated on the coming evening's events and the men who would be their companions at dinner.
"Same as last time, I'll bet," Eve suggested laconically. "One tall, dark and handsome – he'll be yours, no doubt. You're a looker so you attract the same."
Nancy laughed but said nothing.
"Then there'll be one short and bald – I'll probably get him," and Eve grimaced and then laughed. "Not that I care. It's all the same to me as long as he seems a nice guy. And one will be filthy rich – Christine will make a play for him, of course. Have you noticed? She's really clever at picking out the rich one and she always gets her way. Then there'll be one other for whoever else is there."
"Who does Christine work for?" Nancy queried.
"No idea," Eve answered. "She's alright though. Good fun, and all that. And that's what the men want, isn't it? Fun and no strings. I get on ok with Christine but I've never seen her outside of Stephen's company."
"So you don't know where she lives or anything?"
"Nope. Never bothered to find out."

The car pulled to a halt at the door to a prestigious property and their host stepped out to greet them. Alerted to their arrival by the beam of headlights approaching down the drive, he stood silhouetted in the doorway against the mellow glow of light from within. The chauffeur opened the door for the girls to alight on the gravel drive and he stepped forward to welcome them, one hand caressing gold cufflinks on the wrist of his other, suave, immaculate and smelling like heaven.
"Good evening, ladies," he crooned. "So lovely to see you. Come on in out of the cold."
The warmth and light of the hallway embraced them and they crowed their appreciation, handing their wraps to a butler hired for the evening. Two men were already with Christine in the drawing room, their laughter and

Monday's Child
Caroline Jones Lewis

conversation audible from the hall as Eve and Nancy made their way to join them. Stephen stood close by but a little to the side of her, confusing Nancy as to whether he and Christine were together or simply friends invited to the same event. Stephen was the toast of the city, the man who must be invited and secured as a guest to enhance the host's social standing. But whether he and Christine were together she could not tell. There was a tall, slim man with a hook nose, receding hairline and spectacles and wearing an immaculate suit that suggested money. The other was shorter and balding with a soft, round, pink-cheeked baby face that looked scrubbed and clean for the occasion, his clothes neat and clean but indicating more modest means.
"Don't think much of yours," Eve whispered as they stepped through the doorway into the room.
Nancy cut short a giggle, turning it into a charming smile and clasping the outstretched hand of the shorter of the two men as he stepped forward to meet them.
"My name's David," he said in a soft gentle voice. "And you are?"
"Nancy," she replied, "and this is Eve."
David beamed a welcome and introduced the taller man as Gerald. Gerald remained where he was standing, now closely attended by a smiling Christine who had moved almost unnoticed to his side.
"The filthy rich one," Nancy concluded to herself, acknowledging Christine's arm placed lightly on Gerald's Saville Row sleeve. Two other girls who were strangers to her joined the party and were introduced and Nancy guessed their participation to be much as her own.
So who's with Stephen, then? she wondered. And where's tall, dark and handsome?
David had already engaged Eve in conversation.
Nancy's thoughts were answered almost immediately by a late arrival. Tall, dark and an older version of handsome entered the room with a smile and an apology for his lateness. He introduced himself with a self-assured handshake as Matthew. Two other girls arrived to compliment

Monday's Child

Caroline Jones Lewis

the company and introduced themselves as Mandy and Shona. Their host joined them from the hallway. Since it was clear there were no other guests still to arrive, champagne was served and the group settled themselves comfortably on the sofas awaiting the call to dinner. The evening progressed much as on the previous occasion though Nancy found Matthew, who had appointed himself her companion, less charming and enjoyable as Ivanov had been. The natural rapport she had experienced then was not evident with this man. Indeed she felt a slight discomfort and unease. She noticed that while his mouth was smiling there was a coldness in his eyes that was disconcerting. She glanced once or twice in Eve's direction but failed to catch her eye and Stephen was engaged in conversation .

"Just remember it's only a job – just for this evening," she thought to herself and despite her reservations about the man, her demeanour betrayed nothing to the assembled company. As the wine flowed and the evening wore on, she relaxed and dismissed her misgivings as a misjudgement, her over-active imagination at work again.

Later, heading towards his room ostensibly for a nightcap, her misgivings returned and she tried to disengage herself on the excuse of tiredness.

"Really, Matthew," she attempted. "I've had enough to drink already. I'd rather just like to go to my room to bed, if you don't mind."

But Matthew was not persuaded. He was intent on getting his way.

"Oh, just the one, surely," he insisted, taking her arm firmly and propelling her into his room. "You'll be telling me next you have a headache," and he gave a brief snort of laughter.

Barely into the room, he grabbed her roughly and pressed her hard against the wall.

Monday's Child
Caroline Jones Lewis

"Don't," she began, attempting to extricate herself from his grasp and the situation but he was strong and held her firmly in his control.

"Don't what," he responded. "I've paid for this, lady. Just remember that," and he thrust her towards the bed. He pulled her dress down around her legs and she lay on the bed in her underwear feeling exposed and vulnerable while he quickly undressed.

"Take them off," he ordered, indicating her underwear. She slipped off her briefs and bra, afraid to defy him and determined to get it over with as quickly as possible, then return to the security of her own room but Matthew had other ideas. He locked the door, put the key into the pocket of his trousers and turned to study her.

"Your body is beautiful," he said, walking towards her on the bed. "Just what I asked for," and he ran his hands across her breasts.

He was not the gentle lover that Ivanov had been and took her roughly, entering her hurriedly without any pretence of tenderness or consideration. He raised her arms above her head, pinning her beneath him. His face was close to her own, his hot, alcoholic breath on her cheek and the clammy dampness of his body felt crushing against her. In the shadow of the half-lit room, his face gripped in arousal had a cruel quality. She felt an anger welling up inside her, but not just anger. There was something else. As he momentarily relaxed his grip, slowing his rhythm to postpone his climax, she rolled him forcibly onto his back and straddled him, anger and lust taking control of her and she took from him what she wanted as ruthlessly as he had from her until they were both spent. Alcohol and tiredness took over and she lapsed into sleep. In the night he woke her and took her for a second time, roughly as before. She submitted without protest.

When she woke in the morning she was alone. She felt stiff and sore and when she moved she felt something rough scratch against her thigh. She threw back the sheet

Monday's Child

Caroline Jones Lewis

and tucked between her legs was a £20. note marked with a kiss. She crumpled the note in her hand and rolled over groaning. Her legs were bruised, her wrists too and her head throbbed explosively. She remembered Ivanov and the luxury of their intimacy in contrast to the harsh lust of the previous night. She buried her head in the pillow letting her hair tumble like a curtain around her. The recollection of her own promiscuity was a shock to her, the enjoyment of sex and the part she had played in last night's indulgence. She knew now what she really was and knew that, whatever her mother had done in taking her lover, it was not comparable to this. She saw no way back to the person she had been. She had grown up and become a different person in a few short months – and that person, just at this moment, was not to her liking.

She sneaked back to her own room and after showering and dressing, she sat on the bed unwilling to go down to face Eve and the others. The telephone seemed to stare at her from the bedside table, inviting – even challenging. She contemplated. Unable to resist the nostalgia that was surging inside her, she picked up the receiver and dialled Hugh's number still secure in her memory and the sound of Hugh's soft, gentle voice flowed through her like an ungent soothing a wound. Dear gentle, lovely Hugh.
"Nancy. Nancy. Where are you?"
"I'm at a friend's," she lied, trying to sound bright and cheerful. "How are you, Hugh?"
"I'm fine. But how are you? We've all been so worried about you. Your parents have been half out of their minds trying to find you. They still are."
Her resolve re-emerged, still unwilling to concede to a need of her family.
"Hugh, I'm fine. Really. Just fine. Tell them I'm fine though I'm surprised they really care."
"Nancy, how can you say that? Whatever's happened between you and your parents you must know they adore

Monday's Child
Caroline Jones Lewis

you. Always have done. Of course they're worried. They miss you desperately. Won't you ring them?"

Nancy couldn't stand to hear any more.

"Hugh, I've got to go now. Just tell everyone I'm fine. How's Liz?"

"She's fine too. Enjoying uni. Look, I've got a number for her there to give you. Hang on, just a minute. I've got it here somewhere. I'll get it for you, then you can ring her yourself. But she's going home for Christmas right now. You could ring her there?"

He paused but Nancy made no reply.

"But if you'd rather not," he continued, "You can ring her in Halls. Unless we're going to see you over Christmas."

The reference to Christmas brought an immediate response.

"No. And I can't take her number right now, Hugh. I don't have a pen. Just give her my love and tell her I'm fine and I'm glad she's enjoying uni."

"Nancy, don't go, please."

"I have to, Hugh. My friends are waiting."

"Well, will you ring me again? Please."

"I will. Yes. I will, I promise."

"Will you call your parents?"

"No. 'Bye Hugh," and she was gone.

She replaced the receiver trying to stem the sudden longing that was welling up in her but failing, and the tears came anyway. For she knew that she could not face her family now, not after her behaviour of the previous night.

By the time she joined Eve downstairs Nancy had composed herself and told herself that ringing Hugh had been a mistake. She was fine. She would stick to her plan, make money and become successful before she would return to anyone in the family. Little did she know that she would travel a dangerous road as a result of that decision. Last night had just been a bad night, she convinced herself, an unpleasant experience with Matthew which she would not repeat. But her mood was subdued. In the limousine

Monday's Child
Caroline Jones Lewis

back to town Eve sensed her mood and asked what was wrong.
"Just tired," Nancy replied. "That guy …. "
"You did it?" Eve questioned.
Nancy nodded.
"I had no choice," she wanted to confide to her but she refrained, the memory of her own participation shaming her into silence.
"Demanding?" Eve asked.
Nancy nodded again.
"Home to bed then," Eve said.
"Home to bed," Nancy echoed. "On my own."

The following evening Adam called for her to come to his office.
"I've had a request," he began. "From Matthew. From the party?"
Nancy nodded her recognition.
"He wants to see you again. Privately – at the flat."
"No," she blurted. "No."
Disappointed, Adam considered his next move.
"You sound surprisingly adamant," he ventured, as casually as possible. "Is there any particular reason?"
Nancy pulled back the cuffs of her blouse to reveal the bruising. Adam's expression darkened.
"He did that?"
Nancy nodded.
"They're not the only ones," she muttered quietly.
"Leave it with me," Adam told her. "You won't see him again."
When Nancy had left his office, Adam telephoned the host of the previous evening at once. Neither he nor any of his clients approved of violence against the girls. And it could only lead to trouble. Nancy would be out of circulation now until the bruises had faded, or could even be put off altogether, not wishing to go to any further parties. That was bad news as he recognised her potential. Such potential and she knew how to conduct herself, not like

Monday's Child
Caroline Jones Lewis

Catherine who was becoming a greater imposition with each passing day. He had already decided that Catherine had to go and take with her the bleating adoration, the puppy dog devotion and vacuous expression that, once so appealing, was now irritating to the point of distraction. But Nancy was an asset to be nurtured. Then he spoke with Stephen, made him aware of what had happened to Nancy. Stephen was the must-have guest at every social gathering. He could make sure that Matthew would be excluded from every guest list with the girls forthwith.

Monday's Child

Caroline Jones Lewis

Chapter Six – Out of Control

Christmas Day was a strange occasion for everyone. At James and Miranda's, Nancy's disappearance was an ever-constant ache. The elephant in the room. The knowledge that she was alive and apparently safe and well was a comfort at least, and now there was hope that, having contacted Hugh, she would do so again. But it was still a strange day with her conspicuous by her absence. In the early evening James and Miranda kissed their guests goodbye and the family left with a sigh of relief that the day was almost over.

Nancy had to work constantly to keep thoughts of home and family at bay until the day was dying and the alcohol had numbed the senses. It was an unreal day. Bizarre. No decorations, no family and of course no presents to speak of to give or to take. It had been a fantasy when she was at home, the thought of just her and Jacs doing exactly what they wanted instead of being tied to boring home and family stuff. But the fantasy, now it had become a reality, did not live up to expectations. She spent the day at Eve's, the two of them lolling about the flat, nibbling on pre-cooked food and chocolates, drinking champagne and watching a tv loaned by Eve's cousin. He worked in a tv rental shop, a spotty youth smelling of Old Spice and resplendent in flared trousers and an open-necked shirt with a huge collar. In an act of kindness for his favourite cousin, he had smuggled them a surrendered rental model with a 9" screen that flickered black and white images into the room.
"I'll 'ave to 'ave it back on Boxing Day," he told them. "Boss isn't in on Boxing Day so I can get it back into the shop before 'e knows it's missin. E's takin' his wife to the sale at Selfridges on Boxing Day," he confided. "So I'll 'ave plenty o' time. I'll pick it up in the mornin'."

Monday's Child
Caroline Jones Lewis

The two girls lunched on chicken joints and cooked in a rarely used oven. Eve, who had rejected an invitation to home to spend the day with Nancy and who was marginally more domesticated than her, cooked potatoes and frozen peas and followed it up with Mrs Peek's Christmas pud and cream – a relative banquet compared to their usual junk food diet. At 3 o'clock, they watched the Queen's speech. To Eve's amusement, Nancy launched into her imitation of the Queen, a party piece she often used to amuse the family.
"My husband and I," she began irreverently, as the National Anthem faded to silence, "are thrilled by the little Telstar so that now we, and the corgis, can watch you, our Commonwealth subjects, about your little daily lives. God bless you all."
Eve spluttered with laughter.
"My Mum would love that," she giggled. "She always watches her. Tradition, isn't it. They've always been for the royals. In the East End. Ever since the war."
"What would you be doing now – if you were at home?" Nancy asked.
"Oh, we'd be round at Auntie Ethel's by now, me, Mum, Dad and sis, with Auntie Ethel and her friend Edith, As soon as the Queen's Speech is over," Eve told her. "Auntie Ethel is Mum's sister. She lives just round the corner in a prefab. All net curtains, Camp coffee and carbolic."
Nancy giggled.
"What do you mean – all net curtains and carbolic? Who on earth uses carbolic these days?" Except Mrs Hale, she thought, her mind flashing back to Abberley. "What's a prefab?"
As Eve enlightened her as to the answer, it occurred to Nancy how little she had chosen to change in her now independent state. Tradition had still dictated the menu, she had still watched the Queen's speech and neither she nor Eve had any plans for the evening other than to watch more tv. How futile, she thought. What was the saying –

Monday's Child
Caroline Jones Lewis

about grass being greener on the other side? Eve's voice brought her back to the moment.

"Auntie Ethel's house was flattened by a buzz bomb. Lucky she wasn't in it, they say. She was down the underground with all her neighbours. Their houses were flattened, too. Gerry got the whole street. So now she lives in her prefab, after all these years an' she's still waiting for the new house she was promised.

"And uses her carbolic," Nancy interjected affably.

Eve nodded.

"Yep. She's always used carbolic, ever since I can remember. When I was a child she used to kiss me on the cheek and I hated the smell. I've tried to ween her off it but it doesn't work. Last Christmas I bought her some Imperial Leather. Everyone likes Imperial Leather, I thought. A gift set. You know, soap, talc and bath cubes. Really pretty, it was, in a nice flowery box with a ribbon round it. So next time I went I expected the house to smell nice and scenty. But no, back to the carbolic. The place reeked of it. I don't know what she did with the Imperial Leather I bought her. Gave it away I expect. Too old to change, Mum said. Brought up on carbolic so now she can't use anything else. She's our family's answer to Ena Sharples, hairnet and all."

"Ena Sharples?" Nancy echoed. "Who's Ena Sharples?"

"You *know*," Eve crooned. "Coronation Street. The three old dears. Ena, Minnie and – oh, who's the other one."

Nancy looked blank.

"Martha, that's it. Yes, Martha," Eve concluded. But I don't suppose you watch Coronation Street in your house. All Panorama and the Wednesday Play, I spose."

"We don't watch much tv," Nancy reminisced. "I'm not allowed. My father thinks it's all time-wasting rubbish. But we always watch the Queen's Speech. And nature programmes and films sometimes."

Eve noticed the use of present tense. Still hope, then, she thought.

"It isn't too late, you know," she ventured. "To go home."

Monday's Child

Caroline Jones Lewis

"No," Nancy snapped and turned away. Eve made no comment.
Bing Crosby's voice filled the room.
White Christmas again, thought Nancy, listening to Eve amiably crooning along. Sounds and images flooded Nancy's mind of earlier Christmases at home. Her mother loved Bing Crosby, even her father whose usual musical preference was more classical. She had been raised on a musical diet of Bing and Sinatra as light relief from her father's Beethoven, Mozart and Vivaldi, though Sinatra had fallen from grace a little of late on political grounds. Hugh's preference was the jazz scene - Brubeck, Chleo Laine and Ella Fitzgerald. They did not care for the new generation artists of which she was a fan. Cliff was tolerated, as had Buddy Holly been before his tragic and early death but Elvis met with disapproval, the Beatles viewed with scepticism and the Rolling Stones positively vilified.
"Music, they call that music," her father would grumble. "They won't be around long. In six months time they'll have died a musical death and gone. You'll see."
She had the freedom now, she thought; freedom to choose what she wanted. But just at this moment, the sound of Bing's warm and familiar voice caused the knotting of the stomach muscles that thoughts of home and family seemed to prompt. An image of the family gathered around the Christmas tree in her aunt's sitting room refused to be dismissed. Unwrapping presents. Laughing and kissing their thank yous and seated around the beautifully decorated dining table for a luxurious Christmas dinner wearing party hats from the Harrods crackers. She thought of Jacs. She and Jacs had always called each other on Christmas morning to exchange gossip about their presents, their parents, whether they had the colour lipstick in their stocking that they wanted or the right nail polish. She wondered what Jacs was doing today, whether she was missing her, Nancy, and their telephone call. But the dye was now cast, she told herself. If they knew what she had

Monday's Child
Caroline Jones Lewis

now become they would not want her back anyway. They would be so ashamed. So, like Eve, her New Year resolution would be to earn as much money as possible as quickly as she could to move on to another life. She had no idea what that life would be as yet but something would present itself, she was sure. She severed her train of thought and turned back to the present. Eve had watched Nancy intently, guessing at what was going through Nancy's mind and she resolved to do what she could to help Nancy return home.

Nancy changed the subject.

"What does your sister do?" she asked.

"She works in Cheltenham. At GCHQ," Eve replied.

"Doing what?"

"Don't know exactly. It's all hush hush there, you know. Trackin' the Ruskies,, Dad calls it. He doesn't trust the Russians, thinks they're up to no good. But my sister never says a word, never lets on even when Dad's sounding off about them. Just grins and winks at Mum and me."

"I sometimes wish I had a sister," Nancy said dreamily. "Maybe I'd be less selfish if I'd had a sister. If I had learned to share more. It must be nice."

"It's not all it's cracked up to be," Eve muttered. "Like – we used to fight cat and dog when we both lived at home. Over really daft things sometimes. She'd get really annoyed with me because I'd pinch her make-up and stuff. And I'd get annoyed with her because she was always up before me and she'd get the bottle of milk off the doorstep before me and take the cream off the top for her cornflakes. I could never beat her to it. Then there was school, of course. She was brilliant at everything and I wasn't. I was always her not-so-clever sister instead of just me so I suppose in the end I just stopped bothering. I used to mess around or bunk off from lessons altogether so when I left school I had no exams. I regret that now, of course. Wish I'd worked harder. Mum and Dad are so proud of sis. They don't say much but I know they don't

Monday's Child

Caroline Jones Lewis

think that about me. I know they love me but it isn't the same, is it?"

The day ended with both girls sleepy from eating and drinking to excess and a tv diet of Benny Hill and Dick Emery. Nancy could not help but feel that the day had been wasted. She had done nothing exciting as she had always imagined she would when she had grumbled at having to spend the day at home. The two girls lay back on the armchair and sofa, toes and hands splayed to dry the shocking pink nail polish Eve had given Nancy for Christmas and had decided to sample, breathing in the acrid fumes that invaded the room like venom.
"Looks better on you," Eve pronounced. "I don't think it's my colour, do you?"
"No, you're a sort of – ah, deep red. You're a deep red person. We could go to the sales tomorrow and get some."
"Good idea," Eve agreed. "And we could write out our New Year resolutions, couldn't we?"
"Oh, if you insist. What's yours, then?"
"To make lots of money," Eve said determinedly. "Your turn. What's yours then?"
Nancy thought for a moment, then grinned.
"To make lots of money," she replied. "Lots of money. Really lots," and they laughed together for several minutes.
"Money isn't everything, though, is it?" Eve mused, becoming more serious. "Just look at Marilyn. Never brought her happiness, did it? Not her looks or her money. Who would ever have thought that the great Marilyn Monroe would kill herself and die a sad person?"
"Ah, well, that was because she chose the wrong men," Nancy declared. "Mummy said. She did, didn't she? Her marriages, then John Kennedy. She let herself become a victim. I won't do that, believe me. I won't."
She paused, holding her hand out in front of her to study the nail polish.
"I wish this stuff would dry more quickly, don't you?" she said, changing the subject, blowing on her nails then

Monday's Child
Caroline Jones Lewis

waving her hands around to hasten the process. "If someone invented a nail polish that dried quickly they'd make a fortune."
She tentatively touched a nail, impatient for it to dry.
"I know," Eve agreed. "Don't. Nanc. Let it dry properly. You'll only mess it up. Then you'll have to clean it all off and start again. That's what I always end up doing."
"That's because you're such a fidget," Nancy retorted. "You should learn to relax, Eve. Like me. I can relax."
"I have noticed," Eve laughed. "You're just a slob."
"Mmm. I know," Nancy crooned with satisfaction. "I know but I like it. Life's too short to spend polishing and cleaning. A bit of dust doesn't bother me."
Eve grinned.
"I've noticed that too."
Along with the resolve, Eve noticed a new mood in Nancy, a toughness even. Nancy had shown Eve the bruises from that dinner. She had confided about Matthew but omitted the details about herself. It was herself she was most afraid of. And she had told Eve about Adam's reaction, his assurance that there would be no more.
"You could always go home, you know," Eve had ventured. "It isn't too late, Nanc. Your Ma and Pa would have you back, no question. You're not really cut out for this kind of life. It gets harder, you know. The men, well, you can't always choose who, what and when. Can't always have things your way. There's always a risk. And the likes of Adam? Puh, he's a shit. All men like him are the same. He'll only care about you if it suits his interests. Maybe you should go home now, before you get any more involved. They wouldn't need to know anything you didn't want to tell them, would they? You could invent a story…"
"No, Eve," Nancy had interrupted her vehemently. "No, I've told you. I can't do that. Not until I've made something of myself. All I have to do is get myself some money. Or meet a man with money – that's an alternative.

Monday's Child
Caroline Jones Lewis

That's what my parents expect me to do anyway, meet a man, make a good marriage and produce the son and heir." She grimaced.
"With your looks, darling, you'll have the pick of the crop," she mimicked her mother.
"Is that what you really want though," Eve had challenged. "Doesn't sound like you, Nanc."
"It isn't," Nancy had responded. "I'm not really interested in marriage and I certainly don't want a sprog. But a man with money ... "
She had paused.
"Who'll be happy to give it to you for nothing in return," Eve had laughed. "You're kidding yourself," and they had both dissolved into hysterics.
"Well, there are men," Nancy had countered at length.
"At the club, you mean? They're nearly all married men just out for a bit of fun on the side."
"What about the ones we meet at Stephen's".
"Ditto," Eve had insisted.
Watching Nancy now Eve still wished she could persuade her somehow to return to the safety and security of home and family. Nancy interrupted her thoughts with a surprise suggestion.
"Well, we could go to Watford," she said.
"Watford? What's at Watford?"
Nancy sat forward enthusiastically.
"The motorway service station. They all go there. All the stars – like the Stones, Marianne Faithfull. People like that. And that actress. The one with the huge eyes. What's her name?"
Eve looked blank.
"Lots of them go there," Nancy insisted. "They go in the early hours of the morning after they've finished a gig. Away from all the fans. I overheard someone talking about it at the Club."
"Oh," Eve sounded interested but pointed out an obvious flaw in the plan. "So how do we get there then?"

Monday's Child
Caroline Jones Lewis

Nancy thought for a moment but came up with no solution to the problem. She sighed.
"I don't know," she replied disconsolately. "I'll have to think about that one. But it's a good idea, don't you think? Perhaps I could learn to drive. We both could, Eve, couldn't we?"
Eve said no more, reflecting again on what she saw as Nancy's naivety but she said no more. She refilled their glasses and by the early hours, both girls lay in an alcohol induced slumber, propped against each other on the sofa as the close-down spot faded in the centre of the tv screen. Rising a little later to go to bed and leaving Nancy to the luxury of the sofa, Eve peered through the break in the curtains into the street below.
"Hey, Nanc. Look," she exclaimed. "It's snowing."

******

By Boxing Day afternoon snow was falling thick and fast and over the following days snowflakes continued to beat down from a heavy sky. They swirled in a dense blizzard of white that drifted into walls of ice, engulfing the country in an arctic blanket frozen solid by a Siberian wind. In the capital, snow drifts two feet deep halted the traffic, whilst the waters of the Thames became glacial, an ice rink that halted the barges that usually flowed to and fro. Boats rested at their moorings in the pale and eerie silence. Ice flows and mini icebergs swelled the waters, closing the dockyards and robbing stevedores of their pay packets while in Chatham an ice breaker was employed to keep the dockyards open – but only just. New Year's Eve was as quiet as the grave.

Waterworks almost froze to a standstill and heaters had to be loaned to Heathrow Airport to prevent a total freeze. Then the power failed and electricity workers abandoned their strike action in the desperate need to restore warmth and light to a million homes.

Monday's Child
Caroline Jones Lewis

Wildlife was suffering from a lack of food and water. Householders in Windsor fed the ducks and swans along their stretch of river and countrywide members of the public demonstrated their ingenuity to provide the birds with water, converting upturned dustbin lids into makeshift drinking troughs heated beneath by nite-lite candles to melt the ice that formed in their bowls. Lizzie and her flatmate and some of their colleagues kept a constant vigil to ensure the birds on the campus were fed and watered.

By mid-January hopes were raised when a hint of thawing began, only to be dashed just days later by arctic winds depositing another four inches of snow to lie frozen solid for several weeks more. Then in February another gust from Siberia brought further snowfalls, more inches that lay on top of what was there already. Transport continued to be a nightmare for weeks more, road and rail in a state of severe disruption and airports intermittently closed. Hugh's business schedule disintegrated into chaos. Deliveries to shops were hampered and supplies of fresh food and essentials became a scarcity, their costs escalating beyond the pockets of the poor. Power cuts were frequent, refuse piled up in the streets and as water mains froze and cracked, tanks were deployed to deliver water when and were possible.

The British people, inventive as ever, did their best to turn the gloom into chaos and fun. A car rally was held on the frozen Thames, cars skidding and sliding like coins across a shove halfpenny board. Skiers were towed across the ice by the more adventurous willing to risk their vehicles. Amongst the crowds on the banks, Nancy and Eve watched them, giggling and slipping and sliding, clutching onto each other in attempts to prevent the inevitable crash onto the backside.

******

Monday's Child

Caroline Jones Lewis

The fallout from the strange Christmas had reached tipping point for James and Miranda. When Nancy had failed to appear, the temperature between them had plunged to the same icy level as the air outside the front door. Anger and recrimination came to a head on New Year's Eve with a bitter argument and a decision to separate, at least for the time being. The next day James had moved to his club leaving Miranda in the London house in the snow-bound freeze. She had sat alone and dejected in Nancy's room and sobbed.

******

Lizzie had returned to university for the new term with the anxiety of Nancy unresolved and hanging over her more than ever. She resolved to join forces with Hugh in an effort to find her which would be difficult to fit into the schedule of her lectures. The weather added further complications. At times she found it difficult to concentrate on her studies and felt far too guilty to persue a relationship with a young man perplexed by her change in attitude towards him that had seemed to take place during the Christmas break. Lizzie trudged in boots from lecture to lecture through mounds of dirty, frozen snow shovelled into the gutters or sat studying in her room in Halls, wrapped in a blanket and sometimes by candlelight when the power failed.

She had hoped and waited for a call from Nancy but as the days wore on, her hopes had begun to fade.
"Well, that's Nancy," she told herself. "If she does ring, it will be in her own time to suit her own agenda."
There was much to occupy her anyway, back in the swing of university life and all manner of things happening in the wider world that held her attention. Though the Cuba crisis was over and the Cold War thawing, the Black Rights movement in the USA was gaining momentum.

Monday's Child
Caroline Jones Lewis

Then there was South Africa and the indignities of apartheid inflicted on the blacks. She felt passionate about South Africa, horrified and outraged at the splitting of families into segregated ghettoes labelled for black, Afrikaan or coloured – heartrending for children of mixed parentage ripped from their parents who themselves were sent in separate directions. The cessation of land by the white minority, too, was grossly unjust. Oh, yes, there was South Africa. A growing awareness of her desire to change things fired Lizzie's social conscience and she joined protest groups and action groups as the term went on. And with these things came another realisation. A dawning recognition that her real course in life was changing, that a different direction was calling her. Politics. If she wanted to change the world for the better it had from within the policy-making machine, it had to be through politics. Why had she not seen it before? All she was learning and feeling impressed it upon her. It made the difficulties and anxieties of her own life and family insignificant by comparison and at times she felt impatient with Nancy for the angst she was causing for what might well be trivia. Even so, she waited in the hope that Nancy would ring.

******

Nancy had fought against a longing for the familiar, the comfortable security that had once been home and family. She steeled herself to stick to her plan and concentrate on the future. Bad days she blamed on the time of the year and the weather. It was always a gloomy time, she told herself, the anti-climax after Christmas and the long dark nights and bad weather. Her mother had always said so. She and Eve took turns to spend time at each other's flats to save on resources, in particular the heating – when there was any. And when there was not they spent their time huddled together on the sofa, wrapped in blankets pulled up to their chins and kept their spirits up by singing along

Monday's Child

Caroline Jones Lewis

to their transistor radios, with girlie chats about make-up and fashion and men – but mostly about men.

In the opening weeks of the New Year, she and Eve had attended more parties, chauffeured in the Jaguar to various locations across the wintry landscape and cossetted in warmth and luxury each night, comparing notes the following days on the men they had met. On one such occasion, she hit a new low. At some point during the evening, marijuana had been introduced and reckless in the glow of alcohol, she had experimented with bravado. As other guests disappeared from the sitting room, she found herself somewhat out of control with two remaining men who were brothers. They sat either side of her on the sofa, laughing and nuzzling her neck, caressing her thighs and loosening her clothing. They led her to a bedroom that was unfamiliar and onto the four poster bed. In the canopy above her a camera recorded for posterity as the brothers took her and in an adjacent room, Adam watched with satisfaction. He felt himself harden. He wanted her too, he knew it, and he would have her. She was stunningly beautiful even in her inebriated state but more than that. She was a wild and insatiable lover.

When they were spent, the brothers left, leaving Nancy stretched naked across the bed. Lulled by the warmth of the room, the alcohol and marijuana, she slipped into slumber. In the early hours of the morning, the door to the room opened quietly and Adam approached the bed, watching her sleep. He slipped off his bathrobe and slid onto the bed beside her, murmuring soft and low and turning her head towards him. He slid his hands down her body, across her breasts and nipples. She responded without question, eyes barely open in the darkness and unaware of who it was that entered her. Adam reflected later that it was some of the best sex he could remember. He left her there uncaring of his departure and only half aware of what she had done and who her partner had been.

Monday's Child
Caroline Jones Lewis

When at last she woke with a fuzzy head and a vague recollection of the night's events, her unease about herself returned. She tried but failed to ignore the cause of that unease, lying on the unkempt bed, her face turned into the pillows until she could stand it no more. She rose, wrapped herself in a crumpled sheet and sat in a chair by the window, gazing out over the gardens still in the grip of the freeze. Music floated up from the kitchens below.

> Are you lonesome tonight
> Do you miss me tonight?
> Are you sorry we drifted apart?
> Do your memories stray
> To a bright summer's day
> When I kissed you and called you sweetheart?

She turned away from the window, tears stinging her eyes and a newly acquired emotion gripped her. She needed Hugh, to speak to Hugh and hear the comfort of his gentle voice. She caught sight of her face in the mirror above the dressing table, the face of Monday's child. How she hated that face right now, hated herself. Feeling desolate and ashamed she turned to the telephone on the table by the bed.

******

Hugh had felt guilty too, guilty that he had been unable to persuade Nancy to come home or even to telephone Lizzie, let alone her parents. Like Lizzie, he resolved to renew his efforts to find her despite having little idea where to start. It would also deflect him, he thought, from the Simon situation from which he was struggling to extricate himself. Every rational cell in his brain was telling him to do so but the pull of the heart still proved stronger than the mind.

Monday's Child

Caroline Jones Lewis

On this morning he was at home, another weekend when Simon had absented himself from their relationship. He was reluctant to ring Simon himself, the recollection of the last time still fresh in his mind.
"Oh, Hugh. Sorry it took so long to answer," he had said. "Still in the arms of Morpheus, old chap."
Hugh had thought he heard a snigger in the background.
"Are you – with someone?" he had asked tentatively.
"Heavens, no, dear heart. But I'm really tired. Busy night at the theatre – you know how it is. Look, can I call you back? When I'm a bit more compos mentis, old chap?"
"Of course. Sorry, speak to you later then," Hugh had replied.
Simon had returned to his companion and Hugh had not been convinced. Needless to say the promised call back from Simon had not come for some time. When the telephone rang on this morning, Hugh debated whether he should answer, trying to break his addiction in the expectation that he would hear Simon's voice, but the heart once more overruled the head and he lifted the receiver. Once more Nancy's voice came as a complete surprise.

She sounded subdued, he thought, but unrepentant about contacting her parents. She assured him she was fine and asked about his life and about Lizzie.
"At least let me give you her number in Halls," Hugh pressed. "It's right here by the 'phone. Do you have a pen?"
"Yes," she said. "In my bag. Wait a minute," then realised she had left it downstairs. She looked around the room and found a biro in a drawer and rushed to the en-suite bathroom and tore a piece of toilet paper from the roll.
"Ok," she told Hugh and penned the number he gave her.
"Thanks, Hugh. I'll ring her."
"Promise?"
"Promise," she replied.

Monday's Child
Caroline Jones Lewis

"Can't we meet somewhere, Nancy?" he pleaded. "Anywhere. Somewhere neutral. I won't tell your parents."
She refused and immediately insisted she must go but with a promise that she would ring again soon. Then the tears overcame her and she sat for some minutes in the grip of her shame and remorse. Once the tears had subsided, she strengthened her resolve once more. She must not crumble. She would go back one day to her lost life and the people in it but with her head held high. She would show them what she could do. Brushing away her tears, she headed for the bathroom to wash away all trace of her regret.

******

Matthew had been inflamed by Nancy's refusal to meet him again and was further enraged by his obvious exclusion from the guest list to all future parties. Smarting from the snub, he was not a man to let a slight go unrequited. He resolved that somehow he would make them regret their insult. Sitting at his desk in his study in a house as silent as the grave since his wife had left taking their daughter with her, he drummed his fingers on the leather inlay and considered. He had met all manner of people through his contact with Adam and Stephen, both famous and inconsequential. Indiscretions had been revealed and embellished over the gin and tonics. He flipped through the cards in his telephone directory until stopping at a card marked 'Newsroom, Daily Mail'. Gazing out of the window at yet more snowflakes settling on the pristine whiteness of the lawn, he pondered on how this could be achieved without implicating himself in any way. Just a hint, just a suggestion, would set the bloodhounds sniffing and in today's political climate, the press would have a field day. By the time dusk was falling over the now still and glistening landscape outside of the

Monday's Child
Caroline Jones Lewis

window, he had made up his mind. He picked up the receiver and dialled.

Monday's Child
Caroline Jones Lewis

Chapter Seven - Scandals

With March came the thaw and spring burst upon a landscape cleansed by rivers of melted snow. Life, it seemed, was returning to a semblance of normality after months of disruption. The nation breathed a sigh of relief and greeted the spring with joy. Only days into this regeneration, the scandal began to break. Matthew watched from the shadows with satisfaction as the story, and the lives, began to unravel.

Sitting on the bed in her room, Lizzie was disappointed that the calling she had decided to follow should be brought into such disrepute and her faith in the integrity of her intended contemporaries shaken, at least for the moment.
"Had to be a Tory," chortled Sarah as they discussed the development over coffee in the Wimpey bar.
"You wouldn't find a Labour politician behaving like this."
"Oh, I don't know. I wouldn't bank on it," Lizzie mused. "I'll bet there are plenty of skeletons in plenty of closets they'd rather not let see the light of day. Buty why do they do it, these men? They have everything. Money. Family. Status. Power. Why do they put it all at risk for sordid sexual excitement?"
"It isn't about sex," said Sarah. "It's about power – and the confidence that in their position of privilege they can get away with it. They've been in power too long."

Nancy stared at the headline of the tabloid in horror. The pictures of Christine and Profumo splashed across its pages stared back at her from the coffee table. She sat on the sofa in her lounge, legs curled under her and her dressing gown wrapped protectively around her body. She folded her arms around her defensively. Eve sat in the chair opposite looking equally stunned.
"Have you ever met this Profumo?" Nancy asked.
Eve shook her head.

Monday's Child

Caroline Jones Lewis

"Don't think so," she shrugged. "I don't recognise him anyway," and she leaned forward to study his photograph again. "Do you?" she asked of Nancy.
Nancy shook her head.
"No, but then I haven't been to Stephen's as many times as you have. When I have you've always been there too. It says here they met in 1961. That's ages before, isn't it?"
"Well, that lets us out then. I didn't go to Stephen's until last year," Eve declared, relaxing back in her seat.
"But Ivanov," Nancy gasped. "We've met Ivanov. I've slept with him, for God's sake. What if they come looking for me? The police. Or MI5? Oh, God," she went on in horror. "What if they do?"
"Calm down, Nancy," Eve urged. "Calm down. Don't let's be over-dramatic. They won't be interested in us. We're not in a position to pass on state secrets, are we? There's no need to panic."
"That won't stop the tabloids," Nancy spluttered. "My father said they make things up as they go along. If they can't find scandal they'll invent it. I don't want my picture splashed all over the paper. I don't want anyone to know. My parents …."
Eve stopped her in her tracks.
"Look, just stay calm , Nanc, heh? There's nothing at Stephen's place to connect us, is there? It's Christine they're interested in – because of this Profumo chap. Not us."
Nancy calmed a little.
"Damn Christine," she fumed. "Damn Profumo. Bloody people."
Eve grinned.
"I've never heard you swear before, Nanc."
"Not allowed at home," Nancy explained. "It's unlady-like, so my mother says. Please don't swear, darling; it's so unlady-like," she mimicked. "As if what she was up to was lady-like!"
Despite her reassurance to Nancy, Eve felt concerned too. The idea of her family knowing the truth about her life was

Monday's Child
Caroline Jones Lewis

not a palatable thought. What on earth would her Dad say, one daughter tracking the Ruskies and the other fraternising with them. The police were bound to make enquiries and Stephen could well lead them back to the Club. He was a member and it was there he met some of the girls he invited. For all she knew, he could have met Christine there. There could be other connections with Adam, too. Mandy's name was also mentioned too and the press were letting their imagination run riot with stories of drugs and orgies, anything that caught the attention of the public and sold more papers.

"We'll soon know if they're looking further afield when we get to the Club this evening. Adam will know," she suggested.

"Perhaps we should ring him," said Nancy. "Before we go."

"Good idea," Eve agreed. "Come round to my place when you're dressed. We'll give him a call."

Adam was cautious. No, the police had not been round to the Club, he told Eve. Why should they? He was not expecting they would come, not to question him or the girls. There would be no records, he insisted, of the parties they had attended at Stephen's. It was Profumo they were interested in, he told her. And Christine because of her connection with Ivanov – national security and all that. Nothing else. All the same, he said, there would of course be no further parties right now and would they please dress conservatively when they came to work, be careful what they said and to whom.

"We've never mentioned anything to the other girls," Eve assured him. She replaced the receiver cautiously reassured. Nancy breathed a sigh of relief, at least for the moment and on reflection, the events in the wider world made the difficulties and anxieties of her own life and family insignificant by comparison.

Monday's Child
Caroline Jones Lewis

Some days later, Nancy sat at the bar in the Club lost in thought. Despite all Adam's reassurances, despite the appearance of normality, she could not completely put to rest her anxiety. Her natural propensity to exaggerate and dramatise was kicking in after months of apparent calm. The floodgates were threatening to open. Which meant she would be trapped in the life she now inhabited. This was not to her liking given her wish to make a success in some more respectable occupation and return to her family triumphant. It was frustrating. She sipped intermittently at a glass of sparkling wine doing her best to appear perfectly relaxed and at ease but it was not a convincing act to those that knew her well. Eve was very aware of the turmoil Nancy was suffering and the reason for it. At this moment, the Club was quiet for the time of day, fewer Clients than usual sat at the tables and the singer had been taken sick so only background music relieved the dullness. At a table nearby, two pin-striped businessmen were discussing the day's latest revelations over their lunch.

"Damned shame, old chap. Damned shame," pinstripe was saying. "He shouldn't resign. It's only an indiscretion, after all. No more than others are up to. He's just been caught out, that's all. A damned fine politician going to waste? It will be a shame if he goes."

"Oh, I don't know," his companion challenged. "Yes, he is a fine politician, I agree. One of the best we've got. But he lied to the House as well as to his wife and people don't like that. Can't be trusted, that's what that means. If he's lied about this, what else."

He paused to munch on his salad.

"I'm not taken in by this security stuff, though. Are you? I mean, it's a bit thin, isn't it? Just the tabloids justifying their sensationalism."

Pinstripe nodded. "Yes, yes. You're right. This Christine – she's hardly a Mata Hari gathering state secrets, is she? A show girl. I ask you. She's just an empty headed floosie, a glorified call girl. A tart."

Monday's Child
Caroline Jones Lewis

His companion nodded. "Unfortunately, though," he said, "it appeals to the masses after all the Cold War hysteria. I think it might well finish him. I really do."
"MacMillan won't let that happen, surely," pinstripe insisted. "We need good chaps like Profumo."
"MacMillan won't have a choice, will he. He's struggling to stay in himself. There's a mood of change in this country. People are fed up with the MacMillans of this world. They're fed up with leaders born with silver spoons in their mouths who they think are greedy and only out for their own ends and who can't relate to the ordinary man in the street. They want change."
Pinstripe stopped eating and dropped his knife and fork onto his plate. He wiped his mouth with his napkin and answered crossly.
"Don't believe it," he contested. "Don't believe it. It's the bloody press again. Whipping up public opinion. Always stirring up trouble, bloody people. They should concentrate on the important issues – policy and stuff. Not this sort of nonsense. Just a bit of hanky panky on the side."
His companion retaliated strongly.
"That's just the point, though, isn't it? Leaders who set a bad example. No, it won't do any more. This country's changing, believe me and the grass roots want leaders who behave themselves and get on with the job. We'll have a Labour government before the end of the decade if the Tories don't pull their socks up, you mark my word."
"Perish the thought," replied pinstripe. "Perish the thought."
He paused for a moment, thoughtful.
"This Ward chap. Stephen, isn't it? He's a member here, isn't he?"
Nancy tensed at the sound of Stephen's name, half turning away to conceal her eavesdropping but straining her ears all the more to hear every word.
"Yes, I heard that, too. A doctor, so they say. Some sort of alternative medicine."

Monday's Child

Caroline Jones Lewis

"Osteopath," pinstripe confirmed. "He's an osteopath. Not quite the same, is it? But he's got some really high profile Clients, so I've heard."

"There's talk of the police charging him," his companion confirmed. "Living on immoral earnings."

Another pause.

"Maybe that's why it's so quiet here today," pinstripe continued, looking around at the vacant tables. "My wife won't like the idea of me coming here, not that she dictates what I do but she always checks the bank statement. She'll know. And she won't like it. Think I might use another Club for a while. There's that new one in Curzon Street. I've heard it's good."

There was a contemplative pause.

"Well, best get back to the office, I suppose," he decided, waving at a waiter standing idle near the bar and indicating that he wanted his bill. "Pile of work waiting, should have been done days ago but pressure of work, and all that. Got to take a break now and then, haven't you. Fancy one more, old chap. For the road, as it were?"

"Not for me, thanks" replied his companion. "I'd best get on, too."

"I say," said pinstripe, "stunning looker over there, don't you think? Blonde one sat at the bar. Beautiful. Wouldn't push her out of bed, heh," he confided leaning forward with a grin on his face.

Nancy stiffened, unnerved by the content of their conversation but also irritated by their attitude. She wanted to protest, to tell them that she was more than a pretty face and a body for sexual gratification, that she had a brain and a mind of her own. She turned away further to avoid their attention.

That's all they see, she fumed to herself. The face. The body. Sex. Like there's nothing else to me. Monday's child, she thought angrily. Her own reaction surprised her and she felt confused. Her looks had always been the key to her fortune. It was Lizzie who wanted to achieve great

Monday's Child

Caroline Jones Lewis

things using her mind and intellect, not her. The resentment she felt at their patronising remarks was a new departure. She had never had feminist leanings but that last remark had irritated her more than she would ever have thought possible. She remembered how she and Lizzie would giggle at the Miss World contestants – professing their wish to travel and help poor people. Is that how people saw her, she wondered. An empty headed bimbo? Her role in recent months could hardly deny them, she thought. And she had allowed it to happen, to be debased and used for exactly that purpose. But what else? How could she turn things around now without conceding defeat and returning home a failure? If she could save no more money how would she break free? And worse. If the Club became outlawed by its Clientele because of Stephen she may not even have a job. Panic was rising and she needed to get away from the claustrophobia of the Club's atmosphere. She needed time to think. She was compiling an excuse for Adam to leave early on the grounds of feeling unwell, a migraine, or a stomach upset, which would be the most credible, when a flash of light startled her out of her reverie. She turned towards its source, her expression like a rabbit caught in the headlights and at once she was blinded by yet another flash.

The press, she thought. Oh, my God, it's the press. She gasped and began to slide from her seat.

"I'm sorry," a voice spoke to her. "I didn't mean to startle you. I just couldn't resist taking your photograph. I hope you don't mind."

Nancy peered in the direction of the voice, her eyesight still blurred by the flashlight.

"You looked so pensive. Uh – mysterious, one might say. I just can't help it," the voice went on. "It's my job, you see. I'm a photographer. Portraits and that sort of thing but I also do portfolio work for models."

A face was coming into focus, a rather good-looking, friendly face. The sort of face you might trust, thought Nancy. If you weren't me.

Monday's Child

Caroline Jones Lewis

"Oh," she said. "I see."
"Are you alright," he went on. "You look almost frightened. Yes, frightened. I'm so sorry. I really don't mean you any harm."
He was concerned now.
"It's alright. I'm fine," Nancy insisted, relaxing a little. He seemed genuine, not a reporter from the gutter press looking to dig up dirt. How could he have known the effect his actions would have on someone with a guilty conscience? Just stay calm. Eve's words echoed in her head. "Stay calm, Nanc. Don't go imagining all sorts of things like you usually do.
"I was just miles away," she replied. "Deep in thought so you startled me."
"Yes, I can see that. I am really sorry. Here," he said, pulling a business card from his pocket. "This is me. This is who I am."
Nancy took his card and read it carefully. Robin Selway, it read. Photographer. He scooped up his glass from a nearby table where he'd been sitting and joined her at the bar. She guessed him to be in his thirties, quite nice looking in a traditional sort of way with an unassuming smile and manner.
"And you are?" he asked.
"Nancy," she replied.
"Nancy who?"
"Just Nancy," she replied cautiously. "So what are you doing here, Robin Selway?"
"Looking for someone exactly like you."
"Ah," she sighed and smirked derisorily, raising her eyes skyward.
"No, no. I'm not handing you a line," he insisted and laughed. "I really am looking for someone like you. To photograph. And I'd really like to take more 'photos of you if you would be interested. I have a studio near the Embankment. South side, that is," he murmured. "Can't afford this side."
"What sort of photographs?"

Monday's Child

Caroline Jones Lewis

Nancy was still cautious.

"Oh, portraiture, fashion, whatever suits. I have a friend who runs a model agency and I compile portfolios for some of the girls on his books. Well, he has guys too but mostly its girls. But I like to work on my own as well. I've just done some really good work for an elderly gentleman who wanted 'photos of himself and his wife to give to their children before they get any older. In case they get infirm or worse. We went out for the day and took some quite unusual ones of them, walking arm in arm in the snow and such. They're a lovely couple and were so pleased with the result. It's really rewarding when you get good results. "

He sipped at his wine.

"Are you a model?" he asked.

Nancy shook her head.

"Well, you should be," he told her. "I'd guess that you're a natural. The camera will like you. Photogenic. "

"You enjoy your work obviously, but how can you be sure of that?" she asked.

"Just instinct."

He paused and drained his glass of its contents.

"Look," he said. "I have to go now. I've an appointment. But I mean what I said. I really would like to take some photographs of you if you're interested. You've got my card with my number. Give me a call, will you?"

"I'll think about it," she told him, still not willing to trust in the light of recent events.

She smiled and waved him goodbye as he made his way to the door, then studied his card thoughtfully, turning it over and over in her hand. Then she slipped it into her handbag and slid off the stool, heading across the Club towards Adam's office. She wanted to leave. She felt tired and anxious without being sure as to why. There had been no sign of the press or the police but the feeling of unease would not leave her. She would tell Adam she felt unwell and go back to the flat, or perhaps to Eve's if she could persuade Eve to go with her.

Monday's Child

Caroline Jones Lewis

The office door was locked.
"He's not in," Nancy heard someone say. It was one of the waiters passing with a tray of empty glasses.
"Not in," she echoed with incredulity.
"Yeah, not in," came the response. "Have you ever known Adam not to be in before? He rang in and said he was taking the day off – at home. He'll be in tomorrow."
"Oh, thanks. Have you seen Eve?"
"She was on her way to the cloakroom last time I saw her. Bored to tears."

Nancy found Eve in the cloakroom being accosted by Donna, a new member of staff who was trying earnestly to court their friendship. A pretty girl with an elfin face and a short chestnut bob, she had little between the ears or anything else to commend her to either Eve or Nancy.
"We're going to the flicks on Sunday, me and some of the girls," she was babbling to Eve. "Fancy it?" she asked as she peered into the mirror and stroked the dark eyelashes with a mascara brush. She spit onto the block of mascara and stirred it with the brush into a gooey mixture, then applied it again to her lashes.
"What to see?" asked Eve, who was equally absorbed in her make-up.
"They're showing the James Bond at the Roxy and we all missed it first time round."
From the corner of her eye, Eve saw Nancy heading towards her and recognised the slightly anxious expression that was becoming a regular feature.
"Thanks but I think I'll give it a miss if you don't mind," she replied to Donna. "Some other time perhaps."
Nancy indicated the door with a nod of the head. Eve dropped her make-up back into her bag and turned to follow her friend who was already halfway back out of the door.
"Don't think I could stand the boredom of her company for that length of time," Eve confided to her friend. "She's ok

Monday's Child
Caroline Jones Lewis

but she's not the brightest thing on two legs, is she? I reckon she'd be as boring as Catherine. Wonder how long it will take Adam to get in there."

"It's her eyes that get me," Nancy declared. "Great big panda eyes. She looks like Dusty Springfield. It's alright in showbiz and all that. But not for her."

Donna came out of the cloakroom behind them and remained doggedly in pursuit still attempting to engage them in conversation.

"Hey, lose it," a voice barked at her.

"What," asked Donna in a startled voice.

"The gum. Adam would go mental if he saw it. Lose the gum," and Adam's Deputy indicated the cloakroom from which she had just come.

With a sigh Donna turned on her heels and disappeared back inside the cloakroom to remove the offending chewing gum, muttering as she went.

"It's a fresh piece," she complained. "What a waste."

Nancy and Eve grinned at each other.

"Think she might be a mistake," said Eve wryly.

"Think you might be right," agreed Nancy.

"Perhaps we should keep her sweet, though, Nanc," Eve considered. "She's the sort of bimbo who could let something slip to the press if they came sniffing around. Don't you think?"

"Yes, fine," Nancy agreed. "I wouldn't think she knows anything, though, would you?"

"You just never know," Eve confided. "See, I'm getting as paranoid as you, Nanc."

"Perhaps we should go to the cinema with her then?" Nancy suggested.

"Bloody hell, Nanc. No need to go that far," and they giggled. All the same, Nancy felt her anxiety hanging on.

"Eve, I want to go home – or to yours," she blurted. "The Club's dead. Adam's not in. Why do you think that is? He never misses. He's always here. I feel all on edge. I need to get out of here."

Eve thought for a moment.

Monday's Child

Caroline Jones Lewis

"Look," she said, "we're due our break now anyway. Why don't we go back to mine and I'll ring and say you're sick and it might be catching so perhaps I'd better not come in either."

******

In Essex, Adam stood at the bottom of his garden stoking a bonfire to which he periodically added fuel. The files and photographs he had removed from his office the previous night curled and singed on the burning embers, disintegrating into a growing mountain of ash. Behind him, some distance away, his wife stood watching, wondering quite what he was up to. Home in the week? Home at all if he wasn't forced to be? He was up to something, she was sure and a feeling of foreboding hung over her brooding and heavy, like a black cloud that had unexpectedly appeared in a blue summer sky.
"What did I ever see in him?" she asked herself. "How on earth was I taken in by him?"
She stepped forward a little and called.
"Adam, what are you doing? What's going on?"
Adam spun around and saw her leaning against the rowan tree, arms folded and a slightly cross expression on her face. He knew that look only too well. She was elegant as ever in classic slacks and sweater.
Classy lady, my wife, he thought. Beautiful, classy – and loaded. A Monday's child, like Nancy as Nancy had once laughingly told him.
"Just getting rid of some old files," he told her. "The office is bursting at the seams. I need to make some room so I've had a turn out."
"Why are you burning them?" his wife challenged.
"Well, why do you think?" he snapped back. "Some of this is confidential. Client details and such. You don't think I can send it to the tip, do you? Wafting around a landfill site? For God's sake use your common sense, woman."

Monday's Child

Caroline Jones Lewis

He turned to face her, meeting her stare. She bristled with annoyance but said nothing.
He's lying, she thought. He's always lying. How I loathe the man. But one day, she promised herself. She wanted a divorce, she knew it, but she needed grounds and so far he had been good at covering his tracks. Divorce was not that easy to get and it must leave her without a blot on her character, spotless and without recrimination if stigma were to be avoided for the children. She knew he lied – often, but so far nothing she had been unable to prove. There must be something - or someone.
A private detective, perhaps, she mused. Yes, a private detective. One day I'll catch you out, for sure and then you'll be on your way, no problem. The very notion of an Adam-free life filled her with blissful determination and she turned to go back into the house to make a call.

She hates me, thought Adam as he watched her figure recede through the pungent smoke rising from the bonfire. She really hates me. She'll get rid of me if she has the slightest excuse. I'll really have to watch my step. First I must get rid of Catherine. Stupid girl. The sooner she goes the better.
He turned back to the bonfire and from the box of films and papers still waiting to be cast into the flames he picked up the reel labelled 'Nancy'. He smiled ruefully, holding onto it for a final second, then with a regretful smile he consigned it to the flames.
I'm sorry to see that one go, he said to himself. Really sorry.

******

Back at her flat later that evening, Nancy sat on the sofa amongst the muddles that were her daily life. She had stayed at Eve's for a while, but then had an overwhelming urge to be alone. Eve had waved her off with concern. On a side table beside her sat the telephone Adam had had

Monday's Child
Caroline Jones Lewis

installed for her, black and glossy beneath the thin layer of dust that was the norm in her flat. On the coffee table ahead of her lay a tabloid newspaper alleging more lurid details of what had been dubbed 'the Profumo affair'. The things that were being reported in the press about Stephen were outrageous. She and Eve had discussed some of the accusations that were bandied about, wilder and more damning than anything they knew to be true so they were disbelieving, refusing to accept they were true about a man they liked and felt was being turned into a caricature of himself. All the same, her mother would have said there was no smoke without fire and the sense of vulnerability that was becoming all too familiar to Nancy sneaked up on her once again. She snatched up the receiver of the telephone and began to dial Hugh's number but then lost her nerve and dropped the receiver back into its cradle. She fidgeted for several minutes and then made up her mind. She fetched her bag from the kitchen and took from the side pocket a carefully folded and stored piece of toilet paper, the one on which she had written Lizzie's 'phone number. She checked her watch. It was four thirty. It was likely, she thought, that Lizzie might be there at this time of day. Lectures would surely be finished by now.

What would she say? she wondered. Why Lizzie but not Hugh? She couldn't answer either question. She only knew that she wanted to hear Lizzie's voice. Longed to hear it. And it wouldn't matter what was said as long as she heard Lizzie's voice. She picked up the receiver once more and dialled.

The telephone in halls was situated on the landing available to all comers. Not surprisingly, therefore, it was not Lizzie who answered but a fellow student. She asked for Lizzie.
"I'll just check if she's in her room," the girl answered. Nancy waited on tenterhooks.
"Please be there, Lizzie," she prayed. "Please."

Monday's Child

Caroline Jones Lewis

It was not long before the girl returned.
"Sorry," she said. "Lizzie isn't there at the moment. She's at the hospital."
"Hospital," Nancy echoed. "What hospital?"
There was a pause.
"Sorry, I didn't ask," the girl replied. "Who is this speaking, please?"
"It's her cousin," Nancy explained. "Nancy."
"Oh, I see. Well, look, let me fetch her roommate. She'll be able to tell you more about it than me. Can you hold on a minute?"
"Yes, yes. I'll hold."
Then another wait until she heard a different voice on the line, breathless and urgent.
"Hello, Nancy. This is Sarah, Lizzie's roommate. Can I help?"
Sarah did not want Nancy to ring off, knowing how much Lizzie wanted to speak to her. She racked her brain for the right thing to say. Nancy saved her the trouble.
"Why's Lizzie at the hospital?" she asked.
"She's gone to see your cousin, Hugh. He's in a bad way."
"Hugh," gasped Nancy, the shock audible in her voice. "What's wrong with Hugh?"
"I don't actually know the details," Sarah explained. "Only that he's very ill. Critical in fact. He's in the Royal Sussex."
"The Royal Sussex? Where's the Royal Sussex?"
"In Brighton. Lizzie's in Brighton."
Nancy's mind was in a whirl. What on earth was Hugh doing in Brighton, she wondered.
"I've got to go," she said in a panic. "Do you know which ward or anything? How do I get there?" She was talking to herself as much as to Sarah.
"I'm sorry, I don't know which ward," Sarah told her.
"Look, Nancy, can I take a number for Lizzie to call you? She's sure to ring at some point."
"No, no," Nancy rushed on. "I'll go myself. To the hospital. Thank you Sarah. Thank you for your help," and

Monday's Child
Caroline Jones Lewis

before Sarah could respond, she had replaced the receiver and sat stunned at the news.

******

The Parakeet Club had been crowded when Hugh arrived, the music loud and drinks flowing freely. Young men and women flamboyantly dressed for the occasion cavorted around the dance floor in a display of Saturday night fever and release from the humdrum of weekly toil. He looked around for Simon who, in an alcohol induced mood of gaiety, had telephoned the night before to insist that Hugh should come.
"It will be such fun, Hugh, dear," he had insisted.
"Jonathan's 30th. Oh, do come, there's a good chap. Chas and Edward will be there and we can stay the night at theirs."
"Do I actually know this Jonathan?" Hugh had asked.
"Well, does it matter?" asked Simon. You'll be with me and I know Jonathan. Everyone knows Jonathan," he had added laughing. "If you know what I mean."
Hugh had agreed to go and took the late afternoon train to Brighton on Saturday with anticipation of a fun weekend – not least of all to see Simon. He walked into the Club, discarding his coat and overnight bag at the cloakroom and moved towards the bar. He looked around as he crossed the dance floor and spotted Chas and Edward seated at a table at the far side of the room. Of Simon there was no sign. Chas and Edward greeted him warmly as he approached.
"Hugh, hi. Come and join us," they urged. "Have you got a drink yet?"
"No, not yet. I'll get one in a minute, when I've warmed up a bit. It's getting really cold out there."
"It's good to see you," Chas went on. "Have you met Eric," he asked, indicating a round-faced ginger-haired young man at their table.

Monday's Child
Caroline Jones Lewis

Hugh and Eric exchanged handshakes and joined in conversation, small talk about the weather, the journey down from town, getting to know you talk.
"Look, this is my round," said Eric. "We're all on Tequila Slammers. Can I get you a drink?"
"Thank you. Then I'll join you," said Hugh. Eric nodded and rose from his seat to make his way towards the crowded bar. Hugh watched him weave his way around the edge of the laughing, jostling dancers. The beat of the music throbbed in the dim lighting and a crowd had formed around an exhibitionist amongst the throng imitating the antics of the singer.

> I can't get no
> Satisfaction
> I can't get no
> Satisfaction
> 'Cos I try
> And I try
> And I try
> And I try
> I can't get no

He mimicked the singer to the amusement of those around him.
"That," Chas confided, "is Jonathan."
Hugh grinned and briefly joined in the banter but in no time his gaze was wandering once more wandering around the room in search of Simon. Chas watched Hugh's expression as he scanned the room anxiously. He knew what was coming next.
"Have you seen Simon?" Hugh asked.
"I don't think he's here yet," Chas replied.
"Oh," surprise from a disappointed Hugh.
"He said he'd be here to meet me. It is his Saturday off, isn't it? You know how scatty he is, he could easily have got it wrong."

Monday's Child
Caroline Jones Lewis

"As far as we know," Chas assured him. "He's probably just late. You know what he's like. Probably still deciding what to wear," he offered, hoping to avoid any further interrogation. He shot a glance at Edward.

"Make an excuse for me, would you?" Simon had asked earlier. "To Hugh."

"Look, Simon, this just isn't on," Edward had protested. "You're putting us in an awkward position and it's unfair to Hugh. He's a decent chap. You should be honest with him. You asked him to come so you should be there, not dashing off in another direction for what you think is a better offer."

"I know, I know, but this is the only chance I will get to see Patrick. He's off to Rome on Monday."

"So why ditch Hugh, then? What's the point if you won't see Patrick again?"

Simon had promised to think about it, to reconsider – but it seemed to no avail. He had not arrived.

"I really think he's pushing our friendship too far," Edward had discussed with Chas. They had agreed that from now on, Simon would be excluded from their social circle until such time as he tried to mend his ways. He must be honest with Hugh about their relationship and treat Hugh with more respect. They would tell Simon so as soon as the opportunity arose. Hugh would be welcome to visit if he wished. In the meantime, it was a delicate situation that needed tact.

Hugh sat uncomfortably for an hour or so while everyone around him partied.

By 10 o'clock Hugh had decided that it was unlikely Simon would appear. He had been late before but not this late and in any case, he felt it was time to take a stand. Through a growing fog of inebriation he asked the question his friends had hoped to avoid.

"Do you know where he is?" he asked of Edward.

Edward hesitated to answer, shamefaced and clearly embarrassed.

Monday's Child
Caroline Jones Lewis

"Please," Hugh pressed him. "I don't want to make life difficult for you but I need to know."
"Not really," Chas offered. "Only that .. uh"
"He's with someone else," said Hugh flatly, finishing the sentence for him.
"We're really sorry, Hugh," Edward broke in. "We weren't sure whether he would go or not but, well, you know what he's like. He's just unreliable."
"Oh, more than that," Hugh fumed. "Fickle. Unfaithful. Uncaring. Amoral. All the superlatives," he concluded sarcastically. "Well, enough's enough. Thanks for your loyalty. If I go now I can catch the last train."
"You don't have to," Edward protested. "We'd love you to stay."
"Thanks for the offer," Hugh slurred. "But I don't think so."
He stood to leave, swaying a little
"Please keep in touch, Hugh," Chas urged. "We'd really like that, you know. You're welcome any time."
"Thanks for that," Hugh answered. "That's good of you. Really. Thanks, thanks. I will," he mumbled and made his way unsteadily to the door.

Outside in the cold night air, Hugh breathed deeply trying to steady himself. He had not realised until now how much he had drank in his anguish, consumed by hurt and anger and disappointment. He paused for a moment in the doorway to steady himself, then set off on foot for the station. In the darkness of the side street he failed to notice two youths across the street who slowed their pace and eyed him with interest.
"What'ya think?" one of them asked the other. "Nice clothes. Looks worth a bob or two."
His companion nodded.
"Yeah, reckon he's worth a go. Wallet in the top left pocket of his jacket, yeah? If we get 'im before 'e reaches the light at the corner. Nice and quiet 'ere. Should do."

Monday's Child

Caroline Jones Lewis

Hugh paused, realising that he had left his bag and overcoat in the Club. He was cold. Impatient with himself he retraced his steps, slipping a little on the icy ground as he turned and lunged at the door of the Club, knocking loudly, explaining to the doorman who let him back into the inky darkness inside. The youths, thinking he was a lost prospect, huddled disappointed in a doorway to light a cigarette, shielding the flame from their lighter from a gusting wind. Discussing their next move, they were surprised to see Hugh re-emerge from the Club doorway.
"Ere, 'e's back. 'E was in that club. You know. The one where the queers go. 'E must be one of 'em. E's a queer. An' 'e's got a bag with 'im now."
His companion nodded, flicking the ash from his cigarette in his eagerness and watching Hugh who had dropped his bag to the ground while he pulled on his overcoat.
"Yeah. Even better," he replied. "Right then. Let's get 'im. 'E deserves it, the puffter."
He drew one more time on his cigarette, then dropped it to the floor and ground the glowing tobacco to extinction on the paving slab with the heavy metal toe of his boots. Together the pair crossed the street and set about Hugh from behind, snatching his bag and crushing him face forward against a wall. One held him there groaning while the other reached into his pockets taking the cash from his wallet and his bank card, ignoring his driving licence but wrenching his watch from his wrist. Then tossing the empty wallet aside onto the pavement, they set about Hugh who was struggling and trying to shout to attract attention but no-one was near. They hit him repeatedly about the head and face, kicking and punching his body as he fell to the ground until he lay bloody and motionless. They snatched up his bag and ran back up the street away from the light to the doorway of an empty building where they rummaged inside, taking anything they thought saleable, then certain they had everything worth taking, tossed the bag over a wall and ran.
"Bloody pufftcrs," a voice growled - and they were gone.

Monday's Child

Caroline Jones Lewis

Hugh lay unconscious and bleeding in the night chill until some time later a solitary passer-by came to his aid. The ambulance men wrapped a warm blanket around his battered body now suffering the effects of hypothermia as well as the beating. They tucked the ransacked wallet inside his coat pocket, the only means of identification the police were to have.

In a side room at the hospital Hugh remained unconscious for days. Urgent remedial action had been taken for a collapsed lung and broken ribs, a head wound still giving rise to anxiety and speculation. In the near empty wallet along with his driving licence was a scrap of paper with a telephone number. On the Sunday morning after the attack, the police called the number and Lizzie, passing the 'phone on the landing after a morning study group, by accident or design or divine intervention, took the call.
"This is Brighton Central Police Station, miss. Hugh Farrell, do you know him? We found this telephone number amongst his possessions."
"Yes, he's my cousin," replied Lizzie in alarm. "What's wrong. Where's Hugh?"
Shocked after their conversation, Lizzie fled to her room, dropped her books on the table and hunted for some coins. One shilling, two shillings and a sixpence. Yes, it would be enough, especially on a Sunday. Rushing back to the payphone, she called her mother.

When Lizzie reached the hospital, breathless and pale with shock, her mother was already at Hugh's bedside. They were both tired from the stress of their respective journeys and the uncertainty of what they would find when they arrived. They sat silently either side of his bed, shocked at the sight of his battered body. Each had called to him softly when they arrived but there had been no response. Emily motioned to her daughter and they left the room to talk in the corridor.

Monday's Child
Caroline Jones Lewis

"We need to speak to his doctor," Emily ventured.
"That's your department, Mum, isn't it?" Lizzie suggested.
"You'll understand what's happening more than me."
Emily agreed.
"I'll go and find the ward sister," she instructed. "You stay with Hugh."
Lizzie nodded. She choked back a sob and Emily put her arms around her in comfort.
"It looks bad, doesn't it?" sobbed Lizzie.
"Well, sometimes things look worse than they are," Emily consoled. "Don't jump to conclusions, love. We must stay positive for Hugh's sake. You go and sit with him. I'll be back as soon as I've found someone who can tell us what his condition really is. And I must ring your Dad. He's at home waiting for news. He'd have come himself but he's on call. Sod's law; he always seems to be on call these days. But he's going to come later."
She kissed Lizzie on the cheek and ushered her back through the door into Hugh's room, then went along the corridor towards the sister's office.

Later, in the waiting room, Emily related to Lizzie what the sister had told her as they sipped at cups of coffee made for them by an obliging junior nurse.
"He's quite stable now," she told her. "Heavily sedated for the moment so sister feels we should go home, get some sleep and come back tomorrow. They've re-inflated his lung but they're still watching him closely. I think it's the head wound they're really concerned about. If we go home for the night we can be back first thing in the morning. Hopefully we'll find out more in the morning. They'll ring us if there's any cause for concern."
"Ok. I'll ring Sarah and tell her not to expect me," Lizzie agreed.
"What about your lectures?"
"Well, I'm off sick, so to speak. If I were there would be no problem, would there? This is compassionate leave, isn't it?"

Monday's Child
Caroline Jones Lewis

"We can keep in touch, Liz, if you want to go back."
"I couldn't possibly, Mum. I've got to stay. In any case I'd never concentrate on anything. I'd be thinking about Hugh and worrying all the time."
"Yes, I daresay you're right. Let's get home as soon as possible then. We'll just tell Hugh, just in case he can hear us. Besides, we have another unpleasant task to do."
"What?" Lizzie asked.
"We need to ring Grandma."
"Oh, heavens. How on earth is she going to take it?" Emily sighed.
"It hasn't been our year, has it? Well, the last 12 months I mean. First Nancy. Now Hugh. Oh, Lizzie," and she buried her head in her hands in tearful exhaustion.
"And I'll have to ring Miranda."
"What actually happened, Mum? What was Hugh doing in Brighton anyway?"
"The police don't know exactly. Only that Hugh was attacked for some reason, they think robbery. Sister said she didn't really have any details. But the police will be here again and we need to speak to them. So let's just go and say goodnight to Hugh and then we'll get home. I don't think I'll ring Grandma until tomorrow, once we have more of the facts. No need to worry her tonight, before she goes to bed. She is getting on, after all. And she adores him. She's bound to want to come straight away and we need to be here to support her when she comes."
So it was decided and they left to take the train back to Kent.

Two days later Lizzie and her mother had left for the station after almost constant vigil at Hugh's bedside, taking Hugh's grandmother back to Kent with them for a good night's sleep. Miranda and James had each decided independently to wait until he regained consciousness, anxious as they still remained to be available at home should Nancy try to make contact. Emily had promised to

Monday's Child
Caroline Jones Lewis

keep them informed. Hugh had roused briefly during the day, opening his eyes and peering in their direction for only seconds before lapsing back into a drug-induced sleep and without giving any sign of recognition.
"It's a good sign, isn't it?" Lizzie had asked.
"The ward sister had nodded.
"Yes, but we don't want him coming round too quickly. He'll probably be in considerable pain and we want him to stay fairly still and quiet. So don't let's rush things," she reassured her.
Lizzie had looked at her mother questioning and Emily had nodded her agreement.
"Don't worry," she had mouthed to Lizzie. "He's doing ok."
There was hope, too, about Nancy as that evening Sarah called. She related to Lizzie the bare bones of her conversation with Nancy and Nancy's intention to visit Hugh at the hospital.
"How long since she rang?" Lizzie asked.
"Just an hour or so ago," Sarah told her breathlessly. "She could arrive any time."
Emily had telephoned Miranda.
"Oh, I must go to the hospital straight away," she said.
"Is that a good idea?" Emily had responded. "If she arrives and sees you there she may rush off again. It's Lizzie and Hugh she's contacted. Would it be better to let Lizzie and Hugh draw her back? It's a bit late for Nancy to go now. More likely she'll go tomorrow, don't you think? Lizzie will be back there in the morning. Perhaps she should go ahead of Grandma and me – just in case."
Reluctantly Miranda conceded but with tears.

******

It was five minutes before the end of evening visiting by the time Nancy arrived. She enquired as to Hugh's whereabouts at reception and hurried along the corridor towards his room. Peering cautiously into the dimly lit

Monday's Child
Caroline Jones Lewis

room she saw with relief that none of the family were now there; Hugh was alone, so she pushed the door open gently and stood quietly just inside the room leaving the door to swish closed behind her. The sight of her cousin shocked and upset her.

"Oh, Hugh," she gasped. "What on earth's happened to you?"

A tear slid down her cheek and she stepped forward, dropping carefully onto the seat beside his bed. She let her bag slide to the floor and took his hand in both of hers, caressing it gently. Bending forward she kissed his swollen cheek, barely more than a brush for fear of hurting him. She whispered his name softly, hoping he would open his eyes and see her there but his eyes remained closed and there was no physical reaction to her touch, no sign of recognition. She was so absorbed in her own actions that she did not hear the door open quietly behind her.

"Oh, I'm sorry. I didn't realise there was anyone here," said a gentle voice.

Nancy turned sharply and saw the ward sister studying her from the doorway.

"Actually, visiting time is over," the sister told her. "I'm afraid I'll have to ask you to leave."

"But I've only just arrived," Nancy protested.

"I'm really sorry," the sister insisted, "but that's the rule, I'm afraid."

"I've come from London," Nancy continued. "Please. Could I have just a little while?"

The sister considered for a moment, confronted by Nancy's pleading face.

"Well, I'll give you just five minutes," she told her. "But if Matron comes in you haven't seen me, alright? I'll be back in five minutes."

Nancy wanted to protest, to plead for longer but decided against it.

"Oh, thank you so much," she breathed.

True to her word the sister returned in five minutes.

Monday's Child

Caroline Jones Lewis

"Sorry but time's up," she said. "Visiting is from 10.30 to 11.30 in the morning and again for an hour in the afternoon and evening. Are you staying in Brighton?"
Nancy had not considered what she would do but on the spur of the moment made her decision. She had brought money with her so there was no reason not to stay.
"I'll stay overnight if I can find somewhere reasonable," she replied. "Can you recommend anywhere, give me an idea where to look? I don't need anywhere fancy. Just clean and comfortable, a decent hotel - but not too expensive. Or a B&B."
"We do have one or two numbers that we keep for relatives," the sister told her. "If you just wait outside while I do Mr Farrell's obs, then I'll be with you."
She opened the door for Nancy who picked up her bag and made to leave.
"See you in the morning, Hugh," she whispered, then left the room.

Armed with the telephone numbers given by the ward sister and some change for the payphone, Nancy rang and found a B&B along the seafront which suited her purpose. She left her bag in her room, then wrapped her coat around her and walked towards the town to find a café to eat. A small group of mods were gathered outside the local Wimpey bar, laughing and revving the engines of their Lambrettas, opening the throttles so the engines phut-phutted in a cloud of exhaust fumes. At their centre a youth who was obviously their leader eyed Nancy as she approached and wolf-whistled, his cohorts joining in.
"Really like to shag that," he said, loudly enough for her to hear and a jeer went up from the others.
"In your dreams," she thought. "Who on earth do you think you are, you common little person?" She cocked her nose in the air in disdain as she neared, refusing to increase her pace despite the nervous churning in the pit of her stomach and a feeling of vulnerability tugging at her heels. The lads laughed and chided as she passed them by,

Monday's Child
Caroline Jones Lewis

pulling her coat protectively around her. Foremost in her mind was the sight of Hugh and the injuries so visible an indication of the intensity of the beating to which he had been subjected, here in Brighton perhaps by these very people, for all she knew. She sought and found a café quickly, warm and well lit, where she gulped down a coffee and a chicken salad sandwich. Then peering out of the door to see if the coast was clear, she returned quickly to her room at the B&B and fell exhausted onto the bed and to sleep.

Her sleep was fitful, interrupted by bad dreams and spectres dancing on the fabric of the thin plain curtains drawn across the window. At 3 am she rose and switched on the light to dispel the images crowding her head, splashing her face with cold water at a basin in the corner. Drawing back the curtains, she gazed up at the stars and the waxing moon, its reflection glistening on a gently lapping sea. The sea's hypnotic movement held her gaze, the waves tumbling one upon another on the pebble beach until, overcome once more with tiredness, she fell back onto the bed and into sleep. She slept unhindered until the grey light of dawn crept into the room.

Nancy took breakfast in the sparse little dining room, fiddling absentmindedly with the plastic flowers in a cheap glass vase on the table, then returned to her room to pack her bag. Feeling better for the food inside her, she left the B&B and strolled along the seafront with her bag slung over her shoulder. It was a cold morning, but sunny and rays of thin spring sunlight danced off the low tide in the distance, lighting the horizon. The snow that had hung around in grubby hillocks since Christmas had thawed to just occasional lumps of stubborn ice in the gutters and the pavement along the seafront was slippery from the overnight frost. Outside the Grand Hotel a porter was loading cases into the boot of a limousine, his warm breath puffing in steamy clouds as he rubbed his cold hands and

Monday's Child
Caroline Jones Lewis

muttered discontent at the weather. On the beach a girl wrapped up to her neck with warm clothing was throwing a stick for her dog, a black Labrador that hurtled along the water's edge, then skidded to a halt in a shower of sand to retrieve and return, tail wagging, to its mistress. She thought of her old spaniel at Abberley and she knew somehow and for certain that her escape was almost over, the adventure she had thought she would have – that soon she would return home. Whether in shame or triumph no longer mattered – she would return home. Soon she would find a way. She whiled away the time until she knew she could return to the hospital, wanting to be there as early as possible hopefully to avoid any other members of the family. The sister had referred to his other visitors which, from their conversation, Nancy had identified as Lizzie, her Aunt Emily and Hugh's grandmother. She could bear to see Lizzie if it could not be avoided but no-one else and she guessed they would all arrive together if they all came today.

At the hospital Hugh's condition had shown little change. Nancy watched him through the window into his room before entering, taking in the machines, the wires, the beeping of the monitor and the hospital smell that made her feel nauseous. What was that awful smell? Disinfectant? Antiseptic? What was it? Awful. She had little experience of hospitals herself, having only been to one once before and that had been a private one. Why did they all smell the same, she wondered? A nurse hurried past her in a striped uniform, a starched white cap and apron. The soles of her flat black shoes squeak squeaked on the lino floor as she passed, smiling at Nancy as she went. Nancy thought of her Aunt Emily, busily nursing at her own hospital and her Uncle Tom the doctor. They were a good family, she thought – her family. She was the black sheep, the one who let them down, selfish and unworthy. Her return would probably provoke

Monday's Child

Caroline Jones Lewis

recrimination and disapproval from all. But she would have to face it – when the time came.

She entered Hugh's room with caution as though he were just sleeping and she did not want to wake him. Taking his hand she sat beside him, talking to him in a quiet, gentle voice, rambling on without reserve, about family, about their holidays at Abberley, anything and everything that came to mind. She knew she would have to leave soon and she wanted him to know that she was sorry for leaving like she did and how she missed and loved him. At 11 o'clock she rose to leave and was wrapping her coat around her when a movement from the bed caught her eye. The fingers of Hugh's hand flickered for just a second.
"Hugh," she called, leaning towards him. "Hugh."
His right eye opened just a fraction, the left one too swollen to move. He could see someone, a misty image of a face.
"It's me, Nancy," she told him.
Yes, Nancy, he thought. But a different Nancy. A Nancy with grown-up hair and lipstick.
"Nancy," he acknowledged through a mouth thick with lips as dry as chaff.
Nancy pressed the bell beside the bed and smiled in encouragement but Hugh had lapsed once more into unconsciousness.
"He woke," she told the sister. "He said my name. He recognised me. But he's gone again."
"That's alright," the sister reassured her. "He will lapse in and out to begin with. But it's a good sign, him saying your name. That's a good sign."
Nancy turned back to Hugh and kissed his hand.
"I have to go now," she told him. "But I'll be back, soon, I promise."

Arriving only minutes later, Emily and Lizzie left Hugh's grandmother at his bedside and went to the sister's office

Monday's Child

Caroline Jones Lewis

for a progress report. The news of Nancy's visit was met with mixed reaction.

"Oh, Mum, we missed her," fretted Lizzie. "And only by minutes from what the sister said. She must still be in Brighton."

"Yes, we missed her. But she came," Emily encouraged. "You heard what the sister said. Nancy promised Hugh she would come again. We're getting closer, Liz. Sooner or later we're bound to catch up with her. It's just a shame it had to be for this reason," she said ruefully. "But he's waking now and he spoke her name. That's really encouraging, Liz. Really encouraging! Come on, let's take Grandma for lunch and who knows, when we come back this afternoon he may wake again."

Monday's Child
Caroline Jones Lewis

Chapter Eight – A step forward and a step back

Arriving back at the flat Nancy went through to the kitchen, dropping her bag onto the table on her way along with the newspaper bought at the station and a brown carrier bag of groceries purchased in the corner shop. She put on the kettle for coffee, pulled a bottle of milk from the carrier bag and shoved a packet of Omo into the cupboard under the sink. Feeling grubby from the train journey and the overnight stay, she went through to the bathroom to wash and change collecting clean clothes from the bedroom on the way. The flat, as usual, was in disarray, all serious attempts at housekeeping having long ago slipped into oblivion and renewed only intermittently for damage limitation purposes or an urgent need for a clean pair of knickers. A thin layer of film covered the furniture having accumulated since Eve had last wielded a duster in despair of her friend's lack of domesticity. In the kitchen, the last used dishes were propped higgledy-piggledy in a corner where Nancy pushed them out of her line of sight. Dressed in her comfy old dressing gown, she sipped a cup of coffee and quickly scanned the newspaper spread out on the floor before her. What greeted her was worse than she ever could have imagined.

The press were having a field day on the Profumo scandal. On the front page his now familiar image and that of the beautiful doe-eyed Christine stared back at her, photographed outside the Club in Soho. And there were others. There was Stephen outside his flat in Marylebone, Lord Astor, who Nancy realised with horror was known to and who knew her father and last but by no means least, Mandy. The realisation that the net was indeed widening was a cause of deep concern. How long until Adam's face joined the others in the tabloids, she wondered, a supplier of female companionship for the parties that the press were now calling 'drug-fuelled orgies'? Would it then be hers and Eve's? She had to get away from this - and now, she

Monday's Child

Caroline Jones Lewis

thought in panic. She could not bear the thought of the shame she would bring on her family, on Hugh lying in his hospital bed. But how? She heard Eve's voice instructing her. Stay calm. It had become her mantra. Stay calm. As she put her coffee cup down onto the table to reach forward and turn the page of the paper, making a space between the nail polish and a ball of abandoned cotton wool, she knocked onto the floor a small business card which she had removed from her purse some days before. It lay face up on the carpet, defaced by dust and a stain from an earlier cup of coffee. She paused, staring down at the print and recalling the conversation with its owner. Its significance had not impressed upon her at their meeting and she had discarded it with little thought, her mind at the time fixated on other matters. Now it was all too obvious where the source of her redemption could lie. She grabbed the telephone from the side table, propped it on her knees and dialled.

The brr-brr of the ring tone seemed to go on for an eternity and Nancy was just about to replace the receiver when she heard a click and the sound of a male voice.
"Hi, Robin," she began. "I don't know if you remember me. It's Nancy."
"Nancy, just Nancy," he replied amiably. "I certainly do remember you. I've been hoping you would call. Does this mean you're going to allow me to photograph you?"
"If the offer's still open," she replied, cheering immediately.
There was no hesitation.
"When can you come? As soon as possible? Tomorrow maybe?"
She considered.
"I could come in the morning – earlyish," she offered.
"After that it would be difficult."
She knew she had to keep Adam sweet for the time being – if she wanted to eat, that was, so early morning it had to be.

Monday's Child
Caroline Jones Lewis

"Ten o'clock suit you?"
"Fine," she replied. "How do I find you? Oh - and what should I wear?"

Fired by a new optimism, Nancy turned on the transistor radio and sang along to the music, with a sway of her hips and a toss of the head, while she ran her bath.

> Dulang dulang dulang
> Dulang dulang
> He's so fine
> Wish he were mine
> That handsome boy over there
> One with the wavy hair
> I don't know how I'm gonna do it
> But I'm gonna make him mine
> Be the envy of all the girls
> It's just a matter of time

She lay in the warm scented water contemplating the possibilities ahead if she were successful, the chance to try all the latest fashions for free, the latest hairstyles by Sassoon and the make-up, all the latest and be paid at the same time. Fantastic, she crooned. Fantastic. She might even make it big if Robin's friend with the modelling agency got her the right contacts.
"Please. Please," she pleaded to an unseen, unnamed deity she had never acknowledged before and was not even sure she believed in. "Please let this work out for me."
Her reverie was interrupted by a knock at the door.
"Probably Eve," she thought. "Who else?" since she rarely had any other visitor except a neighbour who sometimes ran out of sugar.
She rose from the bath water, taking her time to wrap herself in a bath towel. She hoped it was Eve, could not wait to share her news about Robin Selway. As she walked from the bathroom towards the hallway, the knock came again, this time heavier, more urgent and persistent.

Monday's Child

Caroline Jones Lewis

The sight of Eve made her hesitate in her tracks. Eve looked pale, unusually dishevelled and careworn and she brushed past Nancy in a hurry.
"Coffee on?" she asked brusquely.
"Sure, if you want one," Nancy replied absentmindedly, more interested in knowing what was ailing her friend.
"Eve, what's wrong?" she began, her excitement about Robin fading for the moment and any mention of it seeming inappropriate. "You don't look yourself."
Nancy feared the worst. The police had raided the Club. Or Adam had been arrested and spilled the beans, naming all of them. Eve had dropped her coat onto the sofa and headed for the kitchen. She refilled the kettle, switching it on and hunting for a clean mug in the cupboard.
"God, Nancy, you're a slut," she murmured as she cast aside the clutter.
"Yes, I know," Nancy replied dismissively, "but what is it? What's wrong? Eve, you look positively awful."
"Oh, thanks," Eve snapped, rounding on her. "Just what I need to hear, Nanc."
"Then tell me what's wrong," Nancy insisted, almost shouting.
Eve signed. She turned down the radio which was irritating her.
"May I?" she asked belatedly.
"Of course."
Nancy waited.
Eve sank onto the sofa, her cup of coffee on the table before her.
"God, I'm tired," she said, deliberately ignoring Nancy's inquisitive stare. "The Club was so quiet last night, the evening seemed to go on for ever. I rang in sick this morning. Adam wasn't too pleased, especially after you yesterday, but there wasn't much he could say. He asked when you'd be back and I told him you were travelling back today so probably tomorrow. Was that ok?"
"Yes, fine. I was going in today but if he isn't expecting me then tomorrow is better."

Monday's Child

Caroline Jones Lewis

"Just look at this place," Eve grumbled on. "Don't you ever clean anything? You've had too much done for you, that's the trouble," and she laughed, a short, brittle sort of laugh that did little to relieve the tension, quite unlike her usual warm-hearted laughter. Then she smiled, weakly and hugged her friend apologetically.
"Sorry," she said. "I'm being a cow."
Nancy sighed. "You don't have to tell me. But housework's so boring. Day after day doing the same things."
"I didn't mean to be a nag," Eve told her. "I'm turning into your mother," and they both laughed at the ridiculousness of the statement. Eve went quiet again and Nancy picked up the tone.
"Well, are you going to tell me now?" she began.
"Tell you what?"
"Come on, Eve. I've seen you without make-up before and you don't usually look as pasty as this. For God's sake put me out of my misery. Has something happened at the Club?"
Eve shook her head, realising where Nancy's train of thought was heading.
"Oh, no, nothing like that," she assured her. Taking a deep breath and without further ceremony, she announced,"I'm pregnant."
Nancy gasped.
"Eve, how on earth ..." she began. "After all your warnings to me and the help you gave me. How on earth ..?"
She stopped.
"Well, we both know how," she went on.
"Yes, in the time honoured manner," said Eve sarcastically. "What sort of an idiot am I, do you think? How could I have been so stupid? I ran out of pills for a day or two and I thought it would be ok. Well, these things only happen to other people, don't they? They're not supposed to happen to you."
"Are you sure?"

Monday's Child

Caroline Jones Lewis

"Afraid so," was all Eve could answer.
Nancy could think of nothing to say. She leaned back against the cushions of the sofa and let out a deep breath.

The two girls lolled around the flat for the rest of the day considering Eve's options.
"It has to be an abortion ," Eve was adamant. "Has to be."
"But you need to be sure," Nancy insisted.
"Of what? That I'm pregnant or that I want an abortion?"
"Both," she continued. "Have you seen a doctor?"
"No. Neither am I going to. When I missed the first month I hoped I was wrong. But now I've missed a second and I'm throwing up every morning. It's a pretty good indication, don't you think?"
"Well, you could consider keeping it. Some girls do and they manage," Nancy offered somewhat unconvincingly.
"Oh, yes. I can just see that, can't you. Firstly I can't say for sure who the father is and even if I knew, there would be no support from that direction. So it's me in one of those homes for unmarried mothers, then, is it? Definitely not. And then what? Adoption? Going through all that and then giving the baby away? I don't think I could do that, Nanc. Really I don't. If I had this baby I would want to keep it as sure as eggs are eggs and that's not an option. How would we live? I'd be out of the Club the minute Adam got an inkling. So it has to be abortion ."
She finished in a hushed voice.
"What about your parents?" Nancy suggested, clutching at straws to keep the option of abortion at bay. A back-street abortionist. The very idea frightened her.
"Oh, Mum would want me to keep it. I'll look after it, she'd say. Anything to get me to keep it. But it doesn't stop there, does it? We're talking about years and years, caring for a child. And the stigma for the child. A bastard. You know how cruel kids can be? Adults come to that."
Nancy did not. Coming from the background that she did and with no experience to draw on she had no idea. But she took Eve's word for it.

Monday's Child
Caroline Jones Lewis

"I guess you're right, then," she sighed. But attitudes are changing, Eve, aren't they? Slowly perhaps, but things are changing."

"Not in my world, they're not. They might be in yours, I guess there are ways and means when you have money. But not for me. No, Nanc. It isn't possible," said Eve. Nancy thought about her mother, the subterfuge over the circumstances of her own conception. Not even in my world, she thought. It's no different really.

"I can't do it," Eve continued. "I've thought about it, over and over, about little else since the penny dropped. But I can't do it. Truth is, I'm too selfish anyway. If I knew who the father was and I loved him I might feel different but I don't. No, it has to be an abortion. I've made up my mind. Unless you have a better idea, that is."

"I don't," admitted Nancy.

They sat in silence for a moment, two girls each in their own thoughts.

"Do you know someone?" Nancy asked at length.

"No. But I can ask around," Eve replied. "I'll ask Sophie," she said, referring to a waitress at the Club. "I can trust her. She won't say anything to anyone. Adam mustn't know," she panicked. "I don't want anyone else to know."

Nancy grimaced at the thought but she said no more.

"If only the government would legalise abortion ," Eve murmured. "They keep debating it but they never get round to doing it, do they? They've debated it long enough surely. It's time they did something about it. Can't see it happening in the next few weeks, though, can you?"

"There's too much opposition, Mummy says," Nancy replied. "I'm not sure it will ever happen" and if it had, she thought in anger, I might not even be here.

"But, Eve, what about the money?" she went on. "Isn't it expensive?"

"Yes," answered Eve bitterly. "I'll just have to find the money somehow. Not sure how at the moment."

Monday's Child

Caroline Jones Lewis

"If I can help," Nancy ventured. "I have some savings. You will let me help, won't you? And you're not going on your own. I'll come with you. Promise you'll let me come with you."
Eve hedged.
"Eve, promise me," Nancy insisted.
Eve was reluctant but then her own fear got the better of her and hugging her friend in gratitude she agreed.
"And if I do borrow the money from you, I'll pay it back as quickly as I can," she promised.
"Any time," Nancy told her. "I couldn't have managed all these months without you, Eve. I'm grateful and now it's my turn to help."
She prayed silently that her hopes with the Robin connection would bear fruit and his friend would come up trumps with some modelling work. She hesitated to tell Eve her good news, waiting for a more appropriate moment.
"Oh, God," gasped Eve. "I haven't asked you how Hugh is. Tell me how he is and while you're doing that, we'll clean up this mess."

******

Lizzie sat at Hugh's bedside awaiting her mother.
"I'm going back to uni today, Hugh. There's a lecture I really can't miss tomorrow. It's important. You do understand, don't you? But I'll be back as soon as I can. Mum will be here between shifts and Grandma will be coming. They'll look after you between them. And Uncle James is on his way today. We're all here for you, Hugh."
She went on talking to him about university, about Abberley and how they must go as soon as he was well enough.
"It will be lovely in the spring," she told him.
It was some minutes before she noticed that he was trying to open his right eye. The eyelid of his right was fluttering, the left one still too swollen to move. She pressed the bell for a nurse and went on talking to him

Monday's Child
Caroline Jones Lewis

encouragingly. A nurse swung in through the door and with Lizzie stood watching, waiting until gradually Hugh opened his eye. Squinting to focus, he looked at Lizzie and smiled a weak but definite smile.

"Lizzie," he whispered croakily. "Lizzie."

"I'll fetch sister," the nurse announced . "Take note of anything he says or does 'till she gets here," and with a swish of the door she was gone.

To Lizzie's joy, Hugh remained awake for some minutes with no obvious impairment to his mental ability. When the sister arrived, she checked all his vital signs which gave nothing for concern and he took water keenly from a drinking cup Lizzie lifted to his mouth. He said little, but what he did say made perfect sense.

"Nancy?" he asked.

"She isn't here right now," Lizzie told him. "But she's been, Hugh, hasn't she."

"Yes," he breathed. "Yes."

Over the coming days and with Hugh's increasing consciousness, two police officers at his bedside were able to piece together details of the attack from snippets of information he gave in his lucid moments. The hardest part for Hugh came when he needed to relate to his family. In his weakened mental state and the confused telling, he gave away some of the facts about his friends and the Parakeet Club to his grandmother before he realised what he had done. She made no comment, just took his hands in her own and kissed it tenderly. When it dawned on him that she understood, he did not know what to say.

"Yes, dear," she said matter-of-factly. "You're – what's the term? Gay. I know. I think I have known for some time.

"Grandma," he groaned painfully. "How …?"

"Oh, Hugh," she sighed, leaning towards him. "You're my nearest and dearest. I probably guessed it before you did."

"I'm sorry, Grandma," he breathed. "Not the man you expected, am I?"

Monday's Child

Caroline Jones Lewis

"Do you think it matters a jot to me?" she reprimanded him. "Do you think I could love you any the less because now you've told me? It isn't what I would have wished for you, of course. We always want for our children what we have had and enjoyed ourselves. Marriage. A family life. You won't have that, now, will you? And there will be prejudice if and when it becomes public knowledge. But you don't have to tell anyone you don't want to know. The decision of what and who to tell is yours. But it makes no difference to your family. We all love you too much, you must know that."
"Yes. But I'm fed up of living a lie. I'm tired," Hugh confided.
"Then rest," she told him. "And make that decision when you're good and ready, when you're strong enough. There's no hurry. Right now you don't need to do anything at all. Just get better."

Hugh's boss waited at the reception desk to ask direction to Hugh's room. He had been shocked to hear the news of the attack from Hugh's grandmother whose home he had telephoned when Hugh had failed to arrive for work for several days and no message from him had been received. Her daily had passed the message of his call to Emily who had also passed it on, so grandmother had given him the bare bones of the story.
"He was mugged," she told him. "Beaten half to death. It's a wonder he's still alive. He's in an awful state; only conscious for short periods."
"I'll come to the hospital, shall I?"
"Perhaps in a while," Grandma had advised.
He stood at reception now and waited.
"You can't go in for the moment," he was told. "Mr Farrell's only allowed two visitors at a time and there are two with him at the moment. Police," the receptionist confided in a low voice, adding to the element of drama. He decided to wait for a while, not wishing to return to London without having achieved at least a brief visit. His

Monday's Child

Caroline Jones Lewis

patience was soon rewarded, the two police officers plodding back down the corridor, passing the reception on their way to the exit.

"Straight forward mugging," the one was saying. "I suppose the severity of the beating was because of his sexuality. Coming out of that club. They probably thought the chance of some queer bashing was a bonus on top of the cash and the goods they managed to get."

His companion nodded.

"Yes, probably, though he doesn't look like a queer, does he?"

"What does a queer look like?" challenged the first officer. "They're not all obvious, are they? You never know who you're sitting next to these days. Makes your flesh creep to think of it," and they passed by to the fresh air outside.

Hugh's boss froze.

It couldn't be true, surely, he thought. Hugh a homosexual, a pervert? But then it did make sense. All those non-relationships with women. They never went anywhere, never led to anything more than friendship."

Now he thought about it, it made perfect sense. For a good looking young man of Hugh's age who, to his knowledge, had never had a deep and meaningful relationship with a woman despite the many attractive women he met in his line of work, it suddenly made total sense.

A homosexual – working ins his office, his thoughts rambled on. Mixing with my decent staff.

He shivered at the thought. He couldn't have it. Hugh would have to go. He considered leaving right away without putting an appearance in at Hugh's bedside and before anyone knew he was there but thought better of it. His office staff knew he was there. He would have to tell them something when he got back. What would he tell them? He did not want to reveal the truth right now. He must think carefully about how to achieve what he needed to do. He walked steadily to Hugh's room.

Monday's Child

Caroline Jones Lewis

Despite his abhorrence of homosexuality he was shocked
at Hugh's appearance, his battered and bruised body and
the machinery and tubes surrounding the bed. No-one
should have this happen to them, he thought. "No-one. He
softened a little as he spoke. Hugh's grandmother sat by
the bedside holding her grandson's hand. She looked tired.
"Hi, Hugh. How are you doing, old man?"
The conversation was only brief. Hugh lapsed back into
sleep and the man excused himself, leaving behind the
flowers from the girls in the office and a basket of fruit he
had bought himself.
"Tell him I'll see him again later," he said to the
grandmother.
"Thanks for coming," she replied and he left, slipping
quietly from the room.

Chas and Edward came too. The attack had been reported
in the local press and, as was their way, they only read it
several days later when the paper was retrieved from the
mailbox outside the door along with several others. They
naturally were shocked and hurried to the hospital at the
first opportunity, sneaking surreptitiously into Hugh's
room the latest they could in the evening, once they were
sure he was alone. His condition shocked them further and
their anger at Simon, who they blamed uncompromisingly,
intensified.
"The timing that evening," Chas riled at Simon later, "was
entirely down to you. If you hadn't let him down – yet
again, Simon - he would not have been there and we would
all have left together later. This is down to you."
Hugh thanked them for coming and they left him with a
promise of their return.
"Is there anything we can get you?" they asked. "Anything
," but he shook his head as best he could, too tired at the
late hour to speak more. The two friends left him sadly,
Hugh already drifting back into the abyss.

******

Monday's Child
Caroline Jones Lewis

Lizzie tried to concentrate on her lectures but it was difficult. Her thoughts were still with Hugh in the hospital and there with Hugh was where she really wanted to be. She hoped, too, that Nancy would reappear and that this time it would be while she, Lizzie, was still there. It would not matter about the circumstances, only that they would all three be there together. She longed for it to happen, that the unreal quality that life had adopted since Nancy's disappearance would come to an end.
"Please, God," she urged, "let this nightmare come to an end. Hugh needs us all and that means Nancy too."

******

Nancy struggled to keep on track at the Club. She wanted to be gone, wanted to go back to see Hugh again. There were so many things happening now but she needed to stay at the Club to earn money and to see Eve safely through the abortion. She could not abandon her right now. The 'photo session with Robin had gone really well and he was hopeful that something good would come of it.
"I'm taking the 'photos to my friend," he told her, "the one that runs the modelling agency. I think he'll be impressed. You're a natural in front of the camera."
So Nancy was hopeful too. It could be her passport to a new life.

Eve had telephoned the number recommended to her and the appointment was made for an evening when neither of the girls would be working. Eve was confident this could be done without Adam's knowledge. The two girls made their way to the address given and knocked tentatively at the door.

The abortionist looked like anyone's granny, an innocuous grey-haired little lady who greeted them amiably as though they were just visiting for Sunday tea.

Monday's Child

Caroline Jones Lewis

"Come in, ducks," she told them, ushering them quickly into the hallway away from the twitching curtains and prying eyes.
"Now – which one of you is it, then?"
Eve indicated to herself in reply and the woman indicated to the stairs.
"Up the apples and pears, then, luvvie," she told Eve and turning to Nancy continued, "I think you'd better wait down here. You can come up and sit with her for a while when I call you."
She led Eve to a small bedroom at the back of the house.
"Now, make yourself comfy, ducks," she instructed, turning back the covers on the bed to expose a clean white sheet.
"Try to relax. Your troubles will be over in no time."
Then turning to face her she said, "shall we get the business bit over first, then? You've brought the money?"

An hour later the two girls were in a taxi together heading for Nancy's flat where she intended that Eve should stay the night. While Nancy stood making coffee in a kitchen cleaned and tidied especially for the sake of hygiene, she heard a gentle sobbing from the bedroom where she had settled Eve into bed. A sadness overwhelmed her at the pain of her friend. She went to the bedroom and, placing the cup of coffee she had made onto the bedside table, she hugged her friend close.
"I've ended a life, Nanc," Eve sniffed into her hankie. "Snuffed it out like a candle in the wind."
For a moment Nancy could think of nothing to say in response. Then, "You did what you felt you had to," she said. "Better to do that than bring a child into the world that you that you couldn't care for."
"Then why do I feel so dirty?" Eve insisted.
Again Nancy struggled to reply.
Eve spoke in a subdued voice, unburdening her guilt, her feeling of wretchedness.

Monday's Child
Caroline Jones Lewis

"It would have been easier if it had been legal," Nancy observed. "All this back door stuff, the subterfuge, the underhand way of it all, like a criminal. It adds to the guilt."
"I'm not sure I approve of legalised abortion. Does that sound mad?" Eve observed. "Making it easy, abortion on demand, just getting rid of it because having it would be inconvenient. Just another kind of birth control. Is that how it should be? Maybe it's right that people like me should be made to feel guilty. I've destroyed a life. And it feels awful."
Nancy could think of nothing appropriate to say.

In the morning, Eve was pale and weak. The abortion was complete but the emotional trauma remained with her.
"You're calling in sick," Nancy insisted.
"No, I can't do that," Eve argued, attempting to raise herself from the bed. "I must go in. I don't want anyone suspecting anything."
"Of course you can't. You're calling in sick," Nancy repeated. "Say you've got a tummy upset. I'll back you up. Everyone knows we're friends. Just say you stayed here last night because you were too unwell to go back to yours."
Eve shrugged weakly, too disconsolate to argue. She shuffled meekly to the telephone and called the Club, then crawled back into bed grateful for Nancy's care.

******

The Profuma scandal rolled on, the press baying for blood until, falling on his sword and conceding to the wishes of his detractors, Profumo resigned. It was hoped by the government that press interest would then decline but it was not to be. With the opposition whipping up the security angle and the sordid details and exaggerations holding the interest of the public at large, there was to be no respite in a hurry. Rumours of charges against Stephen

Monday's Child

Caroline Jones Lewis

continued to abound but to Nancy's relief, no new names and involvements were bandied about. Nancy crossed every finger and toe and prayed, promising an angelic rest-of-her life to the God above she had never before acknowledged if only this could be avoided, if she could make her exit from the Club unscathed. Robin came to the Club at lunchtime and the news was good.
"He wants you to come and register with the agency," he told her. "He's shown your photos to a client, a big fashion house and they're interested in you. They're looking for a new face to front their campaign for their summer collection. When can you come?"
"In the morning," she announced readily. "Before I come here."
So it was arranged.

The next morning Eve seemed to be running a temperature. There was no question of her going to the Club.
I'll have to ring in and report her sick again , thought Nancy. What can I say is wrong?
But she didn't want to leave her alone either, worried that there was worse to come. What if she had an infection caused by the abortion? What should she do? What if she died? To take her to Casualty would mean awkward questions that could land Eve in trouble. Unless, she thought, unless she dare ring Aunt Emily. Her aunt would not be judgemental, she was sure. Her aunt was fully in favour of legalised abortion, she had said so on many occasions. But whether she could help Eve without compromising her professional integrity was a different matter. Eve was now sleeping fitfully and Nancy decided she would wait a little and see. Before risking anything she would keep her appointment with Robin and then return to see how Eve was. She coaxed Eve to take two tablets of aspirin, then left her sleep once more.

Her first task was to think of how to deal with Adam. The obvious thing to tell him was that Eve's tummy bug had

Monday's Child
Caroline Jones Lewis

worsened and that now she, Nancy, had caught it too. Adam wouldn't like it but there would be little he could do but accept it; he would not want them in the Club spreading their infection to his clients. She was bracing herself for the call and the need to sound convincing when her thoughts were interrupted by the shrill of the 'phone. To her initial consternation it was Adam, like a spirit conjured up out of her own consciousness.

"Don't come in," he blurted. "I want you to stay away for the moment, you and Eve. I've been trying to ring her but I can't get a reply. Do you know where she is?"

Nancy answered with mixed emotions, relief and a thank you to the heavens for the respite but concern as to the reason why.

"She's here," she began. "She stayed here overnight. What's the problem?"

"The police are here," Adam answered. "They're digging for anything they can find on Stephen. I can't say any more. I have to go."

"But for how long," asked Nancy. "Our pay …" she began but Adam interrupted her.

"You'll be paid," he told her. "As long as it takes. I'll send it round," and before Nancy could utter another word she heard the clunk of the receiver dropping back into its cradle and the line went dead.

With one problem resolved, she set about getting ready for her appointment with Robin and his friend the agent. Time was passing and she wanted to create the best impression she could. Deciding to keep her dress simple, she chose her favourite white blouse and jeans and accessorised with a wide belt and boots. They went well with her favourite jacket. The whole effect, with hair left natural and the minimum of make-up, raised her confidence to its best. She called Eve gently, telling her that she was going for her appointment but would be back soon. She repeated it more than once, unsure that Eve had taken in what she was saying.

Monday's Child

Caroline Jones Lewis

"Stay in bed until I get back," she instructed. "Do you understand?"
Eve gazed at her through heavy eyes but nodded. Nancy left relieved, feeling confident that Eve had heard and would do as she had asked her. In a hurry she made it to the station in the midst of the early morning commuters, running down the steps of the underground to the platform. A poster on the news stand caught her attention. 'Ward Charged' it screamed. It made her shudder but she stopped and bought a copy of the tabloid to read on the tube. It was two stations before she was able to get a seat and scan its pages. Once more pictures of Stephen, Christine and Mandy stared back at her.
I've got to get out of this mess, she panicked. Before it's too late. Before my picture's alongside them, too; mine and Eve's. Today has to work for me.

The events of the last few weeks, Eve's abortion and illness and Hugh's misfortune, had wrought a change in Nancy deeper than she would ever have thought possible. Emotions that had previously been alien to her now took precedence to the selfishness of before. Loyalties had strengthened, towards her family, the parents she had treated with such lack of understanding and disrespect, cousins whose concern and care of her she had disregarded. Loyalty to a new-found friend who, like her, had made mistakes for which she was being made to pay. And responsibility for her own transgressions. She could picture the anguish on the face of her mother, anxiety at her daughter's absence and the pain that knowledge of her daughter's present lifestyle would cause. She thought of her father in the same vein. These were things she had to atone for but still her pride overrode any thought of returning home. Robin was her lifeline now and she would cling to that for all she was worth. She formed a plan in her mind. She would lie low, keep away from the Club and anyone connected with it except Eve. If Eve was better in a day or two she could make another visit to Hugh

Monday's Child
Caroline Jones Lewis

and begin the task of repairing the damage she had caused. By the time the train reached her station, she was ready to meet the challenge and headed determinedly towards her goal.

******

At the Club, Matthew sat at a dimly lit table as inconspicuously as was possible. He had been watching at the Club with anticipation since his tip-off to the press and he now observed the comings and goings with satisfaction. Plain clothes police, unmistakeable to all but the naïve, moved amongst the staff, talking to them quietly, questioning, probing, slipping leading questions into their rhetoric in the hope of gleaning information. But they learned little from a staff instructed by their boss to offer nothing. Yes, they agreed, Stephen Ward was a member here, as he was in other clubs. They knew that was the case because he himself had told them. No, they had never seen him with any of the girls. No, they knew nothing of any parties and had been shocked by the revelations in the press. Matthew watched with interest. But there was one thing that stung with bitter disappointment. There was no sign of Nancy and no involvement of her in the investigation.

When the police officers left apparently empty-handed and with no-one accompanying them for further questioning, he fumed silently over his gin and tonic, his initial satisfaction turning to disappointment then metamorphosing into a vicious anger.
The bitch, he thought. That bitch. Why isn't she here? Where is she? She was usually here at lunchtime. He had seen her here even before the introduction at Stephen's dinner party and he knew where she lived because he had followed her once or twice. He vowed that he would find her and make her pay her dues. Well it's up to me, he

Monday's Child
Caroline Jones Lewis

decided. It's me she has slighted so it's up to me to see she gets her just deserts.

******

Once the police had left the Club, Adam decided he had another task to complete as a matter of urgency. It was time to make the break with Catherine who had now become clingy and tiresome. She must go before their affair caused damage to his private life or more. Confident that all the officers had left, he spoke to her quietly.
"I need to talk to you," he said gently. "I'll call round to the flat this afternoon. You will be there, won't you?"
She nodded.
"Of course."
Her mind began to invent all manner of reason why he should need to speak to her privately and so urgently. It occurred to her that his wife had found out about them and was threatening all manner of retribution. "Surely not, she argued to herself. He would have said so. From the tone of his voice her willing reasoning decided that this was something good, good for their relationship. His demeanour had been relaxed and gentle- not terse or angry. Perhaps his wife was now willing to give him a divorce. The more she thought about it, the more she was eager to accept this explanation. This was her moment. Their time had come at last. As the morning wore on she became increasingly excited.

Adam walked towards her flat later with apprehension. He knew this would not be easy. He would have to choose his words carefully. So engrossed in rehearsing the challenge to come, he had failed to notice the unobtrusive individual dogging his steps all the way from the Club, lurking in a doorway as he let himself into the apartment block. Once inside the apartment, the sight of Catherine confirmed to him how difficult this was going to be. Catherine had changed into her most chic and flattering outfit, retouched

Monday's Child

Caroline Jones Lewis

her make-up and hairdo and sprayed liberally with the Chanel No 5 he had bought her. She smiled expectantly when he arrived and stepped forward to share a kiss. Adam avoided the kiss by launching directly into his speech.

"I have a problem," he began, pacing to and fro across the floor.

"Oh," she responded, a crestfallen expression replacing the smile.

"Why don't we sit down?" he offered, and they sat on the sofa, Catherine beside him. Half-turning towards her, he took her hand gently in his own.

"My wife is giving me a really bad time right now. If she were to find out about you I could lose the Club and that means my livelihood. It isn't as if we have just had a casual affair, is it?"

He tried, appealing to her romantic side.

"So I think we'll have to cool things for a while. Just until things calm down a little."

Catherine was shattered. It was not what she had been expecting, what she had convinced herself she was to hear.

"But why can't you just tell her?" she insisted, close to tears.

Oh, God, thought Adam. Not the waterworks. Please, not the tears.

"It's too complicated," Adam continued, dropping her hand and shaking his head. "Like I said – the Club. And then there are the children."

He took his cigarette case and lighter from his pocket and lit a Russian Sobrani, breathing the smoke in deeply.

"She owns most of the shares at the Club," he disclosed with a heavy sigh. "I'd be ruined. Ruined. And she'd take the children away from me. Can you imagine how painful that would be? I just can't take that chance. You do understand, don't you?" he pleaded.

The tears began to flow.

"But for how long," Catherine protested through her sobs. "When would I see you again? I can't bear it, Adam,

Monday's Child
Caroline Jones Lewis

really I can't. I couldn't stay at the Club seeing you every day but not seeing you. It would be unbearable. Please, Adam. Please don't ask me to do this."

"I've thought of that," Adam continued, seizing his cue. "I have a friend who runs another club. I can get you a job there and then we could still keep in touch."

The tears stopped and look of horror on Catherine's face said it all.

"I could see you there," Adam offered. "Come for a drink or a meal and sit with you. We could talk and plan ahead," he added as a sweetener.

"Catherine dissolved into hysterics.

"You don't mean it," she sobbed. "You're just getting rid of me."

"No, no," he protested. He couldn't have her going to the Club making a scene and telling people about them.

"It isn't like that. Come here," he crooned and took her in his arms, cooing reassurance and calming her to quell the avalanche of tears.

Two hours later, after the inevitable tedium of sex, he left the flat with a sigh of relief. The appeal of Catherine had now well and truly palled. He was hopeful that he had stemmed the histrionics for the time being and sold her on the idea of the move, preparing her for the ultimate break. Just outside the door he stopped to tidy his tie. Absorbed in his thoughts, the next phase of extricating himself from the situation, he once again failed to not notice his shadow across the street, watching him from behind a newspaper stand, flicking through the magazines for the hundredth time of his wait. The shadow noted the details with satisfaction. He had gleaned information from a giggly girl at the Club and informed his client. His instruction had been to follow it through. Mission accomplished, he decided. This would surely be enough for his client to proceed. There would be no defence. He left Adam, oblivious of his presence, to make his way back to the

Monday's Child

Caroline Jones Lewis

Club and went his own way, finished for the day. He hummed to music floating from a window above him.

Woke up this morning feeling fine
There's something special on my mind
Last night I met a new girl in the neighbourhood
Oh yeah
Something tells me I'm into something good.

Monday's Child

Caroline Jones Lewis

Chapter Nine - Survival

Hugh's steady recovery from his injuries continued over the next weeks. He had visits from all his family except his Aunt Miranda for reasons that Lizzie explained. Hugh understood. He was preparing for an imminent discharge from the hospital when he received a second visit from his boss. He was sitting in the chair beside his bed when the door opened.

From the moment the man entered the room, Hugh sensed from his manner that something was amiss. The man seemed edgy, fidgety even, though he was effusive and smiling an obviously manufactured smile – not at all the no-nonsense straight-talking man Hugh was used to in the office. The man paced around the room seemingly casually, feigning exaggerated interest and study of an unimpressive picture on the wall as though it were a valuable Picasso. He flicked back his hair and fiddled with the knot of his tie. The conversation was stilted, peppered with everyday niceties but actually saying very little. Please don't let us get onto the weather, thought Hugh. That really would be scraping the barrel.
"I see the machines are all gone," the man commented.
"Yes," Hugh agreed. "I don't need them now."
There was a pause.
"Still a long way to go though, heh Hugh?" said the man, steering the conversation steadily in the direction he needed.
"Yes, I'm afraid so," Hugh agreed. "The doctors say a full recovery will take a while longer yet."
"Hmm." A moment of thought. The man pulled up a chair and sat near the window – but not too close to Hugh.
"I'm afraid this causes us a bit of a problem, old chap," he began.
Hugh looked at him quizzically.
"Oh?" he questioned.

Monday's Child
Caroline Jones Lewis

"Well, it's the clients, you see. They need continuity, the same person dealing with their account and at the end of a 'phone. It's becoming increasingly difficult to – ah."
A light bulb switched on inside Hugh's head. He knew what was coming next and the reason for it began to dawn.
"I'm really sorry, Hugh, but I'm afraid we're going to have to let you go."
There, it was done.
For a moment Hugh was stunned into silence. The man fidgeted uncomfortably in his seat in the starkness of the silence. Then Hugh spoke, quietly and calmly.
"Who told you?" he asked.
The man reddened and loosened his collar uncomfortably, avoiding Hugh's gaze.
"I don't know what …."
"Who told you?" Hugh repeated.
"Really, I don't understand…"
"Oh, don't give me that," Hugh insisted. "Of course you do."
There was no reply and after another silence that seemed to last for hours rather than minutes, the man rose from his chair and made to leave.
"We'll write to you," he said. "You'll receive everything due to you, of course. According to your contract," he reassured.
Hugh said nothing but an angry tinge of pink flushed his cheeks.
"Well, better be off, old chap. Glad you're on the mend. Take care of yourself. We'll be in touch, heh?" and before Hugh could utter another word, he was out of the door.

Hugh slouched in his chair, his head resting to one side, eyes closed. How dare they, he thought. How dare they. After all the time and energy I have put into this job that I'm so good at. What difference does my sexuality make to the job I do? He stared out of the window in disbelief, seeing nothing. Exhausted by his anger, he hauled himself

Monday's Child
Caroline Jones Lewis

back onto the bed, closed his eyes and allowed himself to drift away.

Hugh had a visit, too, from another. After sleeping soundly, he opened his eyes to see Simon standing at the foot of the bed, clutching a bunch of daffodils and looking less than his usually exuberant self. In fact he was shamefaced and, even more unusually, was struggling to find the words he knew he should say.
"Hugh," he began, trying to summon up the courage to say more.
"Simon," Hugh replied but said nothing more.
"How's it going, old chap," Simon attempted. "News is you're on the mend."
Hugh smiled and nodded weakly. He looked at the sad individual before him and felt nothing but pity. The flamboyance he previously saw as engaging he now saw as comic, a faded version of the image he had previously seen. The campness of Simon's dress, the need for him to wear his sexuality like a badge on the lapel now prompted nothing. The love affair was over. You're just weak and pathetic, thought Hugh. Wallowing in a comedic imitation of what you could be, squandering your talent in an orgy of promiscuity and shallowness; no moral fibre at all. In the post Binky Beaumont era of the 50s and the relaxation of censorship in the theatre, the industry was bursting with new talent and opportunity with new playwrites such as John Osborne, Arthur Miller, Shelagh Delaney. They brought new material to an audience embracing the change. Simon also possessed a unique talent and was of that new and young mode of thinking. Hugh had seen flashes of his inspirational ability. He could be riding the crest of a wave instead of languishing in self-destruction.
"I'm surprised to see you," he said at length. Simon coloured.
"I know what you must think of me," Simon replied glumly. "I don't blame you, Hugh. Not at all. But you can't hate me any more than I hate myself."

Monday's Child

Caroline Jones Lewis

"I don't hate you," Hugh told him. "I find you sad, that's all."
Simon shuffled from foot to foot awkwardly.
"Well – had to come," he muttered. "Brought you these," and he stepped forward primly to place the daffodils on the bedside table. They fell silent. Hugh was too tired to continue. It had been a day of surprises and emotion. Simon struggled for something more to say. There was so much he should say, perhaps explain, but he didn't know how. His shame and guilt gnawed at his consciousness continuously and he knew that somehow he needed to regain Hugh's respect, however long it took. Spectres of his past dogged his waking moments and at night invaded his dreams, not only Hugh but his mother and father. He wanted to confide it all to Hugh but he had recognised how selfish that would be.
"Look," he began, then paused. "Umm, I know I'm probably the last person you want to see at the moment but … "
He waited, hoping that Hugh would fill in the gap.
"If there's anything I can do," he tried. "Anything you need, to make amends … "
"There's only one thing," said Hugh softly.
Simon stepped forward expectantly.
"Sort yourself out, Simon. Your life. Not for me. It doesn't matter to me anymore. But for your own sake."
There was a pause.
"Don't know if I can," Simon replied dully. The look on his mother's face that day haunted him, the day he had told her he was gay. Shocked and disgusted, his father's reaction had been worse.
"Well, you'd better put a stop to that, my lad," his mother had told him. "Just stop it and pull yourself together."
"You don't understand," he had told her. "I'm gay. That won't change. I can't change it."
She had become angry, her usually kind face twisted and red with shock and anger.

Monday's Child

Caroline Jones Lewis

"If you loved us, me and your Dad, you'd do it," she insisted. "You'd stop it right now and find yourself a nice girl to marry. And if you won't, then you'll leave here right now and don't come back. Not ever. I never want to see you again. Go on – get out."

He had ran upstairs to his room, churning with hurt and shock and thrown some of his belongings into a travel bag. His mother had been standing in the hall when he returned downstairs, slowly, hoping that the first of her shock had calmed and she would reconsider and be willing to talk. But her eyes were swollen with tears, her face red and she was close to hysterics. He had rushed towards the door.

"Don't come back," she had shouted after him. "Not ever."

He had walked along the terraced street to the tube station with tears stinging his eyes, his breathing laboured and everything around him a blur. Hugh's voice calling in the distance brought him back to the moment.

"Simon. Simon," he was saying. "Are you alright? You've gone really pale."

"Sorry," Simon spluttered. "Sorry. I'm just a bit tired, that's all. Anyway, it's me came to see how *you* are," and he grinned an apologetic grin.

"You can sort your life out," Hugh went on. "If you really want to."

"I'll try," Simon promised. "I'll do my best."

He started to leave.

Turning back to face Hugh at the door he asked "would it be ok if I came again? Would you mind?"

"Of course I wouldn't mind."

Simon took his leave and walked steadily out into the warm sunshine with a growing conviction. Hugh was right, it was time to confront his demons and lay them to rest. Hugh's compassionate response had been generous and one which he felt he had not deserved. He owed it to Hugh to do as he had asked. Time to move on in life and make a success of a career that he loved. And maybe he would find the courage to visit his parents for what could

Monday's Child
Caroline Jones Lewis

be one last time – for better or for worse. Just making the decision made him feel better about himself and he held himself upright, head raised to look the world in the eye. He breathed in deeply, stepped forward with a purpose and hummed and sang as he went.

> Only you can make this world seem right
> Only you can make the darkness bright
> Only you and you alone can thrill me like you do
> And fill my heart with love for only you
> Only you can make a change in me
> For it's true, you are my destiny
> When you hold my hand I understand
> The magic that you do
> You're my dream come true,
> My one and only you

******

Lizzie worked at organising her timetable to fit with Hugh's discharge from hospital. It had been agreed that he would stay with her parents for a few days, then he and Lizzie would go to Abberley for a period of rest and recuperation. Though not divulging all the facts, Hugh had confided to his Aunt Emily the loss of his job and the family, like Hugh, were angered by the treatment he had received. Rest at Abberley, where spring was now breaking and the last of the winter snows had melted, would help to heal his wounds, both mental and physical. The attack had left him nervous of being alone. Lizzie's company would be a bonus and Mrs Hale would be in attendance to care for his every need. Lizzie looked forward to spending time with her cousin and the peace of Abberley would provide a welcome respite after a winter that had been demanding in many ways. Since Nancy's appearance life had seemed to dole out one punishing circumstance after another. Trying to support her family through their anxiety about Nancy and then Hugh's near-

Monday's Child
Caroline Jones Lewis

death injuries, at the same time coping with her studies and the inclement weather, had been draining. Some tranquil days at Abberley with her beloved cousin to whom she now felt closer than ever would be a salver to her soul and she looked forward to it with relish.

Life at university was not easy for a lone girl in a male-dominated environment. Both her contemporaries and the lecturers alike regarded a female student less seriously than her male counterparts, the expectation being that she would meet a young man and abandon her career in favour of marriage and children. She was gathering her books at the end of a lecture and on the sidelines of an ongoing discussion by her fellow students, ventured her opinion. The response irritated her intensely.
"She thinks she's going to be another Barbara Castle," a voice taunted. "As if!"
She turned to face her detractor, one of the male students in her own year.
"And why not?" she challenged, keeping the manner of her response amiable, refusing to rise to the bait or be intimidated despite the irritation she was feeling. But the chiding continued on other occasions as it had done before. It was during one of these exchanges that her own personal ideology took a firm and decisive direction.
"If you want to be a serious politician you have to be a Tory," a male protagonist declared, knowing Lizzie's socialist sympathies full well.
"I don't agree," she retorted. "They're not the only option. It's a time of change. Change is on the horizon."
Her protagonist jeered along with his cohorts. But a male voice from behind them joined the discussion.
"I think the lady has a point, Warren. The country's in the mood for a change. The youth army is on the move and they want a socialist agenda, don't you think?"
Lizzie turned to identify the owner of the voice but was confronted by a stranger.

Monday's Child
Caroline Jones Lewis

"No chance," said Warren. "They have too much work to do. The Tories will be returned to power."
"This coming election, maybe but it will be short-lived. The one after that? The Socialists will have a chance surely. If you've done your homework – which I'm sure you have - you will know how strong the challenge is."
Warren shrugged his shoulders, suddenly unsure of his ground at the strength of this unexpected intervention. He was well aware of the mood of the country. His only intention had been to wind up Lizzie. He stood up, picking up his books and making to leave with his friends.
The slim young man, the owner of the voice, slid onto the chair beside Lizzie.
"Sounds as though your views are pretty much the same?" he said to her.
"Yes," she replied emphatically, turning to face him. "I agree with you."
Mmm, pretty, he thought. Beautiful eyes, clear and open.
"Of course there's a mood for change," she went on.
"People are fed up with the powers that be, old money, the old school, jobs for the boys. They want a government that's in touch with the needs of the man in the street, not a cabinet of wealthy cronies who conduct the nation's business behind closed doors with their own agenda in mind."
"Passionate as well as pretty," he said. "I'm impressed. Are your family socialist?"
"My immediate family," she told him, blushing at the compliment. "They've traditionally been Tory but have increasing socialist tendencies. My parents both work in the NHS. They see the need for change all the time and it's altering their own agenda. But my aunt and uncle and the rest of the family are staunchly Tory. True blue. Old money, public school – you know the sort of thing. They're good people but they vote the way their family have always voted without question. They will probably be horrified by the idea of a socialist politician in the family."

Monday's Child
Caroline Jones Lewis

She grinned at the thought and he noted the use of the word 'will'.

"So your mind is set – on your career?" he asked.

"Oh, yes. I'd like to think I can make a difference in the world. Improve the lives of ordinary people. And socialism is the only way I can see of achieving that. What about you?"

"Oh, socialist to the core," he answered. "I don't disagree with anything you've said. I'm a fully paid up member of the party. Maybe you should be too."

"Maybe I should," agreed Lizzie.

"So what's your name, my budding revolutionary?" he asked with a grin.

Such a disarming smile, she thought. Such a warm, engaging personality – quite charismatic.

"Lizzie," she told him. "Lizzie Hayne. Elizabeth really, but everyone calls me Lizzie. And you are?"

"Graham Morris," he replied and held out his hand in introduction. She shook his hand and then began to pick up her books.

"Nice to meet you, Lizzie Hayne," he continued. "Welcome to the cause."

******

To Nancy's enormous relief Eve's fever subsided as quickly as it had begun and 24 hours on Eve insisted she should return to her own place. While collecting her things together, Nancy related to Eve the events of the last few days, about Stephen and Adam and the Club, then the success of her meeting with Robin.

"He says I'm naturally photogenic," she said. "He has high hopes for my future."

"That's great for you, Nanc. It's a way out for you. You shouldn't be living this life. And when I'm feeling better I'm going to start looking for a way out for myself, too. All I need is a good rest now," and Eve sighed – a tired sigh that almost developed into a sob.

Monday's Child
Caroline Jones Lewis

Noticing Eve's emotional state Nancy was concerned.
"Are you sure you should go back to your own place yet?"
she asked. "You know it's fine for you to stay here.
You're still very weak."
But Eve was adamant.
"I need to be in my own space," she insisted. "I'm really
grateful to you, Nanc, but I need clean clothes and
everything. You know. Manicure the nails, wax the legs,
do the hair, all that stuff. It's just easier to do it at my own.
In any case, you've got things going on in your own life
that you need to get on with."
Nancy understood, though she would have insisted on Eve
staying had she still been really unwell. Now it was just a
matter of rest and recovery for Eve and she could visit her
daily to make sure she was ok. It was a relief to her, too,
to have her own place to herself again not to mention her
bed. The sofa was acceptable for a night or two but the
luxury of her bed to spread out in held increasing appeal.

She took her friend home by taxi, picking up milk and a
few odds and ends on the way to make them both lunch in
a bout of uncharacteristic domesticity and care. Eve teased
her gently and they giggled at the uneven cut of the bread
and unstable heap of sandwich. Nancy left her friend in
improving spirits and in a sudden bout of optimism,
decided to walk home in the warm spring sunshine. Relief
at Eve's recovery and the hope of better days to come
replaced the anxious expression of previous days with a
confident smile. As she approached her flat, she did not
notice a shadowy figure sitting in a discreet corner of the
coffee bar along the street, half concealed by the enormous
leaves of a rubber plant in the window. He had been
watching and waiting, convinced that sooner or later he
would catch sight of her. He watched her approach, noting
the carefree composure and smile and it angered him. He
slipped quickly from his seat and emerged into the street,
following her a little way behind. She let herself into the
building of her flat and unaware of any danger left the

Monday's Child

Caroline Jones Lewis

outer security door to close in its own time, oblivious to the later than usual click as it did so.. Swiftly Matthew slid inside the hallway behind her and ducked into the stairwell to watch her as she climbed the stairs to her door. Got you, my lovely, he thought, then followed her path up the stairs.

Inside her flat, Nancy stepped out of her shoes and dropped her handbag onto the coffee table. She glanced around her. The flat was unusually tidy, a supreme effort on her part for Eve's benefit and she liked it, the orderliness of it that meant she knew where to find things. I'll try to keep it this way, she promised herself. I'll really try. She hummed softly as she filled the kettle for coffee and twiddled the tuner knob on her transistor radio, abandoning the theme tune of Woman's Hour in her search for Radio Caroline. The radio crackled and hummed as she turned the dial, then the explosion of music as she found her goal.

> I'd like to know that your love
> Is love I can be sure of
> So tell me now and I won't ask again
> Will you still love me tomorrow?

The knock on her door took her by surprise and she hesitated. Who on earth? With Eve gone home at first she could think of no-one else who might call, then she remembered that Adam had promised to send their pay, hers and Eve's. In that expectation she padded in her stockinged feet to the door which she opened without alarm or hesitation. The unexpected sight of Matthew filling the doorway was a shock. He flung back the door with a thud. Disorientated, she stepped back and he stepped forward towards her.
"Hello, Nancy," he said. "Nice to see you again," and he closed the door behind him. His mouth was set in a cruel grin.

Monday's Child
Caroline Jones Lewis

"Since Mohammed won't come to the mountain, the mountain has had to come instead," he said and he took her roughly by the arm, leading her into the lounge.
"What do you want?"
Her voice was thin, her throat constricted with anxiety.
"Oh, I think you know the answer to that," he answered. Released from his grasp she turned to flee but he was too quick for her to reach the door and there was nowhere else to go. She was pinned against the door, his hot breath on her neck as he leaned towards her.
"The bedroom?" he asked and the involuntary flick of her eyes betrayed the way. He pulled her roughly into the bedroom and pushed her onto the bed.
"No," she began but he put his hand over her mouth, pinning her down with his body.
"Now don't be a silly girl," he breathed. "You know that you want to."
"No," she repeated and tried to shake her head but his grip on her was too strong and she found herself unable to move beneath the weight of his body. His hand reached up her skirt and ripped her stockings away, pulling her knickers down below her knees. Her mind was in panic, afraid to fight against him afraid he might disfigure her – or worse. Remembering the bruises of their last encounter she feared his ability to wreck her chances of a modelling career. If he killed her it would no longer matter to her – but her parents, her family. She recognised that resistance was futile and he took what he wanted anyway without compassion or remorse. She tried to blank out of her mind what was happening, concentrating on the music that was floating from the radio in the other room.

> Love Love me do
> You know I love you
> I'll always be true
> So pleeease – love me do
> Oh oh, love me do.

Monday's Child
Caroline Jones Lewis

When he was done he withdrew from her, leaving her shocked and sore. He stood over her still, silent body and tidied his dress.
"So good to see you again, Nancy," he told her. "But next time you could make a little more effort, I think, don't you. Be a little more inventive maybe? It's much better when you join in the fun. I like it when you make more effort – like before," and he laughed as he leaned across the bed. Next time. Next time. The words seared into her brain like a hot knife slicing through butter.
"See you again soon," he crooned and bent forward, kissing her dry, trembling lips and stroking the damp strands of her hair back from her clammy forehead. She heard him walk towards the front door, the clink of something else that she couldn't identify. She lay completely still, terrified, waiting for what seemed an eternity, then came the opening of the door and the click of it closing. For several minutes more she remained still, numb, afraid to move, then slowly she raised her head and satisfied that he was gone she went to check the door. In the hallway lay her handbag, its contents spilled across the floor. In the centre of the debris lay her key fob, and she saw with terror that her spare keys to the outer door and her own front door, kept in a typical lack of practicality on the same key-ring as the others, were missing. She sank to her knees and let out a cry.

Nancy lay on the floor for some time, curled in the foetal position, tears rolling down her otherwise calm face. When at last she moved, she rushed to the bathroom and bathed, scrubbing herself trying to rid herself of the smell of him, trying to wash away the feeling of being dirty, soiled goods. She could not stay here, not even for the night. She was no longer safe and the flat was no longer her refuge. Reacting instantly she reached for the 'phone and called Eve.
"Come right now," Eve urged her. "Just put the bare essentials in a bag and get a cab. He won't come back

Monday's Child
Caroline Jones Lewis

straight away. He's had what he wants for the time being and he'll wait to see if you do anything or tell anybody. So the sooner you get out of there the better. I'll be waiting for you."
Nancy needed no persuading. Within the hour she was sobbing on Eve's shoulder, cradled in her friend's arms.
"I suppose it's my own fault," she spluttered through her tears, aware that Eve had no idea of how she herself had behaved with Matthew.
"No," Eve gasped. "No. It isn't. You mustn't think that. He raped you, Nancy. It was rape. You should go to the police – only .. "
"They wouldn't believe me, would they?" Nancy finished the sentence for her. "He'll tell them that I slept with him before and he paid me. They wouldn't believe me."
Eve sighed. "Probably not," she agreed. "And they'd put you through hell in the process. Then there's the Stephen stuff, Matthew would make sure that would come out. But it was still rape, Nancy. It wasn't your fault. He had no right. You do believe that, don't you."
Another sob wrenched itself from Nancy and Eve held her close again, the only thing she could do to help her friend through the pain.

The two girls spent the night curled together on the sofa, talking, comforting each other for each of their troubles, until the early morning light.
"I've had enough, Nancy," Eve confided. "This life is no good for me any more. Nor you neither. This stuff with Stephen - but most of all the abortion. It's changed everything for me. Now this with Matthew, it's a warning for us both. And Dad has called me today. He's been trying to get hold of me for several days, apparently, while I've been at your place. My mother's sick. She has cancer. In the womb."
"Oh, Eve. I'm so sorry. Is she having treatment?"
"Surgery – then radiotherapy," Eve told her. "It was a real shock, I can tell you. I feel so guilty. I've been promising

Monday's Child

Caroline Jones Lewis

to go round for ages. You know how it is. I kept putting it off, tomorrow, the weekend, next week. I've not been a very good daughter, Nanc. Dad has asked if I can go to help sometimes. But I've decided more than that. I've decided to go home and look after her. Dad didn't ask me. He wouldn't. But I'm sure it's what he'd really like to happen. And perhaps when she's over the worst, the surgery and stuff, well, perhaps I could go to night school. Do shorthand and typing, or something. Secretarial training. And get a decent job with decent working hours. I want to leave all this behind."
"Is that what you want for your life, Eve? Really, I mean. It sounds a bit dull after what you've been used to."
"Yeah. Yeah it does. But I want to change my life for the better. Right now dull sounds good. When I started at the Club it was only to be until I got into real theatre. In my dreams, that was, of course. Then Adam got me involved in the other stuff and I wanted to make more money. Like you. Money for my future – that's what I told myself. But it's kidding yourself really, isn't it? Really it's sordid, sleazy and the chances of getting out of it get less and less as time goes by. You get sucked in more and more. Then you end up on the streets. The abortion was the end for me, Nanc. There's no way I can go back now. I want everyday stuff. Respectability. I might even find a nice guy who'd like to make an honest woman of me. Marriage. Kids. I'd like kids if I met the right man. And I think you should get out too, Nancy. This life isn't right for you neither. You're worth better than this. Look at you. You're beautiful. And funny and classy."
Nancy listened to her friend talk.
"Yes," she agreed. "This is the end for me at the Club, too. I'm hoping this modelling chance – a new future. But this Matthew, I've got to get away from him," and the fear etched across her face caused her voice to tremble. This world had now become a frightening place, this London.
"Can't you go home, Nanc. Your parents would welcome you with open arms."

Monday's Child

Caroline Jones Lewis

"No," Nancy was vehement. "No," she said more softly. "I'm too ashamed. You don't know, Eve – the selfish spoiled brat I was. The fuss I used to make over trivial things. The way I treated my parents. I know that now. I have to go back like a decent grown-up. If I can get this modelling up and running, then I'll go back. I'll ask them to forgive me. They know now that I'm ok. Hugh and Lizzie will have told them. But I need to find somewhere to stay – for the time being. Where Matthew won't find me."

"Well, you're welcome to stay here," Eve offered, "but I wouldn't put it past that evil bastard to track you down again. You can stay here for a day or two while we think of somewhere safe for you to go."

"Abberley," gasped Nancy. "That's it. I can go to Abberley. My parents' house in Cornwall. It will be empty just now. I could lie low there for a while – if only I can get all my things. And I'll need money. Our wages, Eve. Adam hasn't sent them."

What a surprise, thought Eve.

"Don't you worry about that," she said. "I'll make a visit to the lovely Adam. He'll pay up quickly enough. He needs to keep us sweet – and quiet. I'll put the fear of God in him. Then I can pick up your stuff and bring it here. But we'll have to do it quickly, before Matthew decides it's safe to pay you another little visit. We can do everything we need tomorrow and the following morning. Then it's you off to Abberley and me home to look after Mum."

Monday's Child

Caroline Jones Lewis

Chapter Ten – A time for healing

James delivered a weak but delighted Hugh to his Aunt Emily. He sank into a chair in the kitchen and savoured his first real cup of homemade coffee for what seemed an eternity. They sat together, all three, munching biscuits and discussing the arrangements for the next few days.
"Lizzie will be travelling down to Abberley with you and Mrs Hale will be coming in each day to attend to your every need. You know Mrs Hale – the original mother hen," said Emily prompting affectionate grins all round.
"I hope she doesn't do too much clucking," Hugh replied. "I remember what she was like if we weren't well as children. I have to get myself up and running again."
"Miranda will be visiting shortly too. Next week probably," Emily continued.
"Are you still apart, Uncle James?" Hugh asked.
"I'm afraid so," James replied weakly.
"I'm really sorry to hear that, Uncle," said Hugh. "Is there any chance …. "
"I don't know," James shrugged. "Right now we're more concerned about you, Hugh," and he went on to change the conversation.
"We're all so glad you're on the mend and I can understand you wanting to get back in the saddle but you must take it slow and steady. Don't overdo it or you could set yourself back again. Have the police made any progress?"
Hugh shook his head.
"If you ask me they aren't really trying," James grumbled. "I think we should make a formal complaint."
"Please don't," Hugh interjected. James and Emily looked at him quizzically, surprised by his emphatic tone. They exchanged glances.
Hugh considered. Was this the moment to tell them, he wondered, or should he wait until Lizzie was here, too. His uncle interrupted his thoughts.

Monday's Child

Caroline Jones Lewis

"Look, I know you don't like to make a fuss, Hugh – being a good chap and all that, but I really do think …"
Hugh interrupted.
"No, Uncle James. No, I mean it. The police aren't interested."
He breathed deeply and then continued.
"You see, I was leaving a gay club. I'd been there to see friends. Gay friends. Because that's what I am. I'm gay. So in the eyes of the police I'm a pervert and unworthy of sympathy. I got what I deserve."
For a moment James and Emily were stunned into silence, sitting open-mouthed in their stillness. Then Emily broke the tension.
"Are you sure about that, Hugh? You wouldn't be the first to have a temporary aberration."
"Yes, I'm sure," he told them. "And if that changes your opinion of me I fully understand."
They both protested without hesitation, James speaking first..
"Of course it doesn't. You're my late sister's boy that we have always loved and cared for all these years. What could possibly change the way we feel about you?"
"Exactly," Emily echoed. "How could that change?"
She reached out and took Hugh's hand in her own.
"Not everyone feels as you do," Hugh told them. "I have a friend whose family disowned him. It's really screwed up his head," he told them, now taken into confidence by Simon.
"And by the way," he went on. "Grandmother knows. It seems she knew some time back. Or at least guessed. Before I did, in fact."
"Well, she would, wouldn't she? She's a canny old stick. Doesn't miss a trick – Grandma," said James and they laughed together.

******

Monday's Child

Caroline Jones Lewis

The house was completely in darkness when Nancy arrived at Abberley, tired from her journey. She had forgotten that since her last visit the local station had been closed as part of the Beeching plan to streamline the railways, so the nearest stop was now in Truro. Then there had been a wait for a 'bus to the village and then the walk from the 'bus stop to the house which was longer than the walk from the station had been. Carrying a bag that felt heavier with each step, she cursed Lord Beeching in her tiredness.

Her first glimpse of Abberley bathed in soft mellow moonlight was a sight for sore eyes. With bags and baggage, she sidled as quietly and inconspicuously as possible around the lane to the back door. Glancing nervously over her shoulder to check she had not been followed, as she had done all along the journey, she dropped her bags and rummaged in her handbag for the key. The spectre of Matthew following her had been a constant concern. Now inside the house, she locked the back door behind her and for the first time in days she felt safe. Tears of relief were close to falling. She listened to the soft swish of the surf stroking the shingle beach and felt comforted. She switched on the light and Abberley, timeless as ever, welcomed her home.

Nancy studied the silent familiarity of the kitchen, the smell of lavender hung beside the fireplace and the garlic above the Rayburn, the gleam of copper-bottomed pans hanging on their hooks above. Tears began to fall when her eyes came to rest on Cassie's empty basket in the corner. It was only now that she recognised just how much she had missed Abberley and all that it encompassed. Unable to contain herself any longer, she kicked off her shoes and ran through the hall, up the stairs to her room and threw herself headlong into the quilted satin softness of her bed. The tensions of the previous days erupted in an uncontrollable flood and she sobbed into the pillows that smelled of a life abandoned so many long, long months

Monday's Child
Caroline Jones Lewis

ago. Finally, exhausted by emotion, she fell into a deeper sleep than she had managed for several nights.

Waking in the early hours, cold and to a room in darkness, it took Nancy a moment or two to collect her thoughts. Though the curtains remained open, the moon had disappeared behind a cloud plunging all into pitch blackness. She she reached across to switch on the bedside lamp. The sudden glare caused her to squint but as her eyes focused she looked around the room. Her old Ted sat on the cane chair as usual and cosmetics and hair spray remained on the dressing table where she had left them. Some of her clothing hung limp and lifeless on the outside of the wardrobe, clean and pressed and ready for her to wear as though she had never left. It felt so good to be back.

She slid from the bed both thirsty and hungry and drew the curtains for privacy, then made her way down to the kitchen. Realising that the house was warm and welcoming and not the cold, closed-up atmosphere she had been expecting, she was grateful that Mrs Hale had clearly been to the house in recent days. It crossed her mind that someone might be expected, a member of the family, but dismissed it as unlikely timing and revelled in her joy at having returned. She retrieved her bags from the floor and unpacked the groceries Eve had insisted on buying and packing so carefully for her. Minutes later she sat up in bed, washed and changed into a clean nightdress, hungrily devouring a ham sandwich and sipping a steaming hot cup of Horlicks. She remembered that she had not 'phoned Eve as she had promised, but at this hour it was too late and would disturb her family. She must do it first thing, she must remember, she reminded herself. She missed Eve already.

Eve was pleased to hear Nancy's voice.
"How are you doing?" she asked.

Monday's Child
Caroline Jones Lewis

"Oh. great," replied Nancy. "Being back at Abberley is so soothing. I'm still a bit sore and really shaky when I remember what happened. But I feel safe here. It's when I come back it will all start again. But what about you? How's your mother?"
"Ok, I guess. She's going into hospital tomorrow. We have to take her at 8 o'clock in the morning. She's quite positive about it on the surface of things but I think she's quite scared really. Dad seems to be taking it worse than she is. It's a good thing I'm here, Nanc. Honestly, I don't think he'd cope on his own."
"I'll ring you again in the morning," Nancy promised. "To see how things go at the hospital. Take care until then."
"Thanks. You too."

Nancy's day passed in a gluttony of nostalgia and the sea air, breathed in deeply on a walk along the beach, saw her ready for bed and sleep earlier than she had slept in months. She woke early the following morning and lay in the semi-darkness of her room. Through her open window came the distant sound of the surf and the cry of seagulls on the wing. Rising from her bed she drew back the curtains and light flooded the room, rays of sunshine bursting across her landscape. Throwing the window wider she breathed in the smell of the sea and the seaweed, taking in great hungry gulps.
"Oh, God," she breathed. "It's wonderful to be back to clean fresh air. To feel clean again."
The grubbiness that her life had become seemed a million miles away. Today she would take out the boat, she decided. While she was here, however briefly, she would cast aside her troubles and wallow in the joy of Abberley and everything that was here. Any days she would need to make a trip back to London to meet Robin. The anxieties would return and the need to find somewhere more permanent that was safe. Right now, she would enjoy everything that was here. She padded downstairs to make herself some toast and coffee and took it out into the

Monday's Child

Caroline Jones Lewis

garden. Still in her nightdress she walked barefoot across the lawn. It was damp with dew and she wriggled her toes in the soft, lush turf, loving the feel and the scent of damp grass in the early morning air. Her Mother would be appalled. She could hear her now.
"Nancy, for goodness sake put something on your feet. You'll catch your death of cold."
Nancy sat on a chair at the bottom of the lawn, looking out to sea. She could see Joe's boat out on the horizon.
"I suppose he knows," she thought. "He and Maggs. I suppose they know what I did, running away like that. Causing upset to all the family."
She wondered how she would ever face these people again.

Back in the house she set about the things she needed to do. She must ring Robin and confirm their arrangements. She would ring Eve, too and enquire after her mother and they could arrange to meet when she came up for her meeting with Robin.

The call to Robin was encouraging.
"We're on the brink of good things, Nancy," he assured her. "I need you to come tomorrow. If you could be here by midday then we can proceed from there."
It was arranged and the thought that she could spend the night in Brighton and see Hugh at the hospital the following morning cheered her more. Perhaps she could find somewhere to stay in Brighton. She couldn't stay here too long, safe though she felt from Matthew there was always the chance that one of the family might come and at the very least Mrs Hale was bound to look in at some point. She just was just not ready for their meeting yet. Or maybe Robin would have some idea of where she could stay, somewhere in a different part of London, the London of which Matthew was not a part. She would ask him.
"Now," she thought. "What next for today?"

Monday's Child

Caroline Jones Lewis

In her room a little later, bathed and dressed and tidying her room, the sound of a taxi pulling up outside took her by surprise.

Lizzie and Hugh let themselves in the front door.
"Hmm, the smell of that sea breeze, Liz. It's wonderful, isn't it?" said Hugh.
He walked gingerly along the hallway followed by Lizzie and the taxi driver carrying the bags. Lizzie paid the taxi driver and in a bout of generosity prompted by her delight in being at Abberley and with Hugh, she gave him a generous tip.
"Thank you, miss," he beamed. "Thank you."
She turned to Hugh who was standing at the kitchen window gazing out to sea.
"Oh, Hugh," she bubbled. "Isn't it lovely to be here. It seems such ages since the last time. So much has happened since then."
"It certainly has," he agreed. "We would never have believed then all the changes we would be going through before our next visit."
He settled himself into a chair.
"Coffee?" Lizzie asked.
Hugh nodded. "Sounds good," he said. "Shall I make it?"
"No," she replied hurrying towards the kettle and to stop Hugh from getting out of his chair. "I'll do it. That's what I'm here for."
"I have to start somewhere, Liz," Hugh insisted. "When I get home ….. "
"Well, you're not there yet. You need to take things easy, take your time."
Lifting the kettle she said in surprise, "the kettle's warm. I suppose Mrs Hale must have been. I expect she had a cup of tea while she was here."
"It wasn't Mrs Hale," said a voice from behind them.
Lizzie spun round on the spot and Hugh turned his head to the direction of the voice.
"Nancy," they gasped in unison.

Monday's Child
Caroline Jones Lewis

After the shock of their unexpected reunion, the cousins hugged and kissed. Tears flowed and over coffee at the kitchen table came the time to talk, particularly for Nancy. She kept details to the minimum, omitting the more sordid events that had overtaken her life since their last meeting; avoiding all mention of Matthew and the rape. She ended on a positive note with Robin and the prospect of a modelling career.

"So what brings you to Abberley then?" Hugh asked. Nancy had to fudge her reply, not wanting to confide her fear and her stalker.

"Oh, I just so needed some time out," she lied. "And after seeing you, Hugh, I did feel really homesick. But I couldn't face going to the house in London. So I thought I'd slip down and have a few days here. I know it's cheeky but …. "

"Are you going to see your parents?"

Both Lizzie and Hugh were anxious to know.

"Not yet," said Nancy. "Please don't tell them I'm here. Please," she begged. "I'm sorry for hurting them but … you don't know the reason that I left. I need to deal with that in my own mind. They know I'm ok. That I'm still alive. I will get in touch with them soon, I promise. But please don't tell them I'm here."

"You know they've split up," Lizzie said.

"No, I didn't," Nancy admitted but in view of the argument she had overheard that day in the dining room, it did not come as a total surprise. Was it anything to do with her mother's lover? she wondered. Was her mother now living with someone else?

"Nancy, they really need to see you," Lizzie insisted. "They've been distraught since you left. Won't you at least ring them?"

"It's true, Nancy," Hugh urged. "It's been heartbreaking for them."

"Look, you two," Nancy began. "There are things you don't know and I'm not going to tell you. It's between my

Monday's Child
Caroline Jones Lewis

parents and me. They will understand. They know. Now they know I'm ok, they needn't worry about me. Will you tell them that? Tell them I'm sorry for leaving the way I did and I will see them soon. But when I feel ready. I just can't do it right now. I have to make sense of my life first, a success. They'll understand that too. My pride, you see. If anybody knows me that well it's them. Will you tell them for me? Please?"

"Alright. But please don't leave it too long," Lizzie asked. "Is there a man involved."

"Oh, God, no," Nancy retorted. But she shivered, the memory of Matthew suddenly bearing down on her. Yes, she thought, there is a man involved but not in the way you mean, Lizzie.

She turned away to conceal the pain in her eyes but not quickly enough. Hugh and Lizzie exchanged looks of concern but neither wishing to draw her on a subject that she clearly did not want to address. So Hugh turned their conversation quite deliberately in another direction.

"How about a little walk before lunch?" he suggested. "Just to prove to Lizzie that I'm able," and he grinned at his cousin, the grin both the girls loved so much. Nancy's heart melted and she kissed him on the cheek. Hugh and Lizzie confided to each other later the change they saw in Nancy, the spoiled-brat schoolgirl who had returned a mature and sophisticated young woman who seemed to have consideration for others as well as herself.

They spent the rest of the day together, all three cousins, in gentle conversation. Nancy announced her departure for London the following morning and was unsure when she would return.

"But I'll keep in touch now," she promised.

The conversation turned to Hugh's attackers the circumstances of the attack and whether the police had made any progress in tracking down their identity. Hugh explained once more, as he had done to his Aunt and Uncle, the disinterest of the police for a particular reason.

Monday's Child

Caroline Jones Lewis

"I'm gay," he told them. "That's why. The police don't care, just another queer who got what was coming."
The girls were both stunned for an instant, then quickly recognised that it made perfect sense. Neither of them cared, they assured him, because they loved him unconditionally anyway and Nancy also because the last six months had taught her valuable lessons, to value those who loved her and to love in return without judgement. Like Eve, she thought.
"You're still with us, Hugh. That's what really matters. But what about you, Liz? Come on, your turn. Spill the beans. Any man on the horizon? No skeletons in the closet?"
Lizzie laughed, but then feigned a forlorn wail.
"No, nothing," she said. "Not even a drunken mishap. How boring am I? I'm such a swat. I've been so engrossed in my studies. I can see I have some catching up to do?"
"And no man on the horizon? All those virile young men at uni?" Nancy persisted, Hugh joining in the leg pull.
Lizzie blushed noticeably.
"Aha," Nancy pounced. "So there is someone. Come on Lizzie Hayne. What's the goss?"
"No, nothing to tell really," Lizzie protested. "Well, not yet anyway. But I hope, well ... perhaps. Yes, there's someone I really like. I think he likes me too but ... "
She paused, unwilling to say more at this point.
"And I promise," she added coyly, "that when there is something to tell, you two will be the first to hear."

******

Lizzie and Graham had become increasingly close, united by their political ideology but more importantly by a natural ease in each other's company. They were, it seemed, soul mates. It was an exciting time in politics. The student army, swelled by hectic building and populating of new universities, was well and truly on the march, protesting

Monday's Child
Caroline Jones Lewis

against anything and everything that smacked of the old order. They demonstrated against nuclear armament and the arms race. They protested against the Vietnam war. They campaigned for the legislation of abortion, for gay rights, for equal rights for women and for improvements in the NHS. With the explosion of the Profumo affair in which a Government minister had branded himself as a liar and a cheat and the defection of master-spy Philby to the Soviet Union, MacMillan's government was teetering on the brink of destruction. Harold Wilson's speech at the Labour party conference took MacMillan and his government apart limb by limb.

"Will it bring him down, do you think – all this scandal?" Lizzie wondered out loud.

"No. I don't think that's the plan," Graham enthused. "Just think about it, Liz. MacMillan's severely weakened now and he's lampooned all the time by the popular press and programmes like "That's the Week". If he remains in office until the election Wilson stands a much better chance of defeating him and the government than if the Tories have a new, clean leader. No, we need Supermac to stay." His excitement at the real prospect of a Labour government was contagious.

"Yes, I suppose that makes sense. He is a dinosaur, isn't he?"

The two young people committed themselves to the promoting of Labour ideals, conscious of the opportunity the coming election would bring for a Labour victory in a social climate ripe for change. Socially they enjoyed the fruits of young talent. They shopped at Biba, ate in multi-cultural restaurants that had sprung up around the capital. They went to concerts and films and watched tv where youth were the stars, the Kinks,, The Hollies, Small Faces, Pinter's "The Servant" and "Billy Liar". With the lifting of the BBC ban on previously taboo subjects – sex, politics, religion, even now the previously hallowed Royal Family – the floodgates had opened for the satirists – David Frost, Ned Sherrin, products of Oxbridge – who poked fun at all

Monday's Child
Caroline Jones Lewis

that had previously been held sacred. Lizzie's world that had been the secure and mellow locality of the Garden of England had metamorphosed into a whole new vista rippling with the vibrant energy of youth.

Then fate dealt what they feared could be a fatal blow to Labour hopes when MacMillan resigned because of ill health.

"It's just what we didn't want," Graham grumbled. "A new Tory leader. If they choose someone really switched on the next election would almost certainly go their way."

"We'll just have to wait and see, won't we," said Lizzie optimistically, an optimism that was ultimately rewarded. To their disbelief the Tories chose for their new Leader a former peer and member of the old school who, far from promising the modernisation the mood of the country commanded, symbolised a continuation of the stagnation under the old order, a regime not only unable to offer change but oblivious for the need of it at all. The Labour campaign team rubbed their hands with glee and returned to their campaign strategy with fervour.

"I should stay positive – like you, Liz," Graham said determinedly. "Promise I will be in the future," and they linked arms and headed smiling forwards.

******

In the house in Wilton Place, Miranda sat on the bed in Nancy's room clutching Nancy's favourite sweater. Her mood was one of desolation and she buried her nose into the soft warmth of the blue cashmere, breathing in to try and catch the smell of her long lost daughter – but there was little trace of her left. Tomorrow would be James' birthday and he would spend it alone. He had asked her to join him for dinner but she had declined, convinced that the evening would either descend into the acrimony that was their relationship these days or just be so strained as to inhibit enjoyment. Better that he spend it with family, she felt. Then her conscience had niggled at her so she had

Monday's Child

Caroline Jones Lewis

suggested lunch instead, perhaps an easier solution and God knows she needed the social contact. People who she had thought were friends of years had dropped her from their social calendar, the awkwardness of an odd number at dinner to be avoided and with her looks and intellect, a threat to the wives though nothing could be further from Miranda's mind. The husband of one had feigned sympathy, a shoulder to cry on but when the deception had given way to his true intention and he had blatantly propositioned her, she had been vehement in her rejection. "How can you. Your wife is my good friend. Even if I had such feelings for you, which I don't, do you think I could do that to my friend?"

"But why should she know?" he had laughed with a suggestion that she was merely being prudish. "Go on, live dangerously," he had chided.

When she had reinforced her rejection, he had suggested to one or two other husbands in their circle that she had offered him favours. Gratefully, since he had been known to them as a cheat and a liar, they had given it no credence but their wives wondered. It may not be true in this instance, but why take chances? Miranda had become all but a social pariah and her life a cultural desert as a result with the exception of one or two loyal friends.

Michael had not telephoned since her return to London following Nancy's disappearance but she had heard of his new paramour through the grapevine, a source of scandal among the gossipmongers who, gladly, had never known of their relationship. Their ignorance of a relationship between her and Michael meant they had no discretion in her company, freely indulging in their prattle around her. She would sit convulsed with pain. She felt herself betrayed on all sides and very much alone. And the greatest pain of all remained – the loss of her daughter.

Monday's Child

Caroline Jones Lewis

Chapter Eleven – Moving forward

Nancy's meeting with the fashion house went extremely well but she realised how out of her depth she was when it came to the contract. She had no idea of how to make head or tail of the legal jargon.

"You need an agent," Robin advised her. "Before you sign anything you need advice. But you shouldn't take too long."

"I won't, Robin, honestly," answered Nancy. "I really want this deal and I'm glad you're taking all the photographs. I just feel comfortable with you."

"Good. So do you know anyone who can act for you? Someone you can trust."

Nancy shook her head. Her father was the only lawyer she knew. He would be ideal, of course. But how could she?

"Not at the moment," she said. "But I'll give it some thought overnight. Could we meet to discuss it in the morning? I feel pretty tired. I need a bath and change and I have some phone calls to make."

Robin asked where she was staying and she described to him the B&B she had booked into near the station, an area she felt confident that Matthew was unlikely to frequent.

"So what are you doing for dinner?" he asked.

"I've nothing planned," she told him. "I haven't really had time to think about it."

"So why don't I treat you to dinner? Pick you up at 8 o'clock? There's a nice restaurant around the corner from there."

From the studio she telephoned Eve.

"How did it go today?" she asked her.

"Ok," Eve replied. "They took tests and things and if everything's the way it should be she'll have the op tomorrow."

"Hysterectomy?"

"Yes."

"How does she feel about that. I've heard it affects some women really badly."

Monday's Child

Caroline Jones Lewis

"She alright. I think Dad has helped her to cope with it. He's made her feel really secure."
"Well, I hope it all goes well tomorrow. I'll call you."
"How did it go with you?" Eve asked.
Nancy related all her news.
"That's brilliant," said Eve. "When are you going to sign on the dotted line?"
"Well, I have a bit of a problem to sort out first. I need someone to advise me on the contract and I don't know who to go to. The only person I know who's good at that sort of stuff is my father."
"Then ask him," Eve urged.
"Eve, you know it isn't that easy," Nancy protested. "You know it isn't."
"Yes, it is. It could be, Nanc. It could be that simple if you let it."
Nancy paused.
"I don't think I can," Nancy went on. "Just turning up out of the blue after the way I left. Not being in touch and then going to see him because I want something. That's typical selfish Nancy."
"I doubt if he'll see if that way. Oh, just do it, Nanc. Stop thinking about it and making excuses and just do it."
"You just want to see us reconciled, don't you?" Nancy challenged.
"Yes, I do. But you have to be brave about it and be prepared to take the flack. Then he'll fall over himself to help you, just to have you back. Because he loves you. They both do. And you love them, don't you?"
Nancy admitted to Eve that she was right but was still hesitant. She paused, and then said,
"I'll think about it. I will – honestly."

Over dinner she confided to Robin about her father, sketching over the details of their separation.
"He's the obvious person," she told him. "He deals with contracts all the time. And of course I would be able to trust him, wouldn't I. He would be acting in my interest.

Monday's Child
Caroline Jones Lewis

The trouble is I haven't seen him for months. I left on less than perfect terms and I haven't been in contact since."
"You had a row?" Robin asked.
"More like a war," said Nancy.
"And you've not spoken at all since?"
Nancy shook her head. "Not a word," she said.
"Do you want to be reconciled with him?"
"I think I do. I just don't know how."
"Well, he's the obvious person, then, isn't he? Perhaps you shouldn't think too much about it. Just take a deep breath and do it. Just pick up the 'phone."
"That's what my friend Eve said. But I don't know if I have the courage," she confided.
"Of course you do. Look at what you've achieved today."
"It's easy with strangers," said Nancy. "They don't know anything about you, do they? Those embarrassing details you'd rather not tell anyone."
"That's true," Robin agreed. "But that's just it with your parents, isn't it? They would forgive what strangers might consider unforgiveable. Their love is unconditional. That's what it means, isn't it?"
Nancy said nothing for a moment.
"I'll think about it," she said.
Robin grinned.
"I will, really," she repeated and grinned back.
"Good. Then shall we get you back to your B&B? You need a good night's sleep, I think. And I'll see you tomorrow."

******

At his office in the City, James Carlisle sat at his desk checking his diary, two silver-framed 'photos to the right of him, one of his estranged wife and the other of his long lost daughter. He greeted both of them in his mind every morning and said goodnight to them each night. His diary showed him that he had a meeting with a Client at two for which he must prepare. He opened the client file on the desk in front of him, placed there by his efficient secretary

Monday's Child
Caroline Jones Lewis

and he began to read. As a successful lawyer in the City he had built himself a reputation a decade before by successfully representing a member of the Sloane set accused of fraud, a contractual matter that ultimately proved to be untrue. Now engrossed in his papers, he paid little attention to the knock on the door, mumbling a brief 'come in' to the middle-aged bespectacled secretary or a junior member of staff that he expected to appear before him. He felt tetchy, a not-uncommon disposition in the post-Nancy post-separation days.

"Come in," he called again tersely when the door failed to open, still eyes down scanning the papers in the file. The sound of the door opening barely impressed him, still studying his papers, hardly hearing the soft footsteps approaching his desk. When no-one spoke he looked up irritably in anticipation of a shy polite junior awaiting his attention. What he saw rendered him speechless, kept him riveted to his seat. Then his eyes stung with uninvited tears.

"Nancy," he croaked. "Nancy."
"Hello, Daddy," she whispered.

Recovering from his initial surprise, he got up from his chair and walked around the desk, arms outstretched and pleading and Nancy sank gratefully, tearfully, into his warm embrace. I should be ranting at her, he thought. For all she's put us through. But I can't. I just can't.

James' secretary rescheduled his appointments for the day and he and Nancy left his office for the peace and privacy of his suite at his club. In the taxi he studied her more closely.

"You look good," he told her. "Different, of course, but good. Your mother will be surprised. So grown up now. And modern," and he grinned. "I'm not sure what she'll make of the skirt," he added and Nancy's hands went to her thighs, part covering the expanse of flesh exposed. She blushed suddenly aware of the length of it, or lack of.

Monday's Child
Caroline Jones Lewis

"Mummy likes fashionable things," she countered, smiling nervously. "She wouldn't mind."
James hesitated, considering her words.
"Wouldn't?" he asked. "Or won't?"
Nancy said nothing.
"I must ring her," James went on. "She'll want to come straight away. She's desperate to see you."
"No, not yet, Daddy, please," Nancy pleaded. "Can't we just talk first, just the two of us?"
Reluctantly James agreed but only too aware of how hurt Miranda would be at her exclusion. Despite her stringent self-defence he knew that she blamed herself for everything, for Nancy's disappearance, for the break-up of their marriage. It would be a blow to her that Nancy had not wanted her there. But he said no more, not wishing to do or say anything that might endanger this longed for reunion with his daughter. And if he were truthful, he was relishing in the joy of the moment for himself alone. He had tried not to be bitter towards Miranda but not always with success.
"It's my fault, isn't it?" asked Nancy. "That you and Mummy have split."
"No," James replied emphatically. "There had been problems between us for a while. You know that from what you heard that day."
"But you might have resolved things – if I hadn't gone off like that. I'm such a prima donna, aren't I? The way I behave. I don't mean to but sometimes I can't help it."
"Nancy, you were hurt. Shocked. That was understandable. Things may still work out between us. We don't know yet. We're certainly not rushing towards the divorce court, neither of us. The outcome will be the same with or without you. But of course we want it to be with you, for both of us."
He did his best to reassure her. This new concerned Nancy was something he wished to preserve but she deserved the truth now so he did his best to put her mind at rest. Nancy said nothing in reply.

Monday's Child

Caroline Jones Lewis

"You can see that, can't you?" he insisted.
She shook her head.
"I don't know. I can't have helped, can I?"
"No, that's true. Your leaving did bring things to a head perhaps sooner than it might otherwise have done. But that's all, Nancy. It wasn't your fault. You must understand that. Now – can you tell me what's been happening in your life? That's what I'm really interested in."
He listened intently as Nancy related brief details of the last six months or so, omitting the less savoury details and rushing on to her current situation. They sat side by side on as sofa at James' club, father holding his daughter's hand in his own as if afraid she may disappear again in a puff of smoke. He said little but inwardly disliked the thought of her in a club environment, of the lecherous type of men he imagined as the patrons, drooling and lusting over his beautiful innocent daughter. Still he let her continue uninterrupted. She came to the matter of her modelling and the contract on which she needed advice.
"Daddy, would you?" she ventured.
"Is that why you've come back, Nancy?" he could not help asking though he did not really care, just as long as she was here with him.
"It's why I came back now, Daddy," she told him. "I was always going to come back. Always. It was just a matter of when. I wanted to come back a success."
She paused and he studied her.
"Do you know what it took for me to walk into your office?" she asked. "I nearly turned round and left but your secretary kept encouraging me to come in."
He nodded, trying to place himself in the shoes of his headstrong and stubbornly proud girl.
"And you trust me – to represent you?"
"Of course I do," she gasped.
"After all you said last summer?"
"Well, you know me, Daddy. I always over-react, don't I? That's just me. That's who I am. Spoiled brat Nancy. But

Monday's Child
Caroline Jones Lewis

I'm trying to change. I really am. I've learned a lot since I left. Will you, Daddy? Please?"
There was another pause, not because James had to think about his answer but because he was too full of emotion to reply. He steadied his trembling heart and voice and raised her hands to his lips. Kissing her fingers, he said "Of course I will, darling. Of course I will."
They talked on and Nancy asked a long-outstanding question.
"My exam results," she said. "How did I do?"
"Ah," her father paused. "I promised your mother, Nancy, that she would tell you. Once we found you. It's a promise I can't break. Won't break."
Nancy bit her lip but said nothing for a moment, then "oh," was her only response, the expected protestation or attempt to cajole him into doing otherwise that would have come from the old Nancy failing to materialise. She nodded her capitulation ruefully. This could work, thought James with satisfaction. He would build up a store of questions that only her mother could answer until Nancy, curious as the proverbial cat, had no choice but to reconcile with her mother. Yes, he could make it work.

******

Adam had really tried with Catherine. I've been patient, he told himself. I really have but there's no avoiding it. The stupid little fool just won't take the hint. She'll have to go. He stood at the mirror in his flat above the Club fastening gold cufflinks into the cuffs of his shirt. He studied his appearance, adjusted his tie and in his vanity approved what he saw. It was time to be brutal, he decided. He had visited Catherine again only days before and stayed in an attempt to please her and soften the blow, stressing his case. But still she hung on, pleading for time. No more time now, he decided. It would have to be official this time, in the office. He went down to his office and sent for her as soon as she came in.

Monday's Child
Caroline Jones Lewis

"I've tried to reason with you," he told her, "but you just don't seem to understand the predicament you're putting me in. So I think it's best if you leave. Today. I've made up your wages to the end of the month and if you go and see this friend of mine, he has a job for you – no problem."
Catherine stood open-mouthed before him.
"But what about us," she stammered. "You and me?"
"I can't see you," he spluttered. "Not right now. I have explained it to you but you're not listening. I'd be ruined if my wife caught us out. And then there's the children. I have tried to make you understand, Catherine. If you'd listened we could have worked something out, got together again in a while. But not now. You just won't help me on this."
"I will, Adam. I will," Catherine protested tearfully.
"It's too late," he told her. "You have to go."
"What about the flat? How can I afford it on my own?"
He pushed the pay packet into her hand across the desk and guided her out of the Club, calling a cab at the kerb and pushing her inside.
"Just go," he snarled. "For God's sake just go."
He gave the cab driver her address and turned away, walking back into the Club without a backward glance as the cab carrying a distraught Catherine slid away from the pavement and turned the corner at the end of the street, the sound of the Supremes blaring from the cab radio.

> Baby, baby – baby don't leave me
> Please don't leave me all by myself
> I've got this burning, burning, yearning feeling inside me
> Deep inside me and it hurts so bad

"Not feeling well," he explained to the bemused staff who had watched her exit.

Back in his office Adam gave a sigh of relief. Two days later an envelope arrived on his desk. It was the keys to Catherine's flat and a handwritten note from her.

Monday's Child
Caroline Jones Lewis

"Dear Adam," she wrote. "I can't believe how you have treated me in the last few weeks. After all the promises you made. I'm going home to my parents for a while. If you remember what we shared and change your mind about our future you can call me. I will always love you. Catherine."

At the bottom of the page was a telephone number. He screwed up the note and threw it into the waste paper bin. "Thank God for that," he muttered and leaned back in his chair, putting his feet up on the desk and stretching his arms out from his chest. He smiled. Home and dry, he thought. Now all I have to do is keep my nose clean and work at retrieving my marriage. Flowers. Chocolates. Perfume. Jewellery perhaps, though his wife had family heirlooms way beyond anything of beauty he could afford. A holiday, maybe – a family holiday. Yes, a family holiday now that it looked as if the Stephen problem was going away. Somewhere warm in the sun. Spain. France. A cruise round the Med. Overseas holidays were a growing industry now. He would pick up some brochures before Friday, then go home for the weekend. He hummed to himself in self-congratulation as he planned.

******

Stephen's trial was a nail-biting time for Eve and Nancy as details of his sordid little social empire were emblazoned across the pages of the tabloids to feed the hungry curiosity of their readers. Nancy was even more ashamed of her involvement now and more determined than ever to put the entire episode behind her. She stayed at Eve's flat for a while with the intention of returning the key to Adam in a few days. Meanwhile she watched the streets carefully for any sign of Matthew each time she left and returned but so far was confident that he did not know where she was. She met Eve for coffee and they both confirmed their intentions to change their lives for the better.

Monday's Child
Caroline Jones Lewis

"We're lucky," Eve observed, referring to the publicity surrounding Stephen. "We seem to be free of it, thank God. The things the press are saying about Stephen. Terrible things. I don't believe some of it, do you, Nanc?"
Nancy shook her head.
"It's awful," she agreed. "And I liked him so much. Everybody did. Now they've all turned on him like a pack of hounds tearing him to pieces. All those people who were supposed to be his friends. You really can't trust anyone, can you? I thought all that stuff about Christine being a spy was just ridiculous. But this is just vicious. It's frightening the things people can say about you and just get away with it."
"He's been made the fall guy, Dad says," said Eve.
"What do you mean?" asked Nancy.
"Well, you know. Had all the blame dumped on him by other people. Dad says they're more influential than him so they've been able to cover their tracks and blame everything on Stephen. Rich people. Powerful."
"Do you think he's right?"
"Probably. Dad's usually right about these things."
"What – even the government?" Nancy was aghast.
"Especially the government. They'll do anything to cover up things they've been up to. You're so naïve, Nanc," said Eve. "Well, one thing's for sure. We've got to make something of our lives now. We've got another chance and we have to make good use of it, don't we?"
"Yes, we have," Nancy agreed. "It's good to be out of the Club stuff, isn't it? We're lucky, at least so far anyway."
Eve nodded. "So how's it going with the modelling?" she asked.
"Fantastic. I've had my first photo session with Robin and the results were really good. Robin was really pleased with them and the client was too. A cosmetic company is teaming up with the fashion house and there's a chance for me there as well. They want me to have my hair cut, though. I'm not quite sure how that will look but I guess I

Monday's Child
Caroline Jones Lewis

have to go with it. My hair's always been long. It will feel really strange to change it."

"You lucky cow," laughed Eve. "I'm green with envy. A hair cut's a small price to pay. Anyway, you'll look fab whatever you do with your hair. You're a natural."

"It's not signed up yet, though," Nancy bubbled on. "I've got all my fingers and toes crossed. You wouldn't believe the people I've met already. Jean Shrimpton – she's fantastic. Really special. I don't suppose I'll ever be in the same league as her but I'm going to have a damned good try. Terence Stamp, he's her boyfriend, you know."

Eve enthused. "Wow. Terence Stamp. God, he's a dish, Nanc. Did you see him in Billy Budd?"

"No, I wasn't allowed to go."

"Oh, well, it's bound to come back. We'll go, shall we? I'd like to see it again."

"Oh, Eve. It's so exciting. I really want to make it. Just think, all those fabulous clothes to wear. The best hairdressers. The best make-up. The best of everything. If I can just make this work ..." and she crossed her fingers in front of her.

"Of course you will. You'll make it big, Nanc, I know you will. You've got all the right things in the right places – and class with it. And what about your Dad? How are things? It's good of him to do your contact, isn't it?"

"Yes, and it's going fine," said Nancy smiling. "We're taking it a step at a time but it's good to be seeing him again. He's trying really hard to get me to see my mother though."

"So? Why not? What's the problem?"

"I don't know. But I'm just not ready to face her. I'm not – really."

Eve was persistent.

"You said that about your Dad, remember?" she said. "But you did it just the same. So what's different with your Mum?"

Nancy had no answer, other than to admit that she had needed her father at that moment, to suit her own needs

Monday's Child
Caroline Jones Lewis

rather than his. That made her selfish again, she acknowledged to herself. It was an uncomfortable admission.

"Alright, don't rub it in," she said, then changed the subject with determination.

"What about you?" she asked. "Your family. How's your Mum?"

"She's doing ok but it's tough," Eve admitted. "She's over the op now and she's having this radium treatment. An implant. It's really weird; like science fiction stuff. We aren't allowed in the room with her. We can only see her through a window. Like, she's radio-active. But it will be over soon and then we hope she can come home."

"How's your father?"

"Oh, Dad's doing fine. He's better now she's had the surgery. The doctor told him it was a success so it's all looking positive. He's talking about taking her away on holiday for a few days when she's strong enough. Nowhere fancy but just a break. And he's talking about buying a bungalow. They're building these nice bungalows at Wapping. Now Dad's earning good money at the docks he can probably get a mortgage so he's thinking about it. He says he's going to take her to see one as soon as he can."

"Wow, that's great, Eve. It will give her something exciting to concentrate on. Let's hope she'll be home soon. And what about you? Have you done anything about your future?"

Eve explained that she had been to the local technical college to make enquiries. She had put her name down to receive a prospectus as soon as they were printed with the intention of enrolling for a course for the autumn term. In the meantime, she was working in one of the local shops which would fit in with looking after her mother at home.

"The money's rubbish," she said, "but living at home I can make do on pennies. It will do for now. I'll start feeling the pinch when I run out of make-up and stuff. I suppose it will be Rimmel from now on instead of Rubenstein or Estee

Monday's Child
Caroline Jones Lewis

Lauder. Awful to be poor," she grinned and they laughed together good-humouredly.

"I don't care though," she went on. "I feel good about myself again which I haven't for ages. That reminds me," she said, scooping up her bag from the seat beside her. "Got to be in the shop in an hour and I need to leave dinner ready before I go so I'd best be off. Let's meet again soon, Nanc. Any sign of the evil Matthew?"

Nancy shook her head. She gave an involuntary shiver at the mention of his name. "But I'm still nervous, Eve," she admitted. "He could reappear any time."

"We'll just have to sort out your living accommodation as soon as possible," said Eve. "Somewhere he isn't likely to find you." She kissed Nancy on the cheek as they left through the door. "But you're ok at the flat for now. Just as long as Adam doesn't start pestering for the keys just yet. Still – we can cross that bridge when we get to it, can't we? Take care, Nanc. See you soon."

As though fate once more were on her side, a solution to Nancy's dilemma came of its own accord. Chatting over coffee with Robin during a break in a photo session, he offered a solution. She told him that she would have to hand in the keys to Eve's flat soon and needed to find an alternative.

"Well, how about that," he exclaimed. "Nancy, I've taken a new studio now I can afford something better. Thanks to you, that is. But I'll still have to watch the expenses. It's in Kensington, much more expensive than the south bank. But there are rooms above that could be used as a flat. I thought it would be a good prospect because I could live there myself if I needed to – if all else failed, give up my own flat and save on the rent. While the money's coming in, though, you could rent it if you like. Reasonable rent," he smiled. "Would that suit?"

"Do you really have to ask?" said Nancy. She grinned and kissed him on the cheek, a feeling that the sun had just come out and its warm glow was washing over her, and that

Monday's Child
Caroline Jones Lewis

not for the first time, a guardian angel was looking down on her.

******

On Friday morning Adam sent one of the girls from his office to buy a bouquet and chocolates for his wife. He would stroll round to the travel agents before he left for home, he thought - pick up some holiday brochures for places around the Med. His weekend bag was already packed and resting on the floor beside his desk. He had planned to get his business bits and pieces tied up early and leave around midday to surprise her. He could even pick the children up from school. Business was picking up now, too. The scare of the Stephen episode was wearing off and he could trust his manager to keep everything in order if he was away. His morning post lay on the desk before him where a staff member had left it and he picked up a silver letter opener, slitting open the first on the pile. Working his way through the letters he sorted them into piles, bills on one side to pass to his bookkeeper, job applications on another and membership forms to yet another and general correspondence that required his personal attention by his briefcase. He came to a cream vellum envelope with black embossed lettering in the top corner. Bartlett, Bartlett and Green, it announced. Solicitors. He studied it with apprehension for a minute before slitting open the envelope and withdrawing its contents. For Adam solicitors' letters were always to be regarded with a slight feeling of alarm. He was right to do so.

'Application for divorce on grounds of adultery' it was headed. "Regarding our Client Mrs Emma Scott-Edmonds," he read. Catherine was clearly named as co-respondent.

"I hope these are what your wanted, Adam," a voice was saying. "I think they've done them beautifully, don't you? And the white bow – that's elegant. Like your wife. She's so elegant," and a bouquet of enormous proportions and

Monday's Child
Caroline Jones Lewis

overwhelming scent obliterated the entire world beyond the jaw-dropping letter he still held rigid in his trembling hand.
"Are you alright, Adam?" the voice went on. "You look – umm – pale."
The doorman stuck his head around the door.
"Where do you want these, boss?" he asked, dragging into the office piece by piece a mountain of luggage.
For a moment Adam looked at him open-mouthed, unable to reply. Then he blurted, "What the fuck are those? Where did they come from?"
"They arrived by cab, boss," the doorman explained. "With this letter addressed to you," and he handed Adam an envelope bearing his name and written in a familiar hand.
"Leave them there," Adam instructed the doorman gruffly. "And close the door on your way out – both of you."
They left silently with raised eyebrows and an exchange of glances between them. Adam tore open the envelope and drew from inside a postcard edged in black.
"Yours, I believe," he read. "All the belongings you're entitled to. Don't bother to come here, Adam. Your key won't fit the lock. I'm sure you'll be comfortable at the Club – while you've still got it. See you in Court."
His wife had signed the card with an elegant and obviously confident flourish. Shock began to give way to a rage of vesuvial proportions. Adam smouldered.
"So," he thought. "She's after the lot, is she? Well, we'll see about that. I might have used her money to buy this place but it's me that's run it, built it up. I've put in all the work. She's not going to get away with it."
And so he began to plot, of secret offshore bank accounts and hidden investments. He would extract every penny that he could and if she wanted the Club, then he would run it into the ground. Only the barest of takings would hit the Club bank account now. Let her and her smart City lawyers do their worst. He was ready for them. He would fight them with every ounce of strength he muster. The bitch and her lawyers – he would outwit them both.

Monday's Child
Caroline Jones Lewis

Matthew saw the bags and baggage arrive from his table in the corner. He heard with satisfaction the comments of the doorman and the girl who left Adam's office. He was hopeful. One glimpse of an apoplexic Adam heading for the bar and a bottle of whisky told him all he needed to know. Things were indeed going badly for Adam – just as he had planned. And Adam would be too busy concentrating on his own problem to give too much thought to anyone else. Matthew knew well enough the torture of divorce, the cost not only in financial terms. He had been there, accused and found guilty of crimes he had sworn to his wife he had never committed. Now it was Adam's turn, a man far more guilty than he himself had ever been. He could leave Adam's life to run its course. Now for Nancy, he thought. Time for another visit to Nancy. The wound of her rejection still smarted and she must understand now, he reasoned, that she was his. She owed him her loyalty. And this time he would leave his mark in a more visible way. He touched the Swiss Army knife in his trouser pocket, feeling the cold steel smooth against the warmth of his fingers. He smiled. He was ready and at the very thought of her his mood metamorphosed from unreasonable anger into that of malevolent obsession. His mood was changing. Nancy, he vowed, was going to be his for good.

******

Hugh and Lizzie wallowed in the warmth and relaxation of the early Cornish summer. Lizzie followed diligently her mother's copious instructions, organising Hugh's diet and routine beginning with a nutritious breakfast each morning. She ensured that he observed his physiotherapy regime, gently improving his stamina and flexibility after a debilitating period of inactivity. In his good-humoured way, Hugh allowed her well-meant supervision fully aware of his Aunt's instructions and the recognition that soon he would be returning to his own flat where he would be able to do exactly as he wished. It was an eternity since he had

Monday's Child
Caroline Jones Lewis

been there and he longed for that routine, to be in control of his own life once amore. Everyone had been so wonderful to him but the stronger and fitter he became, the more he yearned once more for his independence. He felt glad to be alive. Even the reprobate Simon had become a regular visitor during Hugh's last days in the hospital, armed with grapes and apples and his own peculiar brand of humour and promises of help once Adam had returned home. Though there would be no further intimacy between them a kind of mutual respect was developing that served them both and he hoped would prove firm foundations for a future friendship. Simon unknowingly served a purpose in helping Hugh to rationalise his own sexuality. For Simon, Hugh was a crutch to lean on at times as he attempted to confront his demons. Hugh was glad they had remained friends.

So for now, Hugh was content to surrender to Lizzie's cossetting. Each day after lunch he would rest for an hour or so, then gently amble in her company along the coast path around the bay. The grasses were tall now, wafting in a gentle breeze that stroked a landscape dotted with wild flowers in all the colours of the rainbow and frequented by a myriad of insects. Bees and butterflies buzzed and fluttered busily between the vibrant pink of rose bay willow herb and the cool white of wild daisies. Deep in the vibrant foliage of vetch and gorse crickets drubbed a military beat and grasshoppers leaped from blossom to blossom. The day before Lizzie's return to university the two cousins sat together on the cliff top talking and peering out to sea through a heat haze. Hugh scanned the horizon through binoculars, searching for any sign of interesting wildlife in the water. Seals were known to frequent these waters at certain times of the year and sea birds fished the coastline. On this day,though, there was little to see, the sea too tranquil for much activity, the breeze too warm to stir the senses, a soporific stillness settled across the land.

Monday's Child

Caroline Jones Lewis

"What will you do about work, Hugh?" asked Lizzie, lying on her back and gazing up at the cobalt sky. Hugh sighed and let the binoculars fall and swing on their strap around his neck.

"I don't know yet," he replied. "I feel pretty disillusioned with the City right now. I'm lucky that I'm financially independent but I don't just want to drift through life. It would be so easy, wouldn't it? The need to earn a living must be a great motivator. Without that it would be just too easy to drift and while away a lifetime without making any contribution to anything in particular. But I need more than that, Liz."

He paused thoughtfully.

"I don't want to go back into banking," he said. "I know that much. It's really brought home to me what matters in life these last few months. I wonder now how I ever fitted into banking, such a self-centred environment. Everything is about self. About earning as much money for yourself and your bank as you can, not always what's right for the client. No, I'm pretty disillusioned with banking. Funny, isn't it – how you go on doing the same things day after day without question until something happens to make you change course. I never would have questioned what I was doing. I gave it my all. And then to be discarded in such a way ... I want to do something more ..."

He considered.

"What's the word I want.... Philanthropic," he declared. "Something that benefits people who are in need. Deprived. I don't know quite."

"But you will when you find it," Lizzie commented.

"Yes. Probably. I hope so anyway."

"Good idea," said Lizzie. "Yes, life's strange, isn't it? In the last year we all seem to have gone through some kind of change. Nancy, you, me. Nancy seems to have unexpectedly matured and tumbled by chance into a career when she had no idea before what she wanted to do. Suggesting anything to Nancy usually ensured her rejection out of hand. Contrary always. Now you're on the brink of

Monday's Child
Caroline Jones Lewis

discovering a new goal in life and I've changed direction myself."

"Hmm. The mood of the country. Of the decade," Hugh mused. He leaned forward on his bent-up knees and chewed on a blade of grass plucked from its sheaf. "Change is a theme that seems to be cropping up in all directions. Would you ever have thought a few years back, Liz, that young people would have such a say in so many areas of life as we do now. Setting the agenda? I didn't. We always deferred to our elders, our parents deferred to their elders. Now it seems as if the older generations are having to seek the approval of the young."

"Yes, I agree. It's extraordinary. Especially for young women. Young people have greater purchasing power these days so there's a whole new industry grown up around young fashion and music. The pill has given women sexual freedom, the option to determine if and when they have children. So now we can fight for equality in the workplace. Did you know there are more girls looking to go to uni this year than any previous year?"

"The spirit of Emaline Pankhurst renewed," observed Hugh with a smile.

"Yes and I can play my part," Lizzie enthused.

"You're set on a political career, then?"

"Yes, I am. And it's really exciting, Hugh. To be part of all the changes taking place in our society. I really believe that people are looking for change in the political sense. They're fed up with the current regime. Old money with old ideals. It's time for change, a break with tradition and I want to be part of it."

"What does that mean in domestic terms, Liz? A career instead of home and family?"

"Why can't it be both?" Lizzie argued. "Men have both. Does it have to be a choice for women? Wealthier families have always had nannies, domestic help, au pairs. Why not someone like me? I don't mean a full-time live-in nanny but childcare should be feasible. We have to make it possible. Encourage child-care nurseries – lots of them."

Monday's Child

Caroline Jones Lewis

Hugh smiled at her. "I'm impressed," he said. "All you have to do is sell it to the other halves, the men who'd rather have their wives at home warming their slippers."
Lizzie giggled.
"Yes, I guess. But why shouldn't they be happy with it. More money coming into the home. That benefits him as well as the children. A more interesting wife and mother. Wouldn't men like that?"
She paused, lapsing into her own thoughts. Hugh seized the opportunity to ask a question that had been on his lips since the last meeting with Nancy.
"So what's his name, then? This young man that you're so taken with. And does he share your view of the future?"
Lizzie blushed at the inference of Graham.
"Graham," she grinned. "His name's Graham and it's early days, Hugh. We've only been together a short while. Hardly grounds for marriage. But yes, I think we are like minds."
"Socialist?"
"Absolutely. But more to the point," Lizzie answered, "he's very fanciable."
"Lizzie Hayne," Hugh laughed. "I'm shocked. You brazen hussy, you," and he shivered suddenly as the weakening sun went in behind a cloud. Noticing the shiver Lizzie sprang to her feet.
"Come on," she said, "you're tired. Let's walk home and then you'll have time for a rest before Mrs Hale has dinner on the table. She's cooking us a special meal tonight. It's our last evening together and Aunt Miranda has insisted."

They strolled back along the path together, arm in arm in comfortable companionship.
"Wasn't it nice having Nancy back for a while," said Lizzie.
"Yes, it was," agreed Hugh. " A more likeable and mature Nancy, too, I have to say. Not that I disliked the old Nancy. Not really. I've always loved her and I've really missed her these last months. Christmas was so empty without her,

Monday's Child
Caroline Jones Lewis

wasn't it? Clowning about and such. But you have to admit that she could be a pain at times. You never knew when she was going to launch into one of her tantrums over some trivial mishap on someone's part. She could be vitriolic at times. And then it would be over in no time at all, as quickly as it had begun. The change in her is quite remarkable. I wonder if it's permanent though."

"Hmm, not sure about that. I can't help having this feeling that when she's back for real and the dust has settled the old Nancy that we knew and loved will reappear twice as large and making up for lost time," and they laughed together in agreement.

"There was something, though, Hugh," Lizzie added, becoming more serious. "Something's happened to her. Frightened her. I saw it in her eyes, just for a second. And then it was gone."

"Yes, I caught it, too," said Hugh. "I think you're right. Something bothered her. But what? And I hope it hasn't done lasting damage – whatever it is."

With Lizzie gone, Hugh spent much of his time alone reading in the garden, stretched out on the lounger in the warm sunshine, strolling the beach and coast path sometimes with Cassie the spaniel, watching through the binoculars for anything of interest, all punctuated by telephone calls from his watchful family and the attendance of the ever-dutiful Mrs Hale. One afternoon he sat at the end of the garden, book discarded for the moment on the table, lazily listening to the shrilling of a skylark high above. He peered upward to where the tiny dot swirled and looped, its lungs bursting with song. He felt like the skylark, bursting with joy at being alive, bursting with song. How closely his life had come to slipping away. A kaleidoscope of butterflies fluttered in ragged formation around a clump of lavender that edged the lawn and he watched them float between the blossoms, alighting briefly on one and then another. They reminded him of Simon, skittish and restless, then moving on and leaving no trace

Monday's Child
Caroline Jones Lewis

that they had ever been there. He smiled at his own metaphor and felt a tinge of nostalgia for the love he once had felt and for the person he had perceived Simon to be, a sadness at its loss. Out at sea a boat criss-crossed the bay on the horizon and as it neared the coastline, a familiar figure waved in greeting. Joe sailed up to the jetty to speak and Hugh walked down to meet him.
"You on the mend, then, Hugh?"
"Yes, thank you, Joe. Just a bit weak now, that's all. Just need to build up the stamina a little."
"Gave everyone a real fright, you did," Joe went on. "It's been a real worryin' time, what with you so ill and Nancy missin'. But I 'ear she's been in touch again now."
"Yes, she is, thank goodness. Yes, it's not been the best of times for the family, has it? How about you and Maggs? Are you alright?"
"Oh, aye. Can't grumble, you know. Well, why don't you come and see for yerself," Joe suggested. "Come an 'ave tea? Maggs'd love to see yer."
"What – now?" asked Hugh.
"Aye, why not now? Unless you've got someat else planned, that is."
"No, not at all," Hugh replied. That would be lovely, Joe. I'll just go and fetch a sweater and lock the door. Better leave a note for Mrs Hale, too – or the alarm will go off if I'm missing," and he grinned and turned towards the house.

Hugh spent a pleasant few hours with Joe and Maggs in their garden, amongst the hollyhocks and the lupins and the heady scent of roses. The dog lay at Hugh's feet keeping a watchful eye and Hugh stroked behind its ear.
"Is she alright – Nancy? Maggs asked.
"Yes, I think so," Hugh replied. "As far as we can tell right now. But I must say she's playing things close to her chest. Still won't see her mother, either."
"Funny do," said Maggs, shaking her head and Joe sucked on his pipe solemnly.

Monday's Child
Caroline Jones Lewis

"Worryin' for your aunt and uncle," he said. "Good lookin' young girl like Nancy on the loose goodness knows where. Anythin' could've 'appened to 'er."

"Yes," Hugh agreed. "We were all very worried."

"I dare say," said Joe. "Whatever 'appened to make 'er go off like that?"

"I don't really know," Hugh replied. And I wouldn't tell you if I did, he thought to himself, though aware that Joe and Maggs were not given to idle tittle tattle around the village, more an interest out of concern. "Some sort of row with her parents," he continued. " It must have been pretty serious but no-one quite knows what happened. At the end of the day it's between them, isn't it?"

"That man left after they'd gone back to London," Maggs blurted, then reddened, cross with herself that she had spoken out of turn.

"Man? What man is that?" asked Hugh, surprised at Maggs' outburst and her obvious subsequent discomfort.

"The man who'd rented the bungalow in the village," Maggs explained reluctantly. "A friend of your Aunt's, I think 'e was. E'd paid for the rest of the summer but 'e left after they'd gone and 'e's not been back since."

"Oh, yes, him," said Hugh jovially, loyally attempting a cover up in his ignorance of a matter that was only now casting light on a mystery.

"Yes, we were supposed to meet him but we never got round to it with Nancy rushing off like that."

So that was it, he thought. The eternal triangle and Nancy must have found out. It further explained the separation between his Aunt and Uncle. Layers of mist fell from Hugh's eyes like the veils of Salome dropping to the floor. Joe and Maggs would not approve of that, he guessed, any more than they would understand his sexuality.

"More tea?" asked Maggs, leaning towards him over the table and clumsily clattering her cup in her embarrassment.

"Not for me, thanks," Hugh replied. "It's time I was getting back. Mrs Hale will be in to make my meal. She's being very diligent in looking after me. My Aunt gave her

Monday's Child
Caroline Jones Lewis

strict instructions, no doubt. But it's been lovely to see you both. See you again soon, I hope."

He rose to his feet as an indication that he was ready to leave and Joe roused from his chair, knocking his pipe on the leg of his chair to extinguish the smouldering tobacco. "Right then, I'll drop you back," he said and they walked together towards the jetty.

"Thanks for the tea, Maggs," Hugh called as he stepped into the boat. "And the cake, of course. Delicious as ever. You've still got the magic touch, Maggs," and he waved as they pulled away.

"Just you come and see us again now," she replied. "An' you take it easy, mind. Don't you go rushin' about like a mad thing when you get back up to the smoke. Just take it easy."

"I will. 'Bye for now, see you soon."

"Funny business that, heh, Maggs," Joe commented on his return. "Young Nancy running off like that. Some funny goings on there, if you ask me."

"Yes, I think you're right there, Joe," Maggs replied. "I wish hadn't mentioned that man, though. It popped out before I thought. Could've cut my tongue out I felt that embarrassed. Wouldn't wanna cause any more trouble. Seems to me they've 'ad enough already one way an another, what with Nancy an' Hugh an all."

"Can't be 'elped, girl," Joe reassured her. "You meant no 'arm. An' if they will get up to these things … "

He trailed off while he packed his pipe with fresh tobacco,. "Life seems all topsy turvy these days. The swinging sixties, they call 'em. Swinging capital of the world, London – so they say. Don't know what's so different, girl, do you? Nothin' seems to 'ave changed much 'ere about, 'as it, except for the station closin' and that ain't much to be pleased about. Put poor old Ted out to grass, that did. Thirty four years 'e'd been Station Master of that station an' loved every minute of it. Worked 'is way up from porter when 'e was only a young lad. Now 'e's a grumpy

Monday's Child

Caroline Jones Lewis

old man with nought to do all day 'cept work 'is allotment. They'll be sorry one day, Maggs, when there's too many cars on the road and they're wishing people 'ud go places by train. An' there won't be none. All them tracks ripped up an' thrown away. Aye, they'll be sorry, you mark my words if they aint. They're welcome to all this change, it seems to me; all this change up in the smoke. Seems to 'ave brought this family nothing but trouble."
He sucked on his pipe and watched the tobacco slowly glowing red.
"Aye, Joe," Maggs answered reflectively. "Things 'aven't changed much in these parts 'an a good thing too, I reckon. Change is alright for the young uns but we're fine as we are, aren't we?" and the two sat in contented companionship, watching the sunset streak red and orange across the horizon.

******

Miranda arrived for Hugh's last few days at Abberley. She was to travel back with him to London and his flat.
Dressed and groomed to her usual chic, she presented to the world an air of irrepressible joie de vie. But to Hugh, there was an undeniable change. He noted the fine lines that had crept across her previously smooth forehead, the weight loss that had hollowed her cheeks a little and the outline of a breast bone visible between the reveres of an open necked blouse. He felt the burden of secrecy keenly, wishing that Nancy had not imposed on him the promised silence of her visit. Miranda kissed his cheek and hugged his shoulders, almost clinging as though she were afraid to let go.
"Have you enjoyed your time here?" she asked. "Has it helped?"
"Yes, Aunt," he told her warmly. "Very much so. Thank you so much. I think I was just what I needed to get back on my feet. Put my life into perspective, if you know what I mean."

Monday's Child
Caroline Jones Lewis

"Oh, good. I'm so glad," she breathed. "I must say you are looking more like your old self. Thinner, of course, but much more like the old Hugh. Thank goodness you're on the mend. Well, physically, anyway. How about mentally, Hugh? Emotionally. How are you – really?"

"I'm fine. Really," he told her. "At least, I am here. I may find it a bit more difficult when I get back to town, of course. I need to reassess my future. Find a new direction, and all that. I expect something will present itself. I'm ready to go back, that's the main thing. Ready to start afresh."

"Well, that's really good, Hugh. And we'll all still be here to support you, you know that. That just leaves Nancy to sort out. You know she's been in touch with James, I suppose?"

Hugh nodded. He longed to tell her that Nancy had been there at Abberley, with himself and Lizzie and to confide to her all Nancy's plans. But his hands were tied. He and Lizzie had promised to say nothing. At least she was now in touch with her father but Hugh felt for his Aunt whatever had happened to cause Nancy to run away, whether or not it was because of this man he had heard of.

"She won't see me," his Aunt wailed, close to tears.

"Give her time," Hugh pleaded. "At least it's getting closer. Whatever happened between you all to cause the rift, she's coming to terms with it – in her own time. She'll see you when she's ready. And in the meantime at least you know now that she's alright. You know Nancy. It will have to be in her own time," and he smiled meekly to encourage but feeling wretchedly inadequate.

"Yes," she replied, "you're right there. It will be in her own time." She paused, then "but I'm her mother," she whispered. "I'm her mother and she won't see me."

******

Sitting at a table in a Chelsea restaurant following her meeting with her would-be agent, Nancy and her father

Monday's Child
Caroline Jones Lewis

talked over the details of the proposed contract. Fortified by a prawn cocktail and healthy portion of beef Wellington, the details had been refined and by the time the pavlova was served a deal had all but been struck. With the agent's departure, James rested back in his seat and studied his daughter.

"Well done," he told her. "You were very businesslike, darling. I'm so proud of you."

Nance responded with a beaming smile. "I trusted you to guide me, Daddy," she told him.

"Well, there was a moment or two when I thought a Nancy-type tantrum might erupt, but no .... you kept your head. Well done," James declared. "Like the hairstyle, by the way."

He studied her thoughtfully.

"You really have grown up in the last six months, haven't you?" he observed solemnly.

Without our help, he thought wryly. Nancy felt guilty and embarrassed at her father's praise. If only you knew, she thought. The things I've done. Please God you will never know.

She raised her head and looked her father directly in the face.

"All those childish tantrums," she began. "So selfish. They must have driven you mad."

James grinned.

"At times," he agreed. "I won't deny it."

"Over such trivial things – I see that now, Daddy. But I couldn't see it then. Leaving home has done me some good, don't you think?"

James looked crestfallen.

"Of course. It's taught you to be independent, I'm sure. And resourceful."

He paused.

"It's taught your parents something, too," he continued purposefully.

Monday's Child

Caroline Jones Lewis

Nancy was quiet, ponderous, while her father took exaggerated time and effort lighting a cigar. Nancy broke the silence.

"I'm sorry, Daddy. I've hurt you more than I thought. I was so angry. I didn't think you cared that much."

"Oh, Nancy, how could you," he protested. "How could you really think that? You're the light of our lives – always have been. You must have known that, surely?"

"But you didn't really want me, did you? I was a mistake."

"Nancy, it isn't the conception of a child that makes a true parent – it's what follows, the love and care you put into raising a child for the next twenty years. It's a long-term contract being a parent."

"But Mummy considered an abortion. Why did she do that if you wanted me?"

"She only considered that when she thought I wouldn't want you or want to marry her," James protested. "But I would always have married her. I loved your Mother from the day I met her. There was no question for me. I didn't care two hoots what people would think of us when they knew she was pregnant. Telling people you were premature was really for her parents' benefit. To save their blushes. They were more conservative than mine. Once she knew that, you were as wanted by both of us as any baby in this world. There was no question."

Nancy thought for a moment.

"But you were tetchy with me so often," she explained. "When I heard you having that row I thought it was because you had never really wanted me."

"There are times for any parent when they lose their patience, when you sound off. And you must admit, have already said, there were times when you could really try our patience. But you don't stop loving, darling. There are times when you don't like things about your child, about their behaviour, but you never stop loving them - never. We've missed you so desperately. We're just relieved that you're safe and well after all the worry. Anything could

Monday's Child
Caroline Jones Lewis

have happened to you. There are some bad people out there."
Nancy knew all too well. Tears welled involuntarily in her eyes.
"I'm sorry," she repeated.
"Come on," James suggested, wishing to alleviate the touchiness of the subject, "let's go and walk," and he signalled the waiter for the bill.
"It's been settled, sir," he was told. "The other gentleman."
"Fine, thank you," and James rose to his feet and guided his daughter gently to the door.

They turned towards the river and strolled along the embankment towards the City, arm in arm, talking intimately until they reached Vauxhall Bridge where Nancy would go on to meet Robin.
"Thank you, Daddy," she ventured. "For everything. I'll make it up to you, you'll see."
"And you mother?" he asked. "Will you meet her and make it right with her, Nancy?"
"I'll try – soon," she promised.
"Whatever the rights and wrongs of what she did to me, she's your mother and she loves you. She's always loved you, always will. The first step needs to come from you, you realise that, don't you? It was you who rejected her. So it's you who must take the first step back."
Nancy nodded.
"I will. I will, I promise. I'm just not ready yet."
"The longer you put it off, the harder it will become to break the ice. So don't leave it too long, will you?"
Nancy agreed.
"When will I see you?"
"I'll ring you," she said. "In a day or two."

James kissed her forehead and waved as she crossed the road, heading towards her meeting with Robin. He watched her recede into the distance before resuming his own journey to his office. He would ring her mother and put her

Monday's Child

Caroline Jones Lewis

mind at rest. His anxiety over Miranda's health and welfare increased each time they met, their meetings becoming more frequent now that a state of impasse had been reached between them. He still loved her and was hopeful that one day they, too, would be reconciled. But it was Miranda who set the pace, he recognised and believed that Nancy was crucial to that process. Please, he thought, let it be soon. In the meantime, Miranda's state of mind remained fragile, racked with guilt and confusion as to her own purpose and future. Please, Nancy, he repeated, let it be soon.

******

Hugh stood at the window of his sitting room drinking in a view he had been longing to see for months. It seemed to him an eternity since he had looked out on this familiar tree-lined street, the elegant terrace of houses sweeping grandly into the distance. It was a haven of tranquillity in the hustle and bustle of the busy capital. His Aunt had now left and at last he was alone and where he belonged. It was a luxury. The flat was immaculate, cleaned and polished to perfection by Aunt Miranda's daily who had been despatched with instructions to make it ready for his return. A vase of fresh roses from her garden scented the living room and the smell of lavender polish was all around him. On his desk his latest post was piled neatly for his attention and by habit he picked it up to open it, then changed his mind, deciding it could wait until tomorrow. Today, he told himself, he would just enjoy the luxury of being home. He emptied his case and put away his belongings, clean clothes in the bedroom, dirty ones in the laundry bin. Then equipped with a freshly made cup of coffee, he settled himself in an armchair by the window to read his daily paper.

To his satisfaction the tedium of the Profumo affair had been replaced on the front pages by a daring raid on the

Monday's Child
Caroline Jones Lewis

Glasgow to London mail train. Over £2. Million in used banknotes had been stolen by a gang that held up the train in the Buckinghamshire countryside. He whistled in astonishment. "£2. Million," he muttered. "That must have taken some planning." Any admiration for the perpetrators was short lived when he read on and learned of the serious injury inflicted on the train driver who clung to life following a blow to the head that had rendered him unconscious. They were reduced in the eyes of the public to no more than a gang of thugs. There was much else happening in the world too. In France, President De Gaulle continued to be a thorn in the side of the British over their application to join the European Community. In the USA, President Kennedy continued to woo the world following his recent 'Ich bin ein Berliner' speech and Martin Luther King carried a groundswell of public affection in his fight for black equality. Closer to home, black clouds marred the horizon in Ulster where sporadic protests and violence erupted on a daily basis. The world was truly changing, not just his world but the wider world around him.
"Perhaps I'll get a tv," he thought. "It would be good to see these things on tv." It seemed to be the thing these days and since he was toying with the idea of going into journalism, he needed to be well informed. There were really good programmes on current affairs now. His former colleagues at the bank were regular viewers. He set himself a task for the following day, a first gentle trip to Oxford Street to buy a tv, maybe refresh his wardrobe a little with one or two new pieces of clothing to change his image. His joy at having survived the attack had inspired a desire to reinvent himself, to discard the old persona of the bank employee and emerge as a new and younger version of himself. Maybe he would have a new hairstyle, too. He was mulling over the options when his telephone rang and he answered to hear Simon's voice down the line proposing a visit with Chas and Edward over the weekend. While chatting to his friend, Hugh's eyes fell absentmindedly on an advert in the Evening Standard. "Required by the

Monday's Child
Caroline Jones Lewis

Homosexual Law Reform Society' it read; "Financial Administrator." He knew at once that he would apply. He was sure in his mind that he would be successful.

******

Despite the warmth of the day, Miranda shivered as she heard the news report on the radio. She sat in her daughter's bedroom hugging a scruffy worn teddy that had been Nancy's 'comfort blanket' as a small child. She mourned her absence. Her girl was safe and well, she knew that much, thank God. But Nancy's avoidance of her mother was a wound in Miranda's breast that ached and agitated alternately depending on the time of day. In daylight hours it was almost bearable but in the darkness of the early morning it swelled to a crescendo that sent her wandering around the empty house, gravitating towards the kitchen and the kettle to make a cup of coffee. She would sit at the kitchen table staring down into her cup and wondering for a millionth time where her missing girl might be just at that moment. Today a young girl had been reported missing. The Manchester police were searching. 16 year old Pauline Reade had disappeared without warning, without reason, without a word of explanation on her way to a disco Her family were in limbo, desperate for a solution and her return but dreading the knock on the door that may bring them unwelcome news. For Miranda it had re-awakened the shock and fear of Nancy's disappearance. She had taken a walk to her local church, sitting in a pew for what seemed hours, praying with her head bowed and tears in her eyes. "Don't do this," she told herself. "Stop torturing yourself. Your child is not missing. Not now. Only absent. And one day she'll come home – to you. One day."

She rose and crossed the nave, lighting first one candle, then another – one for her own daughter and one for Pauline Reade. As she placed them in the holder a shaft of sunlight broke through the stained glass window behind

Monday's Child
Caroline Jones Lewis

her, piercing the gloom and sending streaks of light cascading across the flagstones in a kaleidoscope of colour. "You see," she comforted herself. "You see, he is listening. God is listening. They'll come home, both of them. You'll see." She could not know how wrong she would be.

Monday's Child

Caroline Jones Lewis

Monday's Child
Caroline Jones Lewis

Chapter Twelve – Falling back

Now installed into the flat above Robin's studio, Nancy felt a little more secure – but only a little. The fear of Matthew still shadowed her every time she stepped out of the door. She rarely left the building alone. On good days her natural spirit would rile against it and she would promise herself that tomorrow she would break out of the cocoon her life had become, trapped like an animal in a cage. She would not allow him to do this to her life. But when tomorrow came, her fear would close in once more and though she had been nowhere near the Club or her old flat, London these days seemed a very small place where, she was convinced, Matthew was bound to find her. She had told no-one other than Eve about the rape though once or twice Robin had asked her if something was wrong, curious about her lack of friends and social activity. For someone as gregarious and sociable as Nancy, it seemed to him to be strange. Then there had been the time when, coming up behind her, he had lightly placed his hand on her shoulder, not in a sexual way – more in the manner of affection. The unexpected touch had made her jump, to withdraw from his touch as though she had been stung. He felt that something was wrong. He had asked her tentatively if everything was alright with her but she had denied any problem and for the time he had let it be, concentrating on their professional involvement and the success for them both that he knew was within their grasp. Even so, he took care not to repeat the incident and was watchful of others around her.

Nancy had declined the offer of a loan from her father, determined to remain independent now that financial solvency was within sight. All efforts to reunite her with her mother had so far failed. Stephen's trial continued to give vent to lurid reporting by the tabloids ensuring that both she and Eve kept their heads down, though there had been no mention of the Club or of Adam, which hopefully was a sign that no connection had been made. One

Monday's Child
Caroline Jones Lewis

Tuesday evening, however, Nancy arranged to meet Eve at a 'pub south of the river where Eve now lived. They both felt the area would be Matthew free, his lifestyle restricting his movements to the fashionable part of town. The shock news of Stephen's suicide in prison had rocked them and they both felt the need to share their feelings in a way they could do with no-one else. Nancy took the Circle Line to Tower Bridge and on a whim decided to cross the bridge on foot. She emerged into the street at the side of the Tower in the fading light of evening. She had no way of knowing that Matthew had taken to occasional trawling of the south side of the river in search of ladies of the night willing to indulge his particular sexual preferences. So it was quite by chance that from a telephone box beside the Tower, scanning the business cards wedged in the window panes, he caught sight of her approaching the bridge. Quite by chance, too, that to read the cards he had donned his spectacles which, out of vanity, he rarely wore. Without them he may never have spotted her, his myopic vision would have made it impossible to identify her features at such a distance. He could barely believe his luck. It was – unmistakeably – Nancy. It must be destiny, he thought, to find her so unexpectedly, so naturally, like spotting an old friends across a crowded room. All the times he had watched for her at the Club, waited around her flat, with no success. Now here she was, alone and within his grasp.

Immersed in her thoughts as she crossed the bridge, being a little early and feeling confident for a moment in her safety, Nancy had paused to watch a barge edging its way to the south bank and mooring alongside a warehouse. It was only a moment, but her guard was down. On a fine evening like this she would have liked to stroll along the river, relaxed and chatting with her friend. Then remembering the constant risk that stalked her, she moved on and entered the 'pub where she and Eve had arranged to meet. Matthew watched her and found himself a discreet vantage point to await her reappearance. Emotions simmered inside his

Monday's Child
Caroline Jones Lewis

head. Questions bombarded him. Was she meeting a punter, some other man who had no right to her as he did? Why else would she be visiting this side of town? Concealing himself amongst the bushes outside a boarded up building, he settled in anticipation of a long wait.

Inside the 'pub Eve and Nancy commiserated over a drink or two, confiding their shock and sadness at Stephen's demise, the manner of his passing and a sense of injustice at the treatment he had received. They caught up on the events in their lives.
"Hair looks fab, Nanc," Eve complimented. "Told you it would. You can get away with anything."
"Yes, I really like it now. But it takes ages to do in the mornings. I have to comb and comb it until it's just right. Long hair is much easier, Eve."
Noticing the fading light outside Nancy rose to leave and her nervousness was building.
"I need to get back to the studio," she said. "I don't like being out too late," and understanding her anxiety Eve agreed.
"Don't worry," she told her, "I've got us a cabbie. He's a friend. I've just told him you had a bad experience – a guy who followed you. He's a big chap. He'll see you're ok. Anyway, I'm coming with you and then he'll drop me home."
"Oh, thanks, Eve. I can't imagine Matthew would be in this part of town but … well, I just can't seem to .. "
Nancy paused, choking on her words and Eve touched her shoulder in comfort, then made a phone call from a pay phone in the corner of the bar. The toot of a horn in the street signalled the cabbie's arrival and the two girls piled into the cab and were whisked away. From his hiding place Matthew watched and simmered in anger and disappointment. He emerged back into the street, walking blindly towards the bridge in his frustration.

Monday's Child
Caroline Jones Lewis

"No matter, Miss Nancy," he fumed. "Now I know where I can find you. You'll be back no doubt - you and your friend – and I'll be waiting."
He walked back across the bridge towards the City. Aroused by his anger, he needed a woman, a whore on whom to vent his frustration. He knew of a girl, off Whitechapel. He called her from a phone box and then headed towards her address.

******

Some days later and with a growing confidence of her safety on the South Bank, Nancy had no problem in meeting Eve at the same place. She missed Eve's company and the down to earth support that Eve gave her. This time she took a cab to the 'pub and Eve was already there waiting. Matthew was not there when she arrived but he was certainly there when she left. Peering through the windows into the smoke-filled bar he had spotted the two girls seated at a table and engrossed in conversation. He had hired a car for the purpose, an inconspicuous beige Cortina like every other beige Cortina on the road. Parked just on the corner, the 'pub door was visible from the driver's seat where he sat awaiting her departure, a trilby pulled down across his forehead and dark lenses clipped onto his spectacles. After about an hour, the girls emerged and flagged down a passing taxi.
"Belvedere Mews," Nancy told the driver and kissing Eve on the cheek she climbed into the cab leaving Eve to head in the opposite direction. As Eve closed the taxi door, she caught sight of the driver of a beige Cortina spurting into action, turning into the road and setting off in the direction of Nancy and her cab.
"Oh, my God," she gasped. "It's him. It's Matthew."
Then, "Nancy, she thought, he's after Nancy. She slid open the partition window between herself and the driver as both Nancy's cab and the Cortina disappeared over the rise of the bridge.

Monday's Child
Caroline Jones Lewis

"Take me to Kensington," she instructed. "Belvedere Mews. Quickly. It's urgent."
Fired by the urgency of her instruction, the cabbie swung the vehicle in a tyre-squeaking u-turn and headed back across the bridge.

Nancy was astonished to open the door to her friend's urgent yelling.
"Oh, Nancy. Thank God," she breathed and pushed her friend back into the flat, slamming the door behind her and shooting the bolts at the top and the bottom.
"He was there," she explained, confronted by Nancy's vacuous uncomprehending stare. "Matthew. He followed you. He was grinning, Nanc. A horrible evil grin."
Nancy paled. Eve propelled her into the studio and hurried to peer through the slats of the closed blinds. The street was virtually empty except for a beige Cortina which, having parked further along the street when first arrived, now slid away, its driver confounded from his purpose by the sight of Eve's urgent arrival.
"He followed you," she gasped. "I saw him – see, that car there," and they both peered out of the window just in time to see the Cortina turn the corner and disappear from the street.
"I'm staying with you tonight," Eve announced. "Where's the 'phone? I just need to ring Dad. I'll tell him you're sick, or something. And in the morning we'll get you into a hotel or something. Anywhere as long as it isn't here."
"But I can't," Nancy spluttered. "I can't move again, Eve. I like it here. And it's so convenient – working with Robin and all that. I can't let Matthew do this to me. Not again. What am I going to do?"
They faced each other, neither able to provide an answer. But one thing Nancy did know for sure. The anger at Matthew's rape and his subsequent threats that until now had been subjugated by fear was gathering momentum. She was getting stronger, the spirit that had been bruised by the experience of Matthew was healing and she was not

Monday's Child
Caroline Jones Lewis

prepared to have her future continuously dictated by fear. It was time to take a stand. Even so, sleep eluded her and she rose next morning looking peaky and ill-prepared for a day before the camera.

Matthew was ecstatic at his success in tracking Nancy down. It had been frustrating that his ultimate goal had been foiled on this occasion but no matter, things were at last going his way. He would return the car first thing in the morning – it had served its purpose. Then he would do a proper reconnaissance of the area. It would be easier on foot as parking was so difficult in this part of town. In the darkness he had parked around the corner and walked back past the building into which the girls had disappeared, hugging the side of the buildings for cover and noting the security arrangements in place. 'Robin Selway', the sign had read. 'Photographer'. So that was it. There was another man involved. Well, not for long, he vowed. He would deal with him if necessary. Now he had found her again he had no intention of letting her go. He returned home and slung his keys on the table, pouring himself a whisky and taking a large slug in one gulp.
"At last," he muttered. "Things are going my way."
And when I get her, I won't punish her, he thought. I'll be forgiving. Magnanimous. She'll see then that I'm good for her and we are meant to be together. For always. Here in my home. She'll grow her hair again and be the person she used to be, not this image other people had turned her into and he glowed at the prospect of the pleasure that would bring.

******

On Sunday morning a week or so later, Nancy telephoned Hugh from the studio.
"Can I come round, Hugh?" she asked. "Are you going to be home today?"

Monday's Child
Caroline Jones Lewis

She felt lonely. Eve was busy with her own life right now and Nancy had made no other friends since leaving the Club. Though spring had eased into mid-summer, the morning's weather was dismal, a warm drizzle saturating the City streets so the pavements shone as though they were polished. Despite her resolve not to be forced by fear to find another bolt hole, Nancy felt imprisoned once more by the ever-present threat of Matthew. She had seen nothing of him since the last outing with Eve, but had made sure she did not set foot outside the studio alone. Today Robin was not working, visiting family and so absent from the studio. The thought of the entire day alone and trapped in the building was more than she could bear. If she went to visit Hugh she could taxi either way and ask the driver to wait and see her safely back through the studio door.

"Now where else would I be on a day like this?" Hugh replied laughing. "Why don't I make lunch?" he suggested, "and I know Liz is home this weekend so I could ring and ask her if she's free to come, too. If she caught the midday train we could all have lunch together and have a real catch up on the gossip."

"Oh, Hugh, that would be great. I'll come round, then . As soon as I've done my hair."

That gives me an hour or so, thought Hugh, grinning to himself.

Lunch, as usual where Hugh was concerned, was of culinary excellence. Mellowed by good food and wine, the three cousins indulged in gossip and reminiscence and general chit chat about their lives as they sat comfortably around the table. The fruits of Nancy's first modelling sessions were beginning to appear in fashion mags and as usual she held centre stage, bubbling on about the ins and outs of the modelling profession. She dropped a famous name or two, well-known celebrities of the fashion world that fell on stony ground with a bemused and fashion free Lizzie whose clothes were bought for practicality and economy. Lizzie was contemplating her second year at uni

Monday's Child
Caroline Jones Lewis

with relish, securely focused on a political career with a socialist agenda that left Nancy unmoved. Hugh had secured the job with the Homosexual Law Reform Society and found himself immersed in a world a million miles away from his banking background. All three cousins were in positive mood and encouraged for their future prospects.

Lizzie and Hugh had been intrigued in recent weeks about the unseen but ever-present Robin who perhaps, they pondered, was the subject of a romantic interest for Nancy. "She talks about him such a lot," Lizzie had observed to Hugh during an earlier telephone conversation. "That's usually a sign of attraction. But she's never mentioned anything like a date. Well, not to me, anyway."
"No, not to me either," Hugh had replied. "I don't know if it's purely professional or something more. We'll have to ask a few probing questions when we get the chance."
Lunch presented the opportunity.
"So what about this Robin, then, Nanc?" ventured Lizzie with a grin, raising her eyebrows and throwing a knowing glance at Hugh. Whether Nancy was oblivious to the implication or merely side-stepping the issue was hard to tell as she babbled on.
Oh, he's lovely," she cooed. "He's so enthusiastic about his work. You can see just by watching him that he loves what he does. And God, he's so patient with me. He just points out to me how I could stand or move or raise my head or whatever. He never gets tetchy with me or anything, me being so inexperienced and everything."
"He sounds interesting," Lizzie persevered. "Perhaps we'll get to meet him sometime."
"Well, why don't you come back with me to the studio," suggested Nancy. "He's going to be back about tea time. He's usually there all day on Sundays but he had family stuff to do today. He just loves showing people his work and I'm sure he'd like to meet you. Oh, do. Please," she begged. "And I could show you the flat at the same time. Please," she cooed.

Monday's Child
Caroline Jones Lewis

So it was agreed.

"Now, couz. Come on, give us the gossip on this Graham of yours. Are there wedding bells in the air?"

"Oh, Nancy, for heaven's sake," Lizzie defended. "That's the last thing on my mind right now. I have to get my degree first. Then my career. That's the next thing."

"What about Graham," asked Hugh. "What's he planning to do?"

"Journalism, he hopes. Political. Actually he'd like to get into TV. Political satire is all the thing now. You know – Ned Sherrin, Peter Cook, David Frost. He loves 'Beyond the Fringe'. Never misses it. The TV in the common room is always on for that. But in any case journalism of some sort."

"Not another would-be politician, then?"

"No. He just wants to report it or comment on it – not be in Parliament himself. But he's very supportive of me. We both want to make changes for the ordinary people in the world. Did you hear Martin Luther King's speech in Washington? We did. 'I have a dream that my four children will one day live in a nation where they will not be judged by the colour of their skin but by the content of their character'" she quoted verbatim. "It was so inspirational." Hugh nodded but, to the surprise of neither, Nancy shrugged her shoulders in ignorance.

"And the thing is," Lizzie went on, "it applies just as much here to other groups, too. You know that, Hugh. You should never have lost your job because you're gay. But there was little you could do, was there?"

"No – nothing. They would have found a way to justify what they did. As long as homosexuality remains a criminal offence it won't change."

"Then there are women's right too," Lizzie went on. "Why should women be discriminated against in the workplace just because of their gender. They should be rewarded equally if they are making an equal contribution. His speech was a rallying cry for other groups, not just for the

Monday's Child
Caroline Jones Lewis

American blacks. How about you, Hugh? How's your new job going?"
"Oh, fine. It's good to be doing something constructive and beneficial for a change instead of just helping people who already have money to make more money. And of course I'm working with like-minded souls so I don't have to pretend to be someone I'm not. We hope to get new laws on the statute book but changing attitudes is another matter altogether. There will always be those who are prejudiced, convinced that we are evil beings out to pervert the innocent."
As he spoke Hugh wandered over to the radiogram and from his new selection of 45s he picked a Beatles record which, while not entirely his cup of tea, he was sure the girls would like. He set it on the turntable and gently guided the needle into place. Neither he nor Lizzie were prepared for the change in Nancy when the sound of the voices hit the air.

> Love Love Me Do
> You Know I Love You
> I'll always be true
> So please – Love me do
> O oh, love me do

"Nancy, whatever's wrong," gasped Lizzie, discarding her coffee cup onto the table and leaping to her cousin's side. Nancy's face had drained of colour. Her eyes widened with fear and she trembled, shook like the tremor at the start of an earthquake, her hand raised to her mouth. Hugh was aghast.
"Take if off. The music. Please," begged Nancy, struggling for breath.
Hugh leapt to his feet quickly and hurried to the radiogram, scratching the record with the needle in his haste to stem the flow of music. He dropped the arm and needle into their cradle and joined Lizzie at Nancy's side.
"Nancy, what is it? Tell us, please," pleaded Lizzie.

Monday's Child

Caroline Jones Lewis

"I can't," Nancy spluttered. "I can't. You'll despise me."
"Nancy, there's nothing you can't tell us," Hugh insisted. "We're your family. We're here to help and support you like you've helped me in recent months. Not to judge you. Don't you think I was afraid to tell you all that I'm gay, afraid of what you would think of me. But you were there for me because you're my family. Now it's our turn to help you – me and Lizzie. Whatever it is, Nancy, you can tell us."
"He's right," said Lizzie. "Something really bad is troubling you, Nancy and you need to deal with it. Tell us and we'll help you do that."
"You can't," whispered Nancy. "I have to deal with it myself."
She took a deep breath. The colour was returning to her cheeks and her breathing was steadying now. She so wanted to tell them, to pour out everything and unburden herself of her shame and her fear but she knew she could not. Shame and pride prevented her. So she simply said ...
"I was raped. And now he's following me – this guy .... "
The revelation hit her cousins like a bombshell and for a moment they were silent, lost for words and absorbing the implications of the confidence Nancy had just imparted. Then Lizzie broke the silence.
"Have you been to the police?" she asked. Nancy shook her head.
"But don't you think you should?" Lizzie gasped.
Hugh nodded his agreement.
"No, I can't," Nancy protested. "Don't even ask me to do that. I can't."
"But Nancy," began Lizzie but was interrupted abruptly.
"No," Nancy reaffirmed, pausing and then,
"I got involved with some people .... I've done some things I'm not proud of. It would be made public and I couldn't bear for Mummy and Daddy to know."
Lizzie tried again, pleading with her.
"But Nancy, your life could be in danger. Better they know those things than ... "

Monday's Child

Caroline Jones Lewis

"No, no," Nancy interrupted. "I'll deal with it – myself. If he ever tries it again I'll be ready for him next time," she said categorically. Both Lizzie and Hugh knew that she meant it – every word.

It was early evening by the time the three cousins arrived at the studio. Matthew had watched Nancy leave by taxi and had waited patiently for her return. Now he watched all three arrive together, wondering who were the other two, the girl in the hippie style skirt and blouse and the good looking young man. There was no way the girl was a whore. She looked like everyone's girl-next-door. And the man – not the type he would expect Nancy to be involved with – too gentle and innocent looking. In any case, didn't she already have this Robin? He wasn't entirely sure about that. He had never seen them together and they seemed to come and go independently of each other. His earlier optimism was waning, turning to frustration at his failure to get closer or to find a way of getting Nancy alone. The studio light was lit. Robin was working.

Matthew watched the trio disappear into the abyss that lay beyond the security door, a door that was locked against him. He knew he had to find a way of gaining access, of bypassing the entry system – when this Robin was out and Nancy was alone. When he saw the two leave later without Nancy he guessed his watch was over for the day and that Nancy would not be going out again that day. Once again his frustration was threatening anger and there was only one way he knew to vent his feelings. First he needed a drink to put fire in his belly. And then a woman. He found a telephone kiosk and rang the girl in Whitechapel but she told him no, she was not available. He would have to look for a woman elsewhere, he decided; any woman maybe out there on the streets somewhere, in the darkness – but not here, not too close to his quarry. His hand went to the pocket of his jacket, to the Swiss Army knife that he had taken to carrying in readiness for Nancy.

Monday's Child
Caroline Jones Lewis

He turned on his heels and hurried away, trawling the streets for his prey as he had taken to doing more in recent times.

******

Speaking on the telephone the following day both Lizzie and Hugh expressed their concern to each other over Nancy's revelation and her refusal to go to the police.
"I don't understand why she won't go," Hugh confided.
"I don't think that's uncommon," Lizzie explained. "Most women feel the police are biased against rape victims. And they get put through hell in court."
"But it's all wrong. The man needs to be caught – before he does it to someone else."
"He probably has already," said Lizzie flatly.
"That's awful," Hugh replied. "Awful."
"What do you think we should Hugh? If anything happens to her and we've done nothing …."
Her voice trailed off.
"Yes, I know," Hugh agreed. "It caused me a disturbed night, too. I've been racking my brains to find an answer. I do wish she'd go to the police herself. But I did ask our legal chap in the office today – not giving too much away, you know. I didn't mention the rape because she won't; just the following her. He said that really the police wouldn't do much unless the chap actually made a definite threat against her. As things are he doesn't seem to be doing that – just frightening her."
"So there's nothing much we can do then?"
"Apparently not. I just hope Nancy doesn't do something rash."

******

For Hugh and Robin – to the astonishment of both himself and Lizzie given their earlier speculation about Robin and Nancy, it was love at first sight. The man that the two cousins had thought may be a partner for Nancy was to

Monday's Child
Caroline Jones Lewis

become the love of Hugh's life. Since it became clear in an instant there was nothing more between Nancy and Robin than a working relationship, both the girls were delighted for Hugh though well aware that, for both Hugh and Robin, they must keep this confidence to themselves. While Lizzie's parents were not unused to encountering homosexuality in their professional lives and were more open-minded in their thinking, she could make no such assumption where Graham was concerned. In upper class circles homosexuality was an open secret and one which Nancy had discovered amongst her father's social acquaintances in the past. Whilst not exactly blasé on the matter she was not troubled by the idea of Hugh having a lover, particularly as it was Robin. Strange to say, she thought, Robin's sexuality had not in the least occurred to her, but it was a secret she was happy to keep to herself.

******

Autumn trundled on with the usual recipe of news and events around the new Government administration, the usual British obsession with the weather and a sprinkling of seasoning in the form of showbiz personalities. James Carlisle grumbled at the sight on newsreels of screaming, fainting teenage girls at London Airport as the Beatles returned from Sweden. Hugh viewed it with mild and fleeting amusement and Nancy thought they were fab, while Lizzie barely noticed at all, so engrossed in her studies. On a dismal November evening when the light had already faded into dusk, leaves of gold and brown once more skittered around the ankles and fluttered on the breeze to litter the parks and pavements from almost barren trees. Lights glowed mellow from the windows of the university where students were now well into another year of study. They gathered in groups around the campus, cosy in a coffee bar or a 'pub or in the common rooms discussing and debating the burning issues of the day. In a popular bar Lizzie and Graham, as ever, were flying the Labour flag to

Monday's Child
Caroline Jones Lewis

fellow students, pleading the case of the underprivileged and infirm. A roar of dissent and lively laughter from the opposing group was quelled by the sudden opening of the door and a terse and shocked announcement from a reluctant messenger.

"Kennedy's dead," he announced. "He's been shot. He's dead."

Quiet disbelief spread around the group who flew in a disjointed clutter to the common room where other students had already assembled as the news had spread. The TV in the corner flickered images, playing out the tragedy in Dallas, the motorcade of the American President, the crack of gunshots, the President slumped against the blood-spattered jacket of his soon to be widowed wife who cradled his head in shock. The sombre voice of the commentator confirmed the gravity of the situation. John F Kennedy, the youngest ever president of the United States of America and golden boy of the Kennedy clan, was dead.

"Oh, God. It's awful," a voice whispered. "He was their future, the best … "

"Do they know who did it?" asked another voice.

"I think they've got someone," came an answer from somewhere within the crowd.

Then came the tributes, the eulogies, the unsavoury knowledge that there would be those celebrating the President's demise. Over the ensuing days the assassination prompted debate on the reason for killing, on American foreign policy, the Vietnam war, the invasion of Cuba and the incarceration of political prisoners at the Bay of Pigs, some of whom had been detained for years after the invasion. What would a change of leadership in the USA mean for Britain and the world at large? The campus buzzed with speculation. In another bizarre turn of events, Kennedy's assassin, Lee Harvey Oswald, was himself assassinated whilst in police custody by one Jack Ruby.

"It's one long catastrophe," was the general concensus. Kennedy's funeral was transmitted around the world and pictures of the diminutive figure of John Junior, standing to

Monday's Child

Caroline Jones Lewis

attention and saluting his father's coffin, dominated the press and tugged at the heart strings.

******

The church to which Miranda had returned was silent as she sat head bowed in one of the pews in melancholy mood. Another child was missing, this time a boy. John Kilbride was 12 years old and like Pauline Reade he had vanished without a trace. Once more the Manchester police were searching. God had not been listening after all, she decided, for Pauline Reade remained missing and Nancy had still not returned home. What was the world coming to? Who could do this? Who could abduct a child and leave their family confused and frightened and fearing the worst? Only a monster. And where were you, God, when the children needed you? Where were you? She dismissed her thoughts as immature rantings and ramblings but the sadness persisted. She walked across to light three candles, one for each of the missing children and one for Nancy. They glowed like glow worms in the winter gloom. Again shafts of light broke through the stained glass window in a kaleidoscope of colour as the winter sun pierced through the rain clouds skudding across a heavy sky. But now she doubted that anyone was listening to her prayers and wondered why she was here at all.

Amidst the atmosphere of drama and agonising suspense plans, were already being made for yet another Christmas and New Year celebration - without Nancy it seemed for despite pleas and pressure from her cousins and a heartfelt request from her father , she remained reluctant to meet her mother and return to the fold. She could not tell them that while the spectre of Matthew stalked her consciousness she could not risk leading him to a home and family that she loved.

******

Monday's Child
Caroline Jones Lewis

Walking to a nearby shop in the late afternoon, with dusk descending rapidly in the murky drizzle of a December day, Nancy was preoccupied with these thoughts and the impending Christmas celebrations. With memories of the last Christmas spent with Eve and aware of increasing pressure from her father and cousins for Christmas to be the ideal moment for the reunion, she put herself under constant mental debate. Cowardice was not usually her style but increasing unease at her recent past and behaviour and the hurt she had caused was making it difficult for her to concede to what she knew must be her course of action – to meet her mother and say she was sorry. Eve had suggested she and Nancy should meet at some point on Christmas Day, feeling it appropriate to afford her parents some privacy after the traumas of the year. Eve's sister was also coming on Boxing Day as part of the plan. This offered Nancy the let out she needed but her conscience would not cease niggling at the very bones of her.
"Well, I can go to my aunt and cousins," Eve offered, "but I really would like it if we could meet up as some point, Nanc."
"Auntie Carbolic, you mean?" grinned Nancy and Eve had giggled her reply.
"Yeah, Auntie Carbolic. She's not a bad old stick, though, and she's been a brick in supporting Mum and Dad this year."
Nancy had noticed a change in her friend in recent months, since the return to the safety of the family fold. The toughness that had been evident in Eve when they first met had mellowed.
"You're getting soft," Nancy had teased.
"Mmmm – suppose I am. Mustn't get too soft, though. I don't want to stay at home for ever."
"Aren't you seeing Jerry over Christmas?"
Eve now had what Nancy insisted was her boyfriend but that Eve protested was merely a friend. Jerry had been a teddy boy in a dissolute youth of reckless abandon and

Monday's Child

Caroline Jones Lewis

cockfights but the lifestyle of a Jack the Lad had palled. His long velvet-collared jacket and blue suede shoes were now consigned to the back of the wardrobe and he was studying at the same night school as Eve, learning a trade with a determined intent to build himself a future.

"No," Eve had replied emphatically. "He did ask – suggested I might like to go round to meet his parents but … "

"But?"

"Well, it all smacks of us going out, doesn't it?" Eve had explained. "And we're not. Not as far as I'm concerned anyway."

"Are you sure?" Nancy had teased.

"Sure!"

Eve was emphatic.

"But you do like him, don't you?"

"Yes, I do. But honestly, Nanc, I've only just got out of the club scene. I don't know what I want to do with my life yet. I'm certainly not ready to be tied down. Mum thinks I'm mad, of course. She thinks he's the bee's knees. But then what else was a woman's future when she and Dad were young? It just isn't what I want for my life."

"Yes. We're so lucky, aren't we?" said Nancy. "So many more options. Like me, for instance."

"How's it going?"

"Oh, brilliant. I'm going away again this week for a 'photo shoot. Lake District. Not that I'm looking forward to the cold weather but otherwise it will be fun. I've got this heavenly fur coat to model."

They had chatted on for a while until the subject returned to the Christmas break.

"How about meeting for the day?" Nancy suggested.

"What – all of it?"

"Why not?"

There was a pause.

"Well, you are going to see your family, aren't you, Nanc? Your Mum?"

Monday's Child
Caroline Jones Lewis

Nancy had been evasive. So even Eve was pressing her to take that first step. If only she could be rid of this Matthew, of all that linked her with her past indiscretions. Maybe then she could face her mother and maybe then she would feel safe that he would not follow her to her family. If she brought her family into danger she would never forgive herself. She wondered if she would ever have a relationship in the future, whether she could stand another man touching her, making love. Right now the very thought of it was anathema to her. There had been offers of a date or two in recent weeks but she had shied away, the thought of any physical contact abhorrent. In this respect, the future looked bleak. Returning now from her trip to the local shop. she was so engrossed in these thoughts that she failed to notice Matthew hovering in the vicinity.

His vigilance had been paramount in recent weeks, each evening after business and over weekends, increasingly assiduous. He was sure now there was nothing between her and this Robin who seemed to spend more time in the company of the good-looking young man. They had both been dismissed with disinterest. Matthew had been making preparations to his home so that when the opportunity arose he would be ready. He had bought an inconspicuous little van that he kept in a lock-up on the south side of the river and which he parked in an unlit side street near the studio on each visit, practising the routine for when it would be put to the use for which it was intended. In the event of it being noticed at all, whoever would connect the likes of him to a tradesman's van that could be delivering or collecting, or simply the transport of a plumber or electrician attending to a call in the area. It was the perfect vehicle. But it would not be before Christmas, he had decided. Christmas would be difficult. His mother would want to visit, a ritual he knew he would have to endure for the sake of cordiality and all must appear as normal as possible. He would make sure the cellar and small bedrooms were kept locked away from her prying eyes. So

Monday's Child

Caroline Jones Lewis

the New Year it had to be. And the New Year was not very far away. He relished the thought as he doggedly followed Nancy's footsteps in the now familiar routine of the only journey she seemed to make alone and that only rarely, walk to the shop for bread and milk, greengrocer for apples and bananas, newsagents for a magazine, then scuttling back to the studio where she remained for the rest of the day. She seemed to have few friends to visit, just the good-looking young man who often left with this Robin, the other girl from the Club and occasionally the pretty girl dressed like a hippie. Sometimes she seemed to go away for a few days – disappeared into thin air – but then returned as quickly as she had gone. Some weekends she went out with her friend from the Club, all dressed up as though they were going to a party or a disco or sometimes casual, maybe to the cinema. They always took a taxi which left him adrift until their return. Those times he went to the Club for a drink just in case but the girls never appeared there and seemed to have nothing more to do with either the Club or with Adam and his cronies. The frustration of those evenings often prompted the need for sex which he indulged with any woman he could find, whether willing or not. He contented himself in his vigil with thoughts of the future he had planned with Nancy. On this evening, dressed casually, unremarkably, with his collar turned up against the December mist and a cap pulled down over his face, he saw Nancy approach the door on her return. She dropped her keys, bending to retrieve them from the pavement and in a muddled manoeuvre to avoid drawing alongside her, he bumped into another passer-by, knocking off his cap and sending it spinning to the ground.
"Heh, steady, old chap," complained the stick-thin elderly gentleman gruffly, rubbing the elbow that took the butt of the collision. At the sound of the altercation, Nancy turned just in time to see Matthew retrieving the cap from the pavement behind her. At the sight of him, she sucked in her breath and in near panic fumbled with her key in the lock of the door. She dropped her magazine which, in her

Monday's Child
Caroline Jones Lewis

panic to reach the sanctuary inside, she left saturated on the pavement, scrambling inside and slamming and bolting the door behind her. She slid to the floor in the hallway, her heart thumping nineteen to the dozen, breath rasping and fear making her head pound like a hammer. It was him, right behind her, following her like a shadow. How could she ever get away from him? And what was he planning to do to her this time? She remained on the floor for a while unable to move, still breathing hard and struggling against her panic, then calming herself she raised to her feet and gathered up her shopping. She trudged up to the studio and the telephone, feeling suddenly weary and dialling Eve's number. She prayed that her friend would be at home.
"It was him," she told her dully. "He's still following me, Eve. It's scary. What am I going to do?"
"You *must* go to the police, Nanc," Eve told her. "You must."
"I can't," wailed Nancy. "What would I tell them? That I think I'm being followed by a man who paid me to have sex with him at a party? At one of Stephen's parties."
"No, just that you're being followed by this man and you're scared."
"Do you think they'd believe me? Seriously? Without me telling them about everything – that I slept with him at a party? Because if I didn't he would. He'd deny the bad stuff. Do you think they'd even listen to me after that?"
Eve considered for a moment and then had to agree.
"Probably not," she affirmed.
"Well, you need to defend yourself then," she counselled.
"A course on self-defence, or something."
"I need a weapon," Nancy breathed. "A knife or something. A baton."
Eve was reticent. She did not like the idea of Nancy wandering around with a lethal weapon on her person but right at the moment she had no better idea to suggest.
"Let me ask Jerry," she suggested. "He might have an idea. He used to carry a flick-knife when he was a ted but it's not

Monday's Child
Caroline Jones Lewis

a good idea for you to be carrying a knife, Nanc. Jerry might have another idea,"

"Why not," Nancy protested. "It would only be to defend myself, Eve. I'm not going to cause mayhem in the streets just for kicks."

"All the same, Nanc – carrying a knife, well. It's ... " Her voice trailed off.

"But Eve, I have to do something. I have to defend myself somehow. I just don't know what this guy is up to."

"Have you told your cousins?"

"Absolutely not," Nancy replied emphatically. "Neither am I going to."

"God, you're so stubborn," Eve spluttered. She conceded with a sigh.

"Let me see what Jerry and I can come up with," she suggested in a conciliatory tone but she still did not like the idea of Nancy carrying a knife. If Matthew were to overpower her and take the knife from her, even the smallest knife, the damage he would inflict could be fatal; or simply disfiguring which may well be what he would prefer. Whichever way it went it would turn out badly for Nancy.

******

Outside in the street, Hugh had arrived to let himself into the studio with a key of which he was now the proud owner, a testament to the commitment he and Robin already shared. On the pavement, Nancy's magazine, wet from the drizzle, lay stuck to the flagstones. Guessing its ownership, he peeled it off the floor and carried it dripping indoors, smiling to himself at the title. Nancy had clearly graduated from Jackie to Vogue. He let himself into the hallway and nearing the door into the studio, he heard a voice and understanding that Robin would be elsewhere was curious to see who was there. Stepping through the doorway in his usual quiet manner, Nancy did not hear his approach and continued with her conversation. Alarm bells

Monday's Child
Caroline Jones Lewis

jangled in Hugh's head as he grasped the jist of the content. Without reference to Nancy, who had still not noticed his presence, he decided he must do something to secure her safety from this fiend. Confiding in Robin would be his first step, not all the detail, the rape and whatever was in her shady past, but this man that was following her. Between them perhaps they could warn him off.
Suddenly realising she had company, Nancy spun round as she replaced the receiver.
"Oh, Hugh – hi," she said, colouring a little.
"Hello, cous," he greeted her, crossing the room and kissing her on the cheek. "Who was on the 'phone?"
"Oh, just a friend," came the reply with an apparently nonchalant shrug of the shoulders.
"I'm just going up to the flat for a wash and brush up," she told him. "See you in a bit."

Nancy's dilemma over Christmas was unexpectedly resolved. The shifting sands that life can sometimes present provided a solution and a 'photo shoot in warmer climes for the coming season's swimwear could not have presented itself at a more opportune time.
"I'm sorry, Daddy," she cooed, "but you do understand, don't you?"
James conceded reluctantly, his hopes of a family reunion and Christmas trogether dashed for another year and the task of breaking it to Miranda once more falling to him. But at least it's a valid reason, he thought to himself, and not a blatant rejection of her mother.
"Well, you just enjoy the experience," he told his daughter. "There aren't many people who get the chance to spend Christmas anywhere exotic. I'm actually quite envious."
"I'm really excited, Daddy," she told him. "But I'll be thinking of you and the family on Christmas Day."
"Good. I just hope we don't get snow here, like last year. I hate the stuff."
Miranda bore the news philosophically and continued with Christmas preparations in the normal way. There would

Monday's Child
Caroline Jones Lewis

still be Emily, Tom and Lizzie and Hugh and his Grandmother for Christmas Day. And of course James would be with them at least for Christmas lunch though she had hesitated to ask him about the rest of the day. She knew nothing for sure, but there was a spring in his step these days and a lightness about him that made her suspicious of someone new in his life. It filled her with confusion. She had begun to hope that perhaps they could put the past behind them and start anew, at least as good friends, maybe even reunited. Neither had mentioned divorce, indeed not even a formal separation but there certainly seemed to be something in the air with James. For herself, at last a healing process had begun and whilst there was disappointment of her continued estrangement from Nancy, now she knew her daughter was safe and thriving, a degree of comfort in that knowledge made life more bearable. One day she would come, Miranda was sure. And when that time came, all would be forgiven and forgotten on her part. So Christmas came and went and 1964 arrived with quiet grace.

Graham, too, had suffered disappointment. Unable to persuade Lizzie to join him at his parents' for even part of the festivities and uninvited to join her at hers, he sensed that the commitment he had continued to hope for remained elusive.

Hugh and Robin had agreed that, for this year at least, the festive season should be spent with their respective families. Hugh's Grandmother was not in the rudest of health and now, in her eighties, her general frailty was a cause for concern. But the New Year, they had pledged, would be theirs and theirs alone.

Monday's Child
Caroline Jones Lewis

Chapter Thirteen – Danger or deliverance?

The year began in constancy for all the family, each going about their business in the usual way. Hugh and Robin's relationship blossomed and Hugh relished his role in his new career. The campaign to repeal the 1956 act on homosexuality was the current focus of the association for which he worked and he endorsed and supported their activities. In 1954 Peter Wildeblood, Lord Edward Montagu and Michael Pitt-Rivers had stood trial accused of incitement of two others to commit 'indecent acts'. During the course of the trial Peter Wildeblood, a former public schoolboy and Oxford graduate, had become one of the first men in Britain to publicly declare his homosexuality. He had been sentenced to 18 month's imprisonment of which he served a year. On his release, in a climate of public clamouring for tolerance and change, he was interviewed by the Wolfenden Committee who were charged with investigating and considering 'the law and practice relating to homosexual offences and the treatment of such offences by the courts'. At the end of their deliberations, of the 13 members of the Committee, 12 – including their chairman John Wolfenden – had recommended that homosexual acts between consenting adults in private should no longer be treated as criminal offences since they were exactly that. Private. But the description in the 1956 Act of homosexual acts between consenting adults as 'unnatural offences' and 'gross indecency' ensured a public upholding of homophobic attitudes reminiscent of Victorian Britain.
"The general public are ignorant where gay people are concerned," Hugh bemoaned to Robin. "They think that gays are perverted and intent on the corruption of the young. It's an insult to people like you and me who are perfectly decent and law abiding and privately committed in a relationship."
"I suppose I'm lucky," Robin observed. "There are more gays than not in the professional world I move in. No-one bats an eyelid. But I suppose it's different in City circles."

Monday's Child

Caroline Jones Lewis

"I'll say," agreed Hugh, relating to Robin the story of his life-threatening beating and subsequent sacking from the banking world.
So Hugh, along with his employer, was totally committed to the repeal of the Act and fuelled by his sense of injustice, he worked tirelessly for legal reform.

Lizzie's preoccupation with world politics was paramount. She fumed at the imprisonment in South Africa of Nelson Mandela.
"But he's a terrorist," exclaimed one of her fellow students.
"It depends which side of the tracks you're on," she argued.
"One man's terrorist is another man 's freedom fighter."
They agreed to peacefully disagree.
The continuing US involvement in Vietnam irked her, dragging on despite the calls of the American public for an end to the conflict and the continuous repatriation of body bags. She was an avid admirer of Barbara Castle and the Labour left and her choice of music inevitably favoured the protest songs of Bob Dylan. But by her choice and to Graham's continued disappointment, her relationship with him failed to grow beyond that which had already become the norm.

Nancy's career went from strength to strength and she revelled in the financial reward and status it was bringing. Her father's outmoded and cosmetic expectations of his Monday's Child and the ambition that had unexpectedly surfaced in recent times were absorbed in one objective.

Matthew fumed at her exposure in the media. All those other men who would be ogling her. She was to be his and his alone and he had to find a way to stop these evil people who were exploiting and corrupting her, encouraging her to publicly flaunt herself without his approval. But no matter. He was almost ready now to act. The cellar was secure and furnished in readiness and she would be comfortable there until she accepted that her place was with him and could

Monday's Child
Caroline Jones Lewis

convince him that she genuinely agreed to stay of her own accord.

Emily and Tom were kept as industrious as ever in a Health Service groaning under the strain of influenza and bronchitis and Hugh's Grandmother struggled with increasing decrepitude.

James and Miranda continued with the status quo avoiding any source of conflict necessitating any in-depth discussion on Nancy's continuing avoidance of her mother. For Miranda there was another heartfelt happening. Another child went missing. Another 12 year old boy. Another frantic search by the Manchester police for a child who had vanished as completely as the previous two. Another trip to the church. Another candle, four now and still nothing. Another question – why did she come? Because she had to believe, she told herself. She had to. If she ceased to believe, for herself, for those other familes, there would be nothing. A plan was forming itself in her mind, that maybe if Mohammed would not come to the mountain, maybe the mountain should take the initiative. She could no longer accept the role forced upon her, was no longer prepared to be regarded as a victim. Her child was not dead, not even missing like the children of those poor families still waiting. She had given Nancy enough time and now it was time for her to take control. James was not sure it was the right thing to do but decided it was not his decision to make, so he gave Miranda the address of the studio and an idea of the best time to call. If Nancy was mad at him then he would face her censure and he would deal with it.

******

Miranda scooped her hair up into a chignon and carefully re-applied her make-up. The weather, as ever, was dismal, a fine drizzle saturating everything in the gloom. She wrapped her Burberry around her over sweater and slacks,

Monday's Child
Caroline Jones Lewis

collected an umbrella from the hallstand and set off by taxi in the falling dusk. Reading James' barely decipherable scrawl, Miranda found her way to the studio from where the taxi had dropped her. Evening was drawing in fast and she peered at the name plaque beside the studio door. When her buzz on the bell brought no response she looked up at the darkened windows, reluctant to leave in case Nancy came bowling along the street. Perhaps she should leave a note, she thought. But what to say? What help would it be? Still, it was worth a try. Rummaging in her handbag for paper and pen she was oblivious to the figure observing her across the street.

Matthew peered through the misty dampness, rain dripping from the brim of his homburg, clouding his eyes and trickling down the bridge of his nose. His hands were thrust into the pockets of his raincoat where he fingered the knife that was there ever ready. He watched Nancy across the street. There was something different about her that he could not quite explain. He guessed she was rummaging in her bag for her keys, hesitating. She must have lost them, or forgotten them and the building was all in darkness. There was no-one else at home. Excitement rose within him, his heart beating fast inside his chest, thump-thumping and the rushing of the blood through his veins echoing in his eardrums. There was hardly a soul about at this time of night and his van was parked in readiness around the corner in the side-street. This could be his chance, the moment he had waited for when all his plans and dreams would come to fruition. He stepped from the pavement into the gutter, crossing the road stealthily and approaching his quarry from behind.

A sudden feeling of someone close by made Miranda swing around to face him. A startled Matthew covered in confusion leered at her awkwardly. The likeness was uncanny but this woman was old compared to Nancy. He could see that now. She had fine lines around her eyes and

Monday's Child
Caroline Jones Lewis

a mouth that had a slight droop at the corner. But such a remarkable likeness – her mother, perhaps or some other member of the family. She stared at him enquiringly.
"Oh, sorry," he muttered ingratiatingly, wringing his hands in a manner that reminded Miranda somewhat of Uriah Heap. His chest constricted with anxiety. He wanted no-one to remember him when the time came to spirit his Nancy away.
"I thought you were someone else. I didn't mean to startle you," he offered in explanation. He attempted a smile of apology, then scurried away, hopeful that the dim light and mist of evening would prevent too accurate a description should she relate the matter of their encounter to Nancy. He really must be more careful, he deliberated. Disturbed by the unexpected interruption, Miranda abandoned her quest for the time being and hurried home.

Matthew became angry, angrier than he had been for a long time. He sat in the van and fumed. But as his anger dissipated he felt cheated. He had come so close and now felt empty. He needed a drink, a stiff one. Then he would find a woman. He returned the van to the lock-up, then took a taxi to the Club and several whiskies. When he left he was intent on finding himself a whore. He did find someone and he took what he wanted at knifepoint – and not for the first time. But she was not a whore. She was a favoured niece of one of the most vicious gangsters in London's history.

******

In the Blind Beggar 'pub in Whitechapel a few days later, Bob "the Butcher" Bailey shook his head and tut-tutted between gulps of his pint.
"Reggie will go fuckin' mad," he predicted in a gravel voice as serious as the grave. "Fuckin' mad, 'e'll be. 'E's got a soft spot for Annie. Somebody's gonna pay for this, you can be sure of that."

Monday's Child

Caroline Jones Lewis

"But Annie won't go to the Bill," his companion explained. "All in pieces – she is. They tried to persuade 'er but she won't go. Says the Old Bill will put 'er through the mill, try to make out it was 'er own fault 'cos she'd 'ad a drink with mates. Says she can't face it so the fucker will get away with it."

"Bad business," Bob the Butcher pronounced, shaking his head. "Bad business. She's a good girl, Annie. Keeps 'erself respectable, not like some of those tarts that ask for it, flaunting themselves with skirts 'arfway up their arses. What will become of 'er now? Takes a lot for a girl to get over rape. It's a bad business."

He drew ponderously on his Rothmans, an inch long pillar of ash tumbling and cascading down his gabardine which he brushed away irritably; then announced "she won't need the Old Bill. Reggie will track 'im down. Reggie will see to it. Same again, Sid," he called to the barman. "And change for the dog and bone," he added, indicating the payphone on the wall in the corner. "I need to make a call."

At Esmeralda's Barn nightclub in Knightsbridge, Ronnie leaned against the bar watching with satisfaction as his midday customers drank and were merry, a well-to-do clientele dotted with the occasional celebrity that gave the notorious duo of himself and his twin brother a modicum of respectability and a wealth of influence. Dressed slickly in a grey mohair suit, his hair sleeked back and a glass of whisky in his manicured hand, he was at ease with himself. A waiter approaching from his side whispered in his ear. "'Scuse me, Mr Kray. Your brother wants you in the office. Says it's urgent."

Ronnie nodded. He emptied his glass of whisky in one gulp, placed the glass on the bar and turned steadily to head for the office where his brother waited. The thunderous look on Reggie's face that greeted him confirmed the seriousness of whatever it was that needed discussion.

"What's up?" Ronnie began.

Monday's Child
Caroline Jones Lewis

"It's Annie," Reggie began. "She's been raped. We need to go and see 'er. I want this bastard and when I get 'im 'e'll wish 'e'd never been born."
"'As she spoken to the Bill?"
Reggie shook his head.
"No. Never mind the Bill. I want 'im," he replied.

Annie, it seemed, had not seen her attacker who had approached her from behind but after much gentle coaxing from her mother a degree of information was elicited from her that gave the Kray brothers their lead. He was taller than her, she thought and he smelled nice, of expensive cologne or something, the smell of which she had tried to rid herself after he was gone but which still hung in her nostrils like a curse would hang on the ear. He wore a ring on his right hand which had bruised her face and cut into her bottom lip as he had held his hand tightly across her mouth, telling her not to scream or he would have to kill her. It felt like a signet ring that had twisted so the widest part was against her face. His hands were soft, not rough like working hands but soft smooth skin that smelled scenty, like expensive soap of some kind. Not Camay like they used at home but some other soap that was scenty. His voice was cultured, like a City gent and quiet and confident, menacingly quiet, not shouting but whispering threats into her ear. Satisfied they had enough to start their search, the twins returned to Esmeralda's and put the word out on the street. It was not long before they reaped their reward.

"Take a seat," began Reggie affably, pointing to a chair placed in front of the large antique mahogany desk behind which he importantly sat. Lola sat before him nervously.
"Tell me," said Reggie.
"There's this guy," she began. "'E frightens me a bit, likes it violent, you know. I don't mind it a bit rough but e's too much. 'E was alright at first but the last couple'a times 'e's been - well, rougher, getting more violent. 'E rang me that night but I put 'im off. Like I said, 'e frightened me last

Monday's Child
Caroline Jones Lewis

time, see. Wanted to tie me hands be'ind me back. I wasn't 'avin' any. I don't do that stuff. Just straightforward stuff, that's me. I managed to talk my way out of it but 'e frightened me. So I made an excuse that night. Said I wasn't free. Just think – it could've been me instead of that poor girl."

"So 'e was a regular then?"

"Yeah. Quite. Well, 'e was. 'E'd been, ooh, dozen or so times, three or four times in the last few weeks, actually. Not short of money neither. Always 'as a roll of notes in 'is pocket."

"Describe 'im," Reggie ordered.

"Well, it's like your chap said. 'E's smart, always really smart. Posh suits and stuff. All 'is clothes, they're expensive. Tall. Dark 'air. Not bad lookin'. An' 'e always smells good. Really nice."

"Age?"

Lola considered.

"40s I would guess."

"Any jewellry? Does 'e wear any jewellry?"

She thought for a moment.

"Watch, I think. Expensive. Gold. Not flashy, though. An' a ring. Yes, a signet ring. Gold and quite chunky but not cheap. With the initials M something. Now what was it? MJB ... MJB... or it could've been a P. MJP. No, it was MJB. I remember now 'cos it's the same initials as my brother. MJB. That was it."

"So how did you meet this MJB? Card in a 'phone box, was it?"

"God, no," exclaimed Lola indignantly. "Give me some credit. I've a bit more class than that. No, I met 'im at Adam's place. You know, the Club round the corner 'ere. Do you know 'im?"

"Yeah, we know 'im," Reggie replied. That wanker, he thought. Thinks 'e's a big player, the pratt.

" Adam doesn't like me going there," Lola continued. "Thinks I'm not posh enough, I spose, but I'd arranged to meet a punter there, see. Well, the punter didn't show and

Monday's Child
Caroline Jones Lewis

this guy buys me a drink and - like - things went from there."
She paused, not sure whether Reggie wanted to know any more. She did not want to annoy Reggie. No-one wanted to annoy Reggie. It did not pay.
"And you went back to your place?" Reggie asked.
Lola nodded.
"Always your place?" he asked. "Never anywhere else?"
Lola shook her head.
"No," she replied. "Always my place."
Reggie said nothing, breathing hard. Then "you've done good, Lola," he told her. "Real good. Now this is what I want you to do. Next time 'e calls I want you to arrange for 'im to come round. Then ring me. Straight away. Understand?"
Lola hesitated, not keen to see Matthew again especially after this.
"Understand?" Reggie urged, leaning towards her and staring directly into her eyes.
"Sure," she capitulated. "But you will come, won't you? Straight away?"
"Don't you worry," Reggie assured her. "We'll be there. I'll be waitin' for your call. And one more thing," he continued. "You tell no-one about this conversation , right? If anyone asks, you know nothin'. This conversation never took place."
"Right. Of course Reggie. I understand," Lola agreed and raised from her chair ready to leave, relief tangible in her body language. "Is that all, Reggie?"
"That's all," Reggie assured her. "Ron, give Lola 'er cab fare for 'er trouble – an' a bit more," he said amiably and Ronnie handed Lola a £10. note.

******

Adam was disturbed by his unexpected visitors, not the clientele he wished to encourage to the Club at this point. The threat of the Stephen episode had seemed to subside

Monday's Child
Caroline Jones Lewis

and to his satisfaction neither Nancy nor Eve had returned to the Club or even asked for more wages. But he had much to do in preparation for his impending divorce and needed to present respectable credibility. Reggie's men, however, would not take no for an answer and for the sake of his own safety he felt it better to co-operate. Their reputation went before them. With reluctance he surrendered the membership book across the desk towards them. They examined it carefully.

"This guy 'ere," one of them asked. "MJB. Know 'im, do you?"

"Vaguely," Adam replied. "Not very well."

"Describe 'im."

Adam pondered for a moment.

"Well, tallish," he began, "dark-haired. Good looking, I suppose. Women seem to find him attractive, anyway."

"'ow old?"

"Mid 40s I'd guess."

"Smart dresser, is 'e?"

Adam nodded.

"Wear any jewellry?"

"Watch, I think," Adam replied, the recollection of a Rolex he coveted coming to mind.

"What about rings? Married, is 'e?"

"Was," Adam offered. "Divorced, I think. I don't honestly remember whether he wears a ring or not."

"Is 'e in the Club tonight then?"

"I haven't noticed him," Adam assured them. "But then I've been in the office most of the evening." Drafting a response to the bitch's solicitor, he thought bitterly.

"We'll be back," they told him. "No need to mention to 'im that we're lookin'. Understand?"

Adam nodded, more than willing to avoid any trouble with the two gorillas whose backs he watched disappearing through his office door. He wondered what Matthew had done to attract such unenviable attention. Whatever it was, he decided, he preferred not to know.

Monday's Child
Caroline Jones Lewis

On his visit to the Club Matthew noticed the limo parked at the kerbside outside but on a high from the success of his night's mission, he gave little heed to the two burly men making their way from Adam's office. He had overheard the men entering the studio talking about Nancy. She would be home from her modelling assignment around 9 o'clock on Friday evening, the one man had said. They would need to leave a light on in the hallway since they would both be out. Matthew looked forward to the event with anticipation, confident that at last he would be able to carry out his plan unhindered. He brushed past the two men leaving the Club and headed towards the bar. Deep in conversation the men barely noticed the contact between them. But as Matthew took a stool at the bar and signalled to the barman with a wave of his hand, at that precise moment one of the men turned and caught the glint of a signet ring caught in the light from the spotlight above the bar. The man nudged his companion and together they returned to the bar.

One either side of Matthew, they made a pretence of searching for something.
"'Aven't seen a set of keys on the bar, 'ave you?" one of them asked Matthew. He shook his head and scanned the bar, raising his glass to expose the clear surface for their inspection. In so doing, he extended his arm towards his enquirer. The signet ring was clearly in his enquirer's line of vision, the initials MJB just as clearly visible in the light from above. With a nod from the first man to the other, his companion approached, shaking a bunch of keys in his hand.
"It's ok," was the response. "My mate's found 'em," and the two men left, nodding their agreement that their quarry had been located. One sat in the limousine outside and the other made a call from a 'phone box further down the road. Matthew remained at the bar with his whisky oblivious that he, the hunter, had now become the hunted, so engrossed in his expectation of possessing Nancy. Equipped with his

Monday's Child

Caroline Jones Lewis

instructions the second man returned to the limousine and it pulled away. Preparation was paramount, Reggie had told him - and a plan that ensured the covering of their tracks.

******

From behind a cloud a full moon crept out to flood the night sky. Its rays streaked out in silver light across the expanse of a quiet city. In the crispness of Friday evening, Nancy returned with bags and baggage, dropped at the kerbside from her taxi. Paying the driver with a 10/-d. note she waited nervously for her change, anxious to reach the safety of indoors without delay. She tipped the cabbie who pulled away with a cheery 'night, miss,' and turned towards her door, fumbling to fit the key into the keyhole in her haste. It was just at this moment that Matthew emerged from the shadows of a nearby doorway. It was definitely her this time and this was his chance. His time had finally come. He could see no-one about apart from the two of them. He felt in his pocket for the knife, clasping his fingers firmly around the handle. Heart pounding in excitement and his hot breath tinged with the smell of whisky puffing into clouds of steam around him, he stepped up beside her, placing one arm across the doorway ahead of her and breathing her name quietly into her ear.
"Hello, Nancy," he breathed. "Good to see you again – at last," and he put his other arm around her neck, the knife gripped in his fingers. The moonlight glinted on the blade clearly and unmistakeably in front of her. She could smell the whisky on his breath, feel the heat of his body pressed against her own. Fear overwhelmed her and she froze.
"Now just be a good girl and do as I say and I won't have to hurt you," he instructed. "You just come with me now, quiet and steady," and with his arm around her he began to guide a terrified and defenceless Nancy back along the street in the direction she had come towards his van parked in the unlit side street. Her bags remained abandoned on the pavement. As they neared the corner, two men emerged

Monday's Child
Caroline Jones Lewis

from a limo parked at the kerbside, sauntering nonchalantly towards them and Nancy shot them a terrified glance, hoping to attract their attention, hoping that her manner would alert them to her plight and prompt their assistance. But they passed without challenge giving no indication they had noticed anything untoward in a couple hurrying by in the frosty night towards the comfort and warmth of home. Nancy and Matthew turned the corner into the side street and approached the van parked in darkness away from the street light. Keeping his arm around Nancy and using his free hand Matthew took the keys from his pocket and unlocked the rear doors of the van. He opened the doors to reveal an interior lined with a rug, a roll of tape and a length of rope placed in readiness by the door. The moon disappeared behind a cloud, its light extinguished like a light turned off at a light switch.

"Get in," he ordered in a voice of quiet menace. A reluctant Nancy tried to protest.

"Can't we talk," she attempted. "There must be something …."

"Don't make me angry, Nancy," he cautioned. "It wouldn't be good for you."

Nancy climbed into the van as Matthew reached for the roll of tape and the rope.

Outside the studio Hugh had returned from another direction to find Nancy's bags abandoned outside the doorway and her keys in the lock but the door still closed - and no Nancy. Looking around him he caught the briefest glimpse of her being propelled around the far corner into a side street. Something was wrong. He did not recognise the man who was with her and realisation struck him that this must be her tormentor. The memory of his own brutal beating reared in his mind and for a second he stood rooted to the spot but then the horror of what may be happening spurred him into action and he began to sprint after them, not really knowing how he was going to intervene, only that he must try.

Monday's Child

Caroline Jones Lewis

As she climbed into the van, Nancy turned to face Matthew, pleading, summoning every ounce of courage she had to face her abductor. As she did so, Matthew's arms flailed in the air, the knife falling to the floor as his body convulsed backwards. Grabbed on either side by the arms of faceless attackers, two massive frames lifted him from his feet and propelled him around and in another direction. Nancy peered into the darkness trying to make sense of what was happening, the confusion of the moment, but uncomprehending of what was taking place.
"Go," a voice growled at her.
She stared blankly into the darkness, paralysed by fear.
"Go," the voice repeated. "Now".
Finding her courage and needing no further encouragement, she sprang from the van and rushed headlong back towards the studio without troubling to identify her liberators, no care as to who they were, just grateful that they were there. Rounding the corner she almost collided with Hugh who caught her shaking and near hysterical body in his arms.
"It's ok," he told her. "It's ok. You're safe now."
"Take me home, Hugh. Please, take me home," she pleaded and with no further delay, Hugh propelled her back the way he had come.

Safely inside the studio with the door locked and bolted and her belongings retrieved from the street by Hugh, she sank onto the sofa and descended into floods of tears. When at last she had recovered sufficiently to speak, she related to Hugh all that had taken place.
"Who were they? Those men," but neither she nor Hugh had any idea.
"I don't know and I don't care," proclaimed Nancy. "Only that they came at the right moment. But I'm afraid. Whatever might happen next? I daren't go out unless I know he isn't there," she spluttered.
"You really must go to the police, Nancy," said Hugh. "He tried to abduct you."

Monday's Child
Caroline Jones Lewis

"I'll wait," Nancy insisted. "I need to know what's happened. Maybe he'll leave me alone now."
Hugh said no more, well aware that Nancy must go to the police of her own volition. He also knew that nothing and no-one would induce her to do something she did not want to do. Best to leave her to make the decision herself. He went with her up to her flat and made her a coffee, then hearing Robin downstairs he left her to rest.
"Please don't tell Robin," she pleaded. "Please, Hugh. Remember how you wouldn't tell any of us what was happening with you. Please don't tell him."
"We'll only be downstairs if you need us," he replied.
"Thank you. Thank you so much," and she hugged him close.
Later, when she had calmed a little, Nancy telephoned Eve and told her what had happened. Eve agreed with Hugh.
"You should go to the police – now," she told Nancy.
"No, I want to wait and find out what's happened," Nancy insisted. "Everything will come out if I go to the police and Matthew might leave me alone now. I don't want my parents to know all these things. Or Robin. Everything's going so well for me now, Eve. If all the Stephen stuff blew up again it could all be ruined."
Eve understood what Nancy was saying but it still troubled her that Nancy would not go to the police. She was afraid for her.
"Can you go to Abberley again? For a few days? While you're away Jerry and I could find out a few things. There are people in the East End…." Her voice trailed off. You'd rather not know, she thought.
Nancy agreed that it was a good idea.
"I'll ring Daddy in the morning," she said. "I'll ask him if I could go for a few days, tell him I need a rest or something. Or that I feel unwell and the sea air would do me good. I'm sure he won't mind. Just until I decide what to do. Robin will understand. We've finished the shoot for now so I'm due a break."

Monday's Child

Caroline Jones Lewis

Her father saw no problem but gave her a timely reminder about her mother.

"Of course I don't mind, darling," he told her. "I'll let Mrs Hale know you're coming. And what about your mother? Shall I let her know? She might want to join you."

"Oh, no, Daddy. Please don't. I'm just too tired. I'll see her when I get back."

"You've been saying that for some time, Nancy."

"I will, Daddy, I promise."

"It's her birthday soon, Nancy. Her 40th. I really think you should make it before then. It would be the best birthday present she could ever have."

"I'll try."

I need to know that Matthew is out of the way, thought Nancy. Leaving me alone once and for all.

"Hmm," her father muttered. He was becoming impatient now with Nancy's intransigence. What was the problem? He had asked her to which she had given very little in reply. If she had forgiven what she saw as his transgressions, why not her mother's?

Nancy rang Hugh who was relieved at her news.

"I'll come with you to the station," he told her. "Just in case."

******

In a half-empty warehouse on the south bank of the river, the men interrogated their terrified captive. They circled his shaking body, seated and strapped to a chair in the centre of an empty room that had once served as an office. His confession of guilt for the rape of Annie took far less time to elicit than the punishment meted out at length by his judge and jury. His screams of pain and terror went unheeded by his tormentors and the world at large. Reggie was satisfied they had identified the culprit and that justice had been done. Matthew's tortured and beaten body was recovered by the river police the following morning from the muddy banks of the Thames. The van rested ghostly and unsuspected on the river bed. Barely recognisable,

Monday's Child
Caroline Jones Lewis

identification of his body was established by sodden documents in his wallet and confirmed by dental records. There was no doubt in the mind of Detective Superintendant Leonard 'Nipper' Read that somewhere along the line his old adversaries the Krays were involved in this killing though the absence of any known motive caused difficulty in persuing this line of enquiry. But it bore all the hallmarks of their appetite for unnecessary and unbridled violence. For what reason and of how he would prove it he had no idea. But he would try, damn it. He would try. The intention of 'getting the Krays and bringing them to justice' was, after all, the raison d'etre of his police force.

Once again, Adam received a visit from the Met at the Club where Matthew was known to be a member. He sighed as he saw 'Nipper' and his sidekick walk in through the door.

******

Eve read the headline with what verged on disbelief. The photograph of Matthew in the Evening Standard, the account of his brutal death and an appeal for information leading to his murder left her reeling. Mostly she rejoiced in the fact that in some way he had got his just deserts and relief that her friend was no longer in danger. But the description of the state of his body gave an indication of the manner in which he was killed and would be disturbing to even the most hardened. The telephone line between Eve and Abberley buzzed hot and loud.

"I wonder who did it," Nancy mused. "Perhaps he did the same to someone else and their family took their revenge."
"No idea," Eve lied. Say nothing, do nothing, Jerry had advised her. Word on the street is the twins were involved so keep your head down and your mouth shut. Nancy needed to know nothing and in any case would probably be ignorant of who the Krays were.

Monday's Child

Caroline Jones Lewis

"Who cares. The bastard deserved to die," Eve went on. "Evil way to go though. Report in the paper says he was beaten unconscious before being thrown into the river." Nancy shivered.

"He was sick," she said. Something wrong inside his head. To die like that though – God, it makes me shiver just thinking about it."

"Then don't," Eve told her. "It's over, Nanc. You can get on with your life now. You can come back and feel safe."

"Yes," Nancy replied. "Yes. And I have so much to look forward to," and she laughed, a slightly hysterical laugh of relief.

"There's no way the police can connect you to Matthew, is there?"

The concern in Eve's voice unnerved Nancy a little.

"I don't think so." She thought for a moment. "No, I'm sure not."

"That's it then. It's over. From here on it's fun all the way. See you as soon as you're back, Nanc."

Nancy considered. The last threads that connected her with Adam and the Club and Stephen and Matthew were all gone and she felt confident that all ties with the disaster and grubbiness of that part of her life were now severed. Adam had made no attempt to contact either of them, nor they him. Sad though it was Stephen was dead and in his grave and the scandal surrounding his activities consigned to the archives. Matthew was dead and soon to be in his. What could there be? She was now a respectable young woman following a successful career. She could start to live normally again. And she was ready now to face her mother.

"Yes, see you soon, Eve."

Nancy replaced the receiver and turned on the radio. The sound of the Beach Boys hit the air and turning the volume up high as it would go she danced with the joy of freedom that Eve's news had brought her.

Monday's Child
Caroline Jones Lewis

Well, she got her Daddy's car and she cruised through the hamburger stand now
She forgot all about the library like she told her old man now
And with the radio blasting goes cruising as fast as she can now
And she'll have fun fun fun 'til her daddy takes the t-bird away

She could not have been more wrong. She had barely been back at the studio and in her flat for an hour before the doorbell rang and she answered the door to find the police on the doorstep.

******

In a locked bedroom in Matthew's house that had once been a nursery an entire wall was devoted to photographs of the model Nancy Carlisle. They were pinned in a collage across the wallpaper, full length photographs of her walking down the street, standing at her door - keys in hand, her face in profile, her face front view, serious, deep in thought, smiling. Nancy with long hair, Nancy with short hair. There were pictures cut from fashion magazines of her modelling dresses and coats, knee length boots and sandals. And a scarf was draped across them that smelled of perfume. The locked cellar they would find to be fitted out as a bedroom with a bath and portable toilet roughly installed behind a partition and an even more sinister tone struck by the pair of handcuffs and length of chain attached to a ring on the wall. The DI investigating this crime had no idea who this young woman was but the females in the station had no difficulty in the least in identifying her. On the table in her flat Matthew's photograph was placed before a nervous Nancy.
"Did you know the deceased?"
Nancy shook her head.

Monday's Child

Caroline Jones Lewis

"So you didn't give him these photographs?" and several photographs were laid out in front of her.
Nancy shook her head a second time.
"So you couldn't know he had them?"
"No. I had no idea. I'm shocked."
She was genuinely stunned at the extent of Matthew's voyeurism and obsession with her life.
"Have you ever seen this before?" the detective asked producing from an envelope the scarf that still smelled of her perfume.
"Oh, my God, it's mine," she gasped. "I lost it ages ago. Where did you find it?"
"With the photographs, miss. Do you know where you lost it?"
"No," she replied bluntly. "But then I'm quite careless with things. I could have dropped it anywhere."
"Did you ever meet him?"
"Not that I recall," she lied.
She coloured a little and felt like she was trembling though her hands appeared to be quite still in her lap. She was aware the policemen were studying her intently but her shock was so genuine that she hoped they detected nothing suspicious in her behaviour.
"What was his name?" she asked, a genuine question since she had never know Matthew's full name. "This man."
"Matthew Bradbury. He was a stockbroker in the City. Is there any chance you may have met him professionally?"
Again she shook her head.
"I don't know anything about stocks and shares," she told him truthfully. "I certainly don't have any."
Nancy stared at the photograph of Matthew, his face leering back at her from the paper and that oh, so, false smile that did not match the coldness in his eyes. Nancy shivered.
"He just isn't the sort of person I would meet," she explained. "He's old, isn't he?" she blurted.
"Well, not really," the DI argued, a little disconcerted at the description of a man so much younger than himself and he, surely, was a man still in his prime. Unable to elicit

Monday's Child
Caroline Jones Lewis

anything further from Nancy and convinced by her genuine shock and her ignorance of the death, he and his sergeant rose to leave. She saw them to the door, listening to the plod plod of their large policeman feet stepping onto the pavement outside. She closed the door with a sigh of relief and leaned against the wall for a moment, steadying her pounding heart and the deafening roar in her eardrums. Outside on the pavement, the two policemen compared their notes on Nancy's behaviour.

"Do you think she's hiding something, sir?"

"Not sure. She was clearly shocked by all the photos – and the scarf - that really spooked her. But I'm really not sure that she didn't know him. Even if she did,, though, I don't think she had anything to do with his death. Can't see it somehow. Can't see any connection. "

Convinced that Nancy was no ruthless murderer and with other cases higher on their list of priorities, they shrugged and went on their way.

"I can't see a queue of people clammering for justice on this one," observed the DI. "Not likely to inspire much rending of garments and wailing, our man. He seems more despised than grieved for."

"Thing is, sir, word on the street is that one of the girls in the Kray family was raped. If that's the case and the Krays had him down as the rapist ... "

"Yeah, could be," the DI agreed. "There are several other recent unsolved rape cases being investigated, too. Maybe this was our man. Judging by what we found at his address it's a possibility."

Leave it to 'Nipper', they decided. Nipper had the Krays in the radar for this one and he was probably right. They would pass on their observations to him.

******

On the morning before her 40th birthday Miranda sat in Nancy's bedroom in the London house and made up her mind that tomorrow she would attempt another visit to her

Monday's Child
Caroline Jones Lewis

daughter. She hugged Nancy's sweater to her, wrapped in thoughts and with memories cossetting her like a blanket. She caressed her cheek with the soft warmth of the cashmere. The smell of Nancy was gone from the cashmere now and longing welled up inside her, squeezing a tear from her eye to moisten the puffy skin beneath and smudge her mascara. How she longed for her daughter, for the smell and the touch of her. She was so engrossed in her thoughts that she did not hear the turn of the key in the front door lock, or the soft footsteps along the hallway. At the sight of Miranda slumped on her bed, Nancy's resolve crumpled and the words she had promised herself she would not say tumbled involuntarily from her lips. She would play it cool, she had decided; talk with her mother and they would each make their apologies to the other. But all her pre-planned agenda flew out of the window.
"Mummy," she said softly. "Mummy, I'm so sorry. Please don't cry."

A jubilant call to James later in the day brought him the news he had longed to hear and over the next several hours, time just rolled away unheeded. There were tears and laughter, explanations and forgiveness, an appraisal of the new and reinvented Nancy.
"I like the style," Miranda told her. "The hair, the dress. What's the word these days? Fab?"
Nancy grinned. They talked over lunch, they talked over dinner until emotion had tired them both. Nancy rose to leave. For a moment, she was thoughtful. Then she asked, "Mummy, would you ever have had an abortion? If it had been legal when you found out you were pregnant."
"Good heavens, no. Your conception may have been an accident but you were always, always wanted. Always loved. And yes, I would have married your father no matter what. I've loved him always."
"Will you get back together? You're not going to divorce, are you?"

Monday's Child
Caroline Jones Lewis

"I can't say, Nancy," said Miranda. "There may be someone else in his life by now. I couldn't blame him, could I?"
Nancy wrapped her coat around her.
"You don't have to go," Miranda told her.
"I don't have anything with me," Nancy replied. "Anyway, I'm quite used now to having my own place. You must come and see it, Mummy. You'll be surprised. I'm learning to be quite tidy these days."
Miranda laughed. "This I must see," she replied.
It was a reluctant but accepting Miranda who waved her daughter off at the front door with plans in place for a visit the next day.

News of Nancy's return spread quickly among the family who left the two women in peace and privacy to repair their damaged relationship. As Miranda's birthday dawned, James and Nancy joined her at Wilton Place. It had been arranged that, with spring on the doorstep and the weather obligingly warm and sunny, the entire family would meet at Abberley for a birthday celebration over the weekend. Having travelled down together, Mr Hale collected a reunited family at the station and Mrs Hale welcomed them at the door. Emily and Tom would be arriving later, as would Hugh and Lizzie. It seemed an eternity since they had all been together and a flood of emotion and gossip accompanied their first evening together. The three cousins spent much time catching up on their current lives, so much had happened for each one of them since that last summer holiday when disaster – and Nancy - had torn them apart. Nancy's rocketing career was already in the public domain, Lizzie's intention to go into politics was greeted with 'oohs' and 'aahs' from a family wondering just how this would work out in a male-dominated environment and Hugh was so at ease with his new career that it prompted no speculation. Teased about 'the man in her life' in the shape of Graham, Lizzie was insistent that no marriage lines were about to be drawn and Hugh's relationship with Robin at

Monday's Child

Caroline Jones Lewis

this time remained a close secret between the younger members of the family pledged to silence. Emily and Tom remained devoted, but there was more.
At a wink from her mother giving permission to speak, Lizzie confided a secret.
"Mum's having a baby," she beamed. "In the autumn. So we'll have another member of the family around the Christmas tree this year."
Congratulations were offered and received in a spirit of celebration. Which left only James and Miranda.

Several days before and on the pretext of discussing plans for her impending birthday, James had invited Miranda for lunch at one of their favourite restaurants. Miranda had accepted the invitation with trepidation. There had been something about James' manner when he had asked her that once more raised her suspicion that he had met and fallen in love with someone new. Talking over the meal, she had been unable to resist the temptation to raise the subject that was causing her more concern. With Nancy still estranged the loss of James would be a devastating blow.
"Why did you invite me to dinner, James?" she asked.
"You know why," he had answered in surprise.
"But it isn't only about my birthday, is it?" she observed. "There's something more."
"Such as what?" he had pressed her.
"Well, you seem so – well, happy .. " she observed. "Like, a new love perhaps? That spring in your step that a new love brings. An almost permanent smile on your lips."
She had been afraid to hear the answer but aware that deep down she needed to know. James had laughed in response.
"Is that what you think?" he asked. "That I've met someone new?"
"Well, have you?" asked Miranda.
James paused. Then "it's just Nancy," he had explained. "We've found Nancy – safe and well. And more mature than when she left. In a positive way. You'll understand

Monday's Child
Caroline Jones Lewis

what I mean when you're reunited with her. That's all. And isn't that enough?"

Miranda had smiled in agreement.

"So there's no-one else, then? You're not going to ask me for a divorce?"

"No," he had replied emphatically. "Not unless you want one, that is. Do you?"

Miranda shook her head vehemently. James had taken his cue.

"There's only one love in my life, Miranda. You're the only woman I've ever really loved and the only one I've ever wanted. I will love you always."

Unable to hold back the tears, Miranda had rummaged in her handbag for a hankie, trying to cover her embarrassment but also her joy.

"And what about you?" he asked.

"I love you too," she had snuffled. "I hate myself for what I've done. All the trouble it's caused."

"And this man?"

"I've not seen or heard from him since we left Abberley that awful summer. Not given him a thought. It was just a silly infatuation. I knew that the minute Nancy had gone. I don't want to make excuses for myself. I don't know why I did it at all. I've always loved you, James. Perhaps I was just unsettled."

"Mid-life crisis? Bored after all the years of our marriage?" James had offered.

"Maybe," she accepted.

"So what are we going to do about it?" he asked.

"I think that's really up to you," Miranda murmured. "I want you to come home. But what do you want to do?"

"Likewise," he answered. "But not straight away. I'd like to take it steady. Court you again. Enjoy some romance. What do you think? Spend weekends together. Perhaps have a holiday somewhere. See how it goes."

And so it had been agreed. On this weekend of Miranda's birthday celebration, the pair confided their planned reconciliation to the family.

Monday's Child

Caroline Jones Lewis

Nancy stood in the garden alone, the place where, for her, the nightmare had begun. The roses around the pergola were in bud awaiting the warmth of sunshine to burst open their petals. In the distance she could see Joe's boat on the horizon as he set about collecting his lobster pots and her boat bobbed at its mooring at the jetty. The stormy seas and winds that had raged destructive through their lives had calmed; the sea now rippled gently and reassuringly to shore. She breathed a contented sigh, then turned to return to the house, to the security of the family who loved her and who she loved more than ever before. Standing in the conservatory doorway, Hugh and Lizzie watched her. Survival had been a close call for two of them but here they all were. Smiling their approval, Hugh and Lizzie stepped forward to meet Nancy. From the radiogram within the house came the beat of Nancy's newly acquired hit record and linking arms the cousins swayed to the music as they moved forward in life once more, all three together.

> Boom boom boom boom
> You drive me wild
> Make me jump and shout
> Make me work it on out
> With that crazy walk
> And that crazy talk
> Yeah walk that walk
> Come on talk that talk
> Wow – tell me baby
> Come on and tell me that you love me
> 'Cos I love that talk
> When you talk like that
>
> Boom boom boom boom

Made in the USA
Charleston, SC
17 January 2016